An excerpt from *Comfort Object*

There were five or six full pages of job description. I smiled, resting my head on my hand. Okay, the high salary made sense now. I began to scan the first page, also written in something akin to legalese.

"I guess you keep your lawyers busy with all these papers and contracts," I said.

"Yes, I do. But I think it's important to have everything perfectly clear and written down in black and white. It's easier for everyone involved."

"Yes, of course."

The document began with more verbiage about privacy, discretion, the outward appearance of normalcy. *Outward appearance of normalcy.* Okay, that was a little weird.

Near the bottom, it got even weirder. *The applicant will tender public displays of affection as needed...*

The applicant agrees to cooperate with photo opportunities and/or candid interviews regarding the love relationship of Jeremy Gray and the applicant with a positive, convincingly affectionate tone...

I stopped reading, my pulse suddenly beating in my ears. "I don't... I'm not... Okay. I'm a little confused."

"About what?"

"So...this sounds like I'm supposed to pretend to be your girlfriend."

"Yes, that is part of the job. A big part of the job actually. The public part..."

Copyright 2009 Annabel Joseph
Re-issue copyright 2011 by Annabel Joseph/Scarlet Rose Press

Cover art by Bad Star Media
www.badstarmedia.com

* * * * *

This book is a work of fiction. Names, characters, places, and incidents are products of the author's imagination or are used fictitiously. Any resemblance to actual events, locales, or persons living or dead, is entirely coincidental.

All characters depicted in this work of fiction are 18 years of age or older.

Comfort Object

By

Annabel Joseph

Other erotic romance by Annabel Joseph

Mercy
Cait and the Devil
Firebird
Deep in the Woods
Fortune
Owning Wednesday
Lily Mine
Burn For You
Caressa's Knees
Odalisque
Command Performance
Disciplining the Duchess
Cirque de Minuit
Bound in Blue
Waking Kiss
Fever Dream
The Edge of the Earth (as Molly Joseph)

Erotica by Annabel Joseph

Club Mephisto
Molly's Lips: Club Mephisto Retold

Question me now about all other matters, but do not ask who I am, for fear you may increase in my heart its burden of sorrow as I think back;

I am very full of grief, and I should not sit in the house of somebody else with my lamentation and wailing.

It is not good to go on mourning forever.

—Homer's *The Odyssey*
Book 19, 115-120

Chapter One:
Mr. Gorgeous

He was beautiful. No, beautiful was not the word for it. He was godlike, breathtaking, astounding, life-changing. I'd been working at the Eden Fetish Club for five years now, and I had never seen a male specimen like this come through the door. He was golden. His faded jeans fit perfectly over his taut, muscular ass, and his black tee concealed a sculpted torso. He was at least six feet two, maybe taller, with wavy dark hair that framed a classically handsome face. Prominent jaw, and the kind of full, sensuous lips that made me think naughty thoughts. His eyes were set deep and communicated an animal sexuality. Even the way he moved reeked of sex. Everyone in the main dungeon, dominant and submissive and undecided, turned to look as he walked by.

He walked around for a while, taking his time, checking people out. He was shopping. Everything ratcheted up. Scenes got louder, harder, more intense. Doms' voices got more authoritative, subs' cries and moans grew more heartfelt and deep. He was new, he was unattached, he was shopping, and he was something else. Was he a top? A bottom? Both? Neither? Who cared? Everybody wanted him.

I was getting my ass thoroughly beaten by a client when the stranger's gaze fell on me. I wondered if he found me attractive at all. I had a nice body, petite and curvy. My heart-shaped ass was a favored target for Eden's doms. My pussy was waxed bare, and I wore the typical submissive's uniform at Eden—a skimpy garter belt and a black O-ringed collar at my neck. I had red hair, which helped me stand out in a crowd, but my eyes were probably my best feature. Besides their unusual pale green color, they looked slightly ethnic, slanted and wide set. I could drop my lashes over my eyes or peer up and bat them innocently. I had long ago mastered the pleading, vulnerable look.

I turned them on the new guy and saw a flicker of interest. My "master" for the moment, a regular named Jack, wasn't too pleased to see my attention wander and tried to regain it by laying the strokes on a little harder with the flogger.

I tried to concentrate on the job at hand, being his devoted slave, because he was paying me to be, but it was difficult. As I writhed and sobbed under Jack's blows, I knew, guiltily, that I was putting on a show for *him*. Yes, I wanted him to want me. Beauty was desirable, but oh so rare in clubs like these. Jack, bless his heart, had long since passed his prime. But Jack was a great dominant and a loyal customer, so God, I tried to concentrate on him. I took my job seriously. I really tried to be a great sub to everyone who wanted to play.

When Jack finished with me thirty minutes later, Mr. Gorgeous was still standing there, watching me come down. Everyone else had gone back to their own scenes. It was clear now he'd made his choice. *I* was his choice. I was a little jittery about it, which was silly, being a professional sub.

Focus, Nell, you idiot. He was not Prince Charming, and I wasn't Cinderella. I was a professional working at the Eden Fetish Club in Los Angeles, and what I was looking at was just another job.

Mistress Amelia glowered at me from the corner, where Jack was bending her ear and gesturing at me in annoyance. Her eyes said it all. *This better be good.* Forget about poor Jack. I'd better convince Mr. Gorgeous that playing at Eden was a lot of fun, that he should come back all the time. Having regular members like him could draw more business, attract more submissive women. There were never enough subs. Mistress Amelia's cherry red lips pursed into a strict line.

Make it work, bitch.

I walked up to the client and got a noseful of fresh, outdoorsy smell, like he'd spent the day at the beach. He was even more delectable close up. His shoulders were so broad, and his arms had that perfect bulge of muscle... *Focus!*

I gave Mr. Handsome my best submissive greeting: a sweet, soft murmur with my eyes cast down. *Would Master like to spend some time with Little Nell? My only limits were the club's limits: no fluid exchange and no severe marking or bloodletting. I was available to play publicly, here in the main dungeon, or in one of the private, themed rooms. Schoolroom? Hospital? Boardroom? Harem? Interrogation room? What did Master wish?*

Master Gorgeous wished to play privately, he said. Mistress Amelia wasn't happy about that as I led him toward the hallway, but the themed rooms were there for customers, so what could she say? I asked which of the currently available rooms he wished to play in, and he shrugged and said he didn't care.

Okay.

I wasn't sure what that meant, that he had no preference. He only kept staring at me with those eyes that seemed to be weighing, measuring, analyzing more than anything else. They weren't warm eyes. They were businesslike, in a strange but not a scary way. I'd actually never felt more like a sex worker, although I suppose that's what I was. I realized then that must have been his fantasy. Pick out a sex worker and dominate her. Cool. I could understand that kink.

I led him to the first open room we came to, the harem, one of my personal favorites. Along with the de rigueur hooks, trestles, benches, chairs, and display of disciplinary tools on the wall, there were piles of pillows, a very cozy sofa, and a massive crimson-canopied bed. I'd cuddled with many a dom after taking a sound whipping on that bed, watching the garish scarves and curtains blow in the breeze of the ceiling fans shaped to look like palm leaves.

Somehow I doubted this dom was into cuddling. Actually, as the door closed behind us and he looked at me, I could tell, with a certainty born of experience, that this gorgeous, staring, studying man wasn't a dom at all. I was suddenly a little thankful for Joel, the club-appointed chaperone who stood in the shadows to monitor the safety of every private scene I did. I had long since ceased to feel embarrassment around Joel, but feeling thankful for his presence was a totally new thing. What did this guy want? I went down on my knees and waited.

He looked at me a long while. I finally murmured, "Would Master like me to suggest ways to best make use of my submissiveness?"

"No," he said tersely.

"I'm yours," I answered in reply and waited on my knees patiently. He looked over at Joel.

"So the rules apply here too? Privately? No sex?"

"No sex, not with the staff," boomed Joel from the corner.

Too bad, I thought. He wanted sex, and Lord in heaven knew I wanted to give this man sex. All women should have given this man sex, and probably did. Any woman walking the planet would have given it up for this piece of maleness, so why this rigmarole, why come to a club and try to buy it? Why? Because he wanted kinky sex. *Sigh.* I wanted kinky sex too. It had been far too long.

What I would have given to take this man's cock out and take it in my mouth, roll it around on my tongue, and make it hard and stiff and then... I would have taken him anywhere. Anywhere he wanted to stick it, I would have moaned and taken it deep. How long had it been since I'd had good S&M sex, been pushed down and fucked hard and silly and then been beaten and fucked again? After work I was usually too tired, too used-up to troll the straight clubs, and the Eden customers and staff, the only "scene" people I knew, were strictly off-limits to contact off the clock.

I looked at Gorgeous. Did I dare try to meet him later? I'd never attempted anything like that before, but I was so, so fucking horny, and his appraising, level stare and Adonis body weren't helping to cool me off. I tried to infuse a spark of *maybe* into the *I'm yours* in my eyes.

"We're not allowed to do any type of fluid exchange here, Master."

To Joel, I hoped it sounded like I was only telling Gorgeous the rules. But I pointedly added the *here*. I hoped Gorgeous heard it. I think he did, because he glanced at Joel, then walked over to the wall of whips, paddles, and floggers impatiently.

"So what, I can just whip you, huh? What if it gets me off and some fluid exchange just...happens?"

I smothered a smile. "As long as it's not from penetration."

"Can I come *on* you?"

I whispered, "Not here."

"Where?" he whispered back.

I looked up at Joel pointedly from under my lashes. Gorgeous sighed in frustration and picked up a wicked-looking leather paddle and lifted me from my knees. He walked me to the couch.

"Bend over."

God, I wanted him to fuck me. I went up on my toes, my stocking-covered legs tensing as I waited. I tried to make my ass look irresistible.

Ow! Fuck. Fuck.

Fuck.

It occurred to me that bulging, golden muscles instead of the typical flabby limbs came at a price. Particularly when those muscles wielded an instrument that already imparted a hearty sting. He rained blows on my ass like a jackhammer, with no moderate warm-up strokes and no pauses to adjust to the pain. I danced from foot to foot and bit my lip hard as the deep, stinging pain suffused my cheeks.

A fucking amateur. Definitely not a dom.

I looked over at Joel in the corner, his arms crossed over his broad chest. Was the fucker smirking? He knew as well as I did when a client didn't know what he was doing, and this one clearly didn't. He wouldn't step in, though, not unless I used my safe word and the client kept going.

And no way was I using a safe word. I needed sex from this man, I really did. But *ow!*

Jeez, how did these guys get past the front door? Well, I knew how this one got in. His body, his gorgeous face. He was definitely a Los Angeles pretty boy. I wasn't even sure he was totally straight, although he acted straight and dominant enough. He *acted*. That was the weird thing. I got the feeling he wasn't that into what he was doing.

Well, a lot of people came to experiment here in a safe, nonbinding place, to see if the "lifestyle" was for them. If you tied up and beat the shit out of your high school sweetheart and decided it wasn't for you after all, it was a lot more uncomfortable a situation than finding out by beating on a stranger you'd never see again.

I whimpered and fidgeted as he went to town. It wasn't an act on my part. It fucking hurt, and soon the fire in my ass reached crisis proportions.

"No severe marking," I finally said when it looked like Joel wasn't going to help me out.

"What?" He leaned close to me.

I let the pretense fall away. He knew I knew he wasn't a dominant. "You're hitting too hard."

"I want to see you somewhere outside of here."

"I'm not supposed to," I whispered.

He pulled back and landed a few more lackluster blows for Joel's benefit. "I'll give you what you deserve, you little slut," he declared in a stern, faux-dominant voice.

I stifled laughter, turning my head as he leaned down again to whisper in my ear.

"I'll give you two thousand dollars if you'll see me tonight at your place."

I shouldn't have said yes. I really shouldn't have. But I heard myself tell him my phone number and that I got off work at two.

* * * * *

The rest of the night at work was a blur. I vacillated wildly between uncontrolled horniness and horror at what I'd done. I finally convinced myself that when he called I wouldn't answer. But I answered, of course, and I told him where I lived. I called my friend Alexis to let her know what was going on, and then frantically tried to remember whether I had pepper spray in the house. But I didn't, I knew I didn't. I was ninety-eight percent sure I wouldn't need it anyway. I figured Mr. Gorgeous was just a vanilla boy with a little bit of kink inside and nowhere to let it loose. I didn't get a sociopath vibe from him. No. He wanted something else.

He knocked on my door at two thirty sharp. I had on a nice, tight little fuck-me dress I could shimmy out of quickly, and my naughtiest thong underneath. I tried to look like I wasn't anxious and wet as hell to see him.

"Hi," I said.

"Hi," he replied awkwardly. It occurred to me that neither one of us knew what the hell was going on. Okay. I would set some parameters.

"I want to tell you first thing that I made a safe call."

He looked nervous for a second.

"What's a safe call?"

"I called a friend to let her know you were here, and that if I don't call her in the morning, to call the cops. That they would know you at the club."

"Oh, okay," he said. "I guess that's smart. But I have no intention of hurting you or killing you or anything like that." He half smiled, half smirked at me.

Gorgeous man, he flirted. But he wasn't a dom. I locked the door and leaned back against it, looking at him expectantly.

"So what is it you want? Because I don't think you're really into S&M."

He met my eyes. *Guilty.* He smiled self-consciously, but his fingertips reached out to touch my waist and trail down over my hips.

"You can tell? I guess after all this time you know it. How long have you been…working as a sex slave?"

"I'm not a sex slave," I murmured, letting his fingers slowly lift the hem of my dress and brush across the tops of my thighs. "But you promised me two thousand dollars for seeing you outside the club, and I'll need it up front."

"So you're a whore," he said, so quietly I almost didn't hear him. But I did.

"Call it what you want." I put my hand over his before it snaked between my legs. "The money first."

"Are you worth it?"

"I'm worth it, yes. Do you have it?"

With a peeved look, he took out his wallet and removed a stack of bills. He handed them to me, but before he let go, he said, "This is for sex, right? There are no rules about fluid exchange here?"

I hesitated. What were the rules here? I was whoring myself, which was a first. I accepted money for "sex" every night at Club Eden, but that was only mental sex, psychological fucking, spanking and toys and silly scenes, prostitution within the confines of the law. This man wanted actual prostitution, to penetrate me for money. More than once, I assumed.

"You have to use a condom," I finally said. "For everything. And you can't scar me or draw blood."

"Jesus." He let go of the money. "I don't know what kind of people you usually hang out with, but I'm not into making chicks bleed."

"Good. Do you have condoms?"

He reached into his coat pocket and pulled out a handful. "They had them at the door of the club. Which is why I thought it was weird that no fucking was allowed."

"Fucking's allowed, only not with the staff. Couples fuck there all the time. Are you married?"

He laughed. "No."

"Just like to fuck around? Try new things?"

He shrugged, looking at me almost defensively. "I have a friend. He's really into this stuff."

"And you wanted to give it a try?"

He laughed again. "Give it a try. Yes."

I wasn't sure what the fuck was so funny, but then his fingers were on me again, and he was drawing up my hem and discovering my thong.

"Okay," I said. "Do you want me to help you, or do you want to do things on your own? I mean, do you want to fuck me as a dominant? You want me to be submissive for you?"

"Yes, I want you to be submissive. Like my…slave."

"Okay. And you know what to… I mean, I can sort of teach you how to be an effective dom, if you want."

"No, I kind of know."

"From your friend?"

He nodded.

"He let you watch. And you liked it. He has a slave?"

"Yeah. Sort of."

"Okay. But just so you know, this is only business. For now, during this session, I'm your slave. Afterward I'm a person again."

"You're not really into this? In real life?"

"No, I mean, I am." His hands, God, they were talented. He found my clit like a hound on the scent. It was getting harder to concentrate. "I...I love being submissive."

"But on your own terms."

"No. It's not... I'm not available right now."

"You have a boyfriend." He pulled my thong down, letting it fall at my feet.

"No. I don't. I'm just not a lifestyler. I can't be submissive all the time. I choose not to be."

"Only sometimes. When someone's paying you."

"When I want to be submissive, I'm submissive. Is that enough for you?" I said, half-horny, half-annoyed by his insistent line of questioning.

"Yes. What's your name?" he asked me then. "Is it really Little Nell?"

"It's Nell. Just Nell."

"Well, Nell," said Mr. Gorgeous. "I just want to fuck you silly. Is that enough for you?"

"Yes, Master. I'm yours."

I'm yours. I've said it a thousand times in my line of work, and it never fails to give me a shiver, make me a little wet. *I'm yours, now what will you do with me?*

"I want you to kneel down and suck me first."

Mmm. Good line, delivered well, like a real dom. I was pretty certain he'd heard it from his "friend." I hoped his friend was a really good lover, because I had a feeling I was about to reenact a scenario Mr. Gorgeous had already viewed and liked a lot. I felt, for a moment, that his friend was a third party in our illicit little rendezvous.

I took his shirt off first, selfishly, because I wanted to see him fully unclothed. Naked, perfect male. His abs were tight, defined bunches of muscle. I wanted to outline each one with my tongue and then lick him from his neck all the way down to his—

Focus.

I knelt and took my time undoing his belt and unbuttoning his seven-hundred-dollar jeans, daydreaming about doing him and his dom friend at the same time.

Rich boys and their naughty habits. Gorgeous looked to be in his early twenties. I was twenty-eight, and I didn't think he was as old as me. Just a young rich boy sowing wild oats. I would show him wild if he wanted it. I'm sure he had no idea how horny I was.

By the time I got his pants off, he was already rock solid. I rolled on a condom as deftly and sexily as I could and took him in my mouth.

God, I wanted it. A big, hard cock jammed in the back of my throat. I'd had a cock like this, attached to a great, straight, dominant, loving man, but he'd left me. Douglas. I hadn't been enough for him. I'd tried to be, but working at the club and needing time for myself, I had never been enough. But this man, he only wanted me right now. One night. One night, I could manage.

Well, manage was one word for it. I licked his rigid tool, reveling in its masculine power, exploring it from base to hard tip until he lost patience and nudged it between my lips. I salivated for him, opened wide for him to take me. For once I wasn't even bothered by the bitter taste of latex. I was too enthralled by the way he completely filled my mouth. His musky, male scent sent me deep into the throes of submission, and the fact that he was a stranger added an extra kinky thrill. I wanted to give him the best hummer he'd ever had, one he'd remember when he was in his eighties. I wanted to show him how much I appreciated his perfect body.

I cupped his balls and tried to coax him deeper into my throat. He made a guttural noise and placed his hands on either side of my head, just light pressure. When I moaned, he tightened his hold and started to fuck my face. I faltered for a moment, terrified that I might gag, but he slowed and let me find a rhythm. I settled into accommodating his deep thrusts, and soon I managed to wrench some erotic groans from him. He stopped abruptly.

"I want to come on you."

I pulled away and whipped off the condom. For two thousand bucks, sure. I expected the facial, but he yanked at my dress.

"I want to come on your tits."

A tit man. Okay. He shot hot cum over my chest, and I received it like a gift. Douglas used to make me rub it all in and lick my hands. Gorgeous rubbed it in himself and got sidetracked pinching and squeezing my nipples. A tit man all the way. *Ohhh*...and I loved tit men. He leaned closer and I braced for pain, but instead he only tapped the taut peaks. Not flicked them. Tapped them. I'd never had my nipples tapped this way, and I was surprised by how intense it felt. It wasn't pain. It was a tease. It made me fidget and left me craving more. With each light tap my clit throbbed. I moaned and leaned into him, desperate for some kind of relief, but he only stroked and tapped my nipples until they were hard as stones. Then he closed his fingers on them and twisted so hard a gasp of protest came to my lips. Fire shot straight to my center. He watched my reaction in a strange, detached manner.

"Do you have any of those, what do you call them? Clips? Clothespins?"

"I have some nipple clamps, Master."

"Go get them. And don't call me Master, that's weird. Call me Kyle."

Mr. Kyle Gorgeous. Fitting. I didn't know whether to crawl for the clamps or get up and go for them. Well, he wasn't much of a dom. I got up and walked, and he didn't correct me. I came back and placed them in his hands. They weren't the most stringent pair I had, but he'd never know. I liked the more painful ones, but I didn't know if he knew how long it was safe to leave them on.

I knelt down again, but he pulled me back up.

"I want you to look at my face while I put them on you. Look right at me."

Again I felt the ghostly friend. I didn't think Kyle had the imagination to come up with this on his own. He closed the clamps, one and then the other, on my hard, puckered nipples. The ache bloomed, then commuted into a rush of wetness between my legs. I gasped, staring at him. His blue eyes looked dark earlier, but now they were light and wide. He watched as if trying to gauge what I was thinking. I don't know if he knew I was daydreaming about his friend.

"Do you like that?" he asked, tugging on the little beads that hung down from the silver clamps.

"Yes, Kyle. I like it a lot."

"Shake your titties, push them together for me."

I did. The hungry way he was looking at me really turned me on. He might not be a dom, but he was sexy. He put his hand between my legs, probing me roughly, and again the submissive inside me exulted. My mouth opened in a moan, and I let his fingers penetrate me as deeply as he wished. I was so wet, my pussy squelched against his fingers.

"You do like it, don't you? You horny little slut."

I stood still and let him take me with his hand. The pressure building in my belly was shooting up to my breasts, snaking down between my thighs. My legs trembled from the pleasure, so I thought I might fall if he didn't support me. Each time his agile fingertip stroked over the little nub, my hips bucked forward in a plea. He tugged on the clamps again, and I gasped.

"I want you to come," he said.

Thank God. I closed my eyes as he tugged and worked my clit with those talented fingers. Did I say he was gorgeous? His fingers were his best feature by far. I put my hands on his shoulders and moaned, thrusting my hips forward. I clung to him and let the rhythm of his fingers drive me higher. My body drew up tight and then convulsed in release.

"Yes, yes!" I mashed my head into his chest and almost closed my teeth on his golden skin. He held me up with strong hands as I rode out the waves of satisfaction. When I came back to my senses, I looked up into his eyes. He was still watching me in that intense way.

"That was cool," he said.

I let out my breath in a rush. "Yes, it was."

His hand was still clamped over my pussy. He looked down at his hard cock with a smirk. "But I'm not quite finished with you yet."

"I sensed that." I smiled.

His hand left my pussy to grasp my upper arm. He pulled me to the sofa and bent me over it.

It wasn't the harem room, but I was finally about to get fucked. I watched over my shoulder as he rolled on a condom. He positioned his dick against my slit and pushed in to the hilt. I went up on my toes and moaned, then twitched my ass back against him. He began to fuck me. I panted and gripped the cushion. The head of his cock pummeled in and out, rubbing over my g-spot. My hips jerked as delicious sensation gathered into a teeming knot at my center.

"Oh…oh…" I couldn't form words. The only sounds in my world were my incoherent exclamations and his urgent grunts. Warm pleasure suffused my entire body. My nipples tingled with a needful ache.

"Spread your legs." I did, and he practically lifted me from the floor with the force of his thrusts. I felt like his creature, his object. I loved the way he was using me. I imagined I existed only to slake his lust. His hands clenched and unclenched on my hips as he pulled me back on his dick. Just as I was about to come, though, he withdrew. He ignored my wail of protest and put his hands on my shoulders. He pulled me from the couch and forced me to the floor on all fours. He knelt behind me and bent over my quivering back. I could feel his sweat-slickened abs against my skin as he whispered in my ear.

"Nell, can I fuck your ass?"

For two thousand dollars? Yes. I moaned and twitched my hips back against him. My pussy juice eased the way, but I still flinched when he worked the head in. I breathed through the pain and clenched my sphincter around him. I waited for him to suggest lube and gritted my teeth when he pressed on without it. The ache was acute but at the same time thrilled me to the core. I reached back to clutch at his thighs.

"Okay?" he asked.

I made a sound of assent and dropped my shoulders forward. He took it for the capitulation it was and slid his thick tool in to the hilt.

God, it had been far too long since I'd had a cock in my ass. I'd forgotten that terrifying, intoxicating feeling of being impaled. The pain of entry turned into unfolding pleasure that spread from my ass to my pussy and up to my nipples straining in the clamps. I tried hard not to start begging and talking dirty. *You're a submissive. Let him fuck you.*

And he fucked me, slow and deep. He reached under me to flick at the nipple clamps, creating sparks of fire that resonated in my pelvis. Then came a series of quick thrusts that made me clench and moan, scrabble for purchase on the rough carpet. It was the surrender that mattered during anal, letting go and accepting my basest desires. I could barely remember my name, or his for that matter. He reached around and stroked my pussy while his cock stretched my tight hole. I felt his fingers delve into my wet slit and then search for my clit. He pinched it. I felt something inside me unfurl and go wild.

I cried out and came like a madwoman, jerking back hard against his hips. While I shuddered and shook through my climax, I felt his dick pulse in my ass. Mr. Kyle Gorgeous Talented Fingers rocked in me another moment and then finally went still. It was a long time before I became aware of the scratchy carpet under my skin.

He pulled away from me and found his way to my bathroom. I heard water running, a flush of the toilet. When he returned I was still exactly as he'd left me, cheek to the carpet with my ass in the air. When no directions were forthcoming, I righted myself and turned. He was looking at me with that same look from the club, studying, assessing.

"Thank you," he said finally. "Um, should I take those off?" he asked, indicating the nipple clamps.

"Okay." He did, almost gingerly. I drew in a halting breath as the blood flowed back to my nipples.

"Does that hurt? When they come off?"

"A little."

"But you like that, huh? Being hurt?"

It was a simplification, but since I figured I'd never see him again, I gave him the simple answer. "Yes."

He walked over to pick up his clothes. As he pulled his shirt on, I squelched the urge to rip it back off again. *Farewell, hottest abs ever*, I thought, then I realized he was talking to me.

"You're a hot fuck. I thought you would be. I enjoyed that a lot."

"I did too." It wasn't exactly a BDSM scene, but it had been hot in its own way. A little tentative perhaps. If someone who fucked you in three holes one after the other could be called tentative.

"I think you're a really good sub. I mean, aren't you? You try hard at it. You like it for real."

I nodded. Now that he was obviously leaving, I started to feel wistful. I knew he wasn't going to be my new master or anything, but he had been fun. And he was as gorgeous as ever, even sweaty and fucked-out as he was.

"Can I get you some water?" I offered. "A beer?"

He looked at his watch. "You know what? It's late. I've got to be going. Thanks, though."

I watched him buckle his belt, lace up his shoes, straighten his collar, all business now. I thought about asking him if it was worth the two thousand bucks, but I didn't want to hear him say no, or hear him say yes while his body language clearly said no. He was no better dom now than he was when he'd arrived, but I got the clear feeling he didn't care about that. I don't know if he'd gotten what he paid the two thousand bucks for, but if he hadn't, he didn't blame me, I supposed.

So why did I feel so guilty? Or did I feel sad? Or did I feel ashamed?

I'd just sold myself for two thousand dollars. And why? Because I had an itch to scratch.

And this gorgeous guy walking out my door?

I guess he'd just had an itch too.

Chapter Two: The Job

The next day, though, a whole lot more got scratched than my itch. Joel met me at the door when I arrived at Eden.

"Is it true?"

"Is what true?"

"Did you meet that guy after work yesterday?"

"Joel!"

"Mistress Amelia got in my face about it. If you did—"

"What did you tell her?"

"You dug him. I knew it!"

"What did you tell her, Joel? Tell me!"

"I didn't tell her anything. But somebody told her. She's spitting mad. She wants to talk to you."

"Holy shit. What do I do?"

"Lie. Or you won't fucking have a job."

I slunk down the hall toward Mistress's office. There was no point making her any more mad by avoiding her. But who would have ratted on me like that? Joel insisted it wasn't him, and I believed him. He was a friend. It had to be somebody making stuff up. Unless someone had been outside my apartment last night and actually spied on me to see if he arrived, and who would have been petty and vindictive enough to do that?

The door was ajar, so I peeked in carefully. Crap. Mistress Amelia was flushed with anger. I entered silently and closed the door behind me and decided on Joel's suggested plan of action. Lie.

"Joel said you wanted to talk to me?"

"If I were you, girl, I would address me as 'Mistress' and I would do it from my knees. Go out and come in again, and know this time that your job is on the line."

Shit. I left and closed the door and took a few deep breaths to calm myself. Mistress and I had a complicated relationship. She hated me because she knew I wasn't crazy about subbing for dommes—that is, female dominants. I just didn't go for pussy the way I went for cock.

She thought I wasn't a good, dedicated professional because I wasn't into women, but she didn't have much choice in keeping me around. Good subs were hard to find and keep, and the demand for us was constant, so I didn't believe for a second she would fire me. Still, I opened the door with my eyes cast down, dropped to my knees, and murmured quietly, "You wished to speak to me, Mistress?"

"I want to ask you one question, submissive. Did you meet a client last night at your apartment?"

"No. I don't know who told you that. I can't imagine why someone would be telling lies about me."

Mistress Amelia came to stand behind me. I half expected her to press a revolver against the back of my skull and pull the trigger, she was that mad. Instead she slammed the door and put her foot on the top of my back. I flinched, but I leaned forward until my face was against the floor. "Stay, you little slut," she ordered.

I watched her feet walk back around her desk and heard her sit. I could hear her fingers *tap tap tap* on her computer for what must have been ten minutes or more. Finally she cleared her throat and said, "I'll ask you once again. Did you meet a client last night at your apartment?"

"No," I said with less conviction.

"The correct answer is 'yes, Mistress,'" she snapped with restrained fury. "I know you did, because the client called and told me you sold yourself to him last night for two thousand dollars, and went on to detail everything you put out for that sum."

I sat up in shock, which was stupid because it gave me away, but I was dumbfounded. That was his kink? Having what wasn't allowed and then ruining that person's life?

"For the last time, you little slut, did you meet a client last night at your apartment?"

"Yes, Mistress," I said, bowing again to the floor, not that it would save me now.

She was quiet a long time. Finally she sighed heavily. "You make a good living here. You have a faithful clientele, and you have been mentored and trained by the best masters and mistresses in L.A. All we ask in return is that you follow the rules and not fraternize with paying clients outside the club."

"Yes, Mistress."

"I'm afraid this is grounds for dismissal. You not only fraternized with a client of the club, you sold yourself to him like a common whore."

"I'm sorry, Mistress," I said to the carpet. My nose was starting to itch.

She paused. "How sorry are you?"

Stupid, horny bitch. Ugly, puffed-up, over-the-hill dominatrix. It was easy for her to judge. I didn't make as much money in a year as she made in a week owning this club. She'd always wanted me, and now she thought she was going to get me by threatening to take away my job. *Ugh.* There was no way I was going to submit to that spiteful, nasty domme.

"How sorry are you?" she repeated, walking to stand over me. "Are you willing to submit to punishment from me in exchange for keeping your job?"

"What kind of punishment?" I asked her fat, leather-encased ankles. I left the *Mistress* off.

"The cane, you impossibly impertinent slut. To begin with." She landed a stroke of the cane across my ass. I screamed in outrage and sat up.

"The cane is on my 'no' list, Mistress Amelia!" Jesus, I didn't do canes. My ass was on fire from the one stroke she'd landed. No way was I submitting to a caning from her. It would probably kill me.

"Do you want your job or not?"

"The cane is on my 'no' list!"

"Letting a customer fuck your mouth, ass, and cunt for money is on my 'no' list, slut, and you did it anyway!"

"I... It was a weak moment, Mistress. You saw him. I swear, I won't do it again."

"Do excuses like that work with your other doms?"

You're not my domme, I wanted to remind her. *You're just my boss.*

She tapped the cane against the wall impatiently. "So let me get this straight. You can play the submissive whore with this client, but you're too good to submit to punishment from me. I see how it is, you uppity slut. I always knew you weren't a true submissive, and since I don't own you, I can't punish you as I see fit. But I can fire you. And I do. Get out of my sight. Leave Eden now."

I stood up slowly, in tears. Cast out of Eden. It hurt. I had no intention of being caned and put through the sexual wringer to save my job, but it hurt to be told to go. It hurt to be told I wasn't a true submissive, because I was afraid, deep down inside, that she was right.

"But my clients…"

"Your clients will live without your services. I can no longer in good faith offer you to them, now that I see you are in actuality a slut and whore and not even, truly, a submissive. Out."

And so I was out, just like that. I cried a little on the way home from my injured pride, but at the same time I thought, So what? There were plenty of BDSM clubs in Los Angeles, and they all had room for an experienced sub like me.

But I was wrong, because by the time I scraped my self-esteem together and started making phone calls, Mistress Amelia had called every BDSM club, dungeon, and bar in the greater L.A. area and had me blacklisted. I was fucked.

* * * * *

Little Nell, professional sub extraordinaire, was thus reduced to folding napkins during the nighttime lull at Buona Italia. Corners together. Fold over. Again. Pull down the petals.

Like a tulip, like a tulip, Nellie.

Grr. My name wasn't Nellie, and I was only working this job out of desperation. This tiny Italian bistro had hired me on the spot, which had seemed like a stroke of serendipity at the time. Now I thought if I had to fold one more napkin into a tulip, I would take my boss, Guillermo, by the neck and shake him like the little chicken man that he was.

Squawk squawk squawk squawk. *Nellie, fold the napkins. Nellie, clean up behind the bar. Nellie, seat Mr. and Mrs. Iovito at their favorite table.* Mr. and Mrs. Iovito made me want to stick nails in my eyes.

But a job was a job, and waitressing jobs weren't easy to come by in Los Angeles, where you couldn't throw a stick without hitting a starving artist. And I wasn't the type to embrace starvation, so… Corners together. Fold over. Again.

Anyway, I'd done this to myself, just like I did everything to myself to somehow make my life as difficult and complicated as possible at all times. And I guess it was better than taking orders from Mistress Amelia. Oh, I knew I could go back at any time and grovel. I could submit to the cane until I was practically crippled, then bury my face in her crotch for the rest of my natural-born life. Sure, I could do that, and I probably would when I got desperate enough.

But more than Mistress Amelia, I thought about him. Gorgeous rat fink.

Why had he done it?

Had screwing me over been his aim all along? To get me fired? I had no more or fewer enemies than anyone else. Certainly no enemies of the life-destroying kind. I couldn't figure it out. I thought about it while I took orders, while I folded tulips, while I vacuumed the carpet at the end of the night.

Guillermo and his family were good people. By giving me a job, they'd helped me keep a roof over my head. But my rent was paid for by a sex worker's salary. A waitress's salary was not enough. The restaurant was upscale, but the weeknights were slow. And I'd lied. I told them I was part Italian, although my bright red hair would convince anyone otherwise. I was just a failure and a liar and, well, a prostitute, I guess.

"Smile, you tired old girl," Guillermo chided from behind the bar. "This frown on your face, it drives the customers away."

"Does it?" I shrugged. "It's almost closing time anyway."

We both turned as the bell on the door rang. *Shit.* It was eight forty-five. Guillermo seated the lone customer at a small table in the corner. Of course he'd come in to eat. He couldn't just grab a quick drink at the bar and go home. Now I'd be here until ten o'clock waiting on him. Guillermo looked at me apologetically.

"Do you mind, Nellie?"

"Nell," I muttered under my breath, crossing to the customer with a menu. He looked up with a tired smile.

"Is it too late? Is the kitchen closed?"

"No," I said, unable to keep the edge of irritation from my voice. But he looked tired and hungry. And familiar.

I handed him the menu, softening. "What can I get you to drink?"

He looked up at me again. "A beer. Whatever's on tap."

I suddenly realized why he looked so familiar. He was an actor, an A-list actor. I think he'd been up for an Oscar last year.

"Sure!" I hoped my *sure* didn't sound too obsequious. A real movie star! I started back to Guillermo with a goofy, excited smile.

"Jeremy Gray would like whatever's on tap, boss. Make it snappy."

"Jeremy Gray!" Guillermo practically simpered. "In my own little restaurant here. You tell him this is all on the house. All of it. Maybe he'll let us take a picture!"

I looked over at Buona Italia's "Wall of Celebrities," which consisted of a "Like a Virgin"-era Madonna hugging Guillermo's wife.

"Maybe. Got your camera?"

Guillermo bustled away in a panic.

I went back to Jeremy Gray's table to find him still scanning the menu.

"Is the chicken parmigiana good?"

"No one makes chicken parm like Guillermo."

"Bring it on." He smiled. "Nell," he read off my name tag. "Unusual name. Unusual hair color. Is that natural red?"

"Yes. My parents' fault. I'll go put in your order. What kind of dressing would you like on your salad?"

"Surprise me."

"How about Italian, since you're at an Italian restaurant?"

He pretended disappointment. "That's not much of a surprise. Can't you do better?"

My God, Jeremy Gray was flirting with me. It almost made getting fired from Eden all worthwhile. Jeremy of the sandy blond hair, the cerulean blue eyes, the ridiculously hard body. He was pushing forty, but it only made him sexier and worldlier and hotter in a naughty-daddy kind of way. Up close and personal, he was even more handsome than he was on-screen. He had those sexy older-man lines around his eyes.

"Raspberry-walnut vinaigrette?" I suggested.

"Better." Sexy, fortyish, sugar-daddy hot man. I wanted him to spank me like the bad, bad girl I was. But this wasn't Eden, this was Buona Italia, so I went to the kitchen to put in his order instead.

"Make it good," I said to Guillermo. "Then all the big movie stars will come to your restaurant."

"From your lips to God's ears," he exclaimed. "Let it be so!"

Later, when Jeremy Gray had finished his parm and insisted on paying for his meal, he agreed to pose for a photograph. Since Maria Rose, Guillermo's wife, had already gone home, Jeremy suggested I be in the picture with him. He put his arm around me and Guillermo crowed, "Say cheese!"

I obediently said "cheese," but Jeremy said "provolone" and looked over at me, so it ended up looking like he was giving me a kiss. We laughed as we crowded together over the small digital-camera screen to look at the photo.

"I'll print it out tonight!" said Guillermo. "Next time you come, you sign!"

Guillermo hummed with excitement as we closed down for the night. As for me, I couldn't get the solid, warm feel of Jeremy Gray's body against mine out of my head.

* * * * *

He did come back a few days later, right before closing time again. I was half-annoyed, half-joyous. A little part of me fantasized that he'd come back to see me. He'd definitely flirted with me last time.

"I'll have the usual," he said when I came to his table.

"Raspberry-walnut vinaigrette and all?"

"Yes, whatever Little Nell suggests."

The name jolted me for a moment. I looked for irony in his eyes, but he only smiled and handed back the menu.

I headed to the kitchen. No, he couldn't know. I was actually rather little, barely five feet tall and maybe a hundred pounds soaking wet. That's probably why he called me Little Nell. If he'd ever been to the club, I would have known. I would have heard the gossip. I went back out with his beer and set it on the table.

"Can you sit and have a beer with me?" he asked.

I glanced around the restaurant. Another couple was still lingering over their meal. "I'm not supposed to sit down with the customers while I'm working."

He smiled. "You're a good little worker, are you?"

"I try to be."

"I need someone like you. I need an assistant. Do you have any friends looking for a job?"

I opened my mouth and then closed it, but he got the hint.

"Or maybe you're looking for a better job. You like waitressing here?"

I shrugged and looked away. All of a sudden, his eyes really intimidated me. Or maybe I was just afraid he'd see how desperate I was for his job. I wondered how much he'd pay. Somehow I knew it would be more than I made working for Guillermo, tips and all.

"You have no idea how tempting that is. But Guillermo…they're so nice here. I would hate to leave him and his wife high and dry."

Jeremy sighed. "And loyal too. There's got to be a way to lure you away from here."

I laughed softly. "I don't know. If you keep talking to me and keeping me from the other customers, maybe you'll get me fired."

"Excellent plan. I'll get you fired, and then you'll have to come work for me."

"Or just offer me a lot of money. A salary I can't refuse."

I laughed, but he looked at me soberly. "I actually would like to find an assistant like you. Pleasant, responsible, loyal"—he smiled—"and a little bit fun. Think about it?"

"Well..." *Don't sound desperate!* "Yeah. I... Yeah. You need an assistant starting when?"

"I'll be traveling a lot in the upcoming weeks. I need someone right away. Someone who's free to travel, who can keep me organized and sane while I work on location."

I looked over at the couple across the restaurant, their empty glasses and frowns of impatience.

"Mr. Gray, excuse me. I have to—"

"Go on. Come and talk to me later. But think about it."

"I will."

Think about it. God, as if I had to think about it. Personal assistant to Jeremy Gray. Travel, exotic locations, and the movie-star life on movie-star sets and in movie-star hotels. Wow. And I would rub shoulders with him all the time. *Him*, Jeremy Gray. Hot, nice, friendly, sexy, famous movie-star man. Every day. I would see him every day, wouldn't I, if I were his personal assistant? What was there to think about?

I filled glasses and gave the other table their check. They gave me a shitty tip when they left, but I didn't care. I was already picturing handing Guillermo my two weeks' notice and riding off with Jeremy Gray into the movie-star sunset. When I returned to his table he was on the phone, so I hovered around the bar and the kitchen, dying to talk to him. Finally, at the end of the meal, he gave me his business card.

"Listen, Nell, I'd love to talk to you more about this job, if you're interested."

"Yes, to be honest, I am interested." I tried to keep the fawning adulation out of my voice.

"Maybe we can meet over dinner to discuss it. What evening would be best?"

"I'm off Monday." Damn, it was only Thursday, but Guillermo really needed me on the weekend nights. "Or we could do lunch."

"I'd prefer dinner. A nice place where we can sit and chat and talk things over. How about Monday night at the Diplomat? Dinner, you and me."

Dinner, you and me. Swoon. He was being very proper and businesslike, but my imagination was in overdrive.

"That sounds great, Mr. Gray."

"Call me Jeremy. Mr. Gray makes me feel old. Tell me your number and where you live, and I'll pick you up."

Oh my God, oh my God.

While I was trying to choke down the thought that I was going to go to dinner with a movie star like Jeremy Gray, Guillermo hustled over with the eight-by-ten photo of us for Jeremy to sign.

He signed it, *To Guillermo and to Little Nell, the best server on earth*, but I was too distracted and excited at that moment to think about what he meant by that.

* * * * *

No, I didn't get it. I was off in outer space, in La-La Land, in Groupieville. I couldn't wait for Monday to arrive, and I actually spent all day Monday primping and plucking and waxing like it was some kind of date instead of a business meeting. I couldn't help it. A little voice inside me kept saying, *He flirted with you. He said you were fun, pleasant. He smiled. He pulled you close to pose for a picture, and it looks like he was kissing you.* I know. I had the picture on my wall. I had begged Guillermo for another copy, and he'd handed it to me with a smile.

Poor Guillermo. He had no idea I was planning to leave him, but if Jeremy offered me a job, I was gone.

On Monday night Jeremy picked me up at my door like a true gentleman, and I didn't invite him in although I had worked all day to ensure my apartment looked chic and organized from his vantage point at the doorway.

This is about a job. It's about a job, I kept reminding myself, but a part of me couldn't stop thinking about how personal a personal assistant might get with a person she helped. Especially if that person was someone nice and handsome and perfect and unattached like Jeremy Gray.

I somehow managed not to simper about how incredibly handsome he looked in his suit and tie, or how totally awesome his big movie-star SUV was. I tried to hide how sexy I thought it was when he tossed the keys to the valet, and how wet it made me when he swept into the restaurant and all the bigwigs started kowtowing to him. I was even able to subdue my impulse to jump him when he led me to the table with his hand barely touching my back. I felt like a princess when he pulled out my chair. Finally we were seated at our private table, wineglasses in hand.

"You look lovely," he said, raising his glass to me.

I tried to look appropriately modest. Sure, I had agonized for almost two days over the simple black dress I had on, the low-heeled but stylish black pumps I wore. Businesslike yet hip and fun. Isn't that what a personal assistant of Jeremy Gray's would need to look like? I knew he was single now, but his last girlfriend had been really beautiful and fun and stylish, just like him. It was like a currency. Style and desirability. I wanted him to want me for the job.

We small talked awhile, mostly him asking questions. *Where are you from? How did you end up in L.A.? Previous jobs?* I edited of course, feeling slightly guilty about it. Would he hire me if he knew I'd worked at a private BDSM club for the last five years? And was it totally dishonest of me not to mention it? There was always a chance that something about my former job might come out and make him look bad. But I didn't think so. BDSM people were nothing if not universally, protectively discreet.

And Jeremy was so encouraging and funny. God, I desperately wanted to work for this man.

The food arrived, but I was almost too freaked out to eat it. My hand shook as I reached for my wineglass. Of course he noticed.

"Are you nervous? Don't be. I've already decided I want you for the job."

"You have?"

"If you want it, yes, it's yours. I decided it a while ago. That first night I met you actually. When I came in late and you wanted to go home, but you were nice to me instead."

I smiled. "I try to be nice to everyone. It's one of the worst things about me."

"No, not at all. I think it's great, Nell. I really do. And I hope you really are available to travel, and you really do think this job would be a good fit, and that you'll find my salary is fair." He told me a number then that made me choke on my salad.

"I know it sounds high." He paused as I tried to compose myself. "But I have to admit, I haven't been completely honest with you yet about the demands of the job."

"You must have a lot of stresses and inconveniences to deal with on location."

"I do. It's extremely difficult to go to one of these shoots, constantly traveling, working, doing PR, all the little things. I need someone with me who I can depend on. I mean, it's a complicated job, but it's really very simple. I need someone to get me what I need when I need it, to keep me happy and focused and able to work."

"Sure," I said, but the look on his face was weirding me out a little. He reached for the small portfolio he'd carried in.

"I brought this paperwork along for you to look over. You don't have to sign anything or agree to take the job right now. This just sort of lays things out for you, what your duties, tasks, expectations would be." He opened it up and handed me a long, single-spaced document in dense legalese.

"To start, this is your typical confidentiality agreement. These are, unfortunately, a necessary evil in my business."

Yes, I thought, my old business too. I had signed many a confidentiality agreement in my old line of work.

"I understand," I said soberly. "Of course you can count on absolute discretion on my part."

"I'm glad to hear that. So perhaps, before we go any further, you might just sign this document. Because the rest of these papers contain more personal details about the day-to-day demands of the job, and somewhat more personal details about me." He looked at me expectantly.

"Of course," I said. "If you like."

I signed the paper after scanning it to be sure it read like all the other ones I'd signed. By this time the food was getting cold, but I was too spellbound by his attention to eat another bite. We were going over *papers*. I was about to learn his *personal details*. *Oh my God*.

"Now, Nell," he said with what almost sounded like a sigh. "Let's talk seriously about the job."

Chapter Three: Requirements

Jeremy slid the papers across the table.

"Why don't you just read them? Let me know if you have any questions."

There were five or six full pages of job description. I smiled, resting my head on my hand. Okay, the high salary made sense now. I began to scan the first page, also written in something akin to legalese.

"I guess you keep your lawyers busy with all these papers and contracts," I said.

"Yes, I do. But I think it's important to have everything perfectly clear and written down in black and white. It's easier for everyone involved."

"Yes, of course."

The document began with more verbiage about privacy, discretion, the outward appearance of normalcy. *Outward appearance of normalcy.* Okay, that was a little weird.

Near the bottom, it got even weirder. *The applicant will tender public displays of affection as needed...*

The applicant agrees to cooperate with photo opportunities and/or candid interviews regarding the love relationship of Jeremy Gray and the applicant with a positive, convincingly affectionate tone...

I stopped reading, my pulse suddenly beating in my ears. "I don't... I'm not... Okay. I'm a little confused."

"About what?"

"So...this sounds like I'm supposed to pretend to be your girlfriend."

"Yes, that is part of the job. A big part of the job actually. The public part."

The public part. I wondered what the private part amounted to. I flipped over to page three, page four.

The applicant agrees to provide sexual relations on demand, to include vaginal, oral, and anal sex. The applicant agrees to comply with regular blood testing and remain monogamous while in the employ of Jeremy Gray, excepting group sexual encounters at the discretion of Jeremy Gray, to include but not limited to m/m/f, f/f/m, f/f/m/m, m/m/m/f encounters.

The applicant understands that she will act as submissive and/or sexual slave to give comfort and relaxation in private, and function as a loving and affectionate girlfriend in public, and under no circumstances will behave in any way that exhibits or suggests her submissive status in public.

The applicant understands the protocols and expectations of the dominant and submissive relationship and agrees to comply with all requested protocols in private, to include obedience, sexual subservience, and constant availability.

Sexual subservience and use may include but is not limited to sexual intercourse, the use of erotic toys and aids, the use of multiple partners and multiple penetration, the withholding and control of orgasms, sexual objectification, and diverse sexual practices, which the applicant may or may not find repugnant.

The papers fluttered from my fingertips. There was more, much more, but I had seen enough. The knot in my throat made it impossible to speak, and I couldn't look at him, so I simply stood and started to walk. Walk away, walk outside, walk home. I didn't care. I didn't care as long as I was walking away from him.

But of course he followed. He took my elbow, and we waited for his car. He helped me in like nothing in the world was wrong, tipped the valet, started driving. I fumed beside him on the seat. How dare he? Just because he was some big-time movie star, that gave him the right to try to hire me as his personal slave? To spring his contract on me, to humiliate me?

"Nell, listen…"

"Please, take me home."

"Talk to me."

I turned on him. "What do you want me to say? You said you wanted an *assistant*. Someone to help you, keep you organized—"

"It does help! It does keep me organized!"

"You lied to me! Do you have any idea how humiliating this is? You wanted to hire me to be your sex slave. You might have mentioned that sometime before now."

"And if I had, what would you have done? The same thing you're doing now. Pretending to be outraged and running away—"

"Pretending? No, I'm really outraged, Jeremy! This…this setup, those documents—it's all sick, reprehensible—"

"Reprehensible? A little perverse, yes. But this is what you do, isn't it?"

He looked over at me, but I refused to meet his eyes. I clamped my mouth shut and crossed my legs more tightly. So he was hot. So what? He didn't turn me on. *If that's true*, a voice inside me whispered, *why are your panties so damp?* I huffed again to myself and stared out the window.

"Look, let's cut the drama. Okay?" Jeremy said. "I know that you're for sale, and that you're available. I know you're a professional."

"You know that how?"

"Because I already have a personal assistant who does things for me. Like find other types of assistants."

"Let me guess." I seethed. "His name is Kyle."

"Yes."

"You and your assistant are the reason I'm out of work!"

"Yes, but I never intended you to be out of work very long. I wanted you to work for me."

"Why this song and dance? Why didn't you just come to me at the club?"

"Come to you at the club? I'm Jeremy Gray. I'm a little bit famous, in case you hadn't noticed. I don't think you or Mistress Amelia or any of the other clients there would have appreciated the paparazzi camped at the door."

"It was your two thousand dollars! You sent him there to—what? Try me out?"

"I sent him to find someone for me. He knows what I like, what I'm into. Yes, he tried you out."

I thought of our daring, exquisite night of pleasure, now reduced to Kyle's tawdry work assignment. "That's…repugnant."

"Repugnant. Another nice word. Kyle's good at what he does. I asked him to find someone intelligent this time. I know you're not stupid, Nell. I know your mind isn't closed. I know you understand the lifestyle, and I know you've lived it. Put yourself in my shoes. How do you get what you need when you're in the spotlight twenty-four-seven? When cameras and gossip rags and web sites are recording your every move?"

I couldn't wrap my mind around it. It was so depraved. I knew rich, superstar actors lived hedonistic lifestyles, but this was just plain sick. "Your last girlfriend—she was this too? *A personal assistant?*"

"Yes, she was. She signed those same papers you read. We worked great together for a while." He said it like it was perfectly reasonable. He was crazy. He pulled up to my apartment. I wanted to get out, to slam the door in his face and go upstairs and shower until I could feel clean again.

But I didn't. I sat still, still as he did, and for some reason I asked him, "What happened? Why did she quit?"

He sat a moment in silence, biting his lip. "They all leave eventually. You will too."

I snorted. "No, I won't. Because I'm not going with you in the first place. I'm sorry that you're in this situation, I really am. But I'm not... I can't—"

"All right," he said. "Before you make any final decisions, I want you to think about this. You're out of work. Your real work. Waitressing can't be paying the bills. You're good at what you do. I'm good at it too. And I think you and I would get along. I know I went about this the wrong way, and I see that I've made you angry. It was never my intention to humiliate you or hurt you. Trap you, maybe. But only to make you consider things. So don't run away so quickly. Take a few days to consider—"

"The only thing I'm considering now is whether I'm going to take out a restraining order on you and your creepy bitch-boy Kyle. Good night." I got out, slammed the door, and went into my apartment without looking back. I don't know how long he stayed there, parked out in front. I was afraid to look. I was afraid to admit I cared.

I was afraid, because under the blazing anger burned a small ember of desire.

Chapter Four: Scared

If I were a nice person, a gentleman, I would have left her alone. I would have let her out at her apartment and never thought of her again. Her reaction to my proposal left no room for misinterpretation. She wasn't interested. Not in the least.

So perhaps I'd miscalculated. I might have perceived signals that weren't there, although as an actor I was pretty good at reading people. But I wasn't perfect, no more perfect than anyone else.

No, if I were perfect, I would let her go. I would move on. I had a few days left, plenty of time to find an acceptable candidate. Unfortunately I was more selfish than perfect. I wanted her.

I stared at the menu, even though I already knew what I wanted. Nell would arrive for work any minute now. I was sitting in her section, and I'd purposely come at a slow time. Of course, she'd be far from happy to find me here. Oh well. I'd deal with her displeasure when it came.

I picked at the sugar packets on the table and rearranged the salt and pepper shakers. Guillermo brought me a drink and thanked me for the fiftieth time for my patronage. I asked if he wouldn't mind sending Nell my way when she arrived.

"Oh yes," he answered with a wink. "I will happily do this for you."

Well, at least someone would be happy about it. I felt sorry for Nell, I really did, but she wasn't taking into consideration the positives of what I proposed. Hot sex. A great income for her. World travel, elegant dinners.

The many trappings of fame and success. Who wouldn't be happy with that life? *You aren't*, came a voice in my head.

Okay, maybe I wasn't completely happy, but that's why I needed someone like Nell. Someone fresh and pretty. Someone to sit beside me while I flew around the world on interminable flights. A woman to talk intelligently with when I was in the mood to talk. A soft, available receptacle for my cock when I wasn't.

Ah, here was the receptacle now. She crossed behind the bar. I watched her put her apron on over her sensible black work slacks, pulling the long strings around from the back to the front. I thought of corsets. I thought of cinching her wrists in those long apron strings.

She greeted Guillermo with a smile. The smile faded as he pointed over to me. They had a short exchange, Nell protesting, Guillermo urging her my way. I knew Guillermo would take care of it. And sure enough, a moment later, there she was. She pursed her full pink lips as she flipped open her order pad. Lovely pique of temper. Well, she was a redhead after all.

"The usual?" she muttered to a spot over my shoulder. Her clear green eyes stared off into space. I'd never win her over if she wouldn't look at me.

"Nell."

She didn't want to look, but she did. That told me something. It told me that she listened, however doubtful she was. It showed me that some part of her felt compelled to listen, even though her pretty face was screwed into a scowl.

"Why are you here?" Her peevish tone prodded the dom in me. I wanted to pull her over my lap. *Don't spank her. Talk to her.*

"You know why I'm here, Nell. What you probably don't know is that I won't stop coming here until I get my way."

"Well, I hope you like Italian food, then," she said, rolling her eyes. "What do you want to eat, Mr. Gray? Because I'm not going to listen to anything you have to say. I'm just going to bring you your food."

"Chicken parmigiana. Raspberry-walnut vinaigrette."

She turned on her heel and retreated to the kitchen. A moment later she returned with my salad and placed it before me on the table with a bang. I figured she'd probably spit in it.

"Do you mind?" I asked, tapping my half-filled glass. She sucked her teeth and swiped my glass off the table. I watched her stalk to the bar to refill it. Guillermo looked over at her and threw an exaggerated wink my way.

"Nell!" Guillermo said in a jovial voice that carried across the room. "Why not go keep Mr. Gray company? The restaurant's empty." Nell cringed and made a frantic hand gesture to quiet him, but Guillermo did not possess the ability to speak quietly. "Go, go! I'll call you when the order is up." She shot a look at me and grimaced.

"Go on. He is a good customer. You make him feel at home for me. Look at him sitting there, so lonely."

Again she tried to quiet him, leaning close to speak in his ear.

"So what? We are family here. And you know, I think he likes you," Guillermo added in a deafening stage whisper. "Go!"

Nell dragged herself across the bistro to my table. I stood when she arrived. "Yes, make me feel at home, Nell." I pulled out the other chair, gestured for her to sit. I didn't touch her, but she was so close for a moment, I could smell the fresh, flowery scent of her hair.

I returned to my chair, leaned back, and looked over at her.

"I sense that you have not yet calmed down from our conversation last night."

"You sense that? How intuitive."

"It's too bad. I hoped we might talk reasonably. Well." I sighed, stirring my salad. "Maybe later tonight."

"I'm working tonight."

"Guillermo already told me when you get off."

She crossed her arms over her chest and pouted so darkly that I chuckled under my breath.

"This isn't funny," she said. "What are you doing here? You enjoy this? Chasing me?"

"No, I don't enjoy the chase. Not at all. That's why I need you to just say yes." I tried to read her face. I needed to find a way to break down her walls, if I was going to get her. "Believe me, I wish you no ill will. I'm disappointed with myself for going about this the wrong way. But I can't go back now. I can only say what I feel."

"Mr. Gray, I mean this in the most literal way." She spoke slowly, enunciating every word. "I will *never* be willing to talk. I will never talk to you about this. That is all."

Her eyes were hard; her mouth was set. If some small part of her was willing to consider my offer, that part was buried away.

"Okay," I said.

She waited for me to say something else, but I knew anything I said to her would fall on deaf ears. A moment later, some other customers arrived, and she bolted with a sigh of relief. I ate slowly, watching her, looking for those subtle signals that would tell me how to proceed. To my frustration, I didn't know her well enough. Not yet anyway.

But I had a plan B. It wasn't a nice plan, and it wasn't a fair plan, but it was my last chance to make her consider what I'd asked. After I left the bistro, I made some phone calls to my assistant, and later, to her landlord.

I thought maybe, just maybe, this next step was going a little far. I felt guilty, sure, and somewhat evil. But I'd always been a firm believer in the cult of "the end justifies the means."

* * * * *

I was huddled beside my things on the stairs when he found me. He didn't say anything, and I didn't acknowledge him. He leaned down to pick up the eviction notice, holding it between his perfect fingers and scanning it with a frown.

"I'm sorry, Nell. Think of it as tough love."

"You're a sociopath."

He sat down beside me, taking off his sunglasses and holding them loosely in his hand. "I'm not a sociopath, just desperate. I'm supposed to leave in four days. And I really, really want you to come with me."

I breathed deeply, considering my next step. Punch him? Call the police? Gouge out his eyeballs? *Listen to what he has to say…*

"There are a million girls in L.A." I said, hugging my knees more tightly to my chest. "A million girls who would probably jump at this opportunity. So why me?"

"Because I want you. There may be a million girls, but I want you. Kyle told me…" His voice trailed off as he thought better of it. "I heard that you were different. That you were smarter, deeper. That you were tough. That you were petite and beautiful. When I met you, I saw it was all true. I want you, not anyone else. If there's someone better out there, I don't know where she is and I don't care. My mind's made up."

"I'm a person, Jeremy. I have a life. I have the right to self-determination."

"I do too. If I want you, I can do whatever is in my power to attain you, within the law."

"Within the law? You used slander and entrapment to get me fired from my job. Then you had me wrongfully evicted from my apartment! Now I'm homeless, and I can't even… I can't even…"

God, I needed my mom, but we hadn't spoken in years. I was estranged from my whole family. I could call my friends, but they wouldn't believe the story of what was going on with me, even if I could make it make sense in the retelling. And I'd signed his stupid confidentiality contract, on top of everything else. I hugged myself, feeling powerless and confused. Why was I even sitting with him? Why, even now, did some part of me want to insinuate myself into his arms?

"The thing is," Jeremy said, "I really just want to help you. I think you and I could have a lot of fun together. I think this could be mutually beneficial, this arrangement I'm proposing. The only reason you can't see that is because you're so angry and afraid of how I went about making it happen."

"It's not happening! I hate you so much, I can't even explain how much I hate you right now."

"It's okay to hate me, to be afraid of me, to despise me. I don't care. Just know that I would never do anything to hurt you, really hurt you, no matter what it seems like. Come with me, and belong to me for a while. Relax into it. Don't think about it so much."

"You're a psycho," I muttered, burying my head in my knees.

We sat there for a few moments, and then he reached over and put his hand on the back of my neck. He threaded his fingers into the wavy curls of my shoulder-length hair and started to rub my scalp and nape. I wanted to tell him to stop, but I couldn't. It felt so good, so comforting. My mother used to caress me that way to soothe me when I was tired or afraid.

"Listen, what do you want more than anything else in the world?" he asked quietly, when I was reduced to putty in his hands.

I didn't answer.

"Because you know what I want? I want you to come traveling with me these next four months. That's all I want. A partnership with you. Simple and erotic and enjoyable and exciting and fun. That's what I want most on earth. Now, what do you want more than anything else? Something I can do for you. Tell me."

I shouldn't have answered, but I did.

"I want to go to college. I want to finish my degree."

"Finish?" he asked in surprise. "What degree have you already started? Medical school? Law school?"

"Comparative cultural mythology."

He laughed. "I see now why you turned to waitressing and sex work."

I pulled away from him and didn't reply.

"Well, listen, if you stay with me for the term of the contract and work for me, then when you're no longer in my employ, I'll pay your way through college. Any university, any degree you want—bachelor's, master's, doctorate, whatever. If you can't get into the university you want, I'll pay your way into it. Anywhere you like. That's in addition to the salary I'm already prepared to pay you, the salary I quoted you before. That's what I can offer you. Maybe it sweetens the deal."

And damn it, I guess it did.

A little-known fact about me—I attended Harvard University for two years following a stellar high school career and a perfect score on my SATs, and began what I hoped would be a lifelong career in the study and publication of papers on mythological tales and documents. But I had to leave because of my fucked-up family; a father sent to jail, a suicidal mother spiraling out of control, siblings with their heads up their asses. I did what I could, then finally washed my hands of the whole morass, but it was far too late to return to my studies, and the money was gone.

The money. Why was life about money? I'd been trying to save, but it was hard. University tuition was steep, and scholarships were hard to win when your application essay detailed your adventures as a submissive for hire. I put away what I could each month by cutting corners where I was able. I quit the gym to save money and exercised at home with workout DVDs from the public library. I stayed out of the pricier lingerie boutiques and shopped the end-of-season sales at Victoria's Secret. I turned down dinner invitations, bowed out of barhopping with friends to put money away for the future. Still, after five years of determined saving, I barely had enough saved to cover one semester at Harvard, much less an entire degree.

But now, after a short stint of indentured servitude, I could get my life back on track. Maybe he was some twisted gift from the universe, this horrible man. He was the money, the influence I needed to move forward.

I crossed my arms over my chest, still refusing to look at him.

"I don't know you at all," I said. "I don't think this is completely safe."

"That's what all the paperwork is for. You know how this works. If you would have looked over the papers completely, I think you would have felt better about everything. Jesus, I paid a lot of money to have them drawn up. Fortunately my lawyer is very discreet."

"And perverted. To write up contracts like that."

"Yes. Sure. The contract is perverse, and by no stretch of the imagination admissible in court. But it's a job, Nell, a job that I think you'd enjoy very much. You live the lifestyle. It's in your heart, it's in your blood, it's in your will. I think that's why this is so hard for you. You want to be my submissive, but I think you're ashamed."

It was true. I despised myself for secretly craving the arrangement he suggested. "You hide too," I pointed out. "You hide the way you are. From the public, from your fans."

"Only as much as I have to. I do have a public persona to uphold. But I'm not ashamed of it. I think power exchange is beautiful. I think you are too. I think everything about you is beautiful."

"You don't even know me."

"Not yet. But if I get my way, I'll know you very well."

I rubbed my eyes. I was too tired to come up with any more protests or recriminations. Deep inside, I knew I'd already made up my mind. He knew it too.

"Finished sulking?"

"For now." I looked over at my things, then back at Jeremy Gray sitting beside me. "But what do I do? What now?"

Jeremy pulled out his phone.

"I'm going to call someone to pick up your things, and we're going to go to my place. We're going to sit down with my lawyer and go over the paperwork page by page. When we're done, I think you'll agree to start a relationship with me, but if you decide not to, I'll get your eviction reversed."

"And if I do agree to this 'relationship'?"

"We'll go to dinner tonight and tip off the paparazzi. Our first date." He turned away from me to bark into his phone. "Kyle, come over. She's ready now."

* * * * *

I stood with a scowl on my face as Kyle and Jeremy loaded my meager belongings into their cars. He was Kyle Gorgeous to me once, but now I hated his guts.

He didn't look at me, not once, and he and Jeremy didn't talk much. Like me, it was obvious Kyle was a means to an end. An errand boy, and I would be the sex toy. Smart movie star, Jeremy. He had all his bases covered.

He drove me to his house in Hollywood Hills, through monitored iron gates that slowly swung open and reminded me of jail. "It's only for security," he assured me. "Overzealous fans. You can come and go as you please, always. I promise."

I nodded, but I still felt imprisoned by circumstances, if not actual bars. His lawyer, a fit, stylish man of about fifty, ogled me as he leaned against his car in front of the house. Or maybe I should call it what it was, a fucking mansion, not a house.

The lawyer, in his smart, tailored suit and shiny Italian loafers, shook my hand and introduced himself as Martin Richards. *Nice sex contract, Mr. Richards*, I wanted to say. *Your mother must be very proud of you.* But I just shook his hand and stared down at his shoes, already feeling submissive and cowed.

"Come on," said Jeremy, leading me toward the door, enthusiastic and bright, like a kid on Christmas morning. Why shouldn't he be? He had me exactly where he wanted me. He directed Kyle and another man, Carson, to take my things upstairs. A housekeeper greeted us, and I learned there were two other housekeepers who ran the place and worked for Jeremy, in addition to Kyle, his driver, his bodyguard, and, well, myself.

One big, happy family, although I assumed I was the only one who would serve as his kink toy. My heart hammered painfully in my chest. His house was amazing, his staff was friendly, and the wine we sipped was incredible.

But I still wondered what the heck I was doing here, and what kind of ledge I was about to jump off.

Chapter Five: Friends

"Now, my dear," said Martin, passing copies of the papers to me and Jeremy. "I'd like you to read over these first and then let me know exactly what questions you have. It's not our intention to trap you into any service or duties you aren't willing to give as a salaried employee of Mr. Gray, so this is the time for you to raise any concerns or misgivings you might have. What Mr. Gray wants, first and foremost, is to find a work agreement that benefits you both."

"Yes, certainly," said Jeremy. "I want you to understand that these documents and agreements are for your benefit and safety, should you choose to accept the job. Please take your time." He nodded to the papers I held cradled in my trembling hands.

I began on page one, rereading what I'd read before. It was an excellently written document as far as BDSM contracts go. It covered public vs. private comportment, methods of address, acceptable expressions of affection, general parameters of sexual availability, and as eloquently as it was written, the meaning behind every clause was implicitly clear.

The applicant agrees to maintain a superlative level of tone and fitness... The applicant shall not get fat and lazy dining in fine restaurants and lying in luxurious beds.

The applicant shall comport herself at all times as a civilized, polite, and well-educated companion... The applicant shall not behave like a ho-bag.

The applicant will maintain a constant and meticulous level of bodily care and hygiene... Every hair shall be plucked, waxed, or otherwise banished from her pubic region, and the sex slave shall shower and brush the cum from her teeth twice a day whether she needs it or not.

The applicant agrees to wear, both in public and private, clothing and underclothing that is either provided by or approved by Jeremy Gray, and will wear whatever accoutrements she is instructed to, even if the applicant finds said accoutrements uncomfortable or unflattering... The applicant will be dressed like a whore at all times under her clothing, and whether she finds the corset, harness, and/or butt plug uncomfortable will not matter to Jeremy Gray in the least.

Sexual subservience and use may include but is not limited to sexual intercourse, the use of erotic toys and aids, the use of multiple partners and multiple penetration, the withholding and control of orgasms, sexual objectification, and diverse sexual practices, which the applicant may or may not find repugnant... In other words, the man you are considering working for is a pervert of the most extreme kind.

Punishment and humiliation will exclude control of natural bodily functions (including breath control and asphyxiation) and punishments related to natural bodily functions... So even though he is a pervert of the most extreme kind, don't worry, he's not going to try to choke the life out of you or piss or shit on you, no matter how naughty you are.

It was all standard, reassuringly standard, quite similar to the contract I'd signed to work at Eden, similar to the contract my clients had to sign to play with me, similar to the contracts dominants and submissives drew up in wildly varying relationships all over the world. This one was more sexually oriented than my contract at Eden, though, since at Eden, I hadn't been expected to provide actual sexual intercourse.

Well, that was certainly a thing of the past. I got the feeling my job duties to Jeremy would include quite a bit of taking his cock in my holes. I wondered if he was good in bed. A man as kinky as he obviously was—he had to be.

I put the papers down and looked up at Martin. I couldn't quite meet Jeremy's gaze.

"Did you understand everything in the agreement?"

"Yes, I did. I've signed similar employment contracts before, at the club."

"Of course. So this is not totally foreign to you. But somewhat different in a lot of ways, isn't it?"

I blushed. "Yes, in some ways."

"It's important to understand that my client will expect a level of sexual availability that you may not have encountered before, certainly not in your work at the club."

"Yes, I do understand that clearly."

"But his sexual requirements will fall within certain parameters meant to protect you. No third parties will engage in unprotected sex with you. Ever. Mr. Gray will not engage in unprotected sex with you until it is deemed medically safe and secure. Are you on any kind of birth control?"

"I was on the pill," I said, blushing even redder. "I can go on it again."

"We'll see my physician tomorrow," Jeremy interjected. "For blood tests and birth control for you." He looked hard at Martin, who cleared his throat.

"It is exceedingly important to my client that no unwanted pregnancies occur as a result of carelessness."

"It's important to me too," I said. "I assure you I won't be careless. I'm not on the pill right now because I hadn't... I didn't... I wasn't..."

"In a sexual relationship?" Martin provided.

"Yes."

"You will be now," Jeremy said with a broad smile. "And I hope you will find it a mutually satisfying relationship. Most of the time."

I looked down at the papers again. "What about collars?"

"What about them?"

"Will I be expected to wear one in private?"

He studied me, his eyes narrowed. "Do you want to wear one in private?"

I blushed. "I will if you want me to."

"That's not what I asked. Do you like to wear collars, Nell?"

I could feel the flush burning my cheeks. "Sure. Sometimes." Why was I feeling embarrassed about my own kinks in front of a world-class pervert like him?

"Well, sorry. I'm not much into collars." One corner of his mouth turned up in a smile. "I'll be perfectly capable of controlling you without buckling anything around your neck."

He flirted. I had to hand it to him. He was attractive and incredibly masculine. For someone like me, someone who got off on being dominated, he was eroticism defined. *But he's a job. He's just a job. He's your ticket back to Harvard. He's a new life, nothing more.*

"The only thing..." I began. Both men stared at me intently.

"I am... I don't... I would prefer not to be caned. I find it nearly intolerable. The pain of it."

They were quiet a moment, considering. I forged ahead.

"I know my job as a submissive is to accept pain, and I do, but it's not as easy for me as, perhaps, some submissives who really enjoy pain. Pain is different for me." I stopped, embarrassed, but Jeremy was watching me in fascination.

"Why is pain different for you?"

"Because I…just… I mean, I want to accept it to please my dominant, but it's not easy for me. And severe pain—it panics me a little."

"You're not a pain whore. Is that what you're trying to say?" asked Jeremy.

"Yes. I'm sorry if that disappoints you, but I can't change the way I am. I've tried. And I'm telling you honestly that I can take most pain, but I can't… I really…"

"You can't deal with being caned."

"Yes." Why did I suddenly feel ashamed?

Because submissives, good submissives, were supposed to take everything their dominant wanted to dish out.

"Okay," said Jeremy after a moment. "Okay, no canes. We'll put it on the 'hard limit' list. If that's your only hard no, I'm happy with that. You'll find I try to be reasonable as far as I can. I really do wish for you to enjoy your life with me. It won't always be wine and roses, but I want you to be happy. Do you know what I mean?"

He was looking at me almost affectionately, and I found myself close to tears.

"What's the matter?" he asked.

I shook the emotion away. It was only this weird situation. The fact that things were moving so quickly. Or perhaps it was the kindness in his deep blue eyes. "I'm just a little nervous. Overwhelmed. You think because I've worked at a club, because I'm a professional, that I'll be good at this job you want me for. But I have to say honestly, this is new to me. Complete sexual availability, a total lifestyle commitment like this."

"I know it's a lot to ask," he agreed, "but I believe the salary I offered you is commensurate with the demands of the job. And you can always resign if you find it doesn't suit you. This isn't a slave contract. These papers don't convey ownership. I don't want to own you. I just want your availability to be used when I need to use you. Do you understand the distinction?"

"Yes, Mr. Gray, I do."

"Anyway, I have every faith in you. If you're worried about being able to satisfy me, put your mind at rest. I'll teach you everything you need to know, and I'll give you time to become acclimated to it all. Like any job, there will be a learning curve. The first few weeks will be the hardest, but you'll figure everything out. Just remember, it's a job. Do your best, and I'll be happy with you, like any other boss."

The applicant shall remember that this is a job, not a relationship, and shall maintain an appropriate mood and mental composure, and shall refrain, to the best of her ability, from becoming emotionally and romantically attached to Mr. Gray, concentrating instead on the duties of her position.

"Okay," I finally said with more conviction than I felt. "If you'll make the change about caning we talked about, then I agree. I'll take the job."

Jeremy smiled broadly and leaned over to shake my hand, and then pulled me close and kissed me hard on the cheek. Strangely, it seemed both too soon and too late for him to kiss me. His face was rough with stubble, and I could feel his hard jawbone pressed against my skin. He was so solid, so male all over, that I felt suddenly hyperfemale, and yes, hypersubmissive to him. I wanted him to take me in some primal celebration, right there, roughly, on the floor. But as I finished signing and dating the last page of the document, I learned he had other ideas.

"So now you're officially my employee. Perhaps it's time to sample the goods." He smiled over at Martin and rubbed his hands together.

"Sounds wonderful to me."

"Take it all off, Nell. Everything."

I put down my wineglass in surprise. Now? Already? *Really?* "I'm not dressed for playing. I dressed this morning to go to work."

"We're not *playing*. You're *working* as of right now, and what you're dressed for doesn't matter, because as I just said, I want you to take it all off. And," he added, "I'm not a big fan of repeating myself." He waited a moment. "The correct response is 'yes, Jeremy.'"

"Yes, Jeremy," I parroted unenthusiastically, standing up and starting to disrobe. I knew I probably looked sullen, not great for a submissive, but I'd only accepted the job thirty seconds ago. I guess I'd expected to be allowed to unpack, eat dinner, perhaps have a little more instruction in his needs and desires before I had to strip and perform in front of his friends.

"I think our little submissive may be slightly out of practice," Jeremy commented drily. "She hasn't worked in a while. Perhaps you might help me get her back into her submissive headspace."

"I might know a way," said Martin, crossing to a footstool in the corner of the room. He lifted the cover and drew out a whippy-looking pink and black riding crop. "This seems to fit her. Pretty but edgy."

"I don't know." Jeremy considered and shook his head. "Perhaps a little harsh for the first time. A paddle, maybe."

"Okay." Martin dived back into the Footstool of Disaster. I was fully undressed now, my clothes folded neatly and placed on the corner of the sofa, where Kyle sat watching with a smirk on his face.

"Shall I stand or kneel, Master?" I asked when no direction was forthcoming.

"'Shall I stand or kneel, *Jeremy*,'" he corrected with mild irritation. "If you can't learn to drop the 'Master' on your own, I'll happily train it out of you. You're not my slave."

I almost replied "yes, Sir," out of long-ingrained habit, but thankfully caught myself in time.

"To answer your question, Nell, when I snap my fingers and point to the floor, you kneel. If I snap again, you lower your forehead to the floor and stay that way. If I don't snap, you don't do anything but stand in front of me and look like the pretty and available submissive you are. Do you understand those directions?" *Oh God.*

"Yes, Jeremy."

"Good girl."

He walked over to me then and circled me. He just looked. He didn't touch, which was almost harder to bear. He was all dominant now, and I wanted him. I craved what he represented, and I creamed for the way he stood and surveyed me. The friendly, considerate Jeremy fell away, replaced by this curt man and his exacting demands. I sucked in air, and every nerve in my body suddenly seemed to end at my clit. I stood still and let him look at me, trying not to tremble. I was terrified that he didn't like what he saw. But a moment later he whistled low and dispelled my fears with a sexy sound in his throat.

"Look at her ass, Martin."

"I've been looking at it."

"She's worth her weight in gold just for that ass. It's bordering on obscene." He reached out and cupped one of my ass cheeks, then squeezed it. His hands were warm, firm. Large and rough. He was slow to let me go.

"You going to paddle her, Martin?"

"You should have the first go at her."

"No, go ahead. I insist. I'll have my fill of her in the next weeks and months. In thanks for your services, you go first."

"Are you sure?"

"Yeah. Anyway, Kyle had her first," he reminded Martin. "Which he also deserved for finding this outstanding submissive for me."

Kyle smiled from the sofa. I had a feeling he didn't really care whether he'd beaten my ass first. He seemed more preoccupied with watching Jeremy than looking at me, perhaps waiting for his cue to run and fetch his boss a condom. I tried not to dwell on what type of duties playing PA to Jeremy Gray might entail.

And me, I stood and listened as they discussed what to do to me. I had no choice or say in the matter. Well, I had a choice. My choice was to stay in my role and submit to them, or to stop playing along and walk out the door. And I couldn't imagine doing the latter, even though I was jittery to be playing with Jeremy for the first time. All these emotions—fear, lust, vulnerability—they all converged into one warm hum. Subspace. I would already be there, if this situation weren't so completely new.

Jeremy stood close to me. I could smell his bracing, masculine scent. Part musky cologne, part clean male skin. Perhaps a touch of shaving oil. I fought the sudden urge to turn and lick his face. If he took any note of what I was feeling or thinking, he didn't show it. He was still taking in my body, looking over the new toy he'd bought. He reached and pinched one of my nipples, sending my clit into a deep, steady throb. I gasped and looked him in the eyes as he stared back at me. *I want you to look at my face. Look right at me.* I remembered Kyle saying it. Jeremy didn't say it, but I knew to do it just the same.

"You're beautiful," he breathed. Then he crossed the room to watch from a distance as Martin approached me with a long, thin paddle in his hand. He positioned me so my back was to Jeremy.

"Bend over. Grab your ankles," Martin said.

I lowered myself into position, spreading my legs for balance.

"Wider." Martin tapped the inside of one thigh with the paddle. I spread my legs until he stopped prodding me. "Better. How many do you think, Jeremy, to get her back in the right headspace?"

"Hmm. Perhaps start with twenty, and then if she needs it, I'll give her a few more."

"Twenty it is, then," Martin agreed. "Nell, you'll count so I can hear you."

He was a decent disciplinarian. He started with some warm-ups, three or four lightish strokes. *Are you watching, Kyle?* I thought, remembering how he'd lit into me with all his strength from the very first stroke. But of course Kyle was watching, just as Jeremy was, and the idea of Jeremy watching really turned me on.

I was spread, bent, vulnerable, my ass and pussy on brazen display. It wasn't an accident that Martin turned my backside to Jeremy. Sucking up to the boss. In fact, I was well aware that although Martin wielded the implement, this entire scene was Jeremy's—giving me to Martin to paddle, letting Kyle watch. It was going to be a very interesting experience, subbing for Jeremy. That was already clear.

Shit, was that six or seven? I'd been daydreaming. "Six...?"

Jeremy chuckled, and Martin murmured, "If you say so." Then he really started to lay them on to make me pay attention, and I did. Paddles stung. They weren't excruciating—they didn't make me dance around like crops or canes—but they had a solid bite. I squeezed my hands around my ankles to ground myself and concentrated on staying still. Each blow nudged me forward. I had to compensate with the muscles in my ass and thighs. As always when I was receiving corporal punishment, I wondered why I subjected myself to this. I hated the pain. Or did I love it? *Breathe. One blow at a time.*

He took me up to twenty—or twenty-one, I suppose—swatting me hard enough at the end that my voice cracked as I counted each stroke. When he finished, I opened my eyes and let out a quiet sigh of relief. I'd been so focused on enduring the paddling and not falling out of position that I'd almost forgotten Jeremy was there. But not quite.

I watched between my spread thighs as he crossed to take the paddle from Martin's hand. I shivered at the assured way he handled the implement. *Be still. Deep breaths.* I was still bent over, clutching my ankles, as both men took time to fondle my tingling ass.

Was he looking at my slit displayed before him? Staring at it? My pussy must have shone with wetness. The idea of him seeing that made me burn with humiliation, which only turned me on more. He was probably thinking to himself, *This slut. One paddling and she's panting like a dog.* I tried to discipline my breath.

"She takes it well," Martin said. "I wasn't soft on her."

"Well, she's a professional." Jeremy's sharp pinch made me tense. "You get what you pay for. But I bet I can get her to go up on her toes a bit."

He slipped a couple of fingers into my pussy, and I let out my breath in a gasp. I felt that quick impulse to react, to pull away, and then the slow subjugation of will. I let him take me. I let myself discover how rough and thick his fingers felt in my cunt. He slid them around, exploring me. Soon it took every ounce of my control not to arch my hips back into his hand.

"Are you sure you weren't too soft on her? Because I think she's enjoying this," he said. "You should feel how wet she is. Actually, would you like to take her, since you made her so aroused?"

"Oh no," said Martin. "This time I really must insist. That honor belongs to you."

Jeremy snorted and withdrew, then placed his hand on the small of my back. I could feel the hot moisture of my arousal on his fingers. "Such formalities. Anyway, again I'm afraid that Kyle beat us both to the chase. Ah, well. Later. We have dinner reservations at seven. I'm only going to paddle her for now."

He stood back, and I braced. I knew he would test me. I knew he would try to break me down. He began, swung his arm back and then forward in a sharp motion, and *crack*! The first blow panicked me. *No, I can't take this. I really can't*. I made an urgent sound and squeezed my ankles until they ached. Martin had only been one long warm-up. I realized that now.

The next blow came, and I had the same feeling, the same certainty that I could not survive this pain. But then he stopped to let me collect myself. Jeremy knew what he was doing. No wild flailing like Kyle. Powerful arms, powerful snap, powerful sting. Each blow required me to make that difficult decision. *Stand. Present. Accept.* Each blow made me certain that I shouldn't be here, every bit as much as it made me want more. I wished for restraints, because my hands wanted to fly up to protect my ass, and it took so much effort to stay in place. My back wanted to straighten and my legs wished to run away, but I subdued those impulses. I imagined him wielding the crop, and it made me feel faint. I was glad we'd agreed, for now, that the cane was a definite no.

But what I really, truly wanted as I counted to ten, and then twenty again, and then five more—the last five actually making me rise up frantically on my toes as he'd said—what I truly wanted and craved was to feel his hands, his palms spanking me. I wanted contact. It scared me how much I wanted contact with him. I wanted his approval, his affection. Perhaps even his admiration, a little bit. And his cock. I desperately wanted him to put his cock in me, whatever way, whatever hole he desired.

But I didn't get his hands or his cock. When the paddling was done, he lifted me and looked into my eyes. I tried to focus. I was still reeling from pain and trying to process the fact that Jeremy's paddling made me hornier than I'd been in my life.

"Here." He pointed at a spot on the floor. I dazedly looked down. What does that mean, when he points at something? He snapped his fingers. "Here!" he said and pointed again. I lurched to my senses and scurried over to drop to my knees.

"Martin." I looked up at Jeremy to see him gesture down at me. "She's yours. Please take her mouth if you like."

The words froze me. Martin looked down at me with a cordial, relaxed expression as he undid his pants. I looked over at Kyle, who smirked from the couch.

I felt deep shame, and with it, an overpowering wave of lust. I felt distaste, and I felt hot excitement. I felt disappointment that it was Martin I would receive, instead of my new boss. Jeremy crossed his arms over his chest and stared at me. There was no hint of softness in his eyes.

"Go on. You serve me. When it pleases me, you serve my friends."

Martin was already hard. With one last look at Jeremy, I took his lawyer's cock in my hands and sheathed it with the rubber Jeremy handed me. I took Martin into my mouth and started to pleasure him, but my mind was fixed on the man at my side. Jeremy stood and watched, fully clothed, detached—an immovable reminder of my status in the room. I was his comfort object, and what he asked for, I did. My molten ass cheeks were a throbbing reminder of that. Each time I shifted on my knees to take Martin's cock deeper in my throat, I felt the sore ache of my welted bottom and thought of icy blue eyes. I wished it were Jeremy's cock I was servicing, and I worshipped the phallus in my mouth as if it were. I licked, I fondled. I abased myself. When Martin came with a grunt, I wondered only if Jeremy was satisfied with me.

And then I realized it. I was already his submissive, and he was already my dom.

I'd already forged that longing, that emotional connection that I hadn't forged with even one of my customers at the club. I'd never even felt like this with Douglas, like I might die if I couldn't make him pleased with me.

It had taken Jeremy exactly one half hour to make me completely and indelibly his.

* * * * *

After Martin left, I was sent upstairs with orders to shower and dress for dinner.

"Your nicest dress," he added. "We're celebrating tonight."

I tore through my bags looking for something appropriate that wasn't too balled-up or wrinkled or dirty or destroyed. Unfortunately I didn't have many nice dresses. I hadn't needed them when I worked for the club. I had enough corsets, stockings, lingerie, and fuck-me shoes to fill an entire armoire, but my dress selection was woefully poor. There was the dress I'd worn the night Kyle came over, but somehow I didn't feel I ever wanted to wear that dress again.

In the end, Bonita, one of the housekeepers, came to check on me. She became my new best friend when she produced a handheld steamer that helped me salvage a half-decent dress in the bottom of my bag. I supposed in the near future I'd receive the *clothing provided by or approved by Jeremy Gray*, but in the meantime I could only wear what I had.

I showered and plucked and perfumed and did my face and hair as best I could with Bonita's help, rooting through my boxes and suitcases and raiding the well-stocked guest bathroom. I wondered if this had been the old girlfriend's bedroom and bathroom. There was no evidence any other woman had been here before me, but I still felt haunted by her. Would he like me better or worse than he'd liked her? Why had she left him? What was I in for? How long would Jeremy Gray be my "boss"?

She would know, of all people, when she saw us together. She would know exactly what was going on. Or would she? Who's to say Jeremy Gray couldn't suddenly decide to fall in love and get a real girlfriend? I was supposed to make it look that way. I thought I could. I thought I already had a scary little thing going on for Jeremy. It was unfortunate, but it wasn't anything I could help. I could act the girlfriend, sure, but otherwise I would have to protect myself. No matter how sexy and kind and charming he could be, I couldn't fall in love.

I couldn't, I wouldn't. I absolutely wasn't going to…even though he gave me a look when I came downstairs for dinner that took my breath away. A look that said, clearly, *You are mine to control, and I like that. You are mine to use in whatever way I want.*

Yes, I'm yours to use, Jeremy Gray, for the price of a salary.

Yes, you got your wish.

Chapter Six:
Dinner

She was mine, but she didn't completely trust me. Not yet.

That was apparent from the uneasy way she sat across from me, and it made me partly frustrated and partly horny. She feared me. It turned me on.

But I wanted her to like me too.

Why? I always wanted them to like me, against my better judgment. This heady new-relationship tension, it was incredible, an erotic shot in the arm. And she was simply spectacular, everything I loved in a woman. Petite. Pretty. Complicated. Sassy, although she tried to subdue it. And scared, although she pretended to be self-assured.

Best of all, she wasn't a pain whore. She wasn't even a masochist. *She was afraid of pain.* When she'd made that little confession in the meeting, I'd almost come in my pants. It was luck, sheer luck, that Kyle had found her. I'd sent him out with the usual general instructions. Find a small, reserved submissive with nice, real tits and a spectacular ass. Make sure she does it all, takes punishment, does oral, and accepts anal with adequate skill.

But uncovering a true submissive versus a self-occupied pain whore—Kyle wouldn't have had the knowledge and experience to judge it. Even I couldn't intuit it sometimes until it was too late. My last girl had turned out to be the worst kind of self-involved submissive, and I'd put up with her because it seemed easier than starting over again.

But Nell wasn't like her. She wasn't one of the ones who actually wanted to be hurt, who craved it, who could be absolutely spoiled by it. She was one of the ones who feared the pain.

The ones who liked it could be depended on to fake the requisite fear and distress, usually badly, but the ones who feared it and submitted to it anyway were rare and wonderful to possess. So she didn't want the cane, she couldn't take it. I could live with that for now, just to have everything else she offered.

Little Nell. She was little all right. Little and curvy and sexy, and as complicated as the academics she pursued. Comparative cultural mythology? I hadn't known whether to laugh or stare. I'd laughed, but at the same time, her hidden intellectual streak fascinated me. As did her ass.

"How is it?" I asked her, gesturing to the barely touched entrée in front of her, some kind of baked Italian chicken with green beans on the side.

"It's delicious," she murmured.

"You should eat more of it, then."

She picked up her fork.

"If you want to," I amended. God forbid I'd force her to eat. I'd force her to do many things, yes, by agreement, but I really didn't care to control everything about her like some doms would. She didn't know that yet, but she would eventually figure it out. She put her fork down and sneaked a look at me. So nervous.

I'd ordered chicken parmigiana myself, to make her smile, and she had smiled. Not quite the real smile I'd hoped for, though. She was still so guarded, and perhaps she was tired. It had been a long day of trials and tribulations for poor Nell. I didn't think I could leave her alone tonight either, so her day wasn't nearly through.

But perhaps I would leave her alone. It would be the kind thing to do. And possibly a savvy thing to do as her new dom. Let her know that she was *so* mine that I didn't have to fall on her right away, that I could make her wait for me, at my beck and call.

I did, though, desperately want to fall on her. I didn't think I could wait.

"You look lovely," I said, stroking the stem of my wineglass. "How do you feel?"

She looked at me briefly, then shrugged.

"Don't shrug, please. Answer. If we were really on a date, you wouldn't act this way. Like this is your last meal before you go before a firing squad."

She fidgeted and attempted another smile, this one not at all real.

"Does your ass hurt, darling?"

That finally brought a true laugh. She'd been a pleasure to paddle, and a pleasure to watch as she'd sucked off Martin too. I'd almost given her to Kyle for a replay, but by the time I'd watched that I would have had to take her myself, and I didn't want to do that yet.

And she hadn't lied—she'd really struggled with the paddling. Her pained reactions hadn't been faked. It had been a test of sorts, and she'd passed it. She didn't crave it, being punished. For her, it really did hurt.

But she'd become aroused by our little scene, that had been obvious. I was fairly certain she got off on being exposed, bent over, spread, studied, stared at. She would get plenty of that kind of exposure at my hands, both mentally and physically.

She'd get exposure of an entirely different kind also, for better or worse. As we'd entered the restaurant, the paparazzi had snapped our photograph like sharks fighting over chum. I'd purposely brought her to one of the paparazzi's favorite Hollywood haunts to introduce her as my new love, my new girlfriend. Jeremy Gray having a new love interest was a tabloid cover item, and great PR for me.

I'm not sure why I did things this way, why I didn't just find a real girlfriend, maintain a true relationship. It probably involved issues like time, stress, selfishness, and basic shallow tendencies. And probably, even deeper than that, basic mind-numbing, bloodcurdling fear. Fake relationships were easier and less potentially devastating. Emotional entanglements were far too stressful for me.

The upside of fake relationships was that they could be arranged to be everything you want and desire, and none of the things you don't. The downside was that the fake girlfriends always left.

I looked at Nell. *How long until you leave me?* I hoped she would at least last until the end of the upcoming shoot, because it would be a long, complicated, grueling one, and I didn't want to slog through it alone. I grasped for some topic of conversation, something to put her at ease.

"Your name—it's unusual."

"Is it?" She shrugged. "It's not my real name."

I don't know why I found that so alarming. I waited for her to elaborate. She didn't.

"So what is your real name?"

"I mean, Nell's my name, but it's a nickname. I don't like my real name, and I don't particularly want to share it." That frown again. Damn. Subject change.

"Have you traveled much?"

"No, not much. Now and again."

"I'd be happy to help with anything you'll need for the trip. We can shop tomorrow or Sunday. Just let me know."

"I… What…what will I need?"

"Do you have an MP3 player to listen to on the plane? A laptop? Books to read? You'll be spending a lot more time on your own than you probably suspect."

"Oh."

"And you'll need comfortable clothes for traveling, nothing too high maintenance. Some of the flights will be long. And you'll need some high-quality, durable luggage," I added as an afterthought, remembering her well-worn suitcases from the stairwell.

"Where will we be going?"

"Thailand, for starters. That's a ridiculously long flight. From there we'll go to Turkey, Bulgaria, a month and a half in Portugal, and then Italy and Greece, I believe. It's an action flick, lots of chasing bad guys around the globe, past striking and recognizable points of interest."

"All in a day's work."

"Yes. And there will be some very, very long days, for me and for you too. But you might enjoy traveling to these locations if you're into history and mythology and all that. If there's anything you'd like to do or see while we're traveling, let me know and I can try to make it happen. I can't always, but sometimes I can."

Why was I trying so hard to win her over?

"Anyway, whatever you need, just tell me."

She shifted again. Ah, the sore-bottomed submissive, so fun to watch. She looked up at me with wide green eyes.

"I'm not sure—I'm a little worried about what to wear."

I shrugged. "You can wear jeans and T-shirts most of the time, if you like. As long as they're tight, and you're naked underneath."

No response.

"It was a joke, Nell. Wear what you like. Whatever makes you feel comfortable and sexy. If I don't like it, I'll tell you to change."

"I just don't want to reflect badly on you. Will they be taking our picture like that all the time?"

"Yes, pretty much. You can't get obsessed about it, though. You have to be yourself. Take the cameras for what they are, an intrusion of privacy and an irritant of the business. They will get on your nerves, and trust me, the gossip sites will say unflattering things about you. You have to ignore it. You have to blow it off."

"This is all just so new."

"I know you're worried, but I also know you'll do fine. It's good that we've already started. The sooner you're used to things, the sooner you'll settle down." I reached out to run my fingertips down the side of her face. "You're skittish now, but you'll be a jaded, world-weary traveler in no time."

"Like you?"

"Like me. I'm incredibly jaded. Jaded enough to hire a girlfriend to go with me, instead of finding a real one."

"I suppose relationships rarely survive travel anyway."

"So you know more about travel than you're letting on." I laughed. "Yes, there will be tedious and difficult times, just like in a real relationship. But you are a very, very wise woman, because you'll be getting paid to put up with the stress."

She smiled and dropped her gaze to her plate, then looked around. Anywhere but at me. It always took time for the girls to get over the money thing, to get over being paid. I hoped Nell might be different. She was the first one I'd hired who was already a professional. But I understood the difference between being paid for actual sex and being paid for work. *Believe me, Nell. I get it, but it has to be this way.*

I leaned forward across the table then and looked right at her. "Tell me about your thing with canes."

"What about them? I already told you how I felt."

"When did you decide it, though? You know. 'No more canes.'"

I already noticed the way her lips tightened when she was annoyed and trying to hide it, the way her gaze moved around the room when she was upset. I was an actor. I was a master of reading expressions.

"What happened to you?"

"Nothing happened. I got caned. I didn't like it. It fucking hurt. Have you ever been caned?"

There she was, the sassy girl lurking beneath the surface.

"No, I can't say I have, and I hope never to be." I took another leisurely sip of wine. "I guess you've had just about everything happen to you in your line of work. Was that the worst, the experience with the cane?"

"I suppose. Yes. It was one of the worst experiences, but it didn't happen to me at work."

"Your first experience?"

"No."

I looked at her. That annoyed purse of the lips again. "We're going to be spending a lot of time together, Nell. You might tell me a little something candid about yourself. Was it one of your first experiences?"

"Yes."

I leaned my head on my hand, watching her avoid my gaze.

"You don't even have that much experience, do you? Aside from the sanitized play at the club. How many serious Dom/sub relationships have you had?"

She sighed and looked up at me. "Not very many. You got me, okay. I'm far from experienced at all this. I've had a few short relationships with dominant partners, but they never lasted long."

"Why not?"

"I don't know," she said to her hands in her lap.

"Listen to me. Look at me, right in my eyes."

She did, and I put on my best reassuring-dominant voice.

"You're exactly what I want, and you're going to please me. I want you to stop worrying about everything, right now. Do you understand?"

She nodded, but her eyes were still clouded by doubt.

"Are you ready to go home?" I sat back and signaled for the check. "I think it's best if we got our first private scene out of the way, don't you?"

I could barely hear her whispered "yes."

* * * * *

By the time we left the restaurant, the paparazzi had grown to swarmlike proportions. She drew back as the doorman opened the door and the mob started to shout and jockey for shots. I took her by the elbow and led her through the crush of bodies and blinding flashes to the waiting car. Inside, as the door shut on the noisy melee, she hugged herself and shrank down in her seat.

"They're crazy," she said.

"They're thieves."

"Thieves? What do they steal?"

"Privacy. I'm sorry you have to deal with it, but it will get easier. I'll protect you from them as much as I can."

I looked over at her, guarded and freaked out and forlorn, hunched against the door.

"Give me your hand."

I took her hand and drew it to my mouth, and brushed my lips across the soft skin there. We drove home in silence, and I noticed more than once that she stifled yawns.

You shouldn't use her tonight, my conscience chided.

But I would.

I couldn't wait. I absolutely couldn't wait to touch her, to possess her, to make her my own. At the house, I guided her through the foyer and stopped with her at the foot of the stairs. The house was dark and quiet.

"Do you have anything sexy to wear in off-white, ivory, beige, something like that?" I asked. "Not pure white. I hate pure white. It looks cheap."

"Yes, Sir," she said, then quickly amended her response at the look on my face. "Yes, Jeremy."

I'd told her I would beat it out of her, and she remembered, because her face went pale.

"I believe this is the second time I'm having to remind you not to call me that. As stated in the contract, you're not to use that form of address. It will only take one slip in public at the wrong time and place."

"I'm sorry."

"Furthermore, 'Please, Master' and 'Please, Sir' are our agreed-upon safe words, which makes your constant use of 'Sir' even more annoying."

"I'm so sorry."

"I'm so sorry, *Jeremy*."

She only stared back, wide-eyed, too afraid now to say anything for fear of saying it wrong.

"I'll ask once again and hope for the correct reply this time. Do you have anything sexy to wear in off-white or ivory?"

"Yes, Jeremy," she said.

"Go put it on now, and have Bonita show you to my room when you're finished. If you take more than five minutes, I'll double the number of strokes you've earned for addressing me incorrectly."

"Yes, Jeremy."

I went into the kitchen for a quick drink, pretending not to notice the way she took off running up the stairs. Not precisely good form, but it was her first day and it had been a long one, so I let it go. I poured myself a shot of vodka and downed it. I wasn't much of a drinker, but some situations called for a drink, like being alone with a submissive for the first time when you thought you might kill her from the force and intensity of your lust.

I looked at my watch. What time had I sent her upstairs to dress? Ah well, she would be there within five minutes no matter what. A sub as pain-reluctant as Nell wouldn't double her punishment if there was any possible way to avoid it. And Bonita would help her, softhearted woman that she was. I started up the stairs to my bedroom, to gather the things I would need for the introductory scene I had in mind.

I wanted to discipline her again, had thought about it all through dinner, but then convinced myself it was too much too soon. But her lapse of address had allowed the weaker, selfish side of me to change my mind. I pulled a crop out of the closet, not unlike the one I'd cautioned Martin against using earlier in the day. Some nipple clamps, rather strict ones, and a length of thin black leather. A condom. I placed them all in a line on the table at the foot of the bed and started to undress. I loosened my tie and took it off, unbuttoned the top buttons of my shirt, kicked off my shoes and socks, undid my belt and hung it in the closet next to the others. When I returned to the bedroom, she was at the door.

"Come in. Come stand here." I pointed to a spot on the floor purposely near the end table where the implements lay. I looked her up and down as I turned up my sleeves. It was impossible to keep the approval from my expression. I didn't try. As I'd suspected, the ivory corset and stockings she wore set off her bright auburn curls and pale skin perfectly, and she had beautiful, understated matching satin ivory stilettos on her feet. The corset was pretty and old-fashioned and expensive-looking, with some satiny ties and muted soft lace. Exactly the classy sort of slutwear I liked best.

I was going to buy her a hundred negligee sets in ivory. Later. First things first. I wanted to kiss her. I wanted to put my hands on her. I took her in my arms and gathered her close. I cupped her ass lightly, then squeezed it hard. She tensed a little, and she was deliciously shivery. I put one hand on the back of her neck to gentle her, to guide her lips to mine. I kissed her hard and thoroughly, testing her reactions. I was thrilled to feel her responsiveness and hear her soft sighs. I loved the way submissives kissed, so restrained on the surface, and yet so passionate underneath. By the end I had her hands pinned firmly behind her back in lovely little fists.

"Turn around," I said quietly. She turned and waited, her lovely ass outlined by the corset and garter laces. At the sight of it, the burgeoning erection in my pants achieved full mast. *Jesus.* I picked up the black leather string and wound it around her wrists carefully. Not too tight, but tightly enough for her to feel it, securely enough for her to feel restrained. I kissed her nape, then licked her upper back and that lovely curve where her neck met her shoulders. I wanted to eat her alive.

"You're mine," I whispered next to her pale, perfect earlobe.

"Yes, Jeremy," she responded, almost too softly to hear.

I snapped my fingers once, and she dropped to her knees. I snapped again, and she lowered her whole body gracefully forward on the floor. A light nudge on the inside of one ankle and she spread her legs wider, balancing carefully with her hands still bound behind her back.

"Arch a little more," I said. "There, just like that. You will hold this pose for ten strokes of the crop. If you remain silent and still, you'll only receive five beyond that. If you fidget and scream, you'll receive another ten."

"Yes, Jeremy," she said, bracing herself.

I gave her ten then, not awful strokes, but hard enough. She made some soft, frantic sounds that she tried to muffle in the carpet, doing an acceptable job. Quietness was one of the things I tried to train into my submissives right away. Hotel walls were thin, and it was always embarrassing when security showed up. She was impressively still too, the only movement the fitful squeezing of her bound fists.

"Good girl," I said. "These next ones will be harder, but you will receive only five more. Try to be quiet, as quiet as you can manage."

For the last five, I really laid into her. She continued to be still, even though her urgent mewling grew louder. I drew actual tears, which I'd wanted to do. She was a beautiful crier, her eyes wide and wet when I pulled her to her feet.

"Okay." I placed the crop back on the table. "I hope now the 'Sirs' and 'Masters' are all gone."

"Yes, Jeremy," she whispered.

My gaze was drawn to the lovely expanse of her décolletage, which rose and fell deeply with each sniffling breath. Her beautiful tits were thrust forward from her hands being pinned behind her. Wordlessly I folded over the cups of her corset to expose her breasts, and not surprisingly, I found her nipples rock hard. I reached for the clamps on the side table. She stared as I lifted the small silver devices and held them in my hand.

I said, "Look at me," but she already was. She gasped almost inaudibly as each unforgiving clamp closed on her nipple, and she blinked at the sudden intense and stringent pain. I studied my submissive—corseted, bound, whipped, marked, clamped. Subjugated.

"How do you feel?"

"I feel desperate, Jeremy."

"Desperate for what?"

"Desperate to come."

I put my fingers between her legs to find her wonderfully, copiously wet. She was well trained. She didn't dance around or try to grind her clit against my fingers. She stood still and watched me, breathless and aroused.

"You're not allowed to come without my permission," I reminded her, fingering her mercilessly. "Not ever. Not even in the privacy of your room. Not even if we're five thousand miles away from each other, should that situation ever arise. Do you understand?"

"Yes, Jeremy."

I removed my hand and pointed at the floor at my feet, then started to unbutton my pants.

"Normally I would have you undo me yourself, but since you're restrained, I'll do it this time."

"Thank you, Jeremy." She knelt before me in a practiced way that brought her mouth to the perfect angle to receive my cock. Impressive, but the object of tonight wasn't flattery and praise. I rolled on the condom.

"By the way, I'm the only one who's going to be coming tonight, to drive the lesson home that you belong to me, and that your desire and sexual satisfaction belong to me too."

She looked up from her knees in silent resignation. I tweaked one of the clamps and used my other hand to guide her lips to the jutting cock I offered.

"I'm sure your skills aren't nearly up to my exacting standards, but all I ask for now is that you do your best. Open up."

I held her head and thrust into her mouth quickly and deeply, seating myself all the way in her throat. She gagged, surprised and unbalanced, just as I'd wanted her to. There was no use letting your submissive think she was already talented enough as she was. I let her flounder a little, throwing her off her rhythm every time she found one, gagging her purposely and aggressively a few more times. While Nell tried hard and obviously knew the basics of fellatio, she was far from a pro. Well, there had been a "no sex" clause at her work. It was nothing a whole lot of practice wouldn't fix. Practice was good. And for all I knew, it was the first time she'd done a blowjob without the use of her hands, which were still firmly fixed behind her back.

I purposely took a long time, as long as I could. I was in no hurry to leave her hot, eager mouth. She never gave up, never flagged. I knew she was tired, so her effort touched me all the more. I watched her, spellbound by her drive to please me, until tears began to squeeze from her eyes. I put my hand under her chin.

"Look up." Her eyes popped open, and she gazed up at me, never stopping. I fell in love a little. A couple of tears overflowed and meandered down her cheeks. My cock swelled, and I tightened my hands on her head. I purposely thrust deep and choked her. She pulled away, an instinctive impulse, and immediately apologized, her voice low and raspy.

"Okay," I said. "Again." Slowly this time, I eased into her throat. She tensed. I felt the impulse to escape again, a tiny jerk of her head, but this time she subdued it. "Good girl." I gave one clamped nipple a hard pull. She moaned against my rigid flesh. "Now finish me off."

I let go of her head, let her take over. She devoured me. She bobbed her face up and down on my cock. She was hot, she wanted it. She was hungry. I stared down at her reddened ass and the hands clenched above it, trying to pull loose from their bonds. Did she want to touch me? Did she truly desire me? This felt like more than an act. I'd fucked girls who had an agenda. I recognized it. This felt like something else.

I watched her slender back, the muscles working as she sucked me in and out. A sound rose in my throat, shaken loose from some primal recess of my mind. She moaned in answer, and the vibration of her voice against my rigid dick sent shocks to my balls. I threw my head back and felt the release roll over me. I grabbed her head again and rode out the orgasm from deep inside her throat, jerking against her mouth. The sensation of her lips closing on me, the feel of her hair under my hands. The musky smell of her arousal mixed with mine. The red welts on her ass, the clenched fists trapped by a thin leather lace. I thought I would never forget any of it. Not even when she was gone.

My mind rebelled at that thought. I'd just acquired her. It was too soon to think of letting her go. I loosened my hands and drew away. I patted her hair, too spent to think of words. She knelt patiently in front of me. She was still tearful. Her back still rose up and down as she struggled to slow her breath. I left to take off the condom. When I returned I took her chin in my hand again, tilting her face up to mine. Her wide green eyes met mine, and I saw the question there. *Are you pleased?*

"Good girl. Up now."

I pulled her to her feet and held her arm a moment longer than she probably needed to find her balance. I removed the first clamp gently, then licked and sucked her nipple to ease away the sting. I removed the other, giving that sore tit the same soothing treatment. She shuddered and pressed her legs together, made a small plaintive sound, almost too soft to hear. A *please...* An *I beg you...*

But no. It would be better to make her wait.

I was soft on a lot of things other doms were strict on, but orgasms were mine, always mine, to control, to dole out, to demand, to withhold. I would not let her come tonight. I kissed her deeply, then tugged and sucked her nipples again, then turned her around to undo the knotted leather tie around her wrists. After I unbound them, I turned her again so we were face to face.

"Show them to me," I said.

She lifted her wrists. The lace had left some indentations but had not chafed or broken the skin. To be sure, I brought each wrist to my mouth. I kissed the fine, pale surface there, the tiny crisscross of veins. I caressed them with my tongue. She tasted of faint, cinnamony perfume and the more sexual scent of leather. She kept her eyes cast down, but her chest rose and fell as I licked her wrists and then right up into her lovely, soft palms. My tongue traced the three lines there. What were they called? Heart line? Head line? Life line? *Love line.*

No, I didn't love her, but I could have licked her forever, every line, every curve, every vein under her skin, every soft hair on her forearms, every wet, hot, secret place. I would too, but not tonight. Instead I only kissed each of her trembling palms lightly, closed her little fists up tight, and said pointedly, "Good night."

Chapter Seven:
The First Time

I cried myself to sleep. I hated myself for it, but I couldn't stop the tears.

I tried to convince myself it was only frustration, the fact that he'd made me hotter than anyone had in my life and then decided, deliberately, not to let me come. But that wasn't really the reason, just one aching symptom of a much more encompassing pain.

I'd left his room and padded down the hall in my ivory heels, my most elegant silk corset absolutely untouched and unsoiled, but I felt like the world's dirtiest whore.

It's just an arrangement. You're doing a job. Get your act together.

When I'd tried for twenty minutes to make myself feel clean again in the shower, I finally let the tears come. It wasn't that anything he'd done to me had been degrading or sordid. It was the opposite. I had never participated in such an affecting scene.

This was a man I clearly should hate. A man who had trapped me, who was using me in the most selfish way, but instead of feeling hatred for him, when he'd licked my wrists before he dismissed me, I'd nearly cried tears, the same emotional tears that threatened to overwhelm me now. Tears of fearful, fascinated infatuation.

Yes, infatuation was all it was.

No, no, I wasn't falling in love with him. It was ridiculously inappropriate to even dream of feeling that way. Wasn't it?

He'd destroyed my life, my career, reduced me to a contractual comfort object, but all I could think was, *I wish he hadn't sent me away.*

I lay in his guest room, cold, lonely, horny. I could have reached between my legs and soothed some of the ache away. He never would have known, but I wouldn't. I couldn't. He'd told me it wasn't allowed, and I desperately wanted to obey him already. I was already hopelessly his.

He had said *You're mine*, whispered it into the hollow of my earlobe. Did he really think of me as his, or did he think of me as Nell, his body for hire? Was he thinking of me right now, lying in bed, as I was thinking of him? Or was it out of sight, out of mind for him?

Well, of course it was. He wouldn't go to the trouble of hiring someone to play his girlfriend in public and his sex toy in private if he wanted to get emotionally involved.

I would need to be so careful, so cautious here.

And I would definitely need to dry my tears.

* * * * *

Jeremy and I spent the next couple of days in a flurry of preparations. We went to the doctor first, or rather the doctor came to us, drew blood, put me through a very thorough and intimate physical to declare me free of disease and in good health.

Then we shopped, and shopped...and shopped. True to his word, he paid for everything I needed for the trip, and for some things I probably didn't even need. Luggage, clothes, gadgets to make traveling easier, and a durable wheeled leather valise for all my mythology books. Dresses, tops, jeans, cardigans, shoes, bathing suits and cover-ups, even though it was early October. And lingerie, what had to be thousands of dollars worth.

Most of the practical items came to the doorstep already selected and paid for by some underling of Jeremy's, Kyle perhaps. The clothing he gave me a budget for, and I went out on my own to put together a nice little wardrobe. He insisted that I dress with my own sense of style, which he professed to like. But the lingerie—we went to buy that together in what amounted to one of the most arousing shopping excursions of my life.

We didn't just pop down to Victoria's Secret. He took me to a small, exclusive boutique I didn't even know existed, a boutique whose tissue paper was out of my price range, much less the fine garments they wrapped in it.

There was no discussion of price, or any visible price tags, only incredibly luxurious and detailed lingerie. I stared in wonder at the fine silk corsets and sighed over perfectly fitted bras. There were risqué garter belts and G-strings. And of course, piles and piles of cheeky, impossibly detailed panties. If he insisted my outward appearance be completely my own choices, it was clear my private appearance would be exclusively his.

But I didn't mind, because it was incredibly erotic to be dressed by him. He selected everything carefully, studying me with his cool blue eyes as Madame smoothed the corsets and adjusted the garters. She highlighted the embellishments and features of each garment she produced.

"You see, Monsieur, how beautifully this presents her décolletage," she would point out, and he would agree, running his fingertips over the tops of my rounded breasts thrust above the silk.

Or she would run her hand beneath the seams of the fine French panties she slid up my legs, pointing out how they exposed the perfect silhouette of the curve of my ass. And he would cup my ass and agree with her in a perfectly normal, modulated voice. "Yes, they suit her well."

I wanted to beg on my hands and knees for sex.

He hadn't touched me since that first night I'd moved into his house. I don't know why he chose not to, and he didn't explain. I hoped that he was just too busy, and I had my own tasks to accomplish before we left, friends to contact, finances to put in order. Still, I waited to be summoned to his room every time he arrived at the house. I would have given anything on earth to be ordered to suck his cock.

So now, with his gaze all over me in the opulent, private dressing room, I found my breath growing short and my clit growing wet. When Madame finally left us to attend to another customer, Jeremy urged her to take her time. My pussy throbbed as he moved closer to me.

I had on a rum pink bra with small, sexy stays cupping my tits and a matching waist cincher. An intricate garter belt held up silk stockings in the same dusky shade of pink. He didn't say anything in the way of preliminaries, just reached between my thighs and parted me, thrusting his fingers so deep inside that I nearly lost my balance. I clung to him, righting myself, and tried not to moan.

"You're killing me, Nell."

Then I did moan as his fingers slipped out of my slick center to pinch and tease my hard, wet clit. If anyone were killing anyone, it was Jeremy.

"Have you made yourself come since you left my bedroom?"

"No, Jeremy." I was glad I hadn't, because in my current condition I would have been unable to lie.

"Good girl. I want you to come now."

Oh Jesus, how I ached to, but my mind flew to the flimsy curtain separating Jeremy and me from Madame and the other customers outside in the boutique.

"You don't worry about that." He stroked me, separating and probing my labia. I looked up at him, wide-eyed. "You just worry about doing as I ask."

"Yes, Jeremy," I whispered.

"Hold on to me. Put your hands on my shoulders if you think you're going to fall."

I reached for him, closed my fingers over his muscular shoulders. I could feel his arms move under my hands as he manipulated me. I was torn between running my fingers all over his shoulders and chest and giving myself up to the growing pleasure at my core. I pressed my forehead against the front of his sweater. "Jeremy." My voice came out a whisper.

"Come on." I drew in a deep breath. I relaxed and pushed my hips against his fingers. "Yes, that's right," he said. "More. I want you to moan."

I threw a wild look at the curtain, then turned pleading eyes on him.

"I want moans, girl." I recognized the obdurate expression already, knew he wouldn't bend. I buried my face in his chest and let the moans come.

And with his fingers, he kept drawing me closer and closer to that terrifying edge of climax, the terrifying loss of control. I didn't know if I'd be able to let go, here, in Madame's dressing room on Rodeo Drive with a curtain the only thing between us and the people outside. My quiet sounds rose in intensity. I shuddered against his front.

"Do it. Obey me."

He stroked and fondled me so my hips moved and swayed of their own accord. His fingers slid over my clit, lubricated by the juices that, by now, soaked the garment I wore. My urgent lust sounds were uttered against soft gray cashmere. I rode his broad hand spread between my legs. As my orgasm drew closer, my movements grew wilder, undisciplined.

"Hurry," his voice rasped in my ear, "or she'll return just as you're coming. Won't you look like a horny slut then?"

I whimpered as his fingers manipulated, scratched, probed. His other hand came around the back of my neck to draw my lips to his. He kissed me deeply, his fingers pressing inside me at the same time.

"Oh." I moaned into his mouth. "Oh God."

"Yes, be a good girl. Come for me. Now."

He pinched my nipple through the bra, once, twice, a third time. I wanted to come, I had to come. I knew I had to let go. The pressure in my center was unbearable. It was painful anticipation, an urge that couldn't be realized.

"Please!" I begged against his lips.

"Now. Now, girl!" he whispered. He bit my tongue softly and pulled me close to him, drove his fingers deep inside.

"Oh, oh! *Ohhhhh.*" He caught my cries of orgasm with his mouth pressed hard over mine. I bucked against him, and he worked my clit while the waves of pleasure took me. It went on and on, sharp, undulating sensation. By the end I clung to his neck, far too weak to stand of my own accord.

"Oh, Jeremy!" He shushed me and slowly drew his sodden fingers out of my slit and up the front of the garter belt and cincher I wore. I watched the broad, blunt fingers slide against the delicate pink material and then snake around my hip. I peered up into avid blue eyes. He looked down at me with an expression I couldn't untangle.

"Thank you, Jeremy," I whispered.

"Don't thank me. I did that for me."

"Monsieur," came Madame's muted voice from outside the curtain. "Will Mademoiselle be needing any more things?"

Mademoiselle got plenty more things, but all Mademoiselle could think about was whether Madame could smell the scent of sex in the air when she came back in to continue the fitting, or perceive the carnal promise in Jeremy's eyes as he continued staring at me. If she noticed the sharp smell of female arousal permeating the small room, she was too professional to let it show. She laid the set I had on, smeared with my essence, on the purchase pile. From then on, each time she produced panties, I stood stiffly to keep from soaking the gussets, while Jeremy looked on with a smile. When she produced a thong, I asked to be excused to the powder room first.

We were there another hour before Jeremy finished shopping and instructed Madame to have it delivered to the house. "Tonight," he specified. "We leave tomorrow on a long trip."

From the way he hustled me into the car and dragged me home, I thought I'd at least be giving him a blowjob as soon as we got inside, but he left me without a word and went off to do other things. I spent the rest of the afternoon packing and double-checking everything with Kyle and Bonita's help. I'd be living out of a suitcase for the next four months, and I wanted to get it right.

While I packed late into the night and Kyle ran around like a chicken with its head cut off, Jeremy went to a "bon voyage" dinner with some friends. I wasn't invited, but I understood completely. By the time he got home after midnight, I didn't hold out much hope that he'd ask for me. By twelve thirty I had brushed my teeth and headed to bed.

I set my alarm and looked over once more at my suitcases, packed and ready to go in the corner. Just as I put my head on the pillow I heard a soft knock.

He opened the door without waiting for a response. He stood watching me for a long while, and I sat still where I was. He was completely dressed, and he didn't look amorous. He looked irate. I was suddenly terrified he'd come to tell me it was all over, that he didn't want me after all.

"What is it?" I finally said, when I couldn't stand another second of anxiety.

"Are you all packed?"

"Yes, Jeremy."

"We leave tomorrow."

"I know."

He was clearly agitated.

"What can I do, Jeremy?" I asked softly in the silence.

He strode over to the bed with a frustrated sigh and sat down on the edge.

"I want to fuck you now, but I didn't want it to be like this, late, when you're tired and I'm tired. You know, the first time."

Oh God. He wanted it to be special. I didn't know whether to snicker or start bawling again.

"You looked so beautiful today, and I've wanted you so badly, but I've been busy. All this stuff at work, stuff I have to do to get ready for the shoot." He waved his hands and grimaced. "Anyway, I don't know why I'm babbling about it to you. It's not your problem."

"It's my job to make you feel better, right? So you can say whatever you like. Vent away."

He smiled crookedly at me. "Good little worker. Yes. I remember."

I looked down at my hands. "I'm yours. You know that. I'm yours to use. If you want to talk to me now, I'm happy to listen to you talk."

"I don't want to talk," he said curtly. He reached out and cupped my cheek with his hand.

"I'm in my ratty old pajamas. I'm not really dressed for—"

"I don't give a fuck how you're dressed."

"I'm yours," I whispered again, and I meant it.

"I had a whole scene planned. With cuffs and a very strict leather strap. A silk corset." His hands closed around my waist. I felt them tighten a little. "A matching ball gag."

"I don't like to be gagged."

"Don't you?" he asked, staring at my lips. "In hotels they're a necessary evil, I'm afraid. How else will we muffle your screams?"

He was half kidding, relaxing at last.

"I'm not much of a screamer. I'm more of a crier," I said. "Sometimes I plead."

Jeremy laughed. "I can already see you're going to be trouble. I knew it all along."

He sobered then and moved his hand to one of my breasts, running the pad of his thumb over it until the nipple stood out in stark relief through my thin shirt.

"I want you over my lap," he said. "Right now."

I did as he asked, although it was hard to feel sexy in my worn department-store tank top and Betty Boop pajama pants. As soon as I was in position, he yanked my pants down to my thighs, baring my bottom and the thong that didn't offer much protection from his gaze.

"Nice." He played with my ass a little, yanking the thong up farther between my legs. He slid his thick fingers into me, then began to tease my clit and the slick channel between my thighs. I moaned, fidgeting in his lap, but he silenced me with a strict sound in his throat and held me hard by the arm.

"Don't be naughty," he said. "I know you're a little whore. And you know what? Next time I spank you like this, you're going to be wearing a toy in your ass under your sexy little thong."

It was the way he said it that turned me on, every bit as much as the raunchy words. The low, exacting rumble tinged with threat. I tried to press my clit against his thigh again and was rewarded with a sharp smack that burned like fire. I'd been paddled by him. I'd felt the bite of his crop, but I was suddenly gripped with dread of a bare-handed spanking from Jeremy Gray. Had I actually wanted it once? Now that the moment was here, I was scared. I buried my face against his leg in silent apology. He thrust his fingers in my pussy and my ass while I tried to lie still.

"Has your ass been fucked a lot, Nell?"

I tried to find my voice, but it was difficult with what he was doing to me.

"N-no...not a lot...Jeremy," I finally said.

"It will be," he promised. "But not tonight."

He withdrew his fingers and wiped them across my quivering ass. I tensed and whimpered as he rested his hand on my cheek. "Scared?"

"Yes."

"You should be."

He drew his hand back and I braced, waiting. His palm fell. "Ouch!" I cried out as the pain of the first blow bloomed on my skin. It was followed by a barrage of smacks that had me squirming and gasping for breath.

"Please! Please." I tried to dodge the merciless hand and was spanked harder as punishment.

"Just lie still. Your 'pleases' aren't going to accomplish anything."

I bit back the next *please* behind tightly clenched lips. His hand rained fire on me. My punished cheeks throbbed. When I couldn't stop my legs from kicking, he pinned them between his thighs. I was truly trapped, and the pain I'd tried to escape became pain I had to endure. I tried to let it flow through me. Soon I felt the familiar sensation of ebbing relief, and the pain began to transform into pleasure. Subspace. Endorphins. Whatever it was, the searing pain in my bottom was joined by a tingle between my thighs. I was aware of every sensation. The roughness of the hands that held me, the tiny hairs on his forearm brushing against my side. The hissing breaths he drew as the spanking grew more physical. The scratchiness of his wool pants against the undersides of my breasts where my shirt had ridden up. It all swirled together and centered in my nipples and my rapidly swelling clit.

When he finally stopped I was breathless, exhausted, broken down. In flames. Not just my belabored ass, but my pussy too.

"Stand up," he said.

I did, on wobbly legs, my pajama bottoms falling to my feet. I still had on the thong and the ratty shirt. I looked at him. He sat and stared back at me, and the energy passed between us, the energy of power exchange. I'd put myself in his hands, and he'd hurt me. His power eclipsed mine, and it shook me to the core. It made me want to sob out my thanks. It made me want to serve him. I dropped my gaze to the floor in submission.

"Undress."

I took off my shirt and kicked my pants away. I peeled off my thong, trying to hide the fact that it was practically soaked through.

"Turn around," he said. "Let me look at your ass."

For a long time I stood there under his gaze. I desperately wanted to look back over my shoulder and see how red and marked I was, but I disciplined myself to stillness.

Finally he stood and crossed to where I waited, turned me in his arms and clasped me close, then walked me backward to the wall. He held me against it, and I reached for him. He pushed my arms up and pinned them to the wall. "Stay." It was a command I understood. I left my wrists resting against the wall above my head. He cupped my sore ass and kissed my neck, then licked at my racing pulse. He moved lower and took my nipple in his mouth and bit it hard enough to make me pull away with a jerk.

"No!" He pushed me back against the wall and again lifted my hands over my head. "Try again." I tensed and made a plaintive sound as he bit down on the other nipple, but I managed to stand still. I was rewarded with a growl, and his lips pressed over mine. He forced my lips open with his tongue and ravaged my mouth. He put a hand behind my head to pull me closer, and I breathed in his smell, nutmeg mixed with aftershave. I lost myself to the punishing intensity of his kiss.

"Undress me," he rasped finally, pulling away. My fingers started tearing at his buttons while he doffed his pants. I pushed his shirt off his back as he straightened, and there he was before me, golden, naked male. He was stunning. He was pure thickness, severe muscle and solid bone. I watched his broad chest rise and fall with each breath he took. His smooth, tanned skin had a smattering of sandy gold hair I wanted to touch. I stared at his coiled abs, at the bulging biceps and triceps that defined his arms. My gaze traveled lower, to the prominent muscles that outlined his groin. And then lower. *My God.*

He let me look my fill. My mouth grew dry long before my gaze meandered back to his. His lips quirked into an ironic smile.

"Nice," I whispered, stating the obvious. His hand came out and pulled me against him, skin to naked skin. The feel of it took my breath away. He was so warm, so solid. I was desperate to feel him, to take his thick, beautiful cock between my legs, or even in my ass, my mouth, wherever he wanted it to be.

"Stay," he said for the second time. This time he left the room. If I thought he wasn't going to come back and finish me off, I would have sunk into the ground and died. But somehow I knew he'd return immediately, and he did, a condom in his palm. He tore the wrapper with his teeth and rolled it on with quick, practiced grace. Without a word, he took hold of me and lifted me onto the tip of his cock.

"Oh, please." I don't know why I kept saying *please*. I suppose because by that point I was desperate with lust. My breath came in fast, jerky pants. He lowered me down over the head of his cock.

"Hold on to me."

I moved my arms up from his shoulders and wrapped them around his neck. He pressed me hard against the wall, then reached down with both hands to draw my knees up high around his waist. I clung to him and squeezed my legs on his hips as he penetrated me to the hilt. He went still, looked down at me masterfully. My pussy spasmed around his cock. I wanted to beg. I wanted to say, *Please, please, move inside me*, but all that came out were incoherent whispers. He was so thick, so hard. He filled me and made me feel like a trapped animal.

I pressed my face against his neck and touched my teeth to his skin.

"No." I drew back and gazed at him. Why wasn't he moving in me? He was biting his lip and staring at a point past my shoulder.

"What is it?"

"Don't move."

I tried to be still. I tried. I only moved my hips the tiniest inch.

He shuddered and groaned, and his hands snaked down to grip my ass. He pressed me to the wall and withdrew, then thrust again.

"God...you...you feel...too perfect. I almost lost control."

I sighed and arched my hips to him. I felt his muscles contract against my skin, felt the rigid control. A part of me wondered what he was like when his control went away. And then my thoughts were silenced as he fucked me hard. He fingered my ass and pushed my legs even wider with his hips. My entire existence centered on the cock that reared into me again and again.

Within moments I knew I was losing it. I was close to the edge. I began to struggle against him, trying not to come without permission. "Please. Jeremy!"

"What?"

"I'm... Please... I'm going to come. I have to come! May I, please?"

"Oh, I don't know. I'm just getting started." He buried his face against the side of my neck. "Can't you wait?"

I answered with a tortured moan of desperation.

"Okay, you naughty little slut, come."

"Oh God," I gasped, writhing in his arms. "You feel so good! I love how you fuck!"

I knew it wasn't my job to critique his technique, but I couldn't get ahold of my mouth in my current crazed state, and I could feel him laughing into my neck as I fell apart.

"You're a little cum whore."

"Yes, yes!" I agreed with each thrust of his hips.

He didn't stop as he carried me across the room to fall on top of me on the bed. He held my hands hard in his over my head, fucking me deep and slow. The way he filled me, the way he moved against me, all urgent, hard, aroused male, I could have lain there and taken his thrusts for hours and hours.

"Yes yes *yes*!" I hated that I was so out of control, but I was completely powerless to stop it. I was under his spell. I was his.

His thrusts quickened. He let go of my hands and wrapped me in his arms until I could barely breathe, until I could practically hear the blood beat in his veins.

"Oh, Jeremy, God..." He was so close, so close to me. No one had ever fucked me like this, not Douglas, not the play doms before him, not the vanilla boys I toyed with in school.

It was like he wanted to get inside me. It felt so new, so amazing, so intimate to be made love to this way, body to straining body, no holds barred. He was rough and intense, but the way he held me felt at the same time incredibly tender and dear.

"Lovely girl." He nuzzled me. "Come again. Come again, with me."

"I can't," I said, even as I felt my clit throbbing and aching.

"No 'I can'ts,'" he said against my ear. "I know you can."

One hand moved down to cup my bottom and draw me closer, the other fastened on one nipple with a vicious pinch. "Oh God," I said. "Please!"

"Please what?"

"Please, harder...again!"

He complied, and again I felt pleasure bloom in my center, as if my nipples were connected directly to my clit. Pain, pleasure, and his thick cock impaling me. All at once, some receptor inside me tripped. I arched up to him as the orgasm ripped through me. My legs kicked helplessly in his grasp, and he clutched me tighter. I could feel my walls clamping down on his dick. He pounded into me as the aftershocks of my orgasm traveled across my nerves. He bucked against me and then grunted out his own release.

We came to rest, entangled in each other, his hard body plastered to my skin. His hips still pressed against my slick, spread thighs, and my sopping channel still undulated around his cock. I stayed still, wanting him to never move.

Soon, though, he shifted to the side so I could breathe. He discarded the condom and rolled back to look at me. I gazed up at him, spent, satisfied...infatuated. I looked away before he could see it in my eyes. *It's sex glow, just like last time*, I told myself. *You don't like him, you don't love him. He's just your boss.*

"Look at me," he said.

I did, guarded now.

"That was good, wasn't it? For the first time."

"It was spectacular. Honestly." I turned my head, but he nudged my chin back.

"Why won't you look at me?"

"Because I'm your submissive."

"Exactly. You do what I want. And I want you to look in my eyes."

I did, and he studied me carefully. I don't know what he wanted to see. If I'd known, I would have given it to him, whatever expression he wanted, whatever would have pleased him. But I didn't know, so what he saw was only guarded confusion and anxiety.

"I hope you liked that," he said. "That's the softest you're ever going to get it from me."

And I knew he didn't mean soft, as in gentle. He meant soft as in, *I just made love to you.*

Then he fell asleep beside me there like a lover, but woke up in the morning the stern boss again.

Chapter Eight: Hours and Hours

"Here, let me help you."

He grabbed my suitcase to sling it into the overhead bin, muttering, "What's in there, bricks?"

Books, mostly, but I didn't reply to what I assumed was a rhetorical question. Anyway, I was too distracted looking at his arms. Lovely, lovely, lustworthy muscular arms and shoulders in a blue cashmere sweater that made me want to rub all over it like a cat.

Enough, Nell. Calm down already.

It was twenty hours to Bangkok, and we hadn't even taken off yet.

Twenty hours to sit next to him in first class, smelling his masculine smell, looking at his masculine hands fidgeting in his lap, feeling his masculine, sweater-encased shoulder pressing against mine. Twenty hours to sit on the sore ass that still smarted from those hands the night before.

He's your boss. Give it a rest.

He was hyperalert and agitated, still trying to manage everything, even though Kyle, sitting behind us, assured him everything was all right. Jeremy sighed, his leg bouncing and jittering beside mine.

"Nervous flyer?" I asked.

"No, just impatient. I hate long flights."

"I hate the take-off and landing."

"That's the time the plane is mostly likely to crash."

"Thanks." I laughed. "Now I feel better."

"You aren't a nervous flyer, I hope?"

"If I were, I don't think I would have agreed to fly all over the world with you."

"Smarty pants." He checked his phone for messages one last time while the flight attendant went over procedures in case of disaster.

In case of disaster. There wasn't a seat belt, life vest, or oxygen mask that could save me if this new job didn't work out. I was flying twenty hours away to Thailand with someone who was more or less a stranger. If you could consider someone who'd spanked and fucked you silly the night before a stranger. I looked over at him typing away with a frown on his phone. A complete stranger, yes.

But everyone else thought they knew him: bystanders, fans, gawkers. Several passengers came up to introduce themselves and chat with him briefly once we were in flight. He was outwardly gracious, but I could hear the tight irritation underneath. After one particularly cloying woman returned to her seat, he turned to me with a frown.

"You're supposed to help me out. Your job is to glare at women like that until they go away."

"Huh?"

"You're my girlfriend. When women are swooning all over me, you're supposed to look annoyed and irritated so they leave quickly. Better yet, stare them off so they don't even come over."

"Like this?" I asked, putting on my best jealous-girlfriend scowl.

"Perfect. That's a big part of why I need you, you know? To fend off female fans."

"Happy to be of service," I muttered.

I turned away and dug in my bag for my well-worn copy of the *Kalevala* and started to read. I found it a very soothing and entertaining piece of mythology, something relaxing to read when my nerves were on edge. It was an epic poem from Finland, not too terribly ancient, but mythological all the same. I was absorbed in the second Väinämöinen cycle when Jeremy shifted beside me and cleared his throat. It was already growing late. The sky was darkening and we were flying over black water through endless dark gray skies.

"What are you reading?" he asked.

"Some Finnish mythology. The *Kalevala*."

"The Kaleva-huh? Let me see."

I handed him the book, and he flipped it over to look at the cover, losing my place.

"You Finnish?" he asked.

"No, it's just a good work I like to read, one of my favorites. Creative, well written, in verse."

"Verse, huh? Sounds gripping."

"It's not for everyone." I accepted the volume back from him and flipped through the pages to find my place again.

"Why are you so into that stuff? The study of mythology?"

"Mythology is what cultures have used for millennia to make sense of the human condition, to make sense of the world. If you gave it a chance, if you read the mythology of several different cultures, you'd be amazed at the similarities they share. Myths tell you a lot about humanity, about cultural perspectives, world views…"

He rolled his eyes. "All those flowery epics and stories are only complicating things. I live by one idea and one idea only—if it feels good, do it."

"Hmm." I looked back at my book. "I do believe that is your credo."

"If it weren't for people like me who live by that credo, you wouldn't have built your nice little career in the sex trade, now would you?"

"Some people want more out of life than hedonism and sexual pleasure."

"Suckers."

"You know, I fall into that group."

"And you're a *sucker*, aren't you?" He sat back with a smirk. "A half-good one, I'll admit."

I hunched over my book. I wasn't going to be baited into a conversation about how I gave head in the middle of the first-class compartment of an airplane, even if everyone else was going to sleep.

He watched me read for a while, fidgeted, scratched his chin, ran his fingers through his hair.

"*Kalevala*," he muttered. "If it's so great, what's it about, then? Tell me one of the stories. I can't sleep. I hate sleeping on planes."

"Are you going to stay up the whole flight?"

"No, I'll sleep eventually, but I'll wake up feeling even shittier than before."

"I hate sleeping on planes too."

"I bet your mythology could put me to sleep."

I sighed and rolled my eyes. "I'll tell you one of the stories if you want, but if you're just going to make fun—"

"Actually, tell me a story from Eden. I'd like that better. Tell me a good story from your old work, a cool scene you did. Something sexy."

"I'm not supposed to do that. I signed a confidentiality agreement."

"Don't use names, just tell me what happened. I want it. Something really, really raunchy and nasty."

"Not much raunchy happened there. No sex allowed, remember?"

He rubbed his face. "Something sexy had to happen at least once. One sexy story. Come on. *Your* mythology. Tell me. Please."

"All right, let me think." I sighed, closing my book. There had actually been a lot of sexy moments at the club, so many I wasn't sure which story to tell him. A few particular clients stood out in my mind, a few scenes I played that changed or affected me. The mythology of Nell.

"There was one couple who came in who always got me going," I began. "A fiftyish man and a younger girl, maybe nineteen or twenty years old. They were hard-core players in a Dom/sub relationship, but they liked to come in and role-play that she was his new wife. That she was being introduced to the lifestyle but was ambivalent about it. Well, sometimes it was more like she was being forced into the lifestyle. Wifely slavery. It was pretty hot. It always began with him introducing her to me formally. He would explain that I was a submissive, that I was the way he wanted her to be. He'd bring out a collar and buckle it around my neck."

"You and your collar thing."

"Oh, collars melt me. Big, black, leather ones—"

"Okay, okay, you pervert." He looked around and leaned closer. "So then what? You're collared and panting…"

"Then he'd leash me and lead me around in front of her while she stared as if she were horrified at what she was seeing. She was a great actress."

Jeremy chuckled. "Maybe I know her."

I shrugged. "She could have been a professional actress. The first time we played the scene I was absolutely convinced she was a novice, a reluctant partner, but by the end I kind of figured out the game. By the fifth or sixth time, I really started admiring her acting talent. Her distress was beautiful. She would stare and gasp while her dom put me through the paces, flogged me, made me masturbate. He'd talk to her the whole time. 'See how she does what I ask as soon as I ask it? Whatever I demand? That's what you'll do too.' Then he would make us stand together, and he'd take whatever he'd put on me and put it on her. Collars, clamps, cuffs, harnesses. Sometimes he made me put it on her instead."

He looked over at me. "You liked it."

"I got off on it a little, yeah. She played the innocent so well. I felt like her sister, her mentor."

"And you and she…" He seemed enthralled by the possibilities.

"Yeah. I would pretend to console her, soothe her while he watched. It went on from there."

"Wait, you can't just say that. What do you mean, it went on from there? Details."

I shrugged. "You know, it went on. He would dom us both then, tell us what to do to each other, make us get each other off while he watched."

"You ate her out? She ate you out?"

"Not allowed. We did other things."

"Like?"

I laughed. "There was lots of licking and sucking. Making out. We kissed and toyed with each other's tits. There was lots of grinding our horny little hips together and talking dirty."

"Oh yeah, that's good stuff." He shifted beside me. "So how did that make you feel?"

"Pretty horny, Jeremy."

"It's making me pretty horny too. Was she talented?"

"Yes. Crazy talented, a hell of a lot more talented than me. And gorgeous. Huge, perky tits, responsive nipples. I could feel them harden right under my tongue, and I'd tug on her nipple rings with my teeth." I was only teasing Jeremy now. He was all but quivering beside me. "And she had this amazing mane of long blonde hair I would twist up in my fists. Even the way she smelled was gorgeous, sort of musky and woodsy when I'd bury my face in the side of her neck."

"Go on," Jeremy breathed.

I shrugged. "Well, it was work, you know? Ultimately the scene was between her and her dom. I was kind of beside the point."

"The facilitator."

"No, not at all. He was the facilitator. I was only the prop. I was always the prop, the thing people used to get off."

"'The thing people used.' Did you really think of yourself that way?"

"Yes, Jeremy, I still do. That's what I am. It's what I've made a career out of. I don't care."

His lips pursed a little, and he leaned close to me.

"I think you do care."

I looked down at my book. I really wanted to get back to Väinämöinen and the Maid of the North.

"What's your real name?" he asked.

"I don't tell anyone my real name."

"Why?"

"I don't know, maybe for the same reason you keep employees instead of girlfriends. Personal space."

He crossed his arms over his chest and sat back with a frown. So he didn't like that. Too bad. My real name was mine and mine only. It wasn't for use at a sex club, by a dominant, or by anyone who was paying me for my time.

"Nell is part of it, though? At least tell me that much. Nell is short for your real name?"

"Yes," I said. "I'll tell you that much. Nell is short for my real name."

"Lucynell?"

I laughed. "No."

"Janelle?"

I closed my book with a sigh and put it away. It was going to be a long, long flight.

"Danielle?"

I shook my head and leaned against the window, trying to wedge the flimsy airline pillow into some semblance of comfort.

"Here," he said with impatience. "Lean against me if you're going to try to sleep." He took my pillow and propped it against his shoulder, and I rested gratefully against his warmth and solidness. He was quiet a long time, until the hum of the airplane had nearly put me to sleep.

"Eleanor?"

I shook my head against his shoulder, and finally, somewhere over the black ocean, I fell into a deep and dreamless sleep.

* * * * *

Taking off had been nerve-racking, but arriving in Bangkok was completely insane. A massive press of humanity waited outside the airport: photographers, fans, crazy people yelling and gesticulating. "Jeremy Gray! Over here! Over here!" My instinct was to hang back, to hide behind someone, but Jeremy propelled me forward.

"Smile and look happy to be with me," he directed under his breath.

I was exhausted and sore from the flight, but I looked up into the wall of blinding flashes and gave what I hoped was a movie-star-girlfriend-caliber smile. The crowd converged on us, and I slowed. There was absolutely nowhere to go.

"Keep walking. Don't stop. They'll move out of the way."

He pulled me closer, guiding me through the crowds. I was jostled and pulled, and then I felt Kyle at my back, urging us both forward. "There's the car," he said.

The three of us dived into the limo, and the driver shut the door. The sudden silence was shocking after the pandemonium outside. I looked down at my hands. They were shaking.

"You okay?" Jeremy asked.

"Yes," I said. "No. I don't know. That was crazy."

I was sitting beside him, and though I wanted him to hold me, to comfort me, instead he leaned away from me, his face drawn and tired. He still looked like a movie star, even exhausted, but I thought I must look like absolute hell. Kyle rode backward, across from the two of us, wearing his usual smart-ass grin.

They talked about Jeremy's work schedule while I drifted. I watched Kyle from under my lids. We'd had a few tense conversations since our rendezvous at my apartment. I flat out hated the man, but the vibe I got from him was more that of a jealous friend. I suppose he'd been Jeremy's golden go-to pal until I got thrown into the mix.

I watched Kyle lean forward and explain the hotel arrangements. There was something between them that struck me. A closeness. No. It couldn't be. Jeremy was straight as an arrow. But it was a little weird, the way they talked to each other. The way they worked so easily together. As if they shared some kind of intimate connection. To be honest, I suspected Kyle wasn't totally straight. The man had highlights in his hair, for God's sake. He was a flaming metrosexual, and looking at his tight, sexy body and supermodel face... I suppose someone as sexy as that could swing any way he wanted to. If I'd learned anything the last few days, it was that anything was possible in the world of the rich.

But no. No. *No.* Kyle was his personal assistant, that was the only reason they seemed so close.

Kyle looked over at me then, and I quickly looked away, but not before I saw it again, that same look. *Jealousy.* A moment later he was looking at Jeremy. Jeremy didn't notice. His face was propped on his hand as he stared out the window. My own eyes started to close. I was too tired to analyze it anymore.

"How far to the hotel?" I asked.

I don't remember any answer. The next thing I knew, I was in Jeremy's arms in an elevator, the beat of his heart against my ear. Then I vaguely remember him carrying me down the hall to our hotel suite and laying me in bed.

* * * * *

When I woke fully rested, I realized to my chagrin that it was night again, nearly ten. I was still wearing my jeans and top from the flight, and my shoes were arranged beside the bed. I was alone in a beautifully appointed hotel room, my suitcases stacked in the corner beside a tufted armchair, a bureau, and a huge decorative vase. There were two paintings and a small desk on the other wall, and a door that opened to the bathroom. The other door, I assumed, let out to the main room of the suite.

So I would have my own room. I lay back on the starched white sheets and pulled the coverlet up. I was wide awake, and the long, dark night stretched ahead of me. It was utterly silent. Jeremy was either away or sleeping or engaged in some activity that made no noise at all. There was no window in my room, which made it feel strangely confining, even though the door was open wide.

I got out of bed with a sigh and ran my hands through my unruly hair. A trip to the luxurious, mirror-walled bathroom revealed that I looked just as bad as I thought I did.

A shower was in order. I went to my suitcase and dug out a pair of the formfitting pajamas Jeremy bought me before we left. Fortunately, they were as comfortable as they were sheer and sexy. I went back into the bathroom, which we apparently would be sharing, since his things were spread out on one side of the counter and his toiletries were in the shower.

I stared at them as the hot water ran over me. Jeremy's soap, Jeremy's exfoliating face wash, Jeremy's shampoo and conditioner right there next to mine. Surreal.

It still felt great to get clean, to shave and wash and stand in the steam and steep. I probably showered for twenty minutes or more, then got out and dried off with a lovely, fluffy thick towel. No thin, sandpaper-like hotel towels at this place. I put on the pajamas, which left nothing to the imagination, and considered the spa robes hanging on the wall. They didn't say *His* or *Hers* anywhere, and neither looked as if it had been worn, so I chose the one closest to me and wrapped up in it.

Taking a deep breath, I went out to the main room, feeling like I was trespassing in someone's house. It was quite large, with a dining area and kitchenette on one side, and a sitting area on the other side with an overstuffed sofa and chairs and a wide-screen television mounted on the wall. It was a lot like Jeremy's mansion, beautifully decorated, only compacted into one oversize room. Beside my bedroom was another door, which I assumed led to Jeremy's room.

I crossed between the sitting and dining area to the opposite wall, which was one huge window from ceiling to floor. I felt like tiptoeing. I didn't belong here. It was too rich, too fine. As I reached the window wall, I looked down and then jumped back with a gasp.

We were high up. We were *high up*. I'd never been so high in the air in any building ever, and I felt a sudden panic in my chest, a sick feeling in my stomach. *If there's a fire...*

"Nell."

I spun with a stifled yelp, clutching my chest.

"Oh God. You scared me."

He stood in the door to his bedroom, sexy man in loose pajama bottoms and no top. He was sculpted like a statue, all pecs and six-pack and biceps enough to make a girl go wild. I was caught between the sudden stab of lust between my legs and the sick, lingering panic at how high up I was.

"What's wrong?" he asked. It was so, so quiet in the room. He didn't move, didn't cross to me.

"It's so high. This room... This hotel..."

"Eighty-fifth floor." He smiled. "Don't worry, though. Hotels almost never fall over."

"It's just so high. God, it's beautiful, though."

He came to stand at the window beside me, looking out at the urban lights and miles of buildings in every direction. "Welcome to Bangkok, your home for the next four weeks. You didn't see much of it from the limo last night."

"Yes. I'm sorry I fell asleep. I was so tired." I looked down self-consciously. "I guess you had to carry me drooling to the room."

He laughed. "It wasn't a problem. You didn't drool much. And you're a little slip of a thing."

"And you work out." I slid a look over at his golden, heavily muscled torso. "That's pretty clear."

"Are you flirting with me?"

"Is that allowed?"

"It's encouraged." He laughed and moved a hand up into my wet hair. He began to knead my nape with skilled fingers. He had no idea what it did to me... or maybe he did.

"Are you cold?" he asked.

"A little. Not too much."

"I'd like you to take the robe off then, if you don't mind."

His tone was like a cold bucket of water washing over me. For a minute it had almost felt romantic between us, but no, he was still my boss. I took the robe off and held it in my hands, the submissive now.

"Go and hang it in the bathroom. I've ordered us some dinner. It should be here soon."

I crossed to do as he told me, knowing full well that his gaze was glued to my ass as I left the room, and to my boobs as I returned. My nipples were hard, poking through the practically transparent cotton of the cami top. He finally met my eyes after staring his fill at my tits.

"I like that look on you. Sleepy pajama girl. We'll both have to try to sleep later, to get ourselves back on schedule, but we'll eat first. You must be hungry."

"I am."

"A little dinner, and then some sex. A nice involved scene to tire us both out a bit."

"Yes, Jeremy," I said, my clit already throbbing. There was something about a half-naked, Adonis-like man letting you know he planned to use you for sex sometime soon.

I was starving, though, I realized. Yes. Food first.

As if on cue, room service arrived with a cartful of late-night goodies. Pizza and salads, exactly what I was hungry for. There was also cold American beer in a silver engraved cooler. We sat at one end of the large, rectangular table, and he dived into the pizza nice and messy like a real man, not the refined movie star he sometimes pretended to be.

"I didn't know they had pizza on the menu in Bangkok," I said, watching him chew and take a deep drink of his beer.

He shrugged. "Everything's on the menu in Bangkok, if you have money. They sent out for the pizza, I think. It's good. Have some."

I took a slice and bit into it hesitantly. It was so delicious, I almost moaned. "It tastes like New York pizza."

"Doesn't it, though? You know me," he said, looking me up and down. "I don't like to go without the comforts of home, no matter where I am."

"Are you flirting with me?" I blushed, my food forgotten. The way he was looking at me…

"Come here."

As soon as I was near enough, he pulled me astride his lap. He toyed with my nipples through the thin material of the pink lacy camisole. Of course, they stood at attention the moment he passed his fingertips over them.

"You're so sensitive."

He sounded pleased, but I was blushing at how tarty my nipples were behaving.

He pulled the stretchy cami down below my breasts, so they were exposed, then slid his hand under the waistband of my pants. I had no panties on underneath. He parted my ass cheeks and stroked me intimately. "I'm going to fuck your ass tonight, Nell."

"Yes, Jeremy," I said, not sure how else to respond to a statement like that.

"That's one of the things I'm going to do to you, anyway." He licked the hollows of my neck avidly before nuzzling under my ear. "I'm also going to put painful little clamps on your nipples. You like nipple clamps, don't you?"

"Yes, Jeremy," I whispered. "I like whatever you like."

He slapped my ass. "I asked if you liked them, not if I did. Do you like nipple clamps, yes or no?"

"Yes, I do like them. They make me pretty hot."

"Everything makes you hot, you little slut," he said, landing another hard slap against my ass. "But only I can let you come. Do you understand that?"

"Yes, Jeremy."

"Now go into my bedroom and kneel on the bed, just as you are, with your ass to the door. I'll be in to use you in a little while. I want you to think about getting your ass fucked while you wait."

"Yes, Jeremy."

I walked to the bedroom with my ass uncovered and my tits hanging out. I crawled into the middle of Jeremy's bed. *I want you to think about getting your ass fucked while you wait.* As if I could think of anything else.

I was no novice at anal play. Toys in my ass were permitted at the club, and plugging me had been a frequent choice of many customers. But I'd been fucked by an actual cock in my ass only a handful of times. It was a lot different than a toy. A lot bigger, for one thing. The toys at the club had been relatively small, as customers tended to get exuberant with them.

I knelt on all fours and concentrated on being relaxed and open, on accepting the invasion when it came. It was easy to feel submissive the way he'd left me: my tits bare and my exposed ass pointed at the door so it would be the first thing he saw when he came in.

When would he come?

Time passed slowly, ten minutes, fifteen, twenty minutes, according to his bedside clock. I could have knelt on all fours for an eternity, yoga classes and all that, but my mind was the thing that really started to ache. Thinking for twenty minutes about getting ass fucked, it got me hot and frustrated. It felt like hours and hours I waited, and I got so horny, I was afraid I'd come the second he touched me. If he put clamps on me, it was all over. Nothing made me more orgasmic than clamps on my tits.

My mind wandered away from ass fucking despite my will to obey, and I started instead to try to calm down, to soothe the ache between my legs by thinking about other things. When thirty minutes had passed, I tried to soothe the ache another way.

I know I really, really shouldn't have tried it, but I figured I was going to come without permission either way. God, I hated my reckless libido.

"You little slut," Jeremy said from the door at the exact moment I almost came.

Chapter Nine:
Bad

"Thirty minutes!" He crossed to the bed and jerked me to my knees. "You couldn't wait thirty fucking minutes for me? Your job is to wait for my pleasure! Your job is to serve me, not jerk yourself off whenever you feel hot."

"I'm so sorry!" I got that terrible sick feeling in my stomach, the one where you know you completely fucked up. I flinched as he gave me a rough shake.

"You ruined a perfectly good scene, one I was looking forward to all day. Do you have any self-control? Any at all?"

"I'm sorry!" I wailed. The worst part was the recrimination in his eyes.

"Was it worth it, you little slut?"

"No, Jeremy!"

"You had your fun," he said, pushing me down to the floor. He stalked away and came back with a condom. "Now I get mine. Make it fucking good."

I fumbled with the drawstring of his pants, but he pushed my hands away roughly when I wasn't quick enough. He was already hard. He'd wanted to take me as I was before, horny and frustrated. What I'd done was very bad form, and I knew it. Thirty minutes. He was right. I had absolutely no self-control.

Tears were already forming in my eyes before his rough thrusts into my throat started them rolling down my cheeks. He didn't slow or stop, only held my wet cheeks between his palms to fuck my face harder still.

"I wanted you all day," he muttered. "I was going to fuck you so good."

I moaned, tried with everything I had to give him a satisfying blowjob, but it took forever because he was angry. I sucked, I licked, I worshipped his cock, anything to make his anger go away. When he came he shoved deep in my throat. I could barely breathe, but I stayed still. When he withdrew and discarded the condom, I stayed as I was, not even able to raise my gaze to look at his face. In fact, I bowed down as if to kiss his feet, but he made a hissing sound that stopped me.

"I'm not your fucking master," he snapped, tilting my head back so I could see his terrible, angry face. "I don't want you worshipping my feet. I want you fucking obeying my orders, you slut! It's not that hard!"

I swiped at my tears and drew a deep breath. "Please forgive me. It was just because—"

"*Just because* doesn't work for me, girl! There's no 'just because' here, not ever. I make rules, you obey. If that's too difficult for you, I can have you on a fucking plane back to Buona Italia within the hour. Is that what you want?"

I shook my head. "No, Jeremy."

"Because I get enough fucking irritation and disappointment from everyone else, without worrying about my goddamn disobedient sub!" His anger was awful. The veins in his neck stood out as he waved his arms around.

"I'll never do anything like that again. I promise!"

"You promise." He blew out his breath. "Well, that means a lot to me."

His words hurt, but I understood the fury behind them. Things had been going well. We had seemed to find a connection. In a way, we'd come to develop a trust. I trusted him to be safe with me. He trusted me to obey. As it turned out, only one of us held up our end of the deal.

"I want to punish you," he said, turning back to me. "I want to beat the shit out of you right now, but it's not safe. I'll punish you tomorrow when I'm calmer. In the meantime, you think about this, you little fuck. You signed a contract in which you agreed that I would control your orgasms. Me, Jeremy Gray. Not you. If you want to have a fucking orgasm, then the most you can do is hope and pray I'll give it to you soon. You're certainly never to reach between your own legs and give it to yourself when you're on orders to wait for me."

"No, Jeremy."

"I know you're not an idiot. I know you understood those instructions, although I'm starting to sense you're not as submissive as you pretend to be. This is not good enough! Out!"

I ran to my room. *Not good enough!* I felt a shuddery tightness in my chest. What if he sent me home? I wanted to go to his room and beg for forgiveness, but I didn't dare. All I could do was wait for his anger to dissipate, and then let him know that I really was sorry. That I really would never do it again.

I finally crawled into bed, too scared of running into him in the bathroom to brush my teeth. I looked at my luggage in the corner, still completely packed except for the one bag I'd pulled my pajamas and toiletries from. I didn't want to think anymore. I wanted to sleep, to dream. But I was wide awake. I couldn't sleep. I couldn't do anything to distract myself from the distress I felt.

I finally crept to the suitcase that held my books and took out some Babylonian mythology that always made me feel terribly sad. I read it into the wee hours of the night, crying ashamed, bitter tears.

* * * * *

I was woken up in the early morning by Jeremy lifting the book out of my hand.

"Nell, wake up." He was fully dressed, and Kyle was standing behind him looking tired and irate.

I sat up and clutched the covers in my hands. "Are you sending me home?"

He snorted. "You wish. If I sent you home every time you disobeyed an order, I have a feeling I'd be spending a lot of money on airfare flying you back and forth. But you're going to be punished, and by the end of it, you'll probably wish I'd sent you home."

I was to learn, quite quickly, that Jeremy Gray was as erotically sinister at creating punishments as he was erotically talented at making love. I was permitted to shower, brush my teeth, eat breakfast, and then I was stripped and cuffed to the bed with my legs spread wide and my arms over my head. Bondage usually turned me on, and I felt a minor note of arousal, but the greater feeling was guilt. Oh, and subtle shades of humiliation. Kyle was staring openly at my snatch as Jeremy fixed me to the bedposts. I tried to pull my legs together, even though I knew I couldn't. "Comfortable?" asked Jeremy, standing back. I pulled at the bonds. They had a little give but not much. "Be honest, because you're going to be there a long time."

"I'm fine, I guess." I tested the bonds again, shifting and pulling. Jeremy looked at his watch and back at me.

"Fuck." He started to unbuckle his pants. "Bring me a fucking condom," he snapped at Kyle. "Get one too if you want her."

Kyle went in the bathroom and returned with a condom. He handed it to Jeremy, and yes, he made no effort to hide the other one in his hand.

"You're going to fucking make me late for work," Jeremy muttered as he thrust inside me with no preliminaries. He fucked me like a toy, like an object, and it didn't turn me on. No, this fucking was punishment. It was meant to put me in my place. Well, that was our agreement. If I messed up, he punished me. His ramming thrusts were methodical, and I shut off halfway through. It was a skill I'd developed at Eden, a way to live through the scenes I really didn't enjoy. Some doms took umbrage and didn't allow it. Jeremy just finished up in me with a grunt.

Kyle went next. He wasn't rough like Jeremy. He wasn't angry. He was fucking me for fun. I looked away and ruminated some more on whether he was secretly doing Jeremy. Jeremy was certainly watching Kyle with an intent expression on his face. Kyle took his time, even played with my tits a little. If my hands were free, I would have swatted his fingers away, because I didn't want to enjoy this. I just wanted it to be done.

When he finished and while he dressed, Jeremy left the room and returned with some nipple clamps, which he wordlessly applied to my tits. God, they were vicious ones. The little metal teeth dug into my tender nipples and spurred a hot ache. He applied them nearer the edge to increase the intensity. I took deep breaths and gazed at him through the pain.

"I'm really sorry, Jeremy."

"I'm sure you are. But since you want to come so badly, then your punishment today is going to be to come, over and over. I'm a great believer in making the punishment fit the crime."

I blinked. Orgasm didn't sound much like punishment, but I didn't dare tell him that.

"Are you a righty or a lefty?" he asked. "When you masturbate?"

"I'm sort of ambidextrous," I whispered. I didn't mean it disrespectfully, but he frowned and yanked at one of the clips.

"Right or left hand?"

"Right," I said.

He released my right hand. "Masturbate. Make yourself come. Do it now."

I looked at him, then at Kyle. It was so humiliating. *You're his submissive, and you're being paid for this*, I reminded myself. *It's just a job*. But was it just a job? Why did Jeremy's displeasure make me feel so horrible inside?

He looked at his watch impatiently. "If you make me any later, so help me..."

I reached between my legs and started to rub my clit. I was pretty wet. I couldn't take clamps, even in punishment, without practically squirting on myself. I closed my eyes and let my fingers slide over the slick little nub. I had masturbated in front of countless clients at Eden. It wasn't the act that would challenge me. It was getting to a point where I could actually come, especially with the nipple clamps throbbing, and Jeremy staring at me from a few feet away. I tried to call up some hot fantasy material.

Mmmm, some gear...a black collar. A thick leather leash. Jeremy's hand yanking me, pulling me down to his cock. I open wide and suck it, desperate to please him. His hand tightens on the leash as his excitement grows. With a groan, he pulls out and splooges all over my face. I look up, wide-eyed, at my demanding master. He nods, sliding his cock across my cheek...

That did it. Pushed me right over the edge. It wasn't a great orgasm, but it was an orgasm. I didn't cheat. The pleasure spread outward and then dissipated quickly. My breath slowed, and my body relaxed. The moment the glow faded, I wanted the nipple clamps off. I looked up at Jeremy and waited for him to release me. But he only stared down and said, "Again."

Holy shit.

I made a mild sound of protest. It was ignored. Okay. More fantasy material. I reached between my legs. My clit felt numb, but I manipulated it anyway, tried to draw some pussy juice up over it to make it slick.

Rope. Scratchy and coarse. It's wrapped tightly around my breasts so they jut out before me, pointed and taut. The rope is circled around my waist, then down through my legs, up between my ass cheeks. It's cinched hard so I'm pulled and spread wide open.

Jeremy takes a shorter length of rope. He wraps it around the front of the makeshift harness, then ties it in a knot. He pushes it down until it rests on my clitoris. He turns me over. The rope knot rubs against my aching center, and I grind down upon the bed. "No! You may not come!" He slaps my spread ass cheeks. I feel cold lube, and a massive butt plug is driven home. My anus clenches on the toy. My pussy longs to rub against the knot.

He flips me over, ties my wrists and ankles to the bed. He lifts my chin and speaks to me. "You will be kept like this at all times when I'm not making use of you, girl. You will only be permitted one orgasm a month. If you deserve it." I begin to cry...

I bucked against my fingers. The rope-knot fantasy got me every time. I jerked myself off faster and faster. *Don't think of them watching you. Rope knot.*

Rope knot! Ahh, there we go. The second orgasm wasn't even as strong as the first one. *If you want to come so badly, Nell...* My tits ached. He just had to release me now.

Jeremy prompted, "Again. Once more." I let out my breath in indignation, but it made no matter. I was at his command.

Again, again, again, again, yes, whatever you say.

I searched my mind for some really nasty fantasies, fantasies nasty enough to get me going when all I really wanted to do was die.

A camping trip. Jeremy wakes me in the dead of the night. The air is heavy with electricity, a gathering storm. I am frog-marched out into deep black woods and pushed against a tree.

"Please, what have I done?"

He ignores me. Rope is wound around my torso to bind me. Around my shoulders, my waist, and the tops of my thighs, so I'm unable to move even an inch. He moves away, and I hear rustling. He returns and starts to spank me, excruciating sting and fire. A switch!

I cry, I beg for help, but we're alone. I realize I can't escape the lash. I press my clit to the rough bark of the tree to somehow soothe myself. "No," says Jeremy. The storm finally breaks, flashing lightning and pelting rain. He cuts the ropes and catches my limp body in his arms.

He carries me to the tent and lies me on the ground facedown. He traces his tongue over my welted flesh as thunder makes the ground shake under me. He takes out his cock and spreads my ass cheeks roughly, forces it home—

Oh Jesus, that one sneaked up on me. The sharp, quick orgasm. My walls contracted, but it was just response, just physiology. I felt no pleasure at all, only relief that it was over, that Jeremy wouldn't want more than three. And that fantasy! What kind of sick pervert was I, to get off on a scene like that? You're a bad, *sick* pervert, I thought. A terrible submissive, who needs to be punished.

And I felt punished. I had the orgasms, but they weren't fun, and they certainly didn't feel sexy. They felt like work. Maybe that's the lesson he was trying to teach me. That I had a job to do, and that job was pleasing him, not doing what I liked. I looked up at Jeremy again and said, "I'm sorry."

Again I was ignored. Without words, he cuffed my free hand back to the bed. He sat beside me to do it but didn't once look down at my face. He took the clips off me, none too gently. I moaned and writhed against the cuffs. The pain of having clamps taken off was almost more excruciating than having them put on. It lingered longer, anyway.

"As we discussed," he said to Kyle as he handed him the clamps, "put them on her every hour and don't take them off her until she comes. Three times."

Every hour? Jesus.

"Let her go to the bathroom and eat lunch around noon, but the rest of the time, she lies right there with her hands tied. Otherwise God knows what she'll do to herself."

Kyle smirked down at me, jingling the evil metal devices in his palm. God, I hated his guts. Then Jeremy finally looked at me, but only to frown.

"As I said, if you have such a desire to jerk yourself off, be my guest. At four o'clock, you'll be untied and your punishment will be over."

I looked at the clock. It wasn't even eight in the morning.

"Have a good day, Nell," he said, leaving without a backward glance.

* * * * *

I was a submissive. I had been for years, but this all-day-punishment thing was totally novel to me. I'd been humiliated, clamped, made to masturbate on hundreds of occasions, but never for eight hours in a row. Eight hours times three plus the three he'd already forced on me was twenty-seven orgasms, not to mention some sore, tender tits. Every time Kyle came in the room, I glared daggers at him, but he only looked back indifferently and produced the biting clips.

Still the tit man, he took his time toying with my nipples, getting them nice and hard before he applied the clamps. The first time he came in to do it, I said, "Don't you want me to look you in the eyes?"

In hindsight, I wish I hadn't said it, because it brought that night back. The night we spent together, when he was an amazingly hot guy and I was still Little Nell, with my own simple life.

Kyle didn't react to my question. He clamped the first tit. I gritted my teeth to hold in the whine. He sighed, moving on to the other tit. "Nell, I was only doing my job. If you're still angry about that, you're stupid."

I pursed my lips in annoyance and looked away. I wasn't still angry. Was I?

"Anyway, you enjoyed that night," he added. "So what the hell do you care?"

"I don't care." We looked at each other. It felt like a mournful moment to me. How did he feel about what he'd done? He looked a little guilty.

"Nell—" He started to speak, then stopped.

"What?" I finally asked.

"Just start fucking masturbating," he said, crossing his arms over his chest.

"You're going to stand there and watch me?"

"Boss's orders. He doesn't trust you to do what you're supposed to when you're on your own."

I sighed and closed my eyes all three times in a row, and every time after that. I didn't want to see him watching me, and honestly, I don't think he wanted to watch. *Now if Jeremy had been here*, I thought to myself spitefully. With each passing hour I grew more and more despondent. I thought I could handle this sadistic little punishment, but at some point, I started to hurt. Not hurt in my clamped nipples or hurt in my chafed clit, but hurt in my soul. I was tired of being tied up, tired of masturbating, tired of my nipples throbbing while I reached between my legs. Most of all, I was tired of feeling like shit.

"You did this to yourself," Kyle reminded me. Horrible fucking man, gorgeous or not.

At four o'clock I managed three last orgasms. I felt too bleak by that time to even feel glad. "Do me a favor," Kyle said as he untied me. "Don't jack yourself off anymore unless he tells you to. I don't feel like doing this again."

"Fuck you," I replied. With a snicker, he left the room.

I rubbed my wrists and ankles and limped to the bathroom, where I soaked in the tub for an hour. I didn't want to think about how I'd spent my day. And what had I learned? I suppose I learned that Jeremy was not fucking around when he gave me rules to obey. Perhaps I learned too that he was not the romantic hero I'd imagined. He was just my dom.

No, he was my *employer*. Fine. *I get it now.*

Now I wanted to move on, move past it. I wanted to shut my mind off. I sat at the table in the silence, then turned on the TV just to hear some noise. There was nothing to watch, only Thai channels, a few international channels, but nothing I really wanted to see. I didn't want to look out the window and freak myself out again, and I definitely felt too restless to sit and read. It had been two days, and already I was about to lose my mind.

Finally I grabbed my coat and headed down to the lobby. I didn't know if I was allowed to wander around on my own, but Jeremy wasn't there to ask. I thought about the contract rules, but it hadn't said anything about my private time, only that I had to be available to him. But he was at work. He would be working until seven or eight o'clock.

I walked through the lobby, waiting subconsciously for someone to stop me, to leap out and say, *Did Jeremy tell you that you could go?*

But no one paid attention or stopped me, so I nodded to the doorman and walked outside. It was crowded on the sidewalk, the local Bangkok citizens going about their business, pushing past me impatiently, but I didn't care. I felt like I'd been sprung from prison, and I wanted to walk. I wanted to enjoy the feeling of being free. I just wished I blended in more. My bright red hair stood out like a siren among the sea of blue-black hair. I noticed heads starting to turn as I continued along.

I should have worn a hat.

I ducked my head and kept walking, taking in the sights, but the only sights were more people and tall buildings. The city streets were crowded with honking cars and frenetic activity. After twenty minutes or so I turned back, having barely made my way down a few blocks. I was worried about losing my bearings and not being able to get back to the hotel.

Even worse, people were starting to follow me, to grab me and speak to me in broken English. I heard "Jer-my Gray, Jer-my Gray, girl-friend, Jer-my Gray!"

I didn't answer. I didn't like the way they were pulling at me, brandishing cell phones and cameras, flashes in my eyes. Soon they surrounded me, and even when I tried to walk, I couldn't move forward through the crowd without touching someone, without having to push someone out of my way.

"Excuse me." My voice sounded panicky and shrill. "Excuse me. I'm trying to go…go over there."

I pointed to the hotel. It seemed miles away, and I was sure I'd never get there. I'd never get out of this crowd.

"Jer-my. Jer-my. Where your boy-friend?"

"I don't know. I don't know."

A policeman or security guard of some sort began to disperse the crowd with shouts and rude gesticulations. I'd never been so relieved to see anyone in my life. I ducked through the crowds to meet him. He took my elbow and attempted to shelter me from the pursuing paparazzi. He led me toward his squad car, but I pointed at the hotel.

"I have to go there. I'm staying there." All I wanted was to run up to the eighty-fifth floor and stay there forever.

He pushed through the crowds, blowing his whistle. It shrilled next to my ear and set my teeth on edge. He smelled bad, and his hands were hurting my forearm as he dragged me along behind him. It felt like an hour before we finally reached the hotel. The policeman accompanied me into the lobby, where Jeremy waited just inside the door, his face a pale, set mask.

He nodded to the officer and thanked him in Thai before pulling me into the elevator and mashing the button with enough force to break it. I stood beside him, not knowing what to say. I was still shaking. My stomach was still in knots from the experience outside, and now I had to face him and his ire. *Jeremy, please forgive me. Please just look at me without that frown.* "Did you have a nice walk?" he finally asked right before we reached our floor.

I leaned against the wall of the elevator and burst into tears. It was enough. His anger, his tone. It was enough for me. I wanted to go to bed, go to sleep, go home, go back to Eden, to Buona Italia, go anywhere but here.

"Okay." He sighed and turned to me and took me in his arms. I clutched at him, falling apart completely. "Okay," he whispered. "You're okay now. I know. It's scary, those crowds. You've had a hard day."

"I'm sorry. I'm sorry," I sobbed over and over. "I'm sorry. I'm sorry. I'm sorry…"

"Shhh, shh, enough." He led me out of the elevator at the eighty-fifth floor, and down the hall to our room. Inside, he held me a long time by the door. He squeezed me tighter and tighter until the cold, shivery shaking started to go away.

"Why are they like that?" I finally whispered into the side of his neck. "What do they want?"

"Me," he said in a tight voice. "They want me. If they can't have me, they go after you, or anyone else connected to me. You can't go walking around, not here. I'm sorry. I should have told you. I didn't think you'd want to go out today." He released me and brushed away the last of my tears. "If you want to go out and sightsee around Bangkok, I have to make arrangements with Kyle for a security detail. And I will, if that's what you want."

"No, I don't want to go back out there. Not ever again."

"You don't now, but you might another time," he said, tipping my face up and caressing my cheek. "I know this feeling is scary. It will go away. You'll get used to it."

"I'll never get used to it," I said, shaking my head.

"You will. You'll find ways to avoid the worst of it, find ways to minimize it. You'll learn how to hide."

How to hide. Like you do, behind your fake girlfriend.

A knock came from the door, and Jeremy let Kyle in.

"Oh, she's here." He looked relieved.

"Yes, she's here," Jeremy snapped, releasing me to stalk over to the kitchen and grab a beer out of the refrigerator.

Kyle glared at me. "If you wanted to go out, you should have said."

"I told her that already," said Jeremy. I could see that Kyle was the one in the hot seat now.

The personal assistant/sex-toy procurer shall not allow said sex toy to wander about the city alone after torturing her with tit clamps and forced orgasms all day.

"Everything's fine now, Kyle. I'll see you in the morning," Jeremy said. After Kyle left with one last frown in my direction, Jeremy looked at me as if assessing my mental soundness. He didn't look impressed with what he saw.

"You know, sunlight helps jet lag. Maybe tomorrow you can come with me to the set. It's closed. You'll be safe from the fans and paparazzi there, and you can get some fresh air and light. Reset your clock."

"Yes, Jeremy," I said. "That sounds fine."

"You look tired. Are you hungry?"

"I ate before I went out. I'm not hungry, no."

"Go to bed, then," he said. "Get some sleep. Tomorrow's another day."

My throat felt tight. Dismissed. I wanted him to hold me some more, but he was right, I was tired. I headed to my room and tried not to think about how wonderful it felt to be held so tightly in his arms, and the fact that I was going to my big, empty bed alone.

The restraints were still there on the headboard and footboard. I tucked them away and brushed my teeth, put on my old, ratty Betty Boop pajamas and climbed into bed. I didn't want to cry again, but I did. I couldn't help it. I felt so lost and sad. I hunched into a ball and let the tears come.

Then he was there, sliding into the bed behind me, pulling me close. He didn't shush me this time, just held me as I sobbed and shook, my back pressed to his chest. He buried his face in my hair and clasped me hard.

"It's all right." He nuzzled against my ear as I shuddered and cried. He kissed my neck and snaked his hand up under my loose T-shirt, caressing me, avoiding my tender nipples as if he knew they ached too much for play. Soon I felt his hard cock nudge against my hip. While I sobbed, he pulled my pajama bottoms down and ran his hand down between my thighs. I heard the rattle of cellophane, then felt the thick head of his cock pushing into my slit. I thought it strange that he would want to fuck me now, when I was weeping and disintegrating.

But as soon as he began to move in me, I felt the strange appropriateness of it. It calmed me. It soothed me. It grounded me. He took me in long, measured strokes, his hands on my shoulders and neck, then down between my legs, stroking, caressing, pressing, and pinching my clit. My bereft, tortured sobs quickly commuted into soft moans of pleasure. He filled me so perfectly, he moved in me so deftly and skillfully, like no lover I'd ever had.

"Better, Nell?" he whispered in my ear as he fucked me.

Yes yes yes, better. Everything's better again.

And I would have been perfectly happy not coming. I would have not come just to prove how sorry I was, just to let him know that from then on, every one of my orgasms would be his. But he urged me to come, stroking my clit the way I had stroked it that morning when I was forced to masturbate myself. I remembered how he'd watched me, studied my fingers as they moved across my slit. It occurred to me that this man was more complex than I realized. I cried even harder to think that he'd done that, watched me in order to learn how to pleasure me later. Punishment…and care. My quaking, sparkling orgasm came in hectic waves of color, waves the color of ice blue eyes.

"Yes," he said as I shook and gasped in his arms. "Good girl."

I thought it was all too much. Too much warmth, too much confusion, too much pain, too much pleasure, too much joy.

Too much fear of living life with him, too much devastation if he were to send me away.

Too much of his cock, and never enough.

Too many feelings that I couldn't come to terms with.

Too many tears and too much pain. Too much risk.

Too many floors up, and way too far to fall.

Chapter Ten: Mine

Jesus Christ. She undid me.

I would just hold her until she fell asleep, and then I'd leave. I might lick her velvet skin, just a little, to soothe her…her shoulders and the luscious little hollow at her nape.

I buried my hand in her lovely, silky, soft red curls and squeezed lightly. I bit her neck, but I didn't mark her.

I wanted to, though.

Mine.

"Go to sleep now. No more crying."

"Yes, Jeremy," she whispered.

My cock was still inside her. I pulled out to peel off the condom, but I didn't pull away. I didn't want to think about what that meant, that I couldn't let her go.

I mean, sure, I liked her. That much was obvious. When Kyle called me, telling me she'd gone missing, my mind had flown at once to the worst possible scenarios. *She's left you. She's lost. Someone's got her.* Unreasonable fears, the worst one being that she had simply decided to bail. *You're too much for her, too sick, too rough, too coarse, too perverse.*

I knew I had been harsh on her, but I had to be. Law was law, and she had to be taught that rules mattered to me. Plus, to be honest, I got off on punishing her. I was a pervert. There was nothing I could do about it.

Anyway, she was a pervert too.

Deep down inside, I believed she was every bit as perverted as me, although she was holding back like any submissive would. There were so many things I still had to do to her, so many ways I still wanted to use her, and I knew she'd enjoy every one. When I thought she had left, I'd had a moment of real panic. *No, not already. Not so soon.*

But she hadn't left. A cursory look in her room showed me her luggage was still there, and anyway, where could she have gone? She didn't have enough money yet to leave on her own. She would have had to ask me to get a ticket for her, at least until she got her first paycheck. And if she'd asked me, I would have—I really would have—but only after I'd done everything in my power to convince her to stay.

But no, she hadn't left. Instead she'd foolishly braved the streets of Bangkok alone, as if no one would notice her. Her picture was plastered all over the daily tabloids, standing beside me with that lovely, tired smile and that ridiculous red hair that made it impossible to look away.

Yes, I'd bought a copy of one of the papers, the nicest, full-color one, left it in my trailer on the set to look at during breaks. I needed to get some erotic pictures of her for my private use. It wasn't in the contract, but I bet I could talk her into it if I turned on the charm.

But not now. For now I had to let her sleep the day off, sleep everything away, so we could start fresh again. I wasn't happy about her wandering off, but I figured she'd been punished enough for that lapse in judgment. When she'd walked into the hotel lobby beside the policeman, my breath had left my chest in a rush.

Mine, I'd wanted to say as soon as I laid eyes on her. *Thanks, Officer. She's mine.*

She was mine. She'd agreed to be. Maybe I'd sleep beside her all night. Why not? That way if I woke up horny, I could use her. I could slip deep inside.

That way, I could sleep all night with her in my arms, and remember that she hadn't left after all.

* * * * *

I stood beside Jess, stifling a yawn. Above us, grips were rigging the lights, and the stunt crew was resetting the ladder Jess and I would climb, so it would fall down again just the right way. Rig, reset, repeat. I was so fucking bored.

Across the soundstage, Nell had her nose buried in a book. Only her. Bring her to a massive studio during the filming of a blockbuster production, and she's more interested in the *Odyssey*. I stared at her, thinking of the things I could be doing if we were alone. I could strap her to the rigging, do some deep character study involving her ass and my cock.

I'd been eager to bring her to the set, to get her out of the secluded hotel room. I thought it would be good for her to get out and about. But she retreated by herself into a quiet corner of the soundstage as soon as we arrived. And her brief meeting with Jess had not gone as I imagined it. Nell mostly blushed and stared at the floor. I tried to figure out what she was feeling, what was making her so moody. Shame? Surely she realized I'd forgiven her for the day before. Punishment meted out. Finished. Time to move on.

But she wasn't moving on.

Jess nudged me when she noticed me looking at Nell. "Really, Jeremy. Another one? When are you going to get a real girlfriend?"

I chuckled. "Well, you're no longer available. I take what I can get."

"And how is this one treating you? She seems a little skittish compared to the last one."

"We haven't been together long."

"She might not be up to the depths of your depravity."

"She's up to it." I looked at her bent over her book, her lips drawn together in a pout of concentration. My cock twitched. "We literally haven't had much time, Jess. I met her...God...a couple of weeks ago."

"And she followed you all the way to Bangkok." Jessamine raised her eyebrows. "You must be paying her a lot. Or she must have been really desperate for work."

"A little bit of both. Anyway, she's not like the last one. She's smart. She's really...real."

"Is she?" Jessamine looked over at her. "Be careful, or you might actually fall in love."

"I won't."

"I did," she reminded me with one of the flirty, sexy smiles she was famous for. "Never say never."

"I didn't say never. It's none of your business anyway."

And it wasn't. Everybody thought we were their business. Everyone who met Nell that day sized her up, not like Jessamine, who knew about my darker proclivities, but like nosy people. I could tell it was difficult for Nell, the scrutiny, the constant prying questions. Having to act like my girlfriend when I didn't think she even liked me very much.

"*How long have you known Jeremy?*"

"*Not very long.*"

"*Where did you meet?*"

"*I was working as a waitress when he came in for dinner.*"

They weren't paparazzi, they were production people, but they were just as persistent with their questions, and Nell wasn't comfortable with the attention. My last girlfriend had loved the attention, wallowed in it from the beginning, to the point where it disgusted me a little.

But Nell was more circumspect. No, not circumspect. She was *afraid*. Afraid of attention, afraid of the press and cameras. I knew it, but I didn't want to admit it to myself. Admit that what she was enduring for me was, perhaps, not so great for her mental health. Well, I was paying her plenty of money to compensate. Wasn't that enough?

On the way to the car at the end of the day, Kyle showed me a tabloid with photos from her foray into the street the day before. God, she looked terrified. Her expression was outwardly calm, but her eyes were filled with fear. If I had any conscience at all, I would have sent her back to L.A. on the next plane with some college tuition and a *thank you very much*. But I had no conscience, of course. I was perpetually selfish. I gave it back to him before Nell could see it.

"Tired?" I asked as we navigated the busy streets back to the hotel.

"No, I'm fine. I just..." She shrugged.

"What?"

"I can't believe...the whole movie thing...behind the scenes..."

"It's overwhelming, isn't it?"

"I see now why you need to unwind at the end of the day. Why so many celebrities get addicted to alcohol and drugs."

"You're better than alcohol and drugs," I said. She didn't answer, just another small frown. I looked down at her hands which were clasped tightly in her lap.

"Do you...? How do you...? Are you unhappy?" Why the hell had I blurted that out? I rubbed my eyes and sighed. "Look, are you really miserable here with me?"

She was quiet a moment, then, "Do I seem miserable?"

"Yes, you do, to be honest." I took a deep breath. "Do you want to go home?"

"Do you want me to go home?"

"Answer my question, please. Do you want to go home?"

"No."

I eased back against the seat. "It will get better. Soon, Nell."

"I know."

We rode a long time in silence. She was rigid beside me. So unhappy. Why couldn't she smile?

"Tell me what's wrong," I said.

She shook her head. "Nothing."

"Something's wrong."

"Nothing's wrong. I'm tired. I just…" Her voice trailed off, and she waved her hand away.

"Smile for me, then," I said.

"I don't feel like smiling."

I don't know why I felt I had to push her at that moment. But I did. "I asked you to smile for me." I used the voice. She looked up at me.

"Do you really want me to smile?" Her voice sounded edgy. Her normally light eyes looked dark and glazed.

"I don't like to repeat myself. I want a real smile, not a forced one."

She waited a moment, gauged if I was serious, then gave me an approximation of a grin.

"Pitiful." I turned away, then turned back again.

"What's your name, Nell?" I wanted a reaction, and I got one. She hissed through her teeth and snapped at me.

"What? Why are you like this? What do you want?"

"I want to know your real name."

"Why?"

"Because I fucking want to!"

She turned to look out the window again. So much anger under the surface, for both of us. I took her hand.

"Look, I'm stressed. Okay? Relax me, talk to me. Tell me another story. A story from your work."

She was quiet for so long, I thought she wasn't going to do it, but then she said, "One time this guy came into Eden. He was really hot, the hottest guy I'd ever seen. But I could tell right off he wasn't a dominant. I had no idea what he was doing there. He offered me two thousand dollars to come to my apartment and fuck me. And he did. He fucked my mouth and my cunt and my ass—"

"Nell—"

"It was so weird. It was almost as if he was trying me out, sampling the goods. And you know what, he actually was. He worked for this perverted movie star who—"

"Enough!"

We sat in uneasy silence. She said she didn't want to leave, but it was also apparent that she thought I was a dick.

He worked for this perverted movie star who—

Who what? Who was an asshole? Who ruined my life? Who got me fired from my job? Who dragged me to Thailand to make me miserable?

"You're a submissive," I said, trying not to let my injured pride sound in my voice. "You're *my* submissive. If you're going to stay, you need to show a little respect."

"Yes, Jeremy," she said in a perfectly docile tone that broadcast *fuck you* loud and clear.

"I mean it. I don't care if you dislike me. I don't care if you're miserable here. Put up with it or leave, just like I offered you. If you want to leave, let me know."

But I didn't tell her that I would have paid for her college anyway if she left, would have gotten her old job back if she wanted it too. I didn't want to make leaving an attractive proposition for her. Perpetually selfish. Hard habit to break.

She chewed her lip, looking away from me.

"I can't wait to get back to the room with you," I said. I let her mind wander over the reason why. I wasn't even sure what I wanted to do with her. Spank her, fuck her, tie her up, sodomize her, kiss her, worship her, make her suck my cock. I was like those adolescent boys who had so many fantasies, they couldn't get it together enough to make even one come to pass.

* * * * *

I didn't take her hand in the elevator. There was no one around, and a day of playing boyfriend and girlfriend on the set had taken a toll on us both. She walked behind me down the hall, then stood still as a statue while I unlocked the door. As soon as we were inside, she turned to me.

"I want to make you happy." Her voice sounded small and tight. "I'm failing miserably, I know. I don't know why I'm like this."

I looked at her a long moment, looked right in her eyes.

"Prunella?"

I said it just to make her laugh. I'd been hoarding it all day. And it worked. She gave me a smile as she shook her head. It wasn't a huge smile, but it was a start.

"You aren't failing." I cupped her chin in my hand to make her look at me. "Listen to me, because I'm not going to keep repeating this. I know you think you're not good enough, that you're not enough for me. That you're going to be exposed for the scared, nervous, inexperienced girl you are. Well, I've seen it already. I know you're scared. I know you haven't had a whole lot of real-life sex, that you're not the most perfect submissive in the world. But I chose you, Nell. I promise you turn me on more than anything else in the world, and God, the way you're looking at me right now…"

I stopped talking and took her face in my hands. I kissed her, because I couldn't stand not to when she looked at me that way, all soft, wide-eyed submission. Her lips were so warm, so giving. I pulled her close and whispered next to her ear.

"Just trust me. I'll take care of everything. All you need to do is submit to me. That's all. The rest will work itself out. If you truly want to make me happy, then do as I ask. Don't be defensive, and don't be angry anymore. You're here, and you say you want to be, so I would like to let the rest go. The way we met, the things I did that made you so mad. The things that happened yesterday. Because we're not going to get anywhere with this anger simmering underneath."

I looked down at her, and she nodded. "I'll try to let it go of it."

"Don't try, just do it. Or if you can't, then please go. I have enough stress in my life. I don't need your disapproval on top of it all."

"I'm sorry, Jeremy. I don't want to go. I just get so worried and scared. I have no one else to talk to, to vent to. I know you're a good person, that you did what you did to get me here out of—"

Love. We both heard it in the air between us clear as day, although her voice cut off with a sharp breath.

"Out of desperation," I said. "And that's your power over me. I was desperate to have you. I still am." I slipped my hands under her shirt to stroke the silky skin of her lower back. "So don't be scared. Just be Nell. Can you do that? Or have you completely forgotten who you are? Is that why you won't tell me your name?"

"I don't know," she said. "I may have forgotten, a little. Or maybe I never knew."

I ran one finger down the side of her cheek.

"Then I'll have to figure you out, won't I? I'm looking forward to it. Come on," I said. "Let's go get you dressed."

* * * * *

In her bedroom, I went through her suitcase until I found the corset I wanted: black matte velvet with ribbons and lace, and tiny, satin-covered buttons up the back. Next I found the back-seamed silk stockings and matching black velvet stilettos. The set had cost me a fortune, but it was worth it. I wanted her to look like my beautiful high-class whore. I beckoned her over from the door and said, "Undress."

I loved watching her take her clothes off. While she did, I tore my own clothes off, and by the time she was finished, I was already rock hard. I pulled her over by the bed and helped her shimmy the corset over her head. I turned her to tighten the laces and fasten the tiny buttons at the top one by one.

"You're beautiful." I breathed down her neck as I worked. She shivered. She was so sensitive. I didn't know how she would handle what I had planned.

When the corset was on, I knelt, taking first one foot and then the other in my hands to put on the stockings and smooth them slowly up her legs. I fastened the garters without even looking. Once, those tiny clasps completely befuddled me, but now I could work them with my eyes closed and my cock otherwise preoccupied. I stayed still on my knees to survey my handiwork. God, her legs were obscene. She was little, but her legs were perfect, strong, shapely. I kissed the top of one thigh, and she moaned softly.

I pulled myself away from her thighs and picked up the shoes. I slipped them onto her feet, then drew her down and said, "Kneel. Head to the floor. Spread your legs."

She obeyed perfectly, but of course I put my hands on her anyway, rearranging her for the sole purpose of feeling her up. "Don't move," I said. "And don't fucking touch yourself. I'll be right back."

I went to my bag of tricks and pulled out a few toys and some lubricant, then went back in her room. She was exactly as I'd left her, although I thought she was probably wetter. I knelt beside her.

"You know what I want to do to you tonight, Nell? I want to play with your ass a little. Do you know why?"

It was a rhetorical question, although she humored me with a "no, Jeremy," mumbled into the carpet.

"Because it's mine now, and I'm going to use it a lot. I'm going to fuck it and play with it and humiliate you by sticking things inside it. Do you like having things in your ass?" I reached out to caress her bottom cheek. She jumped a little. "Look at me and tell the truth."

"Yes, Jeremy," she whispered, peeking over at me. "Most of the time."

The lovely blush, the trembling, the black velvet against pale skin…

"Most of the time?"

"I haven't had a whole lot of…really large things in my ass," she said, her gaze dropping momentarily to my swollen cock before returning quickly to my face.

"Clients played with your ass at Eden."

"Yes, but there was a size limit on the toys they could use."

"What limit?"

"One and one quarter inch in diameter, and five inches long."

I looked down at my cock. "We're going to need to push that limit a little, I'm afraid."

It was a joke, but she looked traumatized at the idea of taking me in her ass. I had absolutely no doubt she could take me just fine. I moved closer and took up the bottle of lube. I squeezed some of the cold liquid onto my fingers.

"You know I won't hurt you, Nell, that's not my kink. Relax. This will all go much easier if you do."

Chapter Eleven: Intimacy

I breached her, taking my time. I used one finger at first, then two fingers sliding up inside her until I felt her relax.

"I'm going to put a toy in your ass now. It's a bit larger than what was allowed at Eden, but not much. It will loosen you up for my cock, which you are definitely going to take tonight."

She made a small, strangled noise of assent into the floor, but I didn't need her permission. I was already sliding in the little glass toy. I liked glass, it was less forgiving. She took it well, moaning softly but not moving at all.

"Good girl," I said when it was fully seated. "Now kneel up and suck my cock. Don't even think about coming from that little toy in your ass either. You don't have my permission yet."

"Yes, Sir." It was a breach in protocol that I'm sure was caused by the distraction of having her ass firmly plugged. "I'm sorry," she whispered when she realized her error.

"I'll deal with it later. First, attend to my cock."

She rolled on the condom I handed her, and then took me in her mouth like any good submissive, intent on pleasuring me first and foremost. I let her lick and suck me for a while, enjoying the warmth of her breath, the ticklish feeling of her tongue tracing over my ridges. This was the Nell I loved, open and eager to please. When I couldn't hold off any longer, I held the back of her head and worked my way into her throat. I advanced, then withdrew, then advanced again, a little deeper each time. I swelled in her mouth, riled up by the sight of her in the beautiful black corset, with the toy in her ass, kneeling on her stocking-covered legs in service to me. She still wasn't skilled at deep throating, but she tried. She didn't pull away.

Eventually her nose was buried in the fur at the base of my cock. She gagged a little, and I released her. *Again.* I slid into her, and this time she accepted my length. I tapped her chin, and she looked up at me. Beautiful. Her eyes were watery, and drool trickled from the sides of her mouth, but she'd never looked more beautiful to me. I withdrew, felt her take in a rush of breath. I felt her gasps tickle down the length of my shaft to graze against my balls. I drew her head back and shoved it down by my sac. She opened and started lapping at my scrotum like a well-trained slut. Her back arched as she groveled before me. My cock twitched at the sight of the toy in her quivering ass. I pulled her back up by her hair and drove between her lips again. Her soft, hungry moans vibrated against my dick as I sawed in and out. She looked transported just to be sucking me. It was too much. I emptied my load with a groan, buried deep in her throat.

She waited as I rode out my climax. Afterward, I put my hand under her chin. Light pressure drew her attention back to my face. She fell away and gazed up at me, waiting to be told what to do. I threw away the condom and went to pick up my pants and draw the belt from the belt loops, doubling it over. It was a nice, thick, broken-in leather belt, perfect for situations like these. She watched, all too aware of what was coming. I snapped and pointed to the floor, and she lowered her torso into position, her ass facing me, ready to be punished. The small trace of reluctance I saw in her movement made the blood beat in my veins.

Without explanations or a grand lecture, I landed the first blow, aiming purposely for the toy. I made her jump, and that pleased me. The nice thing about arrangements like ours was that there didn't have to be a reason for this whimsical disbursement of punishment. It could always be "just because."

I could be punishing her for slipping up and calling me "Sir," but I could just as well be punishing her because she was kneeling there vulnerable and weak, or because I liked the way the black belt matched perfectly with her lingerie. Just because. Just because her ass was gorgeous, just because she was still a novice at so many things, just because I knew she struggled to take it. Just because I knew she was mine.

Just because she was mine.

Another blow and she jerked. Her hands flew down by her waist, although she wasn't foolish enough to try to cover herself.

"Over your head," I said, tapping her with the belt.

She put her fists next to her head and wrapped them in her hair.

Another stroke, and another. Her reactions drove me, her tiny squeaks and jerks. She drew her knees in after a particularly wicked blow.

"Uh-uh. I'll add more." Slowly she unfolded her body and arched her ass up in the air. "This is the least of what you're going to endure tonight," I reminded her. I brought the belt down again, this time aiming for the tender skin at the tops of her thighs. Again, and yet again. *Bliss.* The sound of the belt cracking against her spread thighs resonated in my cock.

Again. Crack! This one caught her under her left ass cheek. I could tell it was a stinger. Her wail of *noooo* moved me, but not in the way she probably hoped.

By the end I'd marked her pretty badly, just as I'd meant to, just as this entire night would be dedicated to marking her as mine, physically, mentally, sexually, in every way I could. It was high time I did. It would make it easier on her moving forward, although it would be difficult, in the moment, to endure. Soon she wept openly, and her plaintive cries approached a volume that might be heard beyond our walls.

"I'll gag you if you aren't quieter," I said. "This is only a belt spanking. Should I get a gag?"

"No, please. I'll be quieter. I don't like to be gagged."

"But you will be, if I want you to be. You have five more to go. I expect you to control the volume."

"Yes, Jeremy."

She managed to be a lot quieter after that. She moaned and tensed, really struggled to accept the pain, which made it that much more thrilling for me. When I finished and dropped the belt, she went limp. I looked down at her a long minute, at her breathless, prostrated form, her plugged ass, her wet pussy, hungry for me even though her cheeks were bruised and welted from my punishment.

"Stand up." I wanted to watch her, wanted to sit and enjoy the view some more. "I want you to go and unpack your suitcases. Everything. Find a place for it. Put it all away."

It wasn't what she'd expected to hear, but it was what I wanted. I wanted to watch her unpack and settle herself into this room where she would stay. Where she would stay with me, in my employment and service.

"Make it good too," I said. "I want to see that lovely ass every time you bend over."

She looked back at me, an unfathomable look, and bent from the waist with her legs spread to unzip the first bag.

"Yes." It was exactly what I'd hoped for. "Good girl."

She unpacked everything and put it all away. The clothes were hung in a row in the closet, the many sets of lingerie lain carefully and neatly in drawers, the books stacked along the back of the desk. God, there were so many. She bent at the waist again to line up the shoes in the bottom of the closet organized by color. This is what I paid her for. What a fucking pro. She gave it all to me, every intimate view, every part of her that other women hid away.

By the time she finished, the redness of her ass was subsiding and the welts were standing out even lovelier against her pale skin. My cock, on the other hand, was red and swollen hard again.

"Come here, you little slut." When she stood in front of me, I reached to slap her sore ass cheeks. I couldn't help it. She gasped beautifully.

"Do you know why I had you put everything away?"

"Yes," she said softly after a moment. "I think I do."

"Why?"

"So I won't think anymore about leaving. So I won't worry anymore."

"That's exactly why. The only thing I want you to worry about is me and what I want. Can you remember that from now on?"

"Yes, Jeremy."

"And what I want now is to fuck your ass. Come on." I took her by the arm and led her into my bedroom. The bed was bigger than hers, an imposing four-poster that, for the duration of my stay, had been outfitted with eyebolts on each post.

"Go and bend over the side." God, I was so hard for her. I grabbed a condom from the end table and played with myself a little to assuage the ache. I couldn't thrust inside her the way I wanted to, not yet. I wasn't hung like a monster, but I was big enough to require using caution.

She watched me warily. From a chest beside the bed, I got some cuffs and a spreader bar.

Mine, mine, mine. She would feel it in a minute, how completely I owned her.

I knelt behind her with the bar, attaching it to her ankles. No need to explain. She knew this hardware as well as I did, that it braced her legs open so she was at the mercy of whatever I wanted to do. The cuffs too were a known evil. She stood and offered her wrists for them, watching docilely as I secured them nice and tight. I picked her up and carried her nearer to the post at the foot of the bed, so she wouldn't stumble in her heels with the spreader bar holding her. I put her down facing the post and pressed her against it. She stood still and waited to be told what to do. She was absolutely beautiful with her legs opened wide by the spreader. I took a moment to nestle my hard cock between the cheeks of her ass.

"Arms up."

She raised them as high as she physically could, not cheating, not raising them only as high as was comfortable for her. And as I'd suspected, she was the perfect height to hook the cuffs into the hidden eyebolts, stretching but not quite straining, lifting only slightly onto her toes, the spreader bar making it difficult for her to balance.

I stood back and looked at her then. Beautiful. *Beautiful.* Bruised ass, naughty toy, spread thighs, straining back, black corset, stockings, stilettos. My lovely, perfect girl. I wanted to punish her again, just to watch her struggle in the bonds. I got out a crop and stroked it lightly down her back.

"Brace yourself," I said. "You won't get very many, but the ones you get will hurt."

I only gave her five. She didn't disappoint me—her reactions were gorgeous. The first stroke had her pulling at her bonds. The second made her dance around. By the time I laid the fifth blow across her ass cheeks, she was stifling screams.

I threw the crop down. I wanted to be inside, and I wanted her to feel every inch of me. I wanted her to come from having me plunge deep inside. I took her roughly in my arms, pressed my dick against the throbbing part of her anatomy that I was about to enjoy. She was still crying a little. I turned her face toward mine and licked a salty tear.

"Is your ass ready to accept my fat cock now?" I asked against her ear.

"Yes, Jeremy." She pressed back against me.

"Are you sure? It's probably much bigger than anything you've taken before."

"I'm yours," she said.

I unhooked her cuffed hands from the eyebolt and released them, then refastened them behind her and bent her over the bed. I took out the toy and set it aside. I rolled a condom onto my dick, adding extra lube for good measure. Later she would learn to make do with less. For now she was still being trained.

I massaged the small of her back and put the head of my cock against her asshole. "If you can accept the toy, you can take my cock," I said. "Open up, don't brace." I forced the head in as she moaned into the mattress, but I could go no farther. Her tight ring tensed around me. I slapped her ass, and she made a plaintive sound. "Don't make me force you. I will if I have to."

I wouldn't, but she didn't know that. I held her hands hard at the small of her back and pressed in farther. With a muffled groan, she stretched to accept me. I drove shallowly at first, letting her get used to the feeling of my rigid cock in her tiny, tight hole.

"Oh God...God." She arched her bottom to me as I withdrew and surged forward again. There was absolutely no doubt in my mind that she loved what I was doing. I bent over her, twisting her auburn curls in my fist.

"I know it feels good, but don't come yet. I'm going to fuck you like this for an eternity. I'm going to fuck you until your ass is sore and your legs are weak, and when I say so, you can come for me. Not before."

"Yes, Jeremy."

She was so hot and tight. I pressed my body to hers and drove deep inside, scratching my chest on the tiny buttons on the back of her corset, feeling the tension and tremors in her buttocks and legs, the clenching and unclenching of her fists.

"Do you like this?" I asked against the side of her neck. "Do you like to feel me reaming your ass? You don't have a choice, do you? You're spread wide open for me."

"Oh God," she cried. She arched her little bottom back to me again and looked over her shoulder as I plumbed her pale white cheeks.

"I think you're an anal slut. Good to know." I drove harder, held her hands even tighter against her back. Her cries reached a fever pitch. "Do you want to come? Do you want me to shoot my hot jizz in your ass?"

"Yes, oh yes, please!"

I let go of her fists to clamp my hand over her pussy and slide my fingers between her slick labia and her swollen clit.

"Oh God!" She braced her hands on the bed and bucked her hips back against me. I stroked her until I felt her pull up into a tense ball of desire, and then I closed my fingertips on her engorged little nub. "Come for me, you little slut." I pinched hard, and I used my nails. She wailed and went stiff, clutching the covers. She gasped and shuddered, and I felt her ass contract around my length. With a groan I went off, driving deep and coming in blinding pulses of release.

I collapsed over her back. We labored to breathe, our torsos rising and falling in a jerky rhythm. Both of us were slick with sweat. We were exhausted from the power of the orgasm we'd shared. I buried my face in her neck and nibbled at the soft skin below her ear. Words escaped me. I only growled into her luscious, soft curls and then reluctantly withdrew. I discarded the condom, then removed the cuffs. After I released her ankles from the spreader bar, she stood unsteadily and turned to me.

"Okay?" I asked.

"Yes," she whispered. She looked up at me shyly, then her gaze darted away. I wanted to hold her close and kiss her for hours at the same time I wanted to run far away. Instead I cleared my throat and spoke to her.

"Well, do you want…? Do you need…?" I frowned, trying to collect myself, again the oversexed, brain-addled teenage boy. "I mean, well…that was a pretty intense scene. Do you need some…cuddle time?"

Cuddle time? Classic. Who was I, Mr. Rogers?

She shrugged. "I don't know. I mean…whatever you like. It's up to you."

We were standing and staring at each other in excruciating silence when my cell phone buzzed. At this hour, it had to be Kyle. I looked down at his message.

911. I'm coming up re: Nell.

I read it twice. No, the words weren't going away. Of all the fucking times.

"I need to talk to Kyle for a minute. Why don't you shower and get ready for bed? You've had a long day."

She bowed her head in assent, leaning down to take off her shoes. She was suddenly inches shorter, vulnerable and tired-looking in the half-light. As she brushed by me, I reached for her hand before I realized what I was doing. She looked over at me.

I don't know what I wanted to say. *Thank you. You look beautiful. You make all this bearable. The money will never be enough.*

I said nothing instead, and a moment later Kyle knocked on the door and she disappeared into the other room. I pulled on some pants and went out into the main room to let him in.

"What the hell?" I muttered.

"I know it's late. You need to see something."

He put his laptop on the table and logged on, pulling up a web site, a simplistic blog. He turned the screen to me as I looked over his shoulder.

"What? You're showing me stupid fan stuff?"

"Uh, no. Read closer."

I sat down and turned the computer screen toward me, scanning the page.

October 1

Jeremy and I arrived in Bangkok today. The hotel is spectacular. I'm too tired to write more tonight, and Jeremy wants me in the bedroom. More later.

October 2

Went to the set today with Jeremy. I met Jessamine. I think the bitch is jealous of me. Jeremy had a few too many drinks after dinner, so here I am, bored and alone. Not much else to write…

I narrowed my eyes. "What the hell? She's keeping an online diary? She's blogging? This doesn't even make sense. She didn't go to the set with me until today."

"It's not her. One of the entries was posted during the time she was tied to the bed. She wasn't blogging. I was there. Another one was posted about an hour ago."

"That wasn't her either. So what's going on?"

"Someone is posing as her and blogging about your life together, for whatever reason. Some of the posts are explicit. Imaginative."

I looked up at him in alarm.

"Not *that* imaginative. It's not someone who knows what she is to you. But someone is making stuff up that's pretty racy. Not to mention defamatory to Nell. This writer paints her as a gold digger, and someone who's using you for sex. Ironic," he added with a smirk.

"It's not funny. I'm not laughing."

"No, I agree, it's not funny. That's why I wanted you to see it right away. It not only reflects badly on her if people buy into this, it reflects badly on you."

"Why? Why would someone do this?"

Kyle shrugged. "I dunno. Jealousy. Sour grapes. Boredom. Overactive imagination. You know how some of the fans get."

I stared at the computer screen. "Fuck." The elusive peace, the satisfaction and calm I'd felt after my scene with Nell came crashing down. "What the fuck? Why are people so idiotic? This person has to stop. This has to come down. Call Martin and see what we can do about this."

"I already have, but I had to leave a message. I'll try again in the morning."

"Let him know I want this taken down. Full press. Whatever has to be done."

"I will."

"And don't tell her about this. She's already—" I waved my hand. "She's not handling the exposure very well."

"Isn't she?" Kyle looked at me and waited. "Do you...? Should I...? Do you want to—"

"No. I'll handle it."

"I never even considered… She didn't seem that shy the night I met her, not the way she is now. If I had known—"

"She's not shy. She's just freaked out a little. We'll handle it, like I said. Jesus, I worked too hard to get her here to let her go now."

"I'm glad to hear it's working out." He looked at me again, an assessing look that annoyed me.

"Anything else?" I asked.

He looked up, and I followed his gaze to where Nell stood in the shadow of the door.

"Hello," he said to her.

"Hi, Kyle."

Nell frowned at him the way she always did, but Kyle… I was trying to understand the look on his face. I sobered when I placed it. Reluctant infatuation. His eyes returned to mine.

"That's all I wanted to show you," Kyle said then, closing his laptop. "I'll leave you alone. I'm sure you're both tired," he added with a barely concealed smirk.

Disrespectful little fuck. He had a smirk for every situation. After the door closed, I turned to Nell, who still stood watching me warily from the doorway.

"Is everything okay?" she asked.

I tried not to let my uneasiness show. "Everything's fine. Some nutjob fan—"

I stopped talking as alarm washed across her features.

"It's nothing, Nell. It goes on all the time."

"There are a lot of them out there, I guess. Crazy fans."

"Yes. But you're not to worry about it. It's not your problem." *Not if I don't tell you about it.* I looked at her, the girl I'd made so vulnerable. What was this novel emotion I was feeling? Guilt? "Look, would you like to sit and have a beer with me before bed?"

"I can't drink a beer before bed. I'm sorry. I don't have your magic metabolism. That reminds me. Do they have yoga classes here, do you think?"

"If you need a yoga class, you'll have one. I'll tell Kyle."

"I can try to find one myself."

"Kyle will help you," I insisted. "I know you aren't crazy about each other, but I trust him to do what I want him to do, and that includes looking after you. There's a great gym here too, downstairs. Tell Kyle when you want to go, and he'll take you. I don't want you going anywhere alone."

The last part slipped out, and the alarm was back again.

"Why can't I go alone if it's in the hotel?"

"Because I don't want you to. Don't question me, okay?"

She gave me a long, probing look. I tried to exude utter nonchalance.

"Okay," she finally conceded. "Anyway, I'll sit with you if you like, but I'll drink some water instead of a beer."

She was leaning against the door in her sexy, transparent pajamas, trying to look awake for my benefit.

"No, go to bed," I said. "But come kiss me first."

She crossed to me as if it might be a trick, as if it weren't possible that all I wanted was a kiss. I drew her into my lap when she was close enough. I ran my hands down her arms, then encircled her waist and pulled her close. I lowered my lips to hers, kissing her softly, gently. She curled into me, pressed against me, open, relaxed, available, sweet.

She smelled clean from the shower and tasted like toothpaste. My fresh, minty girl. I felt dirty and despicable in contrast for what I was doing to her, the freaks and nuts I was exposing her to.

But I need her.

I deepened the kiss, then pulled away just as quickly. I nudged her off my lap.

"Okay, then. Well, good night. I have to look over some lines anyway. I don't want to keep you up."

"Okay. Good night, Jeremy."

I watched her cross to her room and close the door behind her after one last shy glance at me. Kyle's news might have ultimately ruined the evening, but it had still been a success because of that look she gave me. Because of the kiss.

For the first time she hadn't tensed or held herself away. Intimacy bred intimacy, I thought, even if the intimacy was the basely sexual kind. Perhaps *especially* if the intimacy was the basely sexual kind. Things would go a lot easier when she felt more relaxed around me. She'd grow more confident and lose the fear of the photographers and fans. That was the hope anyway, that we would find a symbiosis that benefited us both.

The blogger, though, that was troublesome. Ah well. Until I could speak to Martin, I would try to put it out of my mind.

I looked over lines instead, and when I had a pretty good handle on them, I stood up to drag myself to bed.

To my bed? No.

Without thinking about it, I headed to hers. I pulled the covers down and pulled her close to me, not caring if I woke her. I needed her body against mine.

Maybe I'd ask her from now on to sleep in my bed. Nightly cuddle time. Why not, if that was what I wanted?

She was mine to do with as I pleased.

Chapter Twelve: Routines

I loved the mornings. Well, I actually had two mornings in my life as Jeremy's paid companion. I had the morning before dawn when Jeremy woke me up to fuck me, and the second morning, when I woke later, alone.

The first morning was okay. It was nice actually. Before the end of the first week, Jeremy had decided that while we would keep separate rooms, I was to sleep in his bed, and the morning sex began soon after that.

I was a snuggler, so I had no problem with sleeping in his bed. I loved curling up next to him. The best nights were the nights after a long, intense scene when he'd clasp me close in his arms, and I'd feel my sore, naked ass rubbing against the scratchy hair of his muscular upper thighs.

Then in the morning, always, he woke up hard. He was ridiculously randy for a man his age. If he had to work, he'd nudge into me from behind and fuck me quick and dirty. By this point we'd had follow-up blood tests, so there was no fumbling around with condoms. If it was a weekend morning, or if he had a late report time to the set, he would take more time, demand more adventurous things. Blowjobs, ass fucking, violating me with some kinky new toy while I masturbated him. One blessed morning, I woke up to him lapping avidly between my legs.

But when he had work, he left, and most mornings I stayed in bed a few more hours, luxuriating in the soft, fragrant sheets and the quiet of the empty hotel room, drifting in and out of sleep. I felt like a treasured concubine, utterly relaxed and still humming from morning sex. I had nothing to do, no job but to pamper myself and read or relax until he returned. Not that I did that. Eventually I rolled out of bed to hit the gym or the salon or the yoga studio, with Kyle tagging reluctantly along.

Kyle, that stupid, jerky, gorgeous man. He made a big fuss complaining, to me, never Jeremy, about how he had to drag me all over town. Of course he had no problem tagging along when Jeremy felt like having group sex. He was more than happy to hang out with me then.

The first time Kyle had joined us for sex, we'd been at the set and driven back to the hotel together. Kyle didn't normally come back with us, but this day, he took a seat beside the driver in the front of the black sedan. Jeremy had looked down at me and said, "Kyle is coming back with us to the room."

I looked up at the back of the driver's head. Was he listening? I knew what went on in Jeremy's bedroom was a secret. Of course, to the uninterested party, the fact that Kyle was coming back with us to the room could have signified anything. Dinner, a meeting, documents to sign. But I knew that wasn't why.

Of course, Kyle had already known, already been told that his services would be required tonight in playing with me. I hated myself for the sudden rush of heat between my legs. Jeremy shifted beside me, smiling. Of course Jeremy, of all people, would know that I was turned on by the idea. As much as I despised Kyle, I was excited by the idea of being used by two men at once like the sex toy I was paid to be.

At the same time I was nervous. I mean, I was no stranger to the subtleties of the ménage à trois, but I wasn't completely sure yet what the dynamic was going to be. Was Kyle only a voyeur for Jeremy's pleasure, or something more? I hadn't quite pinned it down yet.

Jeremy still seemed totally straight to me, but Kyle... I didn't know. I still caught the occasional jealous glance that I didn't understand. A kind of baleful stare. As it turns out, I was to be the only focus of our sexual romps together, and the only thing they shared.

At the hotel, we all walked into the lobby together, me in the middle, with Jeremy and Kyle on either side. I felt like I must have had a huge scarlet letter hanging on the front of my cardigan. *P* for pervert, or maybe *W* for whore. There was an energy, an electricity that flowed among us that I couldn't believe everyone else didn't feel. In the elevator, Jeremy took one of my hands loosely, and Kyle took the other hand. It made me instantly wet.

Up in the room, Jeremy had dinner delivered, and we all sat and ate at the table like three business partners, which I guess we were. *Gray, Winchell & Ashton, Limited Liability Pervs. Specializing in the sexual use and objectification of women. All rights reserved.* Although at this particular business dinner, the two of them wore their street clothes, while I sat dressed like a slut. But if anyone could eat dinner in a corset and stockings, I could.

After dinner, my attention drifted in and out of Jeremy and Kyle's casual conversation. I snapped to sudden alertness when they started pushing the wineglasses and plates out of the way.

"Lie here on your back," Jeremy said, patting the table.

Kyle watched with that ever-present smirk as I hopped up on the table and let Jeremy arrange me as he wished, which was spread wide and opened up on display.

First, as always, his fingers found my cleft and thrust deep inside. "Jesus, you little slut," he said. "Kyle, feel her. She's fucking wet just thinking about taking two cocks. Aren't you, Nell?"

The correct answer was, of course, "yes, Jeremy." Kyle also fondled me intimately, wiping the wetness from my slit onto my leg.

"Let's not keep her waiting," Kyle said. He and Jeremy began to undress as I lay there feeling like a sex doll. When Jeremy began to suck my clit, my whole body loosened and started tingling. He nibbled my outer labia and then licked hard all the way up my slit. I arched to him as the ache of arousal ratcheted up. He slid his fingers inside me and started to move them in and out, up and down. When he started to nip at my clit, I cried out and reached down to pull him closer. He made a noise, pulled his fingers out of me, and stopped.

"Bad girl." I gave a soft whine. He motioned to Kyle. "Nell's out of control. Again. Hold her down for me."

I squeezed my eyes shut, partly in shame, partly because when Kyle took my hands and restrained me, my pussy caught fire. Kyle leaned onto the table beside me to hold them over my head. I stared down at his cock and then into his eyes.

Indigo blue, I thought to myself. That's what those dark blue eyes are called. My gaze clouded over with passion as Jeremy buried his head between my thighs again. Kyle's eyes were intent, watching me. I felt hypersexual, hyperfeminine, held down by one gorgeous man as the other helped himself to what was between my legs. I gave myself up to the sharp pleasure Jeremy was visiting on me. My backbone bucked against the hard tabletop, and I sucked in my breath as he pushed my thighs even farther apart. Without realizing it, I began to moan. "Please, please, please, please…"

Jeremy stopped again. *No!* My clit was pulsing, but it downshifted into a low hum when his tongue disappeared. "Please," I whispered.

"Too much noise," Jeremy said. "Kyle, scoot her over. Let's drape her over this edge of the table. Then you can fuck her mouth while I eat her out." They both set about positioning me, then Kyle rolled on condom. I whimpered softly as Jeremy turned my head toward Kyle. "Open," he told me, then to Kyle, "Does that work?" Kyle leaned over the table and guided his cock into my waiting mouth. Yes. It worked. I turned my head a little farther and started to lick his engorged knob. He shoved it in, and my lips closed around it.

"God, that works," said Kyle to Jeremy.

He chuckled. "If you don't keep her mouth occupied, she starts begging like a sloppy little whore. She's just so fucking hungry for cock." My thighs clenched at his words. My nipples ached to be touched. I sucked Kyle, at the same time glorying in the delicious arousal growing in my crotch. The closer I got to coming, the sloppier I got with my mouth. "Mmmm, mmm." I moaned around Kyle's dick as he slid it in and out. I was a drooling slut, but I didn't care. My whole world was the thick cock filling my mouth and the agile tongue tormenting my clit. Jeremy brought me to the brink, then started pistoning his fingers in and out of my pussy. The pressure became unbearable. I drew away from Kyle and threw my head back. "Please, may I come? Please?" I begged.

"Greedy slut," he said against my throbbing clit. "Kyle first."

I turned to Kyle and drew his cock back into my mouth, cupping and stroking his balls. My hips bucked as I sucked him. I heard a chuckle. Kyle said, "I think she wants to come." I whined around his cock, and then both of them laughed. Jeremy licked my clit, then flicked at it, keeping me close, but not close enough to fall over the edge. Kyle sawed in and out of my mouth. In between sucking at him, I made inarticulate, muffled noises, some impatient, some plaintive. At last I felt his testicles tighten, heard his grunt and sigh. When he pulled away, Jeremy slapped the underside of my thigh.

"Okay, girl. Come for us. Show us how much you like to be worked over like a whore." My whole pelvis felt like a rock, stone heavy. Every nerve in my body seemed to be centered there. Every vein and vessel seemed to flow only one direction, and that direction was my pussy. His hot tongue flicked me, licked me. I looked up at Kyle, nearly mad. He was staring down at my tits. Firm tongue on my clit, thick fingers slipping deep inside, and then…then Kyle reached out with both hands and took my nipples in a hard pinch. I cried out. He twisted them, pinched harder, and blood and lust shot out from my clenching center to diffuse my entire world. My cry went on and on, and my body quaked on the hard tabletop. I was racked by spasms of pleasure and pain. Kyle kept twisting until I came to rest. My body untensed and fell open, and Jeremy lifted his head from my crotch.

"Oh, thank you," I said when I could think again.

Jeremy chuckled. "No. Thank you. That was a lovely display. Good girl, you made me hard. Here. Get down."

He pointed to the floor, and I rolled off the table. He put me on my knees with my forehead pressed to the carpet. I heard Kyle return from taking off his condom. Meanwhile Jeremy was rummaging for a spanking implement, an activity I recognized now purely by sound. The drawer opening, the paddles and whips knocking around as he looked through his collection. I was like Pavlov's dog. My previously satisfied pussy began to ache and throb anew at what was coming. What would he choose to hurt me with? How bad would it be?

"I know you're not into spanking, Kyle," I heard him say, "but her ass doesn't look right to me unless it's nice and red. So before we proceed to the main event…"

"Knock yourself out," said Kyle.

The main event. My mind turned the words over, then I looked back to see what he was holding and thought, *Oh shit. Not that.* It was a paddle he favored, made out of thick, rigid leather. It was almost exactly like the one Kyle had misused on me at Eden. Jeremy wielded it with more control, but I think he actually hurt me more. I tried a pleading expression, although I knew it wouldn't work. He made an impatient sound. "Where is your face supposed to be?"

With a sigh, I turned back to the floor.

"Fifteen, Nell. Count for me."

Fifteen. I could take fifteen. *Ouch!*

"One!" Again the paddle struck. "Two!" "Three!" The sting was so excruciating. I ground my teeth and tried to process the pain. By five, my hands were in fists, and by the seventh blow, I started pounding the floor and kicking my feet. "Kyle, hold her." Again I felt Kyle's hands take possession of mine. He pulled them over my head and pressed them to the floor there. I smelled his male scent, faint latex, and sweat. Jeremy continued, each blow getting harder. "Eight!" "Nine!" "Ten!" My ass was flaming, red-hot. The merciless, sharp blows had tears flooding my eyes, and I pulled at Kyle's hands. He didn't let go. At "thirteen," I broke down and started bawling like a baby. Fourteen and fifteen were each harder than the last.

Then Kyle let go, and Jeremy let me rest for a moment. I was a ball of tension from the paddling. Finally my fists unclenched, and I eased my tummy to the floor. I lay still and drifted, feeling the tingle of my punished skin. After a few moments of rest, Jeremy came to me.

"Okay. Up." He lifted me and led me to the couch where Kyle waited. They seemed to understand without words what was coming next, although my mind balked at what that might be. The very perverse and scary possibility of what two men might do to a woman together—a possibility that turned out, in fact, to be exactly what happened.

Kyle was already erect and sheathed, sitting with his thighs slightly spread.

"Get on him," Jeremy said, nudging me. "You're going to take us both, so prepare yourself. That's what's happening here."

Prepare yourself. I'd always imagined double penetration was one of those porn-only fantasies that couldn't actually be accomplished by nonporn actors. I tensed up a little, but his warm, firm hands propelled me forward. "Go on."

Kyle lifted me into his lap and slid me onto his cock slowly. I was shaking, aroused but terrified.

"Kiss him," Jeremy said. "Put your arms around his neck and kiss him like you mean it."

As my master commands. Kissing Kyle felt slightly incestuous, like being forced to kiss your younger brother whom you hated.

"Harder," he snapped. "Use your fucking tongue."

I jammed my tongue in Kyle's mouth, and he kissed me back roughly, both of us doing it for Jeremy and Jeremy alone. I fucked him at the same time, taking his cock deep and then shallowly and then deep again.

"Beautiful." Jeremy ran his hand across my back and down to part my ass. I tensed again. Kyle's cock alone felt like fullness. Another cock in the mix—in my *ass*—seemed impossible.

"You need to relax. I promise you, this is going to happen. You need to accept that."

I shuddered as he thrust some lube into my ass. He knelt behind me and inserted a couple of fingers, stretching me out. I clung to Kyle, who held me and whispered, "You'll be okay. We know how to do this."

We know how to do this. Their strange closeness explained.

At some unseen signal between them, Kyle withdrew from me almost all the way, and Jeremy knelt behind me. I trembled, afraid of the unknown. What if I couldn't do it? What if they broke me or something? My mind raced through the urban legends. Then Jeremy reached around to pull and pinch at my nipples, and thought left me. I gushed wetness all over Kyle's cock.

"The reason I get your ass and Kyle gets your cunt," he said as he pressed his cock against me, "is because you're mine, and I'll take care of you. I know exactly how to use your ass. This isn't going to hurt. It's going to feel good. Do you understand?"

"Yes, Jeremy." I was scared as shit and turned on as hell, sandwiched between two hard bodies, their hands all over me, soothing, stroking, arranging, pinching. With a soft curse, Jeremy added more lube and pushed against my asshole again.

"Open up. Do it."

I was still fairly new to taking his cock in my ass, but I did my best, driven on by Kyle's hot breath against my ear and Jeremy's fingers torturing my nipples. I took a deep breath, and he pushed the head of his cock in, holding my hips still until he'd slid all the way to the hilt. I moaned softly, but it didn't hurt, not after the initial discomfort. He sighed as he felt me relax, then he withdrew slowly and surged forward again.

"God, yes. Good girl. God, I'm deep inside you. Now we're going to fill both your hungry holes with cock."

I moaned. My pussy clenched as he blew breath down the back of my neck. Kyle took my waist and eased himself back into me. As he did, Jeremy slowly pulled out. For a moment they stayed still. Then again, Jeremy advanced, dirty, thick stabbing in my ass, as Kyle withdrew. Then Kyle's long cock again, slipping, sliding upward while I felt my asshole again empty out. In perfect tandem, they fucked me, pressed against me, back and forth, back and forth. There was no pain, only a strange, horrible pleasure. I was just a body with holes that existed to be filled, again and again, by hard, insistent male flesh. And my skin tingled, my flesh sung with gratitude to feel this savage completeness. I was so full, so expertly manipulated between them. Their feral grunts and groans sounded in stereo in my ears.

When I was dangerously aroused by the overload of sensation, Jeremy reached around me to finger my clit. I gasped and bucked between them. I was about to lose control.

"Please, please."

"Please what?"

Please what? What did I want? To be released? To never be released, to enjoy this torture for the rest of my life?

"Please may I come?" I moaned.

"It feels good, doesn't it?" he said against my ear. "You like being violated like this, filled by two huge cocks?"

"Yes, God...yes...please—Let me—"

"You want to come, you little slut?" He was still pumping away in perfect rhythm with Kyle's delicious thrusts.

"Yes, please let me come!"

"Beg me."

I tried to piece words together. My mind was gone, but Jeremy commanded attention. "Please let me come. Having two cocks is driving me crazy. Please, please!"

"Try again. You can do better than that."

"Please let me come! Fuck me hard in both my holes and let me come and milk your huge fucking cocks."

"That's not bad," he said. "Say this. 'I need to come because I'm such a cum-happy little whore, and I love having both my holes stuffed with cock—'"

I repeated what he said, the words spilling over each other in desperation. Finally he said, "Go ahead."

I let go of the breath I'd been holding, and my body tensed. Jeremy held me still, so deep in my ass I could feel his pubic hair tickle against my cheeks. Then Kyle eased in...slowly—*oh God*—and they were both pressed inside me. I clamped down on both dicks, squeezed my thighs, and shuddered. The orgasm that ripped through me sent white brilliant light around the edges of my mind. I came hard, groaning, burying my head in Kyle's neck as if he could ground me in the world and not let me fly off. He groaned too, shuddered and shook under me. Jeremy rocked against my ass and came with a growl and a firm bite on the back of my neck.

I went still. I simply laid still and felt our connectedness. With the orgasm over, I became aware of the base intimacy we shared. I was still gasping against Kyle's chest, and Jeremy's arms were wrapped around me, half to hug me, and half to support himself, I think. We all lay sandwiched together, catching our breath. I finally lifted my gaze to Kyle's, but he was looking past me, staring at Jeremy with an unfathomable look.

At last Jeremy stirred and licked my neck where he'd bitten me.

"One big, happy family," he said.

We all laughed, and for a moment, I melted for Kyle. I melted for both of them pressed against me body to body. I laughed from the sensation of their deep, masculine laughter vibrating in my bones.

Then I remembered Kyle trying to soothe me with the words, *We know how to do this...*

I thought of Jeremy's last girlfriend, that confident, beautiful, model-like woman. She must have been sandwiched between them as I was, not once, but many times for them to become so proficient. Had they done this only with her, or the girl before too? Or the girl before that?

How many times would they do this with me?

And did I want them to do it again...and again...use me this way?

Yes.

I really was turning into a whore. But I was no more a whore than Kyle, because both of us performed for Jeremy at his whim.

Jeremy invited Kyle to join us not so much as a sexual partner for me, but a conduit to live out his own sexual kinks. And he didn't only watch, Jeremy would direct Kyle. *Harder, faster. Doggy-style. Pull her hair. Fuck her ass.* And Kyle would comply beautifully. If Jeremy told Kyle to make me come, he would.

* * * * *

I stretched in bed. Yes, I loved the mornings. My muscles felt slightly strained but relaxed. I could barely remember what day of the week it was, usually. But I knew it had been nearly four weeks of degenerate pleasure now, and we'd be leaving Bangkok soon for a new hotel in Istanbul.

And it had certainly not been all unending pleasure either. There had been plenty of pain, as well as the inconvenience of being more or less trapped within the confines of the hotel and having to ask Kyle for everything I needed.

But Kyle had to give me what I asked for, no matter how much it annoyed him, which created a strange dynamic between us, above and beyond the detached, objectified sex we regularly shared.

Basically Kyle did everything in his power to make me miserable, but all I had to do was go running to Jeremy to get Kyle in trouble in return. We were like siblings locked in an eternal battle, snipping and sniping, and Jeremy was Dad, yelling at us from across the room to cut it out. When he was around we played nice, but when he was away, we were at war, as much at war as people on the same side could be.

Above and beyond the weekly double-penetration extravaganzas and the many instances Kyle was told to fuck me, I got ordered to suck Kyle off now and again because Jeremy liked to watch me sucking a man's cock. God, the smirks I got then. I wanted to smack them right off Kyle's face.

But oddly enough, there were no extra women brought into our little fold. I guess Kyle was okay to play with us because Jeremy trusted him not to talk. However, if he hired a pro or talked a woman into joining us, she might sell the story to the tabloids. I guess his only choice would have been to hire another full-time girl, and I don't think I could have dealt with that. I think I would have been insanely jealous. Silly, since Jeremy was only my boss.

I guess at some point, Jeremy had to stop hiring full-time employees for the sole purpose of getting his rocks off.

While Kyle joined us several times a week, there were many more times Jeremy and I were alone. We fell into a routine that was comfortable and predictable, if somewhat depraved. Sex every morning. Sex in his trailer on the set, if I was there and we could manage it. Sex either before or after dinner, and sex every night. Basically, sex anytime Jeremy wasn't in public or on camera. No wonder he had to hire a girl. No true girlfriend would have put up with it. I was awash in Jeremy Gray's cum from dawn to dusk.

At least it seemed that way sometimes. In truth, there were some days he worked so long and hard that he fell into bed without even talking to me. Other days, if he didn't have much to do, he'd plan an excursion for us somewhere around the city, to a museum or restaurant or park. He did those things for me, because he wanted me to have adventures while I was with him, and not always have my nose "buried in a book," as he said.

But I did bury my nose in books when I could, when Jeremy wasn't using me. Bangkok still frightened me. I had no desire to go out into the crowds, the hullabaloo. I got good at the sex through sheer practice. I could give him a blowjob like a high priestess of fellatio. I could eventually take him anally without any lube but what was on the condom. I could take him and Kyle together with practiced, controlled grace. But I couldn't get used to acting like his girlfriend in front of the cameras, and the flashes constantly going off in our faces. The screams, the fans, the paparazzi. When we ventured out, there was always at least one person who'd jump out at us brandishing a camera or something for Jeremy to sign. My pulse raced and my hands shook even when Jeremy held me close. He never let go of me when we were out in public, but I still woke up in a cold sweat a couple of times a week dreaming about crowds of trampling fans.

Jeremy took it all in stride, though. At least he seemed to. I have no idea how he did it, how he had the energy to work and explore life and be adventurous and brave the crowds of fans and then come home and fuck with the intensity he did. At first I thought it must be drugs. I went nosing around in his room, in his cabinet in the bathroom, in his personal things looking for pills, but there were none. However he managed, I thought, he was good at it. He was good at everything. He could deal with anything. And I finally realized that sex was his drug. Sex was the thing that kept him ticking. Sex was his heroin, and I was the dealer. We were constantly getting "high."

He would come back to the hotel at the end of the day in a ball of stress and exhaustion, and I'd be ready, without fail, to kneel at his feet and take it all away. He'd sit on the couch heavily, gesturing to me, unfastening his pants, and I'd kneel between his legs like a courtesan, in one of the five-hundred-dollar corsets he'd bought me.

He'd usually tell me to suck him, but every so often he'd lift me onto his lap and fuck me deep and slow. If he had a really bad day, we'd go straight to the bedroom and play hard: cuffs, spreaders, clamps, toys, whips, belts. Whatever he needed, I let him take it from me.

And this worked for us very well, at least most times.

The day before we left Bangkok, though, he came into the room in a mood. I tensed slightly, as I always did when he was strung really tight. Not that he ever abused me or made me use a safe word or broke his contractual promises. I just knew things would get intense when he was keyed up the way he was.

He didn't say anything, which wasn't unusual, just sat down and snapped at the floor between his legs. When I finished, I expected to be ordered over his lap for a spanking, or told to go in the bedroom to fetch some terrible toy. But he just sat still.

"Lay your head in my lap," he whispered. "Right here." He made me lay my face against his thigh, and he stroked my hair for half an hour without uttering a word.

Sometimes he got in a mood. Sometimes he got quiet and let the strain show, and this was one of those times. And I loved him at times like these, as much as I let myself love him. I loved that he showed me the weakness and tension that lurked underneath, the self-doubt and exhaustion he hid from everyone, perfect movie star that he was. As he sat and played with my hair for half an hour, I ached with love for him. I began to cry after a while, thinking about saying good-bye to him one day. We were so close, so excruciatingly intimate with one another, and yet so divided that he signed over a paycheck to me every week.

"What?" he asked when he felt my tears falling on his thigh. "What is it?"

"Nothing," I said. Then, "I like to be with you."

It immediately felt like too much to say. He was quiet for a while, then he said, "Tell me your name. Your real name."

It was an awful thing to ask at that moment, when I was desperately trying to keep my heart from falling even harder for him.

"I can't."

"Helen?"

"No."

"Ornelle?"

"Oh, Jeremy. Please call me Nell."

"I want to know! I looked at your passport. It didn't help."

My passport said Nell, like everything else.

"At least I know now that your birthday's next week. What do you want?"

"What do I want?"

"For your birthday. What do you want?"

You. To be able to love you. To stay with you forever like this, even as your concubine, as your whore.

No matter how much I wanted it, I couldn't have it. This life wasn't for me, as much as I was falling head over heels for this man.

"Just tell me what you want. I'll get you anything."

I sighed. "I don't want anything. I hate my birthdays."

He sat still another moment, caressing my nape, then suddenly pushed me out of his lap. "You don't ask for enough, you know that? You'll never get anything out of life."

I stayed on my knees, my hands clasped in my lap, while he glared down at me.

"I would have given you whatever you asked for. You're never going to go anywhere. You're never going to get what you want if you don't learn how to ask."

"Maybe I don't want to go anywhere. Maybe I don't want anything," I said quietly to the floor.

"Come in the bedroom," he said, pulling me by my arm.

He used me hard that night. He was cold and deviant. He gagged me, which I hated, restrained me, and beat me hard. He fucked my ass and my ass only, whispering depraved threats and epithets in my ear. "You're just my whore anyway, aren't you?" he whispered. "I really don't care if I know your real name."

The next morning on the plane, he still seemed angry. I kept silent and shifted in first class beside him the whole way to Istanbul, feeling sore and beaten.

I was his whore, that was for sure, but at least my name was still completely my own.

Chapter Thirteen: Talk

The flight to Turkey was shorter, and arriving in Istanbul was much less insane, the crowds smaller and more manageable. The hotel room was less high up, the food much less tasty. We would be here barely two weeks before making the short journey to Bulgaria, so I wasn't even inclined to unpack. I did, though, in my stilettos and ass plug, while Jeremy looked on.

You're staying right here. Put it all away.

A couple days after we arrived, Martin paid Jeremy a visit. I assumed immediately it had something to do with me and with sex, and wondered if Martin knew how to double penetrate women like Kyle did. But instead I was ordered to my room to "bury my nose in a book" while they talked, and they talked late into the night.

I didn't pay attention to what Jeremy and Martin talked about until they started to argue in loud, sharp voices, which were quickly muffled by another voice, which sounded like Kyle's. So Kyle was there too, and I was banished to my room. They were having some kind of powwow, and I was completely certain it was about me. I crept over and put my ear to the door, but I couldn't make anything out, just legal mumbo-jumbo terms and Jeremy hissing that he wanted it to *stop*.

My body froze. *He was getting rid of me.* My blood buzzed in my ears.

It seemed impossible, but what else could it be? If Martin was here, it had to be about my contract, how to get out of it. I thought of what I might have done to upset him. We didn't always get along perfectly. I wasn't always a perfect sub, but still, he'd given me no indication that he was totally unhappy with me either. Not until now. *I want it to stop.*

I finally couldn't stand the anxiety. I had to know. I opened the door to go to the kitchenette under the guise of getting a drink. I glanced over at them as casually as I could.

They fell silent as the grave, staring at me balefully, all three hunched over Martin's laptop.

"I told you to stay in your room," Jeremy said.

"I was going to get some water."

"Well, get it," he snapped.

I grabbed a bottle of water from the fridge and opened it, standing right where I was.

"Is everything okay?" I asked. I meant to sound offhand, but my voice sounded small and scared.

"Everything's fine," Jeremy said, although his face looked just the opposite.

Martin pasted on a fake smile. "How have you been, Nell?" he asked. "You look great. The job suits you well."

"Yes, it does." I looked at Jeremy again, searched for clues to what they were talking about. As usual, he was impossible to read. All I could really divine was his frown.

"Go, go on. I'll come in later," he said, nodding toward my room.

I went inside and shut the door, my heart hammering. What had I done? Kyle wouldn't even look at me, and Martin's smile had been totally forced. He was looking for a new girl. That had to be it. Going over contracts, figuring out how to trap her as he'd trapped me. I climbed into bed, fighting the urge to start bawling. I wasn't going to cry over him. I had given him everything I could. If I wasn't enough for him, there was nothing more I could do.

But sleep didn't come. My mind turned over and over, analyzing my many shortcomings. I wasn't very good at taking pain, for starters. Wasn't that something doms always wanted in their subs? The ability to take pain without sobbing like an infant? I also had a way of getting carried away when he was fucking me, doing stuff that a good sub probably shouldn't do, like scratching and biting. And I was always begging in a totally undisciplined way to be allowed to come.

Maybe I read too much. Maybe I was too brainy. Maybe I was too shy. Too reticent in front of the cameras. Maybe he sensed that I was falling in love with him despite my best efforts to the contrary. Maybe he was tired of me fighting with Kyle.

I waited, curled up under the covers, until the voices quieted and I heard Martin and Kyle go away. Still, he didn't come. I got out of bed and opened the door.

Jeremy was sitting on the couch, silent, staring into space.

"I'm sorry," I whispered. "If I did something—"

"You didn't do anything." He sighed. "It's just… Listen, it's none of your business. None of your concern."

"Are you finding someone else?" I had to ask it, although I didn't want to know the answer. I had to know. "Another girl?"

He snorted. "Another girl? Why would you think that? Because Martin was here? He's my lawyer. We talk about a lot of things besides you."

I hugged myself, embarrassed at letting my insecurity show. I expected more teasing from the bemused look on his face, but instead he held out his hand. "Come here."

I crossed the room. He pulled me into his lap, and I melted against his solid warmth. I burrowed my head into his neck and breathed in the soothing, familiar scent of his aftershave.

"I'm sorry," I said. "Sometimes I can't get used to all this. And I'm afraid you're not happy with me."

"Why would you think that?"

His fingers stroked up my back to rub my nape. I felt all the feelings I'd kept hidden inside struggle to the surface. "I don't know. I guess, just, sometimes…the stuff you do to me—"

"What stuff?"

"Like sending me off to my room. Not talking to me. Sharing me with Kyle."

"Listen, the sharing stuff, you know, don't read too much into it. I share you because I like to. Because it gets me off. That's it."

"I know."

"And you know as well as I do that kinks are kinks. You can't help what gets you going."

"I guess."

The fingers continued kneading, calming me. I felt his chest lift and drop in a sigh. "I hope you remember that you're not to get overemotional about this job. The whole reason I pay you is so I don't have to put up with this kind of shit."

"Thank you for calling my feelings 'shit,'" I said, pulling away.

"You know what I mean. Babysitting your feelings isn't what I pay you for."

I made an indignant sound that was silenced when he pulled me back against him. The magic fingers began again on my nape. I shivered and cuddled closer. I could feel my body unwind. A moment later his fingers left my neck and his arms wrapped around me tight.

"Listen," he said against my ear. "Let's keep things simple. Let's just remember I pay you to do as I ask. You obey. If you have a need, a pressing, human need, you let me know. But if you start to obsess over stupid shit and get emotional like you're my girlfriend, then I'm going to let you go. I can't deal with it. Do you understand?"

"Yes," I said, and truly, I understood every word he spoke. What I didn't understand was the *why* behind it.

"I mean, I thought things were going pretty well," he said. "I thought you were happy."

"You pay me to be happy, don't you? So I am." I felt him go tense under me. I wished I could have taken the words back. I sat up and looked in his eyes.

"Are you happy, Jeremy?"

He glanced away, then back at me. "Tonight? I'm a little stressed."

"Why are you stressed?" I took his hand in mine, stroking the soft tufts of hair on the back of it with my fingertips.

He shook his head. "I told you. It's not your concern." He took a deep breath and held my hand tighter. "Relax me. Tell me a story. Not a story from Eden. One of the stories from those books you always have your nose buried in."

I laughed. "You must really want me to stop whining, to subject yourself to that."

"There must be something to them, if you like them so much. Tell me a story. Explain humanity to me."

I thought for a moment, mentally sorting through the hundreds of tales I loved and remembered.

"Do you know the story of Rhiannon?"

He rolled his eyes. "What do you think?"

I smiled and lay back on his shoulder. "Rhiannon was a Celtic goddess. She didn't want to wed the god her parents picked out for her, so instead she married a mortal. A king."

Jeremy snorted. "She still made out pretty good, then, I guess, for marrying a mortal."

"Yeah. She had a happy marriage. She and the king had a son and lived for a year in harmony and love. But then the son went missing. The nurses who'd been charged with caring for the son laid the blame for his disappearance on Rhiannon. To back up their claim, the nurses slaughtered a young animal and spread its carcass and bones around and made it look as if Rhiannon murdered and ate her own son."

"That's disgusting."

"What's disgusting is that everyone believed it. Because Rhiannon was different, a goddess and not a mortal. They all turned on her and believed the nurses. The king turned his back on his wife and left her trial and punishment to the people. They decreed that she must wear a horse collar and live outside the grounds as a slave, carrying guests back and forth from the gates to the castle."

"Kinky," said Jeremy.

"You're a perv. Anyway, Rhiannon didn't fight back or mourn the unfairness of her punishment. She accepted it with the grace of a true queen."

"Or submissive."

"Listen, this isn't about BDSM, if you can pull your mind out of the gutter for a few more minutes."

Jeremy smiled. "Okay, I'll try, but it won't be easy with you in my lap."

I sighed as he pulled me closer. I could feel his hard-on rising against my hip. "Through scorching summers and bitterly cold winters, she wore the collar, swearing to anyone who would listen that one day her love and dedication would bring her son home. The same people who condemned her eventually were moved by Rhiannon's courage and dignity, and word of her plight began to spread beyond the castle grounds to the outlying lands.

"One day a nobleman came to the gate holding the hand of a small boy. Rhiannon graciously offered to carry them to the keep. Instead the nobleman placed the boy's hand in hers and said, 'Brave Queen, your son is home.' It turned out the careless nurses had left the son in a field, and the nobleman found him, considered him abandoned, and raised him as his own. The tales of Rhiannon's predicament made him realize whom the boy belonged to. Everyone rejoiced, and Rhiannon was freed from her slavery at last."

"Are you jealous?" Jeremy asked as I paused. "You'd like to be freed too, wouldn't you?"

"Oh, Jeremy. This story's not about me. The point of Rhiannon's myth is that when she returned to the castle, to her husband and everyone who'd wrongly condemned her, she forgave them all. Forgave every one of them and told her husband she still loved him. She endured the terrible hardships of life with courage and dignity. She's the goddess of being strong."

"Is she? Is that why you like her so much?"

"I don't like her," I said. "I actually never would have put up with the crap she did."

"I could get you a collar, if you like."

"That was your favorite part of the story, wasn't it?" I sighed. "The only part you actually heard."

"Yes. Rhiannon, goddess of pony play and enslavement. What other BDSM myths do you know?"

I rolled my eyes, but I couldn't help laughing. He grinned back, then stood and threw me over his shoulder. I shrieked and clung to him as he carried me into his room and tossed me on the bed. His libido, his perversity, God, it was ridiculous, but at least I knew I wasn't going anywhere.

* * * * *

Our time in Turkey flew by. I would have liked to stay longer. Turkey was a land steeped in cultural history and mythology. I told Jeremy stories from Turkish and Ottoman mythology every night, Anatolian myths, Nart sagas, all the local mythology I studied and loved.

In return he threw me a huge surprise toga party for my birthday. While he may have missed the bull's-eye, he hit the target just fine. The endearingly fake Greek decor, the "David" waiters, the entire cast and crew of his movie getting wasted in bedsheets. I took it for what it was: a magnanimous gesture of affection and fun. He beamed at me from across the room, looking like a true Greek god in his toga, and more David-like than any of the half-dressed waiters roaming around.

"Having fun?" Jessamine Jackson's deep, sultry voice sounded right beside my ear.

I turned to her with a smile. I'd talked to her on several occasions by now, running into her on the set and so forth, but she was still larger-than-life to me, even in a toga and nothing else. *Especially* in a toga and nothing else.

"Look at Jeremy." She snorted, waving at him across the restaurant. "He's so proud of himself."

Jeremy leaned on a balustrade, watching both of us with a meditative smile.

"He wanted to find a party theme where everyone could wear the least amount of clothing possible," I laughed.

"That's our Jeremy."

Our Jeremy? It didn't surprise me to hear her say that, but it made me jealous. Maybe she only meant it in a friendly sense, but knowing Jeremy as I did…

I looked over at Jessamine again, this time as a rival.

It was hopeless. She was so much more beautiful than me, elegant, confident, strong, graceful. If Jeremy looked at us side by side, it didn't take much intelligence to figure out where I would end up in that comparison. But Jessamine was married. Her husband, Mason Cooke, was a bigger star than Jeremy, and every bit as sexy and hot. She wasn't competition, but I suddenly disliked her all the same.

"I hope you're having a happy birthday," she said, leaning closer with a smile.

"Yes, I am."

"And how are you enjoying the movie-star life?"

"It's…interesting."

Jessamine laughed, a beautiful, feminine sound. "You can tell me the truth, Nell. I'm in on the game."

The game? What game was she talking about? I slid a look at Jeremy.

"Honey, it's okay. I *know*," she said. "But I'll never tell. Jeremy and I go way back."

"Do you?"

"Yes, we do. I can tell you whatever you want to know about him too."

"Really?" My eyes opened wide, considering the possibilities. Jess laughed.

"I know, where to begin with the questions? He's complicated, yes, but there's something you should know. He has a heart of gold, deep down under all that black perversion. He really does. He'll take care of you."

He'll take care of you. When he lets you go and gets another girl. When he pays you off and moves on with his life.

"I have to say," she said, leaning in, "I like you much more than his last girl. I met her a few times. She was awful. He's so lucky to have found you."

"I… Yeah…we have good times together."

"And having you along on these long shoots, it's great for him. You know, I'll be damned if you haven't changed him. He's happier than I've known him to be in a long time."

I wanted to seize on her words and save them forever. Happier? Changed? I didn't know how he was before.

"Do you think he likes me?" I blurted out before I could stop myself. I was immediately embarrassed. "I mean...not like...you know—"

"Does he *like* you?" Jessamine turned my head to where he still watched us with a drunk, happy smile. "He hasn't taken his eyes off you the whole evening. And this thing with your stalker... He's beside himself. I'm sure he doesn't show you how much he worries over it."

"What? What stalker?" I looked back at her in alarm.

Jeremy started toward us. Jessamine looked over at him.

"I...um...not stalker. Just something Jeremy and I were joking about. You know, those photogs in Thailand. Ha, that picture—your face. Jeremy!" Jessamine exclaimed as he joined us. "Little Nell here is so adorable in her toga!"

Jeremy smiled down at me. "Yeah. She's going to wear it later while we have some Greek sex."

I blushed. I don't know why. If Jessamine knew Jeremy as well as she seemed to, his decidedly perverse tastes would be no surprise to her. She winked at him.

"Bless her heart, then, Jeremy. You know Greek's never been my thing."

Jeremy laughed, then dragged me over to the cake before I could ask him about her stalker comment. After a drunken, rousing round of "Happy Birthday" from my party guests, I blew out the twenty-nine candles on my cake. Jeremy cut me a big piece and eyeballed me as I ate it. His pale blue eyes traveled up and down my curves, barely concealed by the toga I wore.

"I want to smear that icing all over your fucking body and lick it off."

"Because I'm so sweet, yes?"

He chuckled. "Very sweet. You melt when it rains, sugar."

"Mmm," I said, tracing his golden forearm with one soft fingertip. "I'm actually feeling a little wet right now. A little meltish."

I loved his face when I made him horny. Intent eyes, tense lips. He leaned close to me. "I think you have a birthday spanking coming. Twenty-nine licks, isn't it?"

"Twenty-nine licks?" I pulled a small pout. "I don't know. That sounds so...sadistic." I looked right into his eyes. "If they were hard ones, I might not even be able to sit down afterward."

He drew in a breath. His chin jutted out as his jaw tensed. I wanted to lick it, bite it between my teeth.

"Teasing is a very, very naughty habit. Little girls who tease sometimes live with regret."

I barely held him off until we got to the hotel room. If our surly taxi driver looked in the rearview mirror, he probably got a glimpse of ass cheek and groped boobs. Jeremy lifted me in his arms in the elevator. He pulled my legs up to encircle his waist and dug his hand into my slit.

"Jeremy, someone's going to see us!" I was sopping wet, and his fingers were already making me throb. "Jeremy, stop!"

"*Jeremy, stop* is a contractually forbidden phrase."

"I'm serious, if someone gets on this elevator—"

My voice cut off as he closed his mouth over my lips. He kissed me, then sucked on my tongue. He set fire to my pussy with his fingers until I completely forgot where we were. If anyone did get on the elevator, I was too far gone to know it. When the hotel room door closed behind us, I began to grind against his hips. His erection stuck obscenely out of his toga. He'd decreed earlier that I could not wear panties, and apparently he'd decided to forgo underwear too.

I was wild for him. I craved his cock. I wanted to taste it, wanted to feel it in my mouth. I wanted to feel it slide deep in my throat. I knelt, took it in my hands.

"Well," he said. "Forward little slut, aren't you? Birthday or not, you don't get to help yourself to whatever you want. Do you, girl?"

My gaze flew to his. How had I gotten so carried away?

"I'm sorry, Jeremy."

"I'm happy to hear you're sorry, but does sorry take punishments away?"

"No, Jeremy."

"No, it doesn't, does it?"

I shuddered at his feet, but when I looked up from under my lashes, I saw a glimmer of humor in his eyes. He wasn't really angry. But would he capitalize on my fuckup? I had no doubt. His face took on an imperious expression, and he looked down his nose at me.

"Naughty little slave girl. Abase yourself. On the floor. Show your master how sorry you are."

I drew in my breath. *Ohhhh.* Best birthday present ever. He knew it was my biggest fantasy. I'd told him during one of our long talks. My pussy flooded, and my heart burst with gratitude. I peered up at him, and he stared back at me in full slavemaster mode. Playing scenes with actors was a complete rush. He never broke character. I tried to hold up my end, sinking to the floor with a forlorn look. I knelt and then bent forward, legs spread, ass out. I made no motion to draw the toga back over the parts of my body that were exposed.

He stood a long time and looked before he fetched the cuffs and knelt to secure my hands behind my back. Then he stood in my line of sight and kicked off his sandals. A pause. He moved his foot forward in a gesture I could hardly fail to understand. I swallowed and leaned forward on my knees. I kissed his foot, ran my tongue across the top and down to his toes. After a moment, he drew it back. Held it out again, just beyond my reach. I had to shuffle on my knees to reach it. I was being toyed with, and it made me white-hot. My tongue came out. I kissed the proffered foot again. I started lapping. I felt his shudder all the way down to his toes. His arousal fell down over me in waves of electric energy, or perhaps it was my own arousal I felt. The other foot came forward, thrust in front of my face. I worshipped it, licked it. I ran my tongue over the arch, around the ball of his foot. I poked it between his toes. With a soft breath, he pulled his foot away from me. I bowed my head back to the carpet. He walked away.

My pussy was so hot. I felt empty without his cock inside, especially when I felt like this. The musk of my own arousal permeated the air. A primal moan rose up inside me and I swallowed it down, not wanting to make so much as a sound without permission.

Jeremy returned. I heard his feet on the carpet beside me. He knelt next to me and unwrapped my loose toga. I quivered wherever his warm hands brushed against me. When I was nude, he ran his hand across my back and up to my shoulders. Then he ran it down the other way, slid it between my ass cheeks and down to my pussy. He thrust two fingers inside, and I grasped at them, keeping my hips perfectly still. Perfectly arched. *I'm your slave. These touches for your pleasure, not mine.* He took his fingers away, and I squeezed my eyes shut from the ache he left behind. Then he put a hand on my neck. I felt something rough against my skin. I smelled the tang of leather. I couldn't contain my gasp as he drew up the circle and buckled it around my neck.

A collar. Emotion welled up inside me. *For you, Nell.* He didn't say it, but I heard it plain as day.

"Come." He pulled me up by a large ring on the front. "Bad slaves get punished." He brought out something else. A leash. *God, help me.* Could my pussy get any wetter? He clicked it onto the ring he held, then wrapped the long strap around his fist. He pulled me toward him so sharply that I stumbled. I stared into hard blue eyes. "Twenty-nine licks for a very bad slave girl."

He picked up a whippy crop from the bed. He wrapped the leash tighter around his fist, so I was held close and fast by the strength of his arm. He brought the crop down with a *whap* on my left buttock.

"Ah!" I yelped.

Another crack came, and another. Stinging pain bloomed across my shifting hindquarters. He flicked first one cheek and then the other, so I danced at the end of my tether. I sought his muscular body, tried to press against him for shelter, but he only yanked me back into position and continued his assault on my ass. I was overcome with an almost painful lust, straining there on the end of his leash. My neck was chafed and scratched by the stiff leather, but it felt like heaven.

"Oh! Oh!" I cried. My body lurched. I shifted from one foot to the other. My ass sizzled as the crop fell again and again. The short, hard cracks seemed to fall on every inch of my thighs and ass. I grew quite certain he'd long since passed twenty-nine. "Please, please, Master!" I finally burst out.

His arm went still. My cuffed hands struggled to soothe my blazing ass cheeks. Again he yanked me to attention. His hot breath rasped against my ear.

"What? Don't you enjoy being whipped, slave?"

"No, Master!"

"That's a shame for you, isn't it? Because I love to whip you." He laid the crop across both cheeks with a fiery stroke.

I wailed, an incoherent, desperate sound. It spoke more of my horniness than my aversion to the crop.

"Hush," he said, shaking me by my collar. I fell silent. I felt his tongue trace up my ear. I shuddered and whimpered.

"Well, girl," he said. "There is something I enjoy every bit as much as whipping your ass." His hands grasped my flesh and squeezed it. I struggled, tensing my buttocks and dancing away from him. He ignored my protests, drawing me in again and tracing across my welts with his fingernails. Then he gathered some of my pussy juice on his digits and pressed two thick fingers into my ass. I felt stretched open, defiled. My tight hole ached from the invasion. I pulled against the cuffs and threw my head back.

"No, no! Oh no, please…"

"Slave girls don't say no."

I groaned as his fingers pressed deeper. He withdrew them and pushed me down, letting out the leash. He tore off his toga and stood before me in all his glory, a Greek god. He gave me a moment to look before he shoved me to my knees. "Suck me. Use lots of spit, girl. It's the only lube you're going to get when I ram it into your ass."

I opened my mouth to accept him. I sucked him and caressed him with my tongue. I worshipped. I lapped at the bulging head of his cock and then took him deep in my throat. I salivated on his huge tool so it could more easily rend my asshole. I could have worshipped him that way for hours, in thanks for his party. For the leash and collar I wore. For fulfilling my fantasies. But a moment later, he jerked the leash and pulled me back from him. He stood me up and bent me over.

I gasped, struggling for breath. He held my hips in his hands and trapped the dangling end of the leash under his foot.

"Oh please! Have mercy." I didn't know if I was playing the slave girl anymore or if it was actually me crying out for release. He drew the copious moisture from my pussy and rubbed it up over my nether hole. He pressed the head of his cock against me and, with a grunt, popped the head inside.

The pain was terrible and wonderful. He stopped, let me adjust. I moved my hips back toward him. With a groan he drove forward, then back. He began to fuck me, quick, bucking strokes that made me totter on my feet. My arousal was already at a fever pitch, my pelvis ached with the weight of my excitement. I squeaked and moaned as his hands grasped at my hips. Soon I began to pant.

"Master, Master!"

He reached down for the leash, yanked me upward. He wrapped his arms around my waist from behind and squeezed me back against him. My hands were crushed against his abs. I could feel his trail tickling against my ass cheeks. I scratched at the hard muscle I discovered beneath my fingertips. He growled and wrapped a fist in my hair, and shook me hard. He put a finger through the ring in my collar and held me, while the other hand reached around to grasp a straining nipple and twist it. Frantic sounds rose up in my throat.

"Come for me. Come now, right now, slave girl."

A shock of release rolled over me. I convulsed as pleasure emanated out from where he was buried in my ass. It traveled to my tits, to the swollen clit at my center and even up to the collar chafing my neck. He held me with a hand splayed over my throat as I yowled and jerked against him. His cock convulsed in my ass.

"Master!" I turned and gasped into the hollow of his shoulder. I felt the collar press against my flesh, solid and real. I felt the leash dangling down between my outthrust breasts as my chest heaved up and down. The leash ended in his fist—inexorable control over me.

* * * * *

Later we lay exhausted and fucked-out in bed. I told Jeremy a few of the racier Greek myths I knew.

"That's the best mythology, isn't it?" he asked. "That's why I made your party Greek. Not just so I could make you a slave girl in a toga and fuck your ass."

I snorted. "Yeah. You can do that anytime."

"I think from now on I'll do it at least once a week." He had put the collar and leash away with all the other toys. I had a feeling I'd be seeing them again.

We laughed together. It felt so easy and comfortable with him sometimes. He could be so amazing, so creative.

"Jeremy, thank you. It was fun tonight. It was a wonderful birthday. One of the best ever, really."

"You deserve it. It was my pleasure to give it to you."

I looked into his eyes. I hated to ruin the atmosphere we'd created, but there was something I had to know. "Jessamine said something weird to me tonight."

His gaze shifted away. "Yeah, well, she's weird, so that doesn't surprise me."

"She said you were worried about a stalker."

He shrugged. "I have a lot of stalkers."

I thought about him, Martin, and Kyle hunched over the laptop, and the way he wouldn't let me go anywhere alone. "Do I have a stalker, Jeremy?"

"No," he said quickly, but the look on his face gave him away. I watched him, wanting to know more but afraid at the same time. "I mean, there's some weirdo…" He waved his hand. "Doing some weird stuff, but nothing you should worry about."

"What kind of weird stuff?"

"It's just a jealous fan, some woman. Doing stupid shit. Just… Nell…please."

"Why didn't you tell me? This is what you were fighting with Martin about last week. Isn't it?" It all made sense now, his anger, his frustration. The way he'd pulled away from me and punished me for asking too many questions. This was the source of the anxiety that I couldn't place.

He sighed. "Yes. Okay. There's a stalker. And I'm taking care of it."

"Taking care of what? What is she doing?"

"Oh, some web sites she has."

"Some web sites? Plural?" My eyes widened in alarm. There were stalkers, and then there were *stalkers*. "Am I in danger?"

"Calm down. If I thought you were in danger, I'd—"

"Never let me go out alone? Keep secrets from me?"

He brushed my hair back from my face and kissed my forehead. "Don't fret about it. I didn't want to worry you about something that was out of your control. And listen, that's just what happens when you're in the public eye. I wish Jess had kept her mouth shut. You're worried about something that's not worth worrying about, believe me."

"She said you were alarmed."

"Well, she's an actress. She lies and tells stories. She exaggerates." He couldn't look at me. I could tell from his body language that Jessamine didn't lie. "Anyway, I wanted to protect you from worrying about it. And…"

"And what?"

He was quiet a moment. "I didn't tell you because I didn't want you to leave me. I don't. I don't want you to leave."

He looked so lost, so terrified for a moment, it took my breath away. All this time I'd been the one afraid of being sent away. Silly. We belonged together. Didn't we? For now anyway. Stalker or no, I didn't want to live without him. I looked into his eyes. "I won't leave you."

His gaze left me. He looked over my shoulder and pursed his lips. "They always leave, and you will too." He looked back at me as if he dared me to disagree. "I mean, you should. This isn't a good life for anybody. But don't leave me yet." He pulled me close and twisted his fingers in my hair. "I don't want you to go yet."

Chapter Fourteen: Good Friends

Jesus, I was going to kill Jess next time I saw her.

For over a month I'd been hiding the secret from Nell, only to have Jessamine blab it out in the open at the girl's own birthday party.

Happy Birthday, Nell. Someone wants to kill you.

For fuck's sake, why couldn't she keep her mouth shut?

I looked down at Nell fast asleep in my arms. For now I thought I'd smoothed things over, but if she asked to see the web sites, if she wanted more information…

Jesus fucking Christ.

It had started innocuously enough, a web site with a fake blog that painted Nell in a decidedly unflattering light. Martin had it taken down fairly quickly, and in truth it had been almost funny with its petty, jealousy-fueled rants.

But another site was fast on its heels, this one not so innocuous as the last. Again we were successful in shutting it down, but another two or three popped up in its place. They were all hosted and maintained by the same person, a woman by the name of Leslie Gray, who was absolutely no relation, although to my horror, I'd recently discovered she believed she was my wife.

I'd done a lot of stupid things when I was drunk and horny, but getting married was something I'd definitely never done. The more Martin learned about Leslie Gray with the help of a private investigator, the less soundly I was able to sleep. The defamatory and vindictive web sites were one thing, but the correspondence we intercepted was another thing altogether. The scrawled notes were pages-long ravings about what happened to whoring home wreckers. The crazy woman outlined scenarios of how to knock Nell off with the most pain and least chance of being discovered. Was Leslie Gray a danger to Nell? She absolutely was.

But I also believed there was no safer place for Nell than with me, for now anyway. While Martin and the police wrangled with the restraining orders, cease-and-desist writs, and other legalities, Nell was relatively sheltered halfway around the world, living in high-security hotels and accompanying me to closed sets. I would have sent her away if it would have been safer for her, but my spotlight was the safest place for her to be.

And she trusted me for some reason. *I won't leave you.* I looked down and watched her breathe in and out, my pervy sex girl, so innocent and hapless in sleep. What on earth did I give her to make her trust me, to offer me the loyalty she did? I wanted to kiss her, lick her, wake her up and make love to her.

Make love to her? Fuck her, anyway.

God, I just really, really didn't want her to leave.

* * * * *

The next day I left Nell at the hotel and jumped on Jess the moment I saw her on the set.

"You fucking bitch."

"I'm sorry, Jeremy," Jess said. "But I can't believe she didn't know! I can't believe you didn't tell her. I really think that's wrong."

"She doesn't need to know. I'm taking care of it. By the time we get back to the States, this woman will probably have gotten over Nell and moved on."

"I don't know, she sounds like a pretty deep wack job to me. I don't know that she's going to get over you and the fact that she wants to kill your girlfriend. Not in the next couple of months anyway."

"I can take care of it. I can keep Nell safe."

"Are you sure? I wouldn't take a chance."

"Well, what do you suggest I do? Send her back to the States? Let her fend for herself?"

"Break up with her! If you cared at all about her safety, that's what you'd do, as quickly and as publicly as possible. You know how to engineer these things. Tip off the paps, sell them some nice 'fight' pics, and put her on the next plane home!"

"I'm not breaking up with her!"

Jess narrowed her eyes. "I thought so."

"Oh, Jesus Christ." I threw up my arms and stalked away, but Jess was at my side like some nagging, unwanted pet.

"If you love her—"

"I *don't* love her."

"If you like her that much, you have to send her away. Pretend. Let her go to ground and hide, and then you can go back and pick her up sometime down the line, when this fan has moved on to another target."

I stopped and spun on her. "*I'm* her target, Jess! I'm not going to live alone for the rest of my life so I don't piss off one jealous, unbalanced fan."

"And what about Nell?" she shot back.

"I told Nell about everything, thanks to you, and she still wants to stay."

Jess looked at me suspiciously. "You told her *everything*?"

"Everything she needed to know. Anyway, why do you care? Why are you so obsessed with the safety of my little toy?"

"She's not a toy. She's a person."

"Yes, you should remember that yourself."

Jess rolled her eyes at me and retreated. By this time in our friendship, we could say a lot to each other between the lines.

"You're the one who needs to remember," she called out over her shoulder before slamming her trailer door.

* * * * *

Nell didn't bring up the stalker issue again, and we left for Bulgaria shortly afterward. I was so busy during the week we were there that I barely saw Nell, and neither of us even bothered to unpack.

We left Bulgaria for a remote and scenic area of Portugal, where we'd spend a month and a half. Instead of a hotel, I had Kyle rent a local property for us. Nell practically swooned when we arrived at the small, secluded villa surrounded by romantic gardens and lovely, rolling woods.

"Jeremy, this is the most beautiful place I've ever seen!" She ran through the tall wildflowers to the trees. "Come look. There's a lake in the woods!"

"It's November. Do you want to go swimming?"

"No, but it's—God, look! The view is beautiful! It's just breathtaking!"

Yes, it is, I thought to myself.

If I'd brought my last girlfriend here, the pouts and complaints would have killed me. I took a deep breath of the crisp fall air and then went to help Kyle bring in the bags. Let her run around and play, I thought to myself. Tonight I would play with her.

It had been far too long since we'd played hard together. The Bulgarian shoot had been mercifully short but one hundred percent wretched. We hadn't had any time to do bondage or punishment scenes, just hurried quickies and blowjobs when I wasn't too tired. But not tonight. Tonight I was going to spend time. I was going to play with my lovely toy.

Kyle cooked dinner for us, and I was reminded again why I paid him such an obscene salary. We ate the fresh chicken and potatoes with a huge appetite, even Nell, who normally ate next to nothing.

"That was really great, Kyle." She sighed when she finished. "Thank you."

"My pleasure." He smiled in return.

I dropped my fork and stared at them. "My God, the world is ending. Kyle and Nell just exchanged a couple of civil words." I made a big show of rushing to the window to look out at the darkening sky.

"He's looking for pigs," I heard Kyle whisper.

Nell and Kyle laughed together, and it was great to see them getting along, although I figured it was a momentary truce. We were all in a great mood. New villa, beautiful surroundings, and the knowledge that we had a good, long time to feel at home.

"You," I said, pointing to Nell with a satisfied grin. "Go in the bedroom and put on something really, really hot."

* * * * *

I stood her against the wall for a long time. She'd put on the ivory corset she wore the first night she and I had played. I had her take her shoes off, because I liked when she looked shorter, more innocent. Her wispy auburn curls were a mess as usual, just the way I liked them. She stood still, patiently…*submissively*. She could be so normal and then turn the submissive on and do it better and more skillfully than any sub I'd ever known. Her lovely little nipples were clamped. I used the gentler ones so I could leave them on a long time. Every time she shifted, the delicate silver chain swung between them.

"How do you feel?" I asked.

She looked up at me shyly from beneath her lashes. "Wet. Horny." She was silent a moment. "Treasured. The way you look at me…"

So it was that obvious. I took up the thin leather lace beside me and turned her to tie her hands behind her back.

"Do you know why I treasure you?" I asked beside her ear.

"No, Jeremy, I don't know."

"Because you're the only one who gives me exactly what I need. You're the only one who ever has." I turned her face to mine to give her a long, lingering kiss. "I've missed you," I whispered against her lips.

"I've missed you too." Her voice shook a little. She was so emotional, this one.

"I've been too busy to take time to tie you up like this. To look at you, and make you do things. I hate being busy like that, too busy to play with you."

Her eyes closed, and she let her body melt against me. "I'm yours."

"I know you are." I kissed and licked her eyelids and trailed my fingers down over her hips. "I love the shape of you, and I love how you smell."

She shivered against me.

"Are you cold?"

"No, Jeremy."

"Just horny? I don't want to have sex with you. I just want to tie you up."

Her squeak of dismay made me laugh.

"Down. Kneel down."

She knelt on the floor and looked up at me with wide eyes.

"Down, Nell. You know what I mean. Be a good girl." She leaned forward, balancing carefully with her hands tied behind her back. I nudged at her thighs to spread her wider. I knelt next to her, stroking the perfect arch of her smooth back and thrusting two fingers up her wet, hot slit.

"How do you feel?"

"Vulnerable. Desperate."

"How desperate? What will you do for me to make you come? How far will you go?"

"I'm yours, Jeremy."

"I want to use a cane on you."

She tensed. I didn't move my fingers.

"Do you trust me? Do you trust me not to hurt you?"

"You will hurt me."

"I hurt you all the time," I said. "Now I want to hurt you this way, and I want you to let me because you trust me."

She was quiet. I let her think it over. It was something I'd wanted to do for a long time, not because I wanted to hurt her, but because she'd told me she couldn't. She wouldn't. I wanted her to, for me.

"How many?"

"Ten. No more."

"Just this once?"

"I can't promise I won't ask again. But I do promise I won't gag you, no matter how noisy you are." *No matter how much you scream*, I had almost said. "We're not in a hotel now. You can be a loud as you want, as loud as you need to be."

"I want to, but I'm scared."

I stroked her back. "I know. I know you are. But I want you to do it for me anyway. It's your hard limit. You have to tell me it's okay."

She was already crying. I don't know why I was asking her for this. Because it was as far as she would go, I supposed, and I wanted to take her there.

"Afterward, I promise I'll make it all better." I withdrew my fingers and smoothed them over her clit. "I'll make you feel so good, baby."

She sniffled loudly, and then she whispered, "Okay."

I took a deep breath and stood to get the rattan cane I'd brought along, just in case. I stood behind her. She was shaking.

"You can take this, Nell."

"Yes, Jeremy."

"You remember the safe words?"

"Yes, Jeremy."

"Either one will work." I tapped it on her ass. "Count each one for me. And don't brace."

As soon as she relaxed, I gave her the first stroke, and the second shortly afterward, while she was still experiencing the fire of the first. She gasped, sobbing. On the third, she jerked with a yelp and nearly broke her stance.

"Okay?" I asked. God, I was a sadist. She was crying terrible tears. She buried her face in the carpet and stilled herself again.

"Four!" she said, nearly a scream. I took my time, letting the fire of each stroke run its course before laying on the next one.

"Five! Six!" She managed to count although she was breathlessly crying. "Seven!"

The eighth was the hardest one yet, and she did scream then, loud and long. "Please! God, Jeremy!"

"Two more, baby. Two more."

"No. I can't!"

"You can. You're doing it." I waited for a safe word, but it didn't come.

"Nine!" she screamed. The marks on her ass were absolutely beautiful: straight, thin, pink welts that would fade into lovely red lines as time went on.

Ten was the hardest, and that scream was the loudest. She went limp before the last echoes of it faded in the room. I looked down at her, watched her collect herself and catch her breath. I would be able to look at those marks for a week or more and remember that she took them…for me. I crouched down and placed the cane next to her, in front of her face. Her eyes were tightly closed. Her mouth looked tense, and her chin trembled.

"Open your eyes."

She opened them and looked at the cane, then shuddered and raised her face to me. Her gaze was still dark with the memory of the pain she'd endured.

I had to be inside her. I fumbled with the lace binding her hands, untied it, ripped it off, and flipped her over, taking her down to the floor.

"Put your arms around me," I growled, roughly parting her legs. She sobbed as I entered her. I grasped her striped ass roughly in my hands to pull her closer to me.

"I own you," I whispered in her ear. "I own you." My voice sounded harsh and strained. She felt so unbelievably perfect. We fit so perfectly when I took her this way, held close, her legs wrapped around me, her arms clinging to my neck. She may have only been mine because I was paying her, but at times like this, I thought I would never, ever let her go, if I had to pay her for an eternity.

"Jeremy, Jeremy." She moaned. "God, Jeremy, yes."

"Yes, I want you to come for me. I want to feel it. I want to feel you come." I tugged at the chain torturing her nipples, so she arched and gasped. "I love how it feels when you come, when I'm inside you."

She fell apart, shaking and practically strangling me as her arms tightened around my neck. The shivers that racked her body transferred to me as she arched against my skin. Her little tummy was taut and velvety against mine. I grasped her hips and bucked into her as she rode out her climax. Her satisfied gasps triggered some deep male center inside me. I felt my balls tense, felt every muscle in my body turn electric. I pumped my cum into her with forceful thrusts that jerked her like a rag doll as she clung to me. When we came to rest, she looked up with those striking green eyes full of wonder.

"Good girl." I licked from her jaw all the way down her neck.

Good girl. She was my good girl. She was my everything girl. We'd been together nearly two months by this time, long enough to get past the infatuation stage, but I found I was eternally infatuated with her, with fucking her, with tormenting her, with not letting her come, with making her come, with staring at her perfection as she came apart in my arms. I watched her now, her chest rising and falling. Her beautiful breasts still bore the bite of my clamps. I tugged at one and then the other, feeling a deep sense of pride, a sense of ownership.

"You're beautiful."

She smiled at my compliment and reached up to run her fingers lightly through my hair. The soft, affectionate gesture caught me off guard. I shivered. *This girl could really hurt me*, I thought. Ironic, considering the scene we'd just completed, but it was true.

She shifted in my arms. I knew, now that she'd come, that the clamps would feel much more uncomfortable. The sadist in me made her squirm awhile before I relented and took them off. She clenched her teeth and drew her breath in at the sudden flood of sensation. Again the sadist in me rejoiced. I flicked one reddened, sore peak.

"Your nipples are sensitive."

"Tell me about it." She laughed. "Yours are too. If I put those on you, I wonder if you'd like it."

"Not a motherfucking chance. I like giving pain, not taking it. Speaking of which..." I nudged her. She turned over, and we both looked at her welted ass cheeks. "Beautiful," I said. "Nell, look at that." She didn't seem to share my excitement. She looked horrified, actually.

"They'll fade," I said. "They look bad now, but..."

"When they fade, will you want to make more?"

"Did it really hurt that much? And no, I don't want to try it. I know. I learned to cane girls by hitting my own thigh. I know it smarts."

"Smarts?" She snorted. "It hurts like bejeezus."

"But you survived." I laughed at the doubtful look on her face. "You did. You took it beautifully. I mean, my God..." I looked away. "I really appreciate..." I drew a deep breath, disciplined my mouth before I said something stupid. She still watched me. Her eyes were transparent as ever. She was worried.

"Look, do I want to make it a regular part of our play? No, we don't have to. I know it's your limit. I try to respect those as much as possible." I grinned.

A small smile quirked the corner of her mouth. "Maybe every so often you could sweet-talk me. But you'd have to be awfully sweet."

"I am awfully sweet," I said, nuzzling her sore bottom. "Sweet is my middle name."

"Ouch. I think your middle name is Pain."

I slapped her ass. "Very soon your middle name will be Pain. Come on. Crawl on top of me backward. I want to fuck you again while I look at your ass."

"You're a pervert." She lowered herself onto my jutting cock, ass first.

"Yes," I said, my hands on either side of her hips, pulling her down. "And you love me that way."

* * * * *

The next week was Thanksgiving, and the largely American crew got a couple of days off. Kyle flew home to the U.S. to be with family for the weekend, but Nell and I stayed and went to the formal, studio-hosted Thanksgiving dinner instead.

It was at a beautiful local restaurant, and Nell sat beside me in the car looking lovely and sweet. I'd bought her a new dress for the occasion, as well as some racy new garments to wear underneath: a vintage black garter belt and see-through push-up bra. The new outfit made us late, since as soon as I'd seen it on her I'd had to fuck her bent over the bed. She should have known better than to turn her back to me in lingerie like that.

I moaned, remembering, and flipped her skirt up above her thighs to look at the luscious white skin above the tops of her stockings. Long since inured to being groped, stared at, and salivated over by me, she only shifted casually to let my hand slide between her legs.

"You look beautiful tonight. As always."

She laughed softly. "You say that every time."

"Because every time it's true." I moved her skirt back down again and leaned back in the seat. "We'll be sitting with Jessamine and Mason tonight. He flew in for the weekend," I said, looking out the window.

"Oh my God, Mason Cooke?" Nell clasped her hands together and pressed them under her chin. She was all but bouncing on the seat beside me.

"All right, settle down." I smiled at her fan-girl swoon. "Don't go getting all wet, you little cum slut. You belong to me, you remember."

"I know. It's just... Wow. I can't get used to being around all these big movie stars."

"You have a big movie star fucking you every day."

"Yeah, but you're just Jeremy by now. Wow, Mason Cooke..." she said and then yelped when I pinched her inner thigh.

Nell managed to hold it together when Jessamine introduced her very famous, and yes, very attractive husband. I understood Nell's excitement. Mason was a hottie, not that I ever swung anywhere near that way. But it was good that she found him attractive, that he excited her, because Jessamine, Mason, and I had arranged some group sex to follow dinner. The only participant who wasn't in on the arrangement was the main attraction herself.

Jessamine, an unrepentant bisexual, was wild for Nell and had been for quite some time. Mason was wild for anything that made his wife wild, and me, well, I was wild for the whole idea. The sharing, the visual feast of Jessamine Jackson having a go at my Nell, and probably Mason too.

But my little subbie had no fucking idea. She sat among us at the table, bright and excited and beautiful like a doll, not noticing the way Jess and Mason eyed her, or the silly winks Jess kept throwing my way. That she didn't know, that she didn't understand what was coming, was part of the foreplay, something that turned the other three of us on. Well, she would be fine with it. She did what I paid her for, and I had no doubt tonight would be a garden of delights for her most of all.

When the dinner degenerated into a drunken party like all studio-sponsored events did, Jessamine smiled brightly at Nell and me from across the table. "Well, shall we?"

"Jess and Mason have invited us back to their villa for some sex," I said quietly to Nell. "Get your coat."

By the time I finished helping her on with it, she'd flushed scarlet. Her pale redhead skin showed every blush.

"Are you going to ride with us?" Jess asked.

"No, we'll bring our own car. We'll meet you there," I said, ushering Nell out. Her gaze was fixed to the floor.

"What is it?" I sighed when we were in the car. "You've done this kind of thing before."

"I know. I don't care. But why didn't you tell me?"

I shrugged. "It was more fun, your not knowing."

"So you could spring it on me in front of them and embarrass me—"

"Embarrass you? You're not as easily embarrassed as that, I know."

"It's just rude," she snapped, wrapping her arms around herself and leaning against the door. "I hate the way you play with me sometimes like I'm some toy—"

"You are a toy! You're my toy. My very expensive and very moody toy, if you want to know the truth."

"I do want to know the truth! Is that really all I am to you? Do you really believe that? I have no feelings, no identity aside from your wants and needs?"

"Yes. To me. Yes, that's exactly how it is. We've gone through this before, and the last fucking time I want to go over it again is right now. I've been looking forward to this for ages. You're going to pull yourself together and fucking play along, you little fuck."

"I know I am," she said. "Believe me, I know how this goes by now."

"What's that supposed to mean?" I muttered, but we were there and I got out of the car, practically dragging Nell out and up the walk. "You just fucking do this," I hissed as I rang the bell.

She looked at me and said in a voice like ice, "I'm yours."

* * * * *

"Jeremy! Nell! Come in, have some wine!"

Jess was already unabashedly naked as the day she was born, save a very tiny pair of panties. She kissed each of us as she handed us wineglasses and then led us down the hall. "Mason, they're here!" She turned to Nell and held out her hand. "Come to the bedroom with us."

Nell took her hand, my beautiful, confused, sexy girl. Mason and I brought up the rear. The bedroom was dark, lit by candles, soft Euro breathy sex music already playing. I had to hand it to these two, they knew how to play. Mason crossed the room to watch the show, a man after my own heart. Nell stopped halfway to the raised bed, and I stood near her, willing her to relax.

"I'm so glad you came, you two. I really am," said Jess.

"You don't care about me." I snorted. "It's Nell you want."

"Maybe." Jess laughed. She looked at Nell and put her wineglass on a side table. "I think you're so lovely in so many ways."

"Why?" Nell asked.

Jess shrugged. "I don't know. I can't explain. I just know Jeremy is a very lucky man. You make a beautiful couple."

"We're not really a couple," Nell said.

"I know." Jessamine's gaze darted to mine. "I was telling Mason that I fantasized about you two in the bedroom. About what it was like the first time...when you were strangers..."

Nell swallowed. She knew as well as I that this was foreplay. Jess looked up at me.

"Tell me, Jeremy, the first time, were you hard or sweet to her?"

"Both," I said. "And I didn't let her come. But she liked it. She likes sex. She fucks like a slut, and she comes like a supernova."

"Does she?" Jess looked at me. "Do you, Nell?"

"If Jeremy lets me." A charming blush rose in her cheeks, and her voice shook a little.

"Well," said Jess with a light laugh. "In this bedroom you can come all you want. Jeremy's rules don't apply here."

I took Nell's wineglass away as Jess approached. Otherwise I think she would have dropped it. Jess stood in front of her, proud, beautiful, sensual, the candlelight glowing on her naked skin. Nell leaned back against me as Jess began to undress her.

"Oh, Jeremy." Jess sighed when she reached the black lingerie. "Are you trying to kill me?"

I nuzzled Nell's cheek. I could feel her relax against me as Jessamine went about casting her seductive spell. Her fingertips skimmed over Nell's skin.

"I love beautiful, beautiful girls like you," Jess whispered against Nell's ear. She kissed her, lightly at first, then more deeply. Nell wrapped her arms around Jess's waist, her small hands resting on the womanly curves of Jess's hips. Soon her hands opened, began to explore the satiny skin there. Nell leaned closer, craning her head to give Jess deeper access to her pliant mouth. Jess devoured her, then made an urgent sound in her throat and pulled away. She brushed back Nell's auburn hair and whispered to her. "Relax. I'll make you feel good. I promise."

I watched, almost unable to draw breath. Jess took her to the bed and had her lie back against the pillows. Mason and I started undressing madly, quickly, impatiently, as Jess bent over and spread Nell's legs wide.

Chapter Fifteen:
Sideways and Upside Down

Oh my God. Oh my God. Oh my God. Jessamine Jackson was eating me out. She was like a shaman of oral sex. Her tongue explored me wantonly. Her lips closed over my labia and sucked. She probed and laved me until she found a motion or a spot that made me gasp, and then she stoked it, drew out the pleasure there until I felt the world falling away. My moans and cries were impossible to stifle. The musky essence of pussy juices wafted into my nostrils and drove me even higher. Whether the fragrance flowed from her sex or mine, I couldn't tell, and I didn't care.

Mixed in with the sexual fragrance in the air was Jess's own exotic perfume. Her hands clutched at my thighs as I squirmed under her. From time to time I looked down just to see her long, elegant fingers stroking my skin. Jeremy sat behind me, cradling my head in his lap, reaching under my bra to pinch and play with my nipples. I stared up at him through the haze of my arousal. My mouth was open; I could hear my labored breath. "Yes," he whispered to me. "Yes." In my momentary lapses of coherency, I noticed Mason sitting on the other side of the bed, watching, stroking himself.

Oh God...oh God. She was finger fucking me now. Her lovely movie-star fingers slid over my g-spot in an erratic rhythm. Her thumb played over my clit, stroking me with twice as much dexterity as Jeremy ever used. Well, she would know exactly how to touch me, wouldn't she? "Oh God...ohhhh..."

"Yes, so beautiful," she murmured against my inner thigh. "Does that make you happy? Does that make you happy, beautiful girl?"

"Yes," I sighed. She kissed and licked the insides of my pussy lips, then returned to sucking and tonguing my clit. Her tongue flicked and toyed across its slippery surface. I could feel it swelling. With her finger she flicked and scratched the tender skin between my thighs. "Oh God...please... No...yes!"

Jeremy closed rough fingers on the tips of my nipples. My pelvis rose up off the bed. I was so close. With a tortured moan, I threw my head back against Jeremy and twisted my hips under Jessamine's eager mouth. He squeezed harder. Jess pistoned her fingers in and out of me and pressed hard on my aching nub with her tongue. I gasped out Jessamine's name, and the shudders took over me. My walls contracted, and the pleasure shot down my thighs and up to my nipples. Jess lapped at my slit while I swirled through the aftershocks. I reached down and twisted my fingers in her hair. I loved her.

But Jess gazed up at Jeremy first.

"I told you so," he said.

She laughed and crawled up over me with a beatific smile. Her long, lean thighs straddled my hips, and she leaned down to kiss me. I tasted my own pungent pussy juices, licked them from her lips and tongue. She held my face in her tapered fingers and looked down at me then, a sweet look of wistfulness.

"Thank you, Nell."

"I... I..." I was completely tongue-tied, but it didn't matter, because she'd already turned her attention back to Jeremy. She leaned right over me to kiss him. The feelings of satisfaction that flooded me a moment earlier disappeared in that space of that one kiss. I watched from below as Jeremy's rough, full lips warred with hers. She pulled away abruptly, as if remembering I was still there.

"Thank you for sharing, darling," she said, cupping his face in her hand.

"My pleasure."

"Now what are we going to do about your little problem there?" She peered down at his swollen cock. "Or big problem, rather."

She rolled off the bed, and Jeremy followed. I watched them for a moment, feeling abandoned and jealous until I noticed Mason Cooke was crawling between my legs. *Oh my God. Mason Cooke!*

"Hi," he said.

"Hi—"

My voice was silenced by his deep, urgent kiss. *Mason Cooke is kissing me.* Why did this all have to be so strange and crazy, and why did I have to feel so horny about it at the same time? I looked to the side to see Jeremy pushing Jess against the wall, lifting her legs to straddle his hips. I felt jealousy, yes, but something else too. Admiration. They were beautiful people. It was impossible for some small part of me to not get excited seeing them wrapped together in an animalistic embrace.

Mason's hand crept over my hip, and my gaze returned to him. He didn't speak. I wondered why. Did he know what I was feeling, the jealous thoughts I was trying to subdue? I had no real rights to Jeremy. Hell, Jess was Mason's *wife* and he seemed happy to share. I took a deep breath and tried to stay in the moment. Mason's hand slid down my belly to probe between my legs. I felt embarrassed by how wet I was. He reached over to the side table and grabbed a condom, then threw one to Jeremy across the room. He rolled it on while he kissed my shoulder, my neck, my jaw, the soft skin below my ear. "Can I make love to you?"

I drew in a hard breath and stared up at him. Across the room, Jeremy was fucking Jess against the wall. "It's up to you," Mason said, "but I'd really like to."

I looked up into his marine blue eyes, the eyes I'd seen and swooned over on the movie screen. Now they were focused on me. His hands soothed and cradled me. His huge cock nudged between my thighs.

"Go on. Go ahead and take her," Jeremy called out over Jess's horny shrieks and moans. "I pay her. She's not allowed to say no."

Mason's eyes looked into mine, the same kind, friendly eyes that had gazed at me over dinner, made me feel interesting and pretty, so I'm sure he saw me flinch. All along, he knew he'd be fucking me in a few hours.

"I'm yours," I said in a voice that didn't sound anything at all like mine.

With a sigh, he reared between my legs and entered me. I let out my breath in a long gasp as I felt every inch of his cock pry me open. He was huge, thick. He stretched my sensitive walls. When he was fully seated in me, I felt impaled, trapped. I felt a flash of panic. *What if he hurts me?* I looked over to Jeremy for courage but only got an eyeful of his naked ass pumping between Jessamine's flailing legs. My gaze darted around the room. I didn't know where to look. Not in his eyes, they were too intense. Not over at the wall. I could still hear the racket Jess was making as Jeremy drilled her.

"It's okay." Mason traced his fingers down the edge of my jaw. Was it okay? Something in his eyes, his gentle manner, made the anxiety begin to fade. He moved in me, a deep, slow stroke. It didn't hurt. It felt great actually, and I shivered at the sensation. Every part of me felt like it was being caressed, stroked. He held me close and cradled me like I was breakable. He moved over me, hard abs and thick, dark pelt on his chest to grab and bury my fingers in. He didn't try to pin me down. He didn't try to subdue me. He simply drove in and out and visited sensation on me again and again.

I got braver. I reached up and ran my hands over his shoulders, behind his neck. I twined them up into his soft black hair, and he sighed.

"Nell..."

I drew them away as if I'd been burned. But soon enough, I felt that shivery, hot pleasure stroke inside my walls, and I had to reach for him again. I wanted it to be ugly, horrible, mechanical like when Kyle and I had sex for Jeremy, but this wasn't like that at all. "Mason," I heard myself moan. *Mason Cooke.*

By that time, Jeremy and Jess's wall sex was over, and they both came to join us on the bed. Jess stroked her husband's ass as he thrust into me, and Jeremy knelt beside the bed to toy with my breasts and kiss my lips. I felt torn in two different directions, filled and pleasured by Mason, but belonging to Jeremy at the same time. I turned to kiss him, to feel his fingers twist my nipples, but at the same time, I thrust my swollen clit against Mason's pubic bone. I ground my hips and arched them up to receive his deep strokes. He began to swivel his pelvis, driving his cock even more intimately against my walls.

It was too much for me, too much excitement and sensation. A dam broke, and my orgasm flooded out. I tensed and bit off a cry as my pussy contracted almost painfully around his thick cock. Mason came too, driving in me so that he lifted my hips off the bed.

He came to rest, then sighed and kissed me. He stroked my face and lips while Jessamine watched with a smile on her face. They were all looking down at me, all three of them, and a muddle of feelings washed over me. I tugged myself from under Mason and turned to Jeremy's arms. I buried my head in his chest, my face burning.

"Okay, I'm here," he soothed me. "I'm right here."

He crawled into the bed beside me and held me. We all lay still, not speaking for a long time. I don't know why I felt so unbalanced. This felt like depravity...and yet...

I didn't want to think about it. I didn't know what to feel, so I chose not to feel anything except the light fingertips tracing over my belly and my hips. I didn't know who it was, and I didn't care. After a while, Jeremy nudged me.

"Turn over."

I moaned softly, but I obeyed. He crawled over my back and slipped inside my pussy, holding himself over me and sliding in and out of me slowly. I thought I couldn't bear to feel another ounce of pleasure, but soon enough the familiar throbbing heaviness began to build. I heard Jessamine moan as Mason drove into her from behind, shaking the bed. I looked over to find them both watching us.

It was so erotic, so licentious. It was nothing like when Jeremy watched me and Kyle fuck. I watched them watching me, awash in their own pleasure, and I wondered what I looked like to them. A girl? A body, a cunt? A vessel for sex? The idea of it turned me on so much. Jeremy pulled me up on my knees, and I held hard to the bed frame as he pounded into me. I was exhausted. I thought I would let him use me, just let him take me. I didn't want to come again. I couldn't. I watched Jess and Mason fucking, two sexual creatures giving up every ounce of themselves to the thrill. They moaned and groped at each other. Their mouths fell open, and they threw their heads back with abandon, no thought of inhibition or shame. And behind me, my own lover holding my hips, squeezing my ass cheeks. I felt a flame of desire start to grow. I wanted to let go too. I wanted to let sex take me over.

I reached between my legs and grasped my clit in urgent fingers. It wasn't permitted. I wasn't allowed to touch myself without permission, not ever. I waited for him to reprimand me, to slap my hand away, but he didn't. He was drifting in his own erotic dreams. His hands roved over me with wild intensity. I fingered my clit, drunk on sexual freedom. God, how long since I'd sought my own pleasure? Touched my clit to find my own release, and not because Jeremy told me to? It was like reuniting with an old friend. I caressed my clit, worshipped it. I explored it and pinched it. I rubbed my juices over it. I heard Mason's groan and Jess's cry, and my fingers worked faster. They flew over my aching center as Jeremy's cock filled me. We came together, and I fell to the bed, Jeremy collapsed over the top of me. I left my hand cupped over my pussy and turned my head to the side, spent.

Jeremy stroked my hair, and I heard a soft giggle from Jessamine.

"Is she okay?"

"Jesus." Jeremy laughed. "I think she's finished for the night."

The bed shifted, and I felt Jessamine lean against us. I think she and Jeremy kissed, and then she leaned down to kiss the back of my neck.

"God, Jeremy, she's so sweet."

"She's the sweetest little harlot you ever saw."

They chuckled, and Jeremy kissed the back of my neck this time. "You are," he whispered in my ear, "and I adore you for it."

"She must love getting her ass fucked," Mason said. *Holy hell. Please, no.*

"She does," agreed Jeremy. "But I'm a little possessive of her ass. That, I don't share."

"Oh, I understand completely," said Mason. "And those beautiful marks…wow." I flinched as he explored the faded welts with rough fingertips.

"Those are almost a week old," said Jeremy. It sounded like he was bragging. He gave me a hard pinch to make me jump. The welts burned now from being handled, but I didn't think of putting my hand back to rub the ache away.

Mason must have given Jessamine a look then, because she said, "Oh no, lover. Not a chance."

"So, what, you did this with a belt?"

"No, a cane. They really hurt."

"You have some kind of Master/servant thing going on?"

Jessamine tittered as Jeremy answered, "No."

"Daddy/daughter?"

"Ugh, no."

"Domestic discipline? You spank her on a schedule?"

That made even me laugh.

"I discipline her when I'm in the mood for it. She doesn't like it, especially the cane, but she does what I ask her to do. She submits when I ask her to submit."

Jessamine made a low whistle. "That's pretty hot. I would love to see you spank her gorgeous little ass."

I tensed, but Jeremy calmed me with a caress. "I don't think so. My cherub is tired."

"Stay here with us tonight?"

I looked up at Jeremy, imbuing every ounce of the word "no" that I could manage in my eyes.

"Come on. We'll have breakfast in the morning. No more sex if you don't want. Please? I had so much fun. Don't run off. Let's sleep together like kittens," Jessamine begged.

I knew he wanted to, but I desperately wanted to go back to our villa and crawl into bed.

"We'd better not, not tonight. Next time, maybe," he finally said.

He did take me home, and I went right to sleep, but things went sideways and upside down the next day.

* * * * *

He had the day off, which I think made things more difficult. Instead of his leaving after he fucked me in the morning, he hung around. I retreated to my room, which was rarely used now, but at times like this I was glad it was there.

I was still processing the night before, so I didn't really want to be around him. The more the shock wore off, the more indignant I felt. *Go ahead and take her*, he'd said to Mason. *I pay her. She's not allowed to say no.* Jeremy let me mope and sulk until it was almost lunchtime, and then he came to glower at me from the door.

"What are you doing?"

"Reading."

He came in and nudged me over, then lay down beside me in bed. He grabbed my book, losing my place as he always did.

"The Babylonian stuff. You always read that when you're pissed."

I grabbed it back. "Why? Why do you always lose my place? Every time!"

"You've already read it anyway. I know, I've seen you read that book at least three times, so who cares?"

"I care! Why do you *not* care? Why do you not care about anything you do to me, ever?" My voice trembled and cracked on the last word.

He scowled at me. "Okay, fine. Let's get this over with." He raised his voice into a squeaky, nasally imitation of mine. "'Why are you so mean to me, Jeremy? Why do you make me sleep with your famous friends and have mind-blowing sex and earth-shattering orgasms—'"

"That's not the point." I rolled off the bed and stalked out of the room. I didn't want to have this conversation, because it always ended the same, with a cold and biting reminder that I worked for him, so my problems, my feelings, didn't matter, and I should shut the fuck up and stop whining.

"What, Nell?" He followed me with an exasperated sigh. "Explain to me. How was last night any different from you, me, and Kyle?"

"Because that's just—not the same. How can you not see that?"

He threw up his hands. "Same tired phrases, every time. 'That's not the same,' 'that's not the point,' 'you just don't understand.' You never make sense! I never have a clue what you're talking about."

"Because you never hear me!" I turned on him. "You don't listen to me. You don't see me. You don't see anything but a plastic sex toy you can drag around from place to place! Last night, you never asked. You never told me. You just dragged me there—"

"And you enjoyed it, you moody little slut!"

"Yes, I did!" I said, bursting into tears. "That was the worst part!"

"Jesus Christ," he said, storming away. "Here come the fucking waterworks! What do you want from me?" He spun on me. "I keep you in beautiful hotels, in this villa you love. I buy you clothes and meals and toys. I fly you around the world. I introduce you to famous people, and in public I treat you with utmost respect. In private I play safely with you. I give you pleasure! What more do you want, Nell? What would satisfy you? Do you want me to fall in love with you? You won't even tell me your fucking name! You want me to be your real boyfriend, and *honey* and *sweetheart* and *baby* you all day and marry you and give you fucking babies and live the rest of my life wrapped around your little fucking finger."

"No! I want you to... I just want... I want to feel like you'd care if I lived or died. That you wouldn't just shrug and send Kyle to find a replacement."

"A replacement? You little fuck." He crossed the room in three strides and took me by the elbow to yell in my face. "You think I don't care? You think I'm not losing sleep over keeping you safe, over this fucking woman getting to you—" He stopped speaking.

Getting to me? "What are you talking about?" My heart was beating hard. He dropped my arm and turned away.

"Nothing. I didn't mean to say that."

"But you did!"

"Just—" He paced away from me and back again. "Just please fucking leave it alone, okay?"

"You said it was nothing to worry about, just another crazy fan."

"Yes, it's a crazy fan," he said, avoiding my eyes. "I didn't mean to worry you. I shouldn't have said anything. There's nothing to worry about."

I looked at him a long time. "Then why are you worried?"

"You know what, Nell? I'm a lot more worried about your misguided ideas of what our relationship is than some deluded fan halfway across the world," he said, crossing to the door. "And about last night...just fucking get over it." He grabbed his coat and stalked outside.

* * * * *

Jeremy refused to talk any more about the crazy fan, so my paranoia went wild on its own. I made up terrifying, unlikely scenarios in my head and then convinced myself they would come to pass. Eventually I stole on to his computer one night while he was sleeping and tried to find something by checking his files. He caught me and was probably as angry as I'd ever seen him. As punishment I had to sleep plugged the next five nights with rope panties and a knot placed right on my clit, with no orgasms allowed. He was nothing if not devastatingly creative in tormenting me. I woke up every morning absolutely frantic to be fucked, only to have my orgasms denied.

But I learned nothing of this mysterious stalker. I begged Kyle for information, but he remained tight-lipped. He just kept reminding me, as Jeremy did whenever I brought it up, that I was perfectly safe. And I did feel safe at our remote little villa. If I went with them to the set, I was surrounded by people at all times, even when I wanted peace to sit and read. We didn't play again with Jessamine, although I saw her often. I got the feeling it was more his choice than hers.

Kyle also began to spend less time with us, at least as a sex partner. Without Kyle milling around or joining in, the sex began to feel more intimate than ever before. In fact, it became almost unbearable subterfuge, to play the affectionate girlfriend in public where it was all a lie, and then later, in the deepest, most honest moments of intimacy, pretend I didn't care about him at all.

Pretend. I pretended. I acted. It was all a total lie. I was in love with Jeremy Gray. But I pretended I wasn't, and he pretended I wasn't. Anyway, I kept reminding myself that one day it was going to end.

We left Portugal the next to last week of December to spend the holidays with Jeremy's family in the mountains of North Carolina. Jeremy got mad when I tried to beg off, when I asked to stay in the villa until he returned. He wouldn't even consider it.

"You stay with me," he said. "That's what I pay you for."

But I didn't know how I would handle this meeting. I didn't want to handle it. While Jeremy drove us to his parents' house, I tried to ferret out more information about how I should act, what to expect, but he was in a terrible mood.

It was late, we were both tired, and we drove on a winding road that made my stomach turn. We climbed and climbed in the dark until my ears popped and I thought his parents must live at the crest of a mountain. He'd rented a car with a manual transmission, and now I saw why. I could never have maneuvered these hills and slopes.

Something about watching him drive aroused me. He drove like he made love, recklessly but with breathtaking skill. I couldn't stop watching him shift gears as he coaxed the car up and down the steep hills. But of course, Jeremy Gray could do anything and everything well. That was the appeal.

"Jeremy," I finally asked. "Do your parents know?"

"Know?"

"Know what I am to you?"

He frowned. The muscles in his forearm bunched as he downshifted around a tight corner.

"They think you're my girlfriend, and that's how you'll act. And they'll practically smother you with excitement and affection in hopes that finally I've met a girl who'll make me settle down." He looked over at me in my conservative, girl-next-door cardigan. "They'll go wild for you. You're the least Hollywood girl I've ever brought home."

"So you bring all your girls home?" I made no effort to disguise the sarcasm in my voice.

"I spend every Christmas here in the mountains, so yes, I've brought a few. And you should know"—he looked, for the first time I could remember, deeply embarrassed—"my parents are very old-fashioned and religious, so you'll have to sleep in your own room the next couple of nights."

I burst out laughing. I couldn't help it. Jeremy Gray, the product of a conservative and religious home.

"What's so funny?" He shifted with a little more force than necessary.

"It's just funny. How do you not find it funny?"

"Because it's my fucking life."

"Yeah, well, we all have fucked-up lives," I said. "I just can't believe you ever set foot in a church, much less were raised by religious people."

"What? I'm not that evil. No more so than you."

I snorted. "Whatever."

"Don't make me pull the car over. It's late."

I snorted again, which in hindsight was a mistake. He pulled over and yanked me out. He bent me over the trunk of the car so my feet dangled at least two feet above the road.

"What if a car comes?" I asked as he unbuttoned my jeans and pulled them down to my knees, along with my panties.

"I guess they'll see me beating your ass." He tugged the belt from his pants and doubled it over. "Don't bother to count. I'll stop when I feel like it."

"Are you mad, Jeremy? Because you always say you don't want to hurt me in anger—*Ouch!*"

"I'm not mad," he said. "I'm irritated, and you're acting like a brat."

"Ouch. *Ouch!* I won't even be able to sit down at your parents' house!"

"Yes, that's what I hope for."

The chilled metal of the car against my skin froze my front while my backside was absolutely red-hot. I counted up to twenty in my head before I gave up and started to beg.

"Please, please, stop. I'm sorry! My ass is on fire!"

"I said I would stop when I felt like it."

I buried my face in my arms, trying with all my strength not to reach back and shield myself, or jump off the trunk of the car and run. I'd probably go tumbling down the side of the mountain and be found frozen in a heap at the bottom with my red, bruised ass exposed. Of all the appropriate ways to die...

"Jeremy, you're killing me!" He finally stopped when I started to cry, but he didn't let me down, just put his hand on my lower back and held me still while he undid himself.

"You may find my life funny," he said, thrusting deep inside me, "but you of all people are in no position to judge."

"I was joking, Jeremy." I sniffled. "Why have you been so mad all day?"

"Because I get tired of the lies. Of living this farce."

"Then why don't you stop lying?" I could barely get the words out as he pummeled me with forceful thrusts.

I grunted as he pulled out of me and pressed his cock against my ass. He entered me all the time this way now, with only the lube from my pussy. I clenched against the pain, then willed myself to subdue the protective impulse. He slapped me lightly.

"Open. I want to fuck your ass."

"Yes, Jeremy."

He eased the head of his cock in, then waited for me to relax before thrusting the rest of the way inside. I moaned. I couldn't help it. It was a little painful, as always, but one hundred percent better than the pain of his belt.

"Jeremy." I gasped to the rhythm of his fucking. "If you're tired of the lying, why don't you stop?"

"Hush. Let me fuck you. And don't you come, you little fuck slut. I don't want you to come."

Jesus, I'd really ticked him off.

"Yes, Jeremy."
Yes yes yes, whatever you say.
Not only did he not let me come, but I had to ride the rest of the way up the mountain with my pants around my knees, my bare, sore ass on the scratchy rental-car seat.

Chapter Sixteen:
Lies

Nervous, sore, ass-fucked, horny.

It gave me great pleasure to introduce her to my parents that way. It would have been better to have harnessed her under her jeans with dildos in her pussy and her ass, but I hadn't thought that far ahead.

If I had to lie, if I *had* to lie about everything, let me lie about her too. Let me make her base and dirty instead of the beautiful, intelligent girl she truly was.

As they greeted her with hugs and exclamations, I wanted to yell, *She's just my whore. I'm too worthless and sick to deserve anything more of her.* But I didn't. I just hugged and exclaimed too. All the other girls had been painfully out of place here, but she was so perfect, it hurt.

It *hurt*. Nell shifted on the sofa as my mother brought tea and cookies. I watched her. I'd made her hurt.

Lately I wanted to hurt her all the time. Hurt her the way that she hurt me. Hurt her so she would turn on me and I wouldn't ache anymore over how perfect she was. How much would it take to drive her away from me, far away from me, where she ought to be? Nothing so far had worked, but to take things further, to really hurt her to the point she would leave…it was too difficult. It was a game of chicken I couldn't and wouldn't play.

At least not yet.

My hand went to the pocket of my jacket, to the small box there, the box I'd been carrying since a week ago when I'd come up with a ridiculously stupid idea. It had been such a ridiculously stupid idea that I'd called Martin to run my stupidity past him first.

"Martin, about the stalker. Do you think...? I mean... I wonder how it might affect her if I were to get engaged to someone?"

"Engaged? Like, to be married?"

I could already tell by the tone in his voice that he thought it was as ridiculous as I did.

"I mean, it might put her off, don't you think?"

"Or make her even angrier at Nell," Martin said. "Leslie Gray thinks she's your wife."

"I know, I know. But maybe getting engaged to someone else would make her reconsider that."

Martin was silent a long time.

"So, you mean...get engaged to Nell."

"Yes," I said, my voice tight.

"Well, do you... I mean...are you talking about really getting engaged to Nell, or...?"

"I mean, we would really get engaged. I got a ring."

"Jeremy, what I'm asking is, would you be getting engaged for appearances, or do you...? Are you...? Do you really intend to make her your wife?"

I snorted. "Do I have to think that far ahead? She probably wouldn't have me anyway, so no. I mean, you know. I just want to give her a ring. Let her wear it for a while."

Martin sighed. "Are you sure she would understand a gesture like that? Because I'm not sure it makes sense to me. You have to tread very carefully with things like engagement rings and proposals. You have to honestly explain—"

"Explain what? She works for me. She plays my girlfriend. Now she can play my wife."

"You mean your fiancée."

"Right. My fiancée. Whatever."

He sighed again. I wished I hadn't said anything to him at all.

"Listen, Jeremy, you need to think this through. Playing a girlfriend is one thing. Wearing someone's ring is something else altogether. Especially when..."

"When what?"

"When you're both so emotionally involved already as it is."

"I'm not... We're not emotionally involved. I mean, we've been keeping things professional."

"Have you?"

Fucker.

"Yes," I said. "Actually we have. Anyway, I thought it might get this crazy stalker lady off my back."

"I don't know. I think it might inflame her more. We should talk to the case worker at the police department first, get his opinion. He would probably know better what might play out from a situation like this. You certainly don't want to endanger Nell even further—"

"No, of course I don't want to fucking endanger Nell!"

He fell silent. Now I was the one who sighed. Martin cleared his throat.

"Jeremy. Listen. I've known you for a long time. I've known a lot of your girls. I'm not exactly sure where you're taking this. I can't tell where your mind's at. Perhaps worse, I'm not sure you know where your mind's at. So until you know, I'm advising you not to do anything extreme. Don't do anything without thinking things through and without being brutally honest with yourself first. If you don't know why you're doing this, or what outcome you want, it would be better to just—"

"God, it was only an idea. Don't flip out and go all mental-health counselor on me."

Fuck Martin anyway, and fuck the little fuck at the police department who called me a couple of days later to insist it was a *very bad idea.*

If I wanted to propose to my fake girlfriend on Christmas morning in front of my whole family, then I fucking would. Hell, my parents would be beside themselves with happiness. Even now they were both beaming at her like she was the Madonna herself. I guess since she was the first girl I'd ever brought home who might remotely be considered wife material.

Wife material. I really didn't want her for my wife. I just thought it might be a good idea for the stalker thing. And anyway, it would be fun to pretend to be engaged to her.

My parents were grilling her about her hometown, her parents, her career.

"I'm a personal assistant," she said with a straight face over her plate of cookies. She didn't eat one of them. "I like to help people, I guess."

"She's helped me on this trip, that's for sure," I chimed in with a subtle wink that had her blushing and glaring at me.

"And were you raised with a religion, dear?" my mother asked with a hopeful note in her voice.

"Nell studies mythology," I said. "She's too polite to tell you this, but she believes the Bible is just another book of myths."

She shot me a glare and dropped her gaze into her lap. My mother looked depressed, like she always did when confronted by my godless ways.

"She knows hundreds of stories," I continued. "Mythology from every continent and every era in time. Mythology about how the world began, what people used to believe—"

"The nice thing about being human," Nell said softly, "is that you can determine the reality of the world for yourself. People have always done that throughout time, and mythology can reveal to us what those creative beliefs were. If you believe that God created the universe and everything in it, you're certainly not alone."

Creative beliefs. I had those sometimes. If I could write a mythology, the reality of the world for myself, it would involve me, Nell, a bedroom, and forever after.

"It's late, Mom. Nell's tired, if the inquisition is over."

"Oh, of course you must be exhausted, dear," she said. "She'll be staying in the smaller guest room, Jeremy. Everyone else will be arriving tomorrow, along with all the kids. Do you like kids, Nell?"

She nodded. "I do, but I haven't been around them much."

"Will you want a big family someday? You know, Jeremy is an uncle fourteen times over."

"Mom!" I said. "It's late, do you mind?"

I led Nell down the hall to the guest room after the awkward leave-takings and good nights.

"Fourteen?" Nell whispered. "You have fourteen nieces and nephews?"

"My brothers and sisters are all breeders. Lots of kids."

"How many brothers and sisters do you have?"

"Five. Two sisters, three brothers."

"Wow."

It seemed strange that she didn't know things about me like how many siblings I had. Why had I told her so little about myself? Why did I know so little about her? I thought on the flight back to Portugal I would ask her hundreds of questions. I wanted to know it all.

"Let me guess." She smiled. "You're the baby of the family."

I slapped her ass. "Why do you say that? Because I'm so immature and self-involved? Actually I was one of the ones in the middle. What about you?"

"I have a big family too. But they're all fucked up."

"You'll find everyone in my family is perfect," I said. "Except me."

"Why did you say that about the Bible? You made me feel totally stupid."

"Well, that's what you believe. We talked about it a long time one night."

"Still, if your parents believe in the Bible, why go out of your way to rub my opinions in their faces?"

"Why hide who you are, just to keep some strangers happy?"

"They're not strangers. They're your parents. Anyway, follow your own advice. Why hide who you are?"

"What do you mean?"

"Why not tell them what I am to you, if you're so against hiding the truth?"

"Because some truths they just couldn't handle."

"Because you only reveal the truths that make *me* look bad, not *you*."

I sighed and glared at her. "It's Christmas Eve tomorrow. Why don't you try to summon up some small inkling of holiday spirit and stop acting like such a bitch?"

She rolled her eyes and started into the bedroom. I stopped her for one long, deep, passionate kiss to replace the sex I couldn't have that I so desperately wanted. I could have tried for a quickie, I suppose, but something about being in my parents' house ruined me for sex.

Later, in my own childhood room, I pulled the box out of my jacket and looked at the ring. She would love it. Girls loved rings, didn't they? This one was big but not too outrageous, a brilliant cut, a rare and exceptionally pure diamond. Just like her.

* * * * *

In the morning the parade of arrivals started. By noon the house was crawling with my annoying siblings and their hyperactive kids. Nell was a champ. No one played the innocent, adoring girlfriend better than her. I loved to watch her and picture her as only I knew her. Dressed in corsets or garters, bound, clamped, tortured, fucked, and in the throes of an orgasm. None of my vanilla siblings could ever understand. None of them would ever have what Nell gave me. I watched her mingle with the other women, all wives and mothers. Somehow she fit in.

Well, I suppose she was a woman after all. She had the genes to be a wife and mother. She hadn't been born a sex toy, and she certainly wouldn't die a sex toy. Someday she would become something more. A student, a mythology expert. A girlfriend, a real one. A wife. She would be somebody's wife someday, wouldn't she? She was almost thirty. She would want to settle down soon.

She held the children and interacted with them differently than I did. Instead of looking at them as nuisances or oddities, she treated them like little people. It was very entertaining to watch. And thought-provoking. When she quieted the colicky baby no one else could quiet, I caught myself wondering what a baby of ours might look like.

Anyway, it didn't matter. She wasn't cut out for the movie-star life, and I wasn't settling down into marriage and parenthood anytime soon.

"Jeremy, Nell is spectacular." My squeaky-clean brother-in-law Ed sidled up to me. "She's great with the babies too," he added, poking me in the side and nearly getting punched in the face for it.

She's great in a lot of ways you would never understand. I was absolutely certain Ed fucked my sister missionary-style every time, if they even had sex anymore after three kids.

"She is great," I agreed, moving out of poking range.

"How long have you been together?"

"Long enough. In my line of work, even a month or two is a golden anniversary."

Ed looked at me with pity. I wanted to punch him again.

"Well, don't let this one get away like the other ones."

I was hard-pressed not to snort at the idea of the other ones "getting away." If he only knew. If all of them only knew, I'd be driven out of the house into the cold and thrown off the side of the mountain. Nell too.

By nightfall, the same conversation had been repeated twenty times, including at least four times by my mother. *This one's a keeper. She's so great. Don't let her get away.*

I turned the ring around and around in my pocket. I waited until the end of Mom's interminable Christmas Eve dinner, then stood, pretending I didn't hear my mother's small gasp of joy.

The value of family, the magic of love, the blessing of finding the one you're meant to be with, blah-blah-blah... I looked around the table at the smiling faces of my mother and father, my many brothers and sisters and their husbands and wives. I went on and on in the way someone who's done countless press junkets and interviews learns to do, and it sounded good. It sounded like something from a romantic script. Maybe it was from some script I'd read. Whatever. I couldn't repeat it again, because the entire time I was thinking of the ring in my pocket and thinking about giving it to Nell. By the time I went to her and knelt down, everyone knew what was coming—hell, my mother was bawling openly.

Only Nell stared at me in disbelief.

No, not disbelief. Fear, loathing, outrage. *Don't do this. Don't make a mockery of me.*

"Nell," I said quietly. "I want you to wear my ring."

I emphasized the words *I want* and purposely declined to ask, *Will you marry me?* I shoved the ring on her finger before she could pull her hand away.

* * * * *

We left soon after. I used work as an excuse and paid an extra twenty-five hundred dollars to fly us out of Charlotte on Christmas Eve.

"It's just a ring," I said in the car on the way to the airport. "It's just for—"

"For show. I know. It was a wonderful performance. I just wish you had let me in on it in advance."

"Well, these kinds of things are better when they're a surprise."

"These kinds of things? You mean fake engagements?" She crossed her arms over her chest. She was so irresistible when she was pissed off. "You know, this is like that time you blindsided me with that fucking contract. You're such a sick, sadistic bastard."

"It's supposed to ward off the stupid stalker. Don't flip out. You overreact about everything. You'd think by now you would be able to take this stuff in stride."

She didn't answer, and the silent treatment continued all the way across the Atlantic to the layover in London, where we were swarmed by paparazzi begging to see the ring.

Are you engaged? Show us your sparkler, Nell! When's the wedding?

I sheltered her from the pushing and shoving as best I could.

In our remote little villa, we'd started to let our guard down. The paparazzi hadn't been around very much, but the attention would be ten times worse now that this "engagement" was out. My stupid-ass family. Of course they would have called everyone they knew the instant we left. My mother had probably called in an announcement to the Charlotte newspaper when she'd gotten up to bring the coffee and cake.

Of course I'd known people would find out eventually, but this was a really, really bad time to be battered by the paps. I thought about the end of January, returning to L.A. If Nell stayed with me, which seemed very doubtful at this point, life in the spotlight would get very hard for us both. I had the awards season coming up shortly, then the inevitable premieres and appearances to promote this film and another one being released shortly afterward.

God, what was I thinking, giving her a ring? As if she would stay, as if she would put up with that badgering and picture taking for the rest of her life only for me. I grew more and more agitated, torn between ripping it off her finger and gazing at it mesmerized, imagining what might be. She was engaged to me now, and everyone would know it by the time we reached Portugal. It would be in the morning tabloids, on the covers probably.

But none of these troubling and complicated thoughts deterred me from the desperate feeling of needing to be alone with her. I needed to take her, to fuck her. I let her fume and pout beside me, her monosyllabic answers to my questions arousing in their own way. Foreplay. I had no doubt we would exchange some heated words eventually, when it was just her and me and we could openly say what needed to be said. I think that was the whole reason for this middle-of-the-night marathon trip back to the villa. We needed to be alone, truly alone. Actually we needed to be naked.

"I'm going to fuck you when we get there," I whispered to her somewhere between London and Lisbon. "I'm going to tie you up and whip you really, really hard."

She feigned sleep, but I saw the dark circles under her eyes tense a little.

"Pretending you don't hear me doesn't mean it isn't so," I said. "Just so you know."

* * * * *

We arrived at the villa late Christmas Day, jet-lagged and grouchy. We'd both slept almost the entire way across the Atlantic, so we were an unfortunate combination of wide awake and pissed off.

"Go get undressed," I said as soon as we dropped our bags, "and put on something really sleazy."

"Right now? This instant?"

"Don't try me, Nell. Just do what I say."

"I don't have anything sleazy. You don't like sleazy lingerie, remember?"

I took her arm and frowned down at her. "You don't have anything sleazy? Not one thing? You should, for when I feel like treating you like a fucking whore. Go get something on. Now."

She stomped off to her room and returned a few minutes later in a black push-up bra and garter belt with lace-top stockings. Very nice. Slutty.

Black, for mourning. The ring flashed against the dark lace and ribbons, an incongruous sparkle of light.

"Kneel down here." I pointed to a spot in front of the fireplace and then began to build a fire to chase away the cold.

"Why doesn't Kyle join us anymore?" she asked after a while. "I mean, it's been so long."

I looked at her. She was kneeling where I told her to kneel, but she didn't look very submissive.

"Kyle's in L.A. until tomorrow."

"I know. I'm just asking why, in general, he doesn't join us anymore for sex. I used to enjoy getting fucked by him every once in a while."

I laughed. "You're a terrible liar. Honestly, you suck at it."

"Well, why doesn't he?"

"I don't know." She was purposely trying to annoy me, but I wouldn't take the bait. "Maybe because that's not what I want."

"Are we going to sleep with Jessamine and Mason again?"

"Just shut up, Nell." I stacked the small wood near the bottom and lit a match. The fire started slowly, a small flame igniting tinder, then the smaller branches, then up to lick at the larger logs.

"Do you love me, Jeremy?" She asked quietly, but she might as well have screamed it.

I spun on her. "Tell me your name, you little slut, and then I'll tell you if I love you."

"No. I'm never telling you that. You can't have that, not on top of everything else."

I stared down at her, kneeling, her white breasts heaving above the scanty push-up bra, her hands in little fists at her sides.

"What do you ever let me have, Nell, besides your body? Why would I love you?"

"Why did you give me this stupid ring if you don't love me?"

"I told you why."

"I don't believe you."

"You think I love you?" I turned back to the fire, watching the flames rise higher. "Well, I don't. I pay you a lot of money so I don't have to love you, and you don't have to love me."

"I love you," she said.

I turned and glared at her. "You do not."

"I'm very sure I do, even though I wish I didn't. I really wish with all my heart that I didn't love you."

"You don't. This is just more submission, more kneeling, more offering, more 'I'm yours.' You can say it beautifully, but I don't believe any of it, not a word. I never have. I never will. I don't believe you!"

"I don't believe *you*!" Her gaze locked on mine. "I don't believe you still won't admit you feel something for me! I'm wearing a ring, Jeremy. A ring you bought and gave to me in front of your whole family."

"So what? Do you think that means I love you? It just means…it means—"

"What? What does it mean? Tell me!"

"I don't—Jesus. It—maybe it means that I want to hold you here. That I don't want you to go away. Not yet."

"You don't need a ring to do that. I've stayed long past the time I should stay, and you know why!"

"I do know why. You *need* to stay. You're sticking around to get your fucking college education, but the joke's on you. I would have paid for it anyway. If you'd left me the first week, I would have paid for it. The first day, if you'd left me. You stupid little whore. So go pack up your bags if you want to, if you really want to leave—"

"I don't want to leave!"

"They all leave!" I shouted.

"I'm yours! I'm yours. I have been since the first night we played. You know I am! It's not your stupid contract that holds me here."

"'I'm yours' doesn't mean 'I love you'!"

"How would you know that, Jeremy Gray? You don't know anything about love. You wouldn't know love if it came up and spit in your face. You with your fake life and your fake job and your fake girlfriends and your fake contracts and your fake control. You aren't in control of me. And you sure as hell aren't in control of yourself, of how you feel."

"Oh really? I can be in control, you little fuck," I said, advancing on her. "I'll show you control. I can control you just fine!"

It was a really bad time to play with her, a *really* bad time. A horribly bad time to play with her, but I pushed her down and pulled her arms hard behind her back. I bound her with the only thing I had, the belt I wore around my waist, and it made a sloppy restraint, but I had to tie her up. I looked down at the ring on her finger, the ring she didn't even want. The stupid ring.

I was the stupid one. Why on earth had I ever imagined she would understand, that she would be able to accept it for what it was? Why did everything have to mean *love, commitment, honesty*, whatever it was she wanted?

I fucked her, grappling with her while she fought me. She was angry, but she was wet for me. Her slim torso struggled and tensed below me. There was a beautiful quality to the undulations of muscles straining across her back, but only because the belt kept her bound. Otherwise she would have been in motion, coming at me. Not as beautiful, I thought. Still, part of me was tempted to release her just to see how hard she'd fight.

She'd never fought me before, at least not like this. It was a novel feeling. It made me feel even more powerful, more dominant than I usually did. I fucked her long and hard, enjoying my mastery of her. Her struggling inflamed me so much that when my orgasm came it was painfully intense. The waves of pleasure spread out like fire up into my chest and down through my balls and thighs. I shuddered and shook it off, pulled out of her. I looked down at her still trembling with indignation beneath me. I stood and went for the cane. I came back and dropped it in front of her face.

"Are you really mine? I want to hear it, you little fuck. *I'm yours*. Say it to me."

"I'm yours." She tried to sound strong, but her voice was shaking, and it sounded thick with unshed tears. I remembered that same tremulous voice, scared and nervous, at a meeting ages ago. *I know my job is to accept pain, and I do, but it's not as easy for me as, perhaps, some submissives who really enjoy pain. Pain is different for me.*

"You're really mine? This is what I want, then. I want to hurt you!"

"Why?" she whispered.

I shook my head. "I don't know why. I don't know." I picked up the cane.

She had safe words she could use, and I wanted her to use them. I wanted her to realize that she wasn't really mine. That she was only with me because she had to be, just as I was with her.

I made her cry with the cane, I made her beg, but she never said the words.

Please, Master.

Just say them, Nell. Just say them.

But she didn't say them, although I really wish she had.

Chapter Seventeen:
The Faithful One

He dropped the cane and stalked away. God, he was so angry. My ass ached from the horrible sting, my legs shook, tears bathed my face, but I could still remember the hot pleasure of his cock fucking me hard.

Just use me. Please. Whatever. I'm so sorry for what I said. Please fuck me again and hold me close and forgive me.

I was so, so sorry. I'd ruined everything now. Why hadn't I shut my mouth and worn his stupid ring while he figured out where the hell his head was? This was all so horribly complicated. I understood now. I understood completely why he avoided real relationships. It was too devastating when they went wrong. Now I understood Jeremy's need to cloak himself in contracts and impersonal distance.

Jeremy. Where was he?

I moaned softly. He came back in the room, and I braced. Another implement? A torturous toy? Rough anal sex?

I heard a thud and turned my face to the fire to see my book of Babylonian myths surrounded in a puff of red-hot embers flying up and around it like fireworks. My vision blurred as the smoke billowed and the acrid smell filled my nose. I was confused for a moment. Why was my Babylonian book burning? Another book landed in the fireplace, and another, the flames leaping higher, consuming my treasured mythology books as fuel, books I had collected and loved over a lifetime.

And I watched with a strange, confused detachment as every one fell into the fire. *The Kalevela, The Dictionary of Celtic Myths, The Odyssey, Native*

American Sacred Texts, Colarusso's *Nart Sagas from the Caucasus*, which had cost me almost a hundred bucks.

I started to cry.

"That one is so rare, Jeremy. It's so hard to find!"

He ignored me, and he didn't stop until every book was burning. I'd brought all of them, all the ones I owned. They were all gone now.

"Why did you do that?"

"Because you're not here for your college education, are you? That's what you claimed. Or were you lying?"

Tears stung my eyes. There was a hollow ache coiled hard in my stomach. A stubborn wish not to believe it. He looked back at me, no hint of remorse in his gaze.

"Those were my books. They had nothing to do with college. I liked to read them!"

"And I like to make you cry. You're my submissive, and if I want to get a hard-on from burning your fucking books, I will!"

He stormed away, then back again. I waited, still bent over, still restrained, still vulnerable, but there was nothing he could do to hurt me anymore, so I just waited, crying softly, for whatever came.

"Tell me your name."

"No," I sobbed. "If you cared at all about me, you would have figured it out by now. I'll never tell you my name. Not now!"

He leaned over me, breathing hard as he roughly released my hands. Then, without a word, he stormed into his room and slammed the door.

But me, I stayed awake a long time watching my books turn to black paper, then ashes, then dust.

* * * * *

It stormed hard that night, appropriately. I lay awake a long time listening to the rain beat on the rooftop. I also strained to hear any sign at all that Jeremy was still up. I wanted him to come to me, I wanted him to kneel by the bed and take me in his arms and whisper, *I'm sorry, I'm sorry*. I would have whispered back, *I'm so sorry too*.

But he didn't, and I didn't dare creep to his bedside, for fear of being sent away. So that was my Christmas: a fake ring on a North Carolina mountain, a red-eye flight back to Lisbon, and my books thrown on a fire while I knelt with my head on the floor and my ass aching from the cane. Santa wouldn't be coming for us, not this year. And next year, next Christmas, I'd be on my own, I was sure.

I finally cried myself to sleep thinking of my mother, thinking of my childhood Christmases, which hadn't been great, but at least my mother had tried. Jeremy hadn't gotten me anything besides the ring I still wore, for some reason, on my left hand. Me, I had bought him a tie the exact color of his eyes with Kyle's help, a paltry little gift. It was still buried in my suitcase and would probably remain there. Why give it to him? He owned a hundred designer ties. What do you get for the man who has everything and all the money in the world?

Submission. Obedience. Comfort. That was what he wanted, what he paid me for, but I hadn't given him that.

When I woke the next morning, I felt even more tired than I'd felt the night before. My eyes were red and raw from crying, and my muscles protested as I eased myself from the bed and took my robe from the back of the chair. I stared at the desk, at the back wall where all my books had been neatly stacked. Gone. They were gone forever now.

And I could buy them again, sure, but those books had been broken-in, loved, familiar. They had absorbed my joy, my pain. Some had been given to me by teachers or good friends. One had been inscribed by the author.

I should have been furious. I should have stood up and fought back until he stopped what he was doing. I should have insisted he stop. I could have used a safe word. I should have.

It hadn't even crossed my mind.

I listened hard for the sound of Jeremy in the quiet morning, but I didn't hear anything. I wrapped my robe more tightly around myself and opened the bedroom door. Jeremy was gone, but Kyle was sitting at the table. His serious expression made my throat go dry.

"Jeremy said if you want to go, I'm supposed to help you."

I leaned against the door frame, hugging myself.

"Go? Where?"

"Leave. Go home. Back to L.A."

I stood still, thinking about those words. *Go home.* I could be gone before he returned. I could drop his ring by his bedside and never have to face him again.

"Does he want me to go?"

Kyle frowned and crossed his arms over his chest. "What happened last night? What did he do to you?"

"He didn't tell you?"

"No."

"He burned all my books."

"He did what?"

"He burned them. He threw them in the fire. Even my Colarusso."

"What the hell? Why?"

"I don't know! I don't know what to do. What does he want? Does he want me to go?"

Kyle came to me and hugged me, led me to the couch and held me close while I cried like a baby into his chest for almost half an hour. In between my incoherent sobs and whimpers, he rubbed my back. "Okay, it's okay…"

When I finally calmed down, he stared at the fireplace and narrowed his eyes. "I don't get it. Why your books? What did he say?"

"He said he wanted to hurt me. It was because of the ring, because I said it was stupid. He gave me a ring."

"I heard." Kyle pursed his lips. "Show it to me."

I held out my hand like there was a poisonous spider perched on my ring finger, and he took it as if there were. He looked down at the ring a long time, then said under his breath, "What the holy fuck is going on? What did he say about it? What did he say when he gave you this?"

"I don't know. Nothing. He said it's to ward off the stalker."

Kyle frowned. "Ward her off? Piss her off, more likely. What the fuck? I don't know, Nell. I just don't know." He dropped my hand and sighed. "What else did he say last night? Why would he burn your books? I thought he was supposed to pay for your college."

I sniffled. "Maybe he isn't anymore. I told him…I told him I loved him. It made him furious."

He looked down at me with a look I couldn't decipher. Surprise, disappointment, something more. "Do you love him?" he asked. "Really?"

"Yes. I wish I didn't. He doesn't love me."

Kyle chuckled, a soft exhalation of breath. "I don't think he knows if he loves you or not. I don't think he has a clue what he really feels."

I looked up at Kyle. I let all our past fights and rivalry fall away. "Help me understand what he wants. Please help me figure this out!"

He looked back at me hard but didn't answer. Instead he said, "I know your real name. We all keep our secrets. Sometimes it's better that way, you know?" He handed me another tissue and headed for the kitchen. "Is ten in the morning too early for a glass of wine?"

We drank wine for a while and talked about things that felt safe. By the time he left to run some errands I was feeling better, but I still dreaded facing Jeremy when he came home.

I walked around the garden outside and tried to imprint the beauty and quiet of the surrounding woods on my mind. Serenity. Why couldn't I find it?

When he finally got home, I was hiding in the bedroom. I hoped to hear him open the refrigerator for a beer, turn on the TV to watch some show.

But he didn't. He came right to my room and stood in the door. I was sitting in the dark, waiting to hear those three awful words. *You're still here?*

But he didn't say anything for a long while, just stood and looked at me while I looked back at him. Finally he came in and tossed a book beside me on the bed.

"Penelope," he said quietly. "The faithful one."

I glanced down at the book, knowing what I'd see. Homer's *Odyssey*. "Did Kyle tell you?"

"Yes. And you're right. I should have figured it out long ago. I would have, if I hadn't been so caught up in myself."

I bit my lip. I refused to cry. I had cried enough tears over him. He stood against the wall, his face betraying nothing as I leafed absently through the pages. It was a beautiful edition in English and Greek.

"Dutiful, virtuous, prudent Penelope," he said. "She waited twenty years for her husband to come home. She fended off one hundred and six suitors."

"One hundred and eight." I don't know why I corrected him, why I sounded so surly. It was a thoughtful gift, and an apology, I was sure. His apologies were never the typical *I'm sorry*, but I understood them when they came. And now he knew my real name. I should have felt happy. I looked down at the embossed cover, ran my fingers across the intricate design. For a moment I let myself imagine Jeremy picking it out for me, although I knew Kyle would have done it. "Did you read this book?"

"No. I Wiki'd it." He paused. "Why didn't you leave today?"

"I don't know. I guess because I'm the faithful one."

He frowned. "Did you eat dinner yet?"

I shook my head.

"Come on." He beckoned me out of bed and out into the main room. We crossed into the kitchen and began to pick through what was there, which wasn't much.

"There's some chicken," I said. "Lots of fruit."

"There are eggs," mumbled Jeremy. "Maybe omelets? French toast?"

I picked up an apple and washed it, then looked in the drawer for a knife. He got out the eggs and put them on the counter, but then he stopped and looked down at the one in his hand, rolling it across his palm. I turned to reach for a bowl and stopped when I felt his hands around my neck.

Not hard. Not like he was choking me or trying to scare me. Just like he wanted to hold my neck in his hands. His careful grasp claimed possession. I stood still and accepted it. *You're mine.* I turned to him, and the tears finally came. He kissed me hard, and I let myself be taken. I reveled in the sensation of his tongue ravaging my mouth. I clung to his solid bulk, and his hard abs felt like a rock wall against my chest.

When his lips left mine, he ran his tongue across each tearful cheek. His fingers loosened, then tightened around my windpipe again. "You're right," he said. "The ring is stupid. I want to put a fucking collar on you. I never understood until now, your collar thing, but now I understand." His thumb caressed my pulse, then moved up under my jaw, across my throat. He tilted my head back and breathed down the side of my neck. "I want you to draw breath because I allow it. I want to own you inside and out."

"You love me," I whispered, the apple still clutched in one hand, the knife in the other.

"Yes, goddamn it. Maybe. I might." He sighed. "Fine, I probably do."

I laughed softly through tears. "You love me. I knew all along that you did."

"Um, Nell. Put down the knife." He pried it from my hand and laid it on the counter. "Take off your clothes."

"Yes, Jeremy."

We did it there on the kitchen floor. He made me kneel and then pushed me forward from the waist. He positioned himself behind me and grasped my hips in his rough hands. I clenched my pussy in anticipation, and he slid inside without preliminaries. "I want you. You're mine."

"Yes," I said. "I'm yours."

He bit my neck, and I pushed back against him, wanting him closer, deeper. He claimed my pussy with long, urgent strokes. His hands caressed me, running up and down my back before closing around my shoulders. Again and again they returned to my neck. He grasped it, brushed his nails down it from beneath my jaw down to my nape. Each time he released it, I would moan low in my throat, wanting him to encircle it again.

I heard Kyle come home in the middle, heard a mumbled "oh, hi," as he bypassed the kitchen and went into his room. Jeremy reached down to cup my pussy. He squeezed and growled in my ear. "You're mine." I bucked against his fingers. He swirled them around my clit, pinching it, flicking it as it swelled to life. He was coarse and insatiable, the same Jeremy I always knew, only there was a difference now.

He loved me.

He admitted it. He loved me, loved me as much as I loved him.

"Jeremy," I cried. I reached back for him, reached for his hand.

He gripped it and wrapped his arms over mine. He held me clutched to him so tightly that for one strange moment I felt we were not two but one. I was so overcome that I collapsed onto my front, and he followed. As I fell, I skimmed my head on the cabinet. We both heard the dull thud. He hissed and I giggled, but I didn't feel it.

He put one hand over my head where I'd bumped it and fucked me against the floor. My pelvis got hotter and tighter. I was rocked by a wave of pleasure so deep I felt I was falling. My clit contacted the cold tile. I pressed it into the smooth, slick surface, driven on by his cock filling my walls, and I came hard with a cry. When I felt his own organ start to pulsate inside me, I pulled his hand down from my bumped head and kissed his palm over and over until he told me to stop.

Later we sat side by side on the couch and watched the fire, the same fire I'd watched with tears in my eyes the night before. Now I watched it overcome with happiness, wrapped in Jeremy's arms.

"God," he said. "I'm so sorry about your books. I'll find them all again for you. I'll set Kyle on it. Give me a list."

"I'll subsist on *The Odyssey* for now."

"Okay, Penelope."

I laughed. "I hate that name."

"I like it. I'm going to use it all the time." He nuzzled me. "It suits you, faithful one."

"I don't know why I kept it from you for so long."

"Probably the same reason I couldn't admit that I loved you, even when I gave you a ring."

I couldn't help giggling. "You asked me to marry you before you could even admit how you felt about me."

"I know. I'm a mess. Believe me, I know."

Our laughter died down, and Jeremy took a sip of his beer. "Poor Kyle."

"I know, having to track down all those books. The Colarusso took me forever to find."

"No, not the books. He has the most pathetic crush on you. How did he take it, when you showed him the ring?"

I laughed again. "What are you drinking? He does not have a crush on me."

"He certainly does. He has for ages. But he's too vanilla for you, in case you're thinking about leaving me for him."

"If I didn't leave you after you burned all my favorite books, I don't see myself leaving you for Kyle. He's too young for me anyway."

"He's a good guy, though," said Jeremy. "Don't rub it in. Don't tell him I told you how he feels."

"I won't." Those glances at Jeremy I'd misunderstood as jealousy *had* been jealousy, I suppose—jealousy over me. How clueless I'd been. *I know your real name. We all keep our secrets. Sometimes it's better that way, you know?*

"So that's why you stopped inviting him to have sex with us?"

"Yeah. In a way. I'll still like watching you with other people, though."

"You'll still share me, even after we're married?"

He frowned and took another drink. "Yeah, if we get married."

I was quiet a moment to see if he'd elaborate on that comment, but he didn't. "So...you said *if* we get married, but maybe we won't?"

"I don't know, Nell. I just... I don't know. Can't it be enough for now that I told you I love you?"

"Yes, and you gave me a ring!"

"Jesus, you're nuts about that ring. What, you have some crazy, girlish fantasies about a dream wedding? A train seventeen feet long, a big-ass wedding cake, and two thousand guests and roomfuls of flowers—"

"I know you sometimes forget that I am actually a *girl*, and that you actually gave me an *engagement ring* and told me you loved me. In that case, we do often begin to plan our weddings."

"Nell, don't flip out on me again."

I pulled away from him. "Why don't we pretend we're married? We're great at pretend. We've had tons of practice."

"We aren't vanilla people, either one of us. Why do we have to get all vanilla now and plan some stupid Hollywood wedding?"

"Ooh! I know, we can throw a pretend wedding and invite the paparazzi. You can have Martin write up a contract first. *The employee agrees to wear a white dress even though she's been fucked more times by the groom in every orifice than any sane person would believe.*"

"Nell—"

"*The employee agrees to pretend to be married for better or worse, for richer or poorer, in sickness and in health, for as long as this contract is in effect—*"

"Nell! Enough. Listen, there are things going on you don't understand. I've told you how I feel. You've told me how you feel. Now I want you to shut the fuck up and go back to the way you used to be. My submissive little whore. God, don't you see? I don't want anything to change between us. I liked things the way they were."

He pulled me back to him, but I kept my arms crossed over my chest. We stared into the fire, the romantic flame between us extinguished. I thought to myself: *This man does not know how to love. This man does not know how to have a relationship that's not outlined in black and white and signed and dated at the bottom.*

And this was the man I loved.

* * * * *

I didn't sleep well that night, my mind too full of frustrating questions. I tossed and turned until Jeremy threatened to make me leave the room. I made a groggy attempt to get up with him in the morning, but he took one look at me and ordered me to stay in bed and sleep. I sunk back under the covers gladly, not even hearing when he and Kyle left for the set.

I did fall back to sleep, but it was just as restive. An amalgamation of burning books, tightening collars, and a massive wedding ring that kept bumping me on the head. *Bang, bang, bang.* I put my hand up to shield myself from the irritating wedding bling, but it came at me again. *Bang, bang, bang.*

My eyes popped open. *Bang, bang, bang!* The banging wasn't a dream. Someone was pounding on the door, and I was alone. I was also completely stark naked in bed.

I jumped up and ran to the closet, heart thumping. I threw on clothes and peeked out the bedroom door into the main room. Again someone banged on the door, even louder this time. I picked up my cell phone from the table and fled back into the bedroom. I locked the door and dialed Kyle.

"What is it?" He was always impatient when I called.

"Someone's at the door. They keep knocking. They're pounding now."

"Who is it? What do they look like?" The alarm in his voice made my heart jump into a shaky rhythm again.

"I don't know. I'm afraid to go look. I'm in the bedroom."

"Don't answer the door. I'm coming right now."

He hung up, and a second later a fist pounded on my window. I screamed, then clamped my mouth shut. Now whoever it was knew I was here. An insistent male voice yelled in broken English. "Hello? Hello? Nell Ash-ton? Please to answer door! I have question, to ask for you!"

The urgency in his voice terrified me. I flattened myself against the wall. The blinds were closed, but I could see his shadow, and I was afraid he could see me through the cracks.

"Miss Ash-ton? Open please. I meet you. Very important to speak me!"

I hugged myself. Police? Landlord? Stalker? Some crazy murderer loose in the woods? Whoever it was, he knew my name and he knew I was here.

The pounding went on until I couldn't stand it. I made sure the chain was on, then cracked the door.

"Please, go away!"

"Miss Ash-ton! I have only few questions."

"Get away from the door! Leave her alone!" Jeremy's voice boomed. Kyle and Jeremy were stalking across the driveway.

"I want ask only of wedding, en-gage-ment ring—"

"That is none of your motherfucking business. Turn that off!" He ripped the video camera out of the pap's hand and gave it to Kyle, who calmly started pushing buttons.

The man protested, although in the face of Jeremy and Kyle's fury—and muscles—he did it under his breath.

"You're trespassing on private property," Jeremy said. "And you've terrified my girlfriend."

"Your fiancée, no?" the pap asked.

"Whatever the fuck she is, it's no fucking business of yours, is it?"

Sirens blared as police vehicles came roaring down the lane. "We'll see him off the property," Kyle said to Jeremy. "Go inside with Nell."

I stood aside, wide-eyed and jittery, to let Jeremy in.

"You okay?" he asked once he came inside the door. He took my face in his hands and brushed his thumbs across my cheeks. "You're so pale. You're shaking. I shouldn't have left you here alone." He pressed his forehead to mine. "I'm sorry."

"It's okay."

"It's not okay. I don't like worrying about whether you're all right."

I looked up at him. There was real relief in his eyes and lingering tension lines around his mouth. He had been scared.

"You thought it was her," I said. "The stalker."

"Nell..."

"You called the police."

"Someone was pounding on the door. You were alone. We didn't want to take any chances."

I looked at the floor. I didn't believe him. I wasn't safe. I would never be safe now that I was with him.

He drew me into his arms and tucked my head under his chin. "I know it's hard, putting up with all this. I promise you, I'll keep you safe. I won't leave you alone again like this. I'll have Kyle stay here with you."

"He's your personal assistant. Don't you need him?"

"For now he's your bodyguard, until I can hire you one of your own."

"A bodyguard? Jeremy!" I pulled away and looked up at him.

"You'll need one at the very least, when we're back in L.A."

The words hovered between us, the unspoken question.

"You will come back to L.A. with me, won't you?"

"I live in L.A.," I reminded him. "I'll go back either way."

The employee shall return to L.A. with her employer and continue to live in a state of constant agitation and confusion about what the true nature of their relationship is.

He let go of me abruptly. "Well. Okay. I have to get back to the set."

Chapter Eighteen:
Love

The paparazzi overran our secluded villa by noon. The sparkly ring on my finger was a top-level news item. It comprised the lead story for hundreds of papers, and they wanted, they *needed*, pictures. They knocked, they cajoled, they pleaded, they begged until the police came and moved them back behind bright orange CAUTION tape, which they walked around as soon as the police left. I wanted to open the door and scream at all of them, *You realize it's all for fucking show! This entire relationship!* It would have felt spectacularly cathartic to do that, but the truth was I didn't know anything more about the nature of our relationship than they did.

No, the only one who seemed to know or understand what our relationship was by this point was Jeremy. He went on as if nothing were wrong, as if there were no blurry lines or unanswered questions between us, or rings of undetermined sentimental worth on my finger. So while the paparazzi grew in number and rudeness, I refrained from screaming anything out to them.

Instead I slumped on the couch and watched as Kyle and another staffer from the set packed everything up. By three we had checked into a high-security hotel in Lisbon. We left a couple of days later for Italy, for another posh hotel in central Rome. By that time I had a new Italian bodyguard, a short, burly, affable man named Arturo, who looked like he could crush a Hummer into a twisted chunk of scrap metal with his bare hands.

Arturo brought some much-needed comic relief to our uptight little family with his broad smile and endless supply of jokes. It didn't seem to matter to him that we didn't understand a word of them. Jeremy was a ball of stress as the end of the shoot neared, and Kyle and I continued to be awkward around each other since Jeremy had outed his crush on me. But Arturo was all goodness and light. He was fun and pure of both heart and soul.

Also, Arturo was in the dark about our true relationship. He assumed Jeremy and I were a typical loving couple, engaged to be married, just not yet choosing a date. Of course, since we didn't speak Italian and he didn't speak English, explaining what confused even us would have been hard.

It should have been a relief that Arturo didn't know, I guess, but I found it grated on me. Jeremy still trumped up his evil little punishments, but now they were carried out in secret, for Arturo's sake. So I'd find myself fidgeting through a day with a toy in my ass or tacks in my bra or a rope knot against my clit, and it was made all the worse because I had to hide it from Arturo.

But when Jeremy returned each night, Arturo left, and then things were comfortingly routine. Kneel in front of the couch, release his cock, suck it, take a break to eat dinner or not, and retire to the bedroom for more cock sucking or ass fucking or getting tied up or bending over for punishment, or whatever Jeremy wanted to do. I still wore his ring and flashed it obediently in public, although we never discussed it privately and certainly never made any plans for a wedding. I finally had to face the fact that it truly was only for show.

At the same time, he still insisted that he loved me. He whispered it in my ear every night when there were no cameras or reporters to convince. He still bought me too much, spent too much money taking me to expensive restaurants, and procured a ridiculous amount of mythology books to replace the ones he'd destroyed. And he still dominated me, as he always had. Lovingly. He had dominated me lovingly from the start.

He was so caring, *so careful*, to give me just a little more pain than I thought I could take, but never, ever too much. He almost always permitted me to find my own pleasure. In fact, his eyes shone with the deepest lust not when he lost himself to orgasm, but when I was moaning in his arms. The way he kissed me, there was no doubt in my mind that he felt love, whatever love meant to Jeremy Gray in his strange, perverse mind.

And yes, of course, I loved him more every day.

* * * * *

In the middle of January we left Italy and Arturo behind to fly to Los Angeles for the Golden Globes. It was to be a short trip, a couple of days before we returned to Greece to finish the shoot. I sat beside Jeremy on the plane and felt, as always, like I was flying blind. What was I to Jeremy? Who was Jeremy to me? My employer? My lover? A friend? Something more? A pretend fiancé, that much was sure. I was staring down at my ring when Jeremy took my hand and leaned close to me.

"Whenever we fly at night, I remember that first flight to Thailand," he said in the darkness of the first-class cabin. "You were so quiet and scared."

"Yes, I was. I barely knew you then."

"I know. That's what was so amazing about it. It was kind of thrilling, knowing how scared you were, and that you were sitting there beside me anyway, flying halfway across the world." He fell silent. I supposed now that thrill was gone.

"Are you getting tired of me?" I asked before I could stop the words.

He scrutinized me. Could he see my insecurity? My fear? He squeezed my hand. "No, I'm not tired of you. Not at all. Why would you think that?"

"What happens when we leave Greece? When your shoot is over?"

"Oh Jesus, Nell. What do you want to happen?"

"I don't know." I cloaked my distress in apathy. I picked at my cuticles, then shrugged. "I guess it's all up to you."

"I thought you wanted to go to school."

I did want to go to school. Now I just want to be with you. I'll sign another contract. I'll do whatever it takes.

"I guess," was all I said out loud. He squeezed my hand again.

"Listen, I want you to be prepared. Things will be wild in L.A. The paparazzi are horrible there. You can't throw a rock without hitting one. You'll need to think about your security. You're not to go anywhere alone. We'll stay in a hotel for added safety. I don't want you at the house."

"The stalker? She's in L.A.?"

"She might be. They can track her movements when she leaves the country, but she can move around the U.S., and we don't really know where she is."

"Have you been tracking her? It's that serious?" His silence unnerved me. "Has she actually left the country looking for you?"

"She was in Thailand, yes," he said finally. "And Portugal for a while. And she's not looking for me, Nell. She's looking for you. I'm not saying that to scare you, just to let you know that you need to be safe. You can't go anywhere alone. You can't run off when you feel like it."

I looked down at the ring, twisting it.

"If I weren't so selfish, I would make you go." He gave me a look so guilty, it was heartbreaking. "If I weren't so selfish, I would have let you go as soon as all this stalker craziness began."

"You can't let one woman change how you live your life," I said.

"But it's not just my life. You're involved too."

"Am I?"

He scowled and shifted beside me. "We won't have much time in L.A., but I'll find time to beat your little ass if you piss me off enough."

And time did fly. As soon as we arrived at the hotel, Jeremy ran off to do some interviews or something while Kyle let in a stylist from the studio with a rack full of designer dresses and three suitcases of makeup, jewelry, and fake hair. He tried out "looks" on me, some of which made me want to laugh, some of which made me want to cry. Kyle's smirk was in overdrive as Leonard remade me again and again. At Leonard's urging, I finally decided on an ivory dress that was simple yet elegant, embellished with rhinestones and pearls.

Jeremy got in late from his movie-star activities and woke me from a sound sleep to turn me over his knee. I chalked the brief but painful spanking up to either stress or frustration. It hurt, but I figured it was my job to help him unwind, and I felt inordinately pleased with my work when he fell into a deep sleep minutes afterward. He still woke up to fuck me at some point during the night.

He was gone again in the morning when Leonard arrived, bright and cheery, to give me the spa treatment from head to toe. It was tricky to hide the bruises from the spanking when he was dressing me, but I did my best. If he noticed them, he was circumspect about it. I'm sure a studio stylist like him had seen it all.

"So lovely," he said when I was dressed and ready to go. "All that's missing is your smile."

I faked a smile for him that hurt my cheekbones. Kyle arrived just as Leonard was preparing to leave with his many suitcases full of stuff.

"God," Kyle said as he closed the door behind the stylist. "Just…wow. Look at you. God."

"What?"

"Look in the mirror." He led me over to the bathroom, and I looked in the mirror at the elegant stranger standing there. Ivory gown, sparkling diamond earrings and choker, perfectly made-up face.

"It doesn't look like me," I said, frowning.

"Maybe. But it's still pretty," Kyle said. "Come on."

He drove me to the Golden Globes preparty. Jeremy met me inside the door, acting the solicitous fiancé in love. I smiled back and accepted his awkward kiss for the photographers. He left me alone then and went off to chat with some of the many other actors and luminaries crowding the room. For God's sake, what the hell was I doing here? I hid in the bathroom as long as I could, then slunk around behind the coatroom, then drifted over by the stairs before Jeremy came to find me.

"What the hell are you doing?"

I shrugged.

"I want you to stay where I can see you—"

"Jeremy! Nell!"

I turned from Jeremy and found myself clasped to Jessamine Jackson's bountiful breasts. She let go of me and hugged Jeremy. Mason winked at me from behind her back.

"We're sitting together. I arranged it! Nell, you look awful." Jessamine frowned. "For God's sake, have a drink. You should be shit-faced by this point. Everyone else is."

I blinked. "It's only four o'clock."

They all laughed like I was hilarious, and Mason squeezed my hand. "It's so good to see you again, Nell." I didn't miss his subtle glance in Jeremy's direction, or the fact that Jessamine still had her hands on Jeremy, practically squeezing his ass.

"Four o'clock," said Jeremy, looking at his watch. "Ready to go?"

The red carpet was terrifying. It was the same yelling and persistent camera flashing as the paparazzi on the street, only now we had to actually cooperate with them. Even worse, there were bleachers and crowds of yelling fans everywhere I looked.

She could be anywhere.

I looked down at my rhinestone-encrusted bodice and thought about the Romanov girls, who couldn't be killed because the bullets kept bouncing off the diamonds hidden under their dresses. But they'd been killed eventually. Their murderers found a way.

"What's wrong?" asked Jeremy, lifting my chin.

"I feel like I'm going to die." I don't know why I said that. He pursed his lips and held my elbow hard.

"Just look happy," he said.

My face grew sore and tired from smiling as Jeremy dragged me here and there. I stood and posed like a mannequin beside him with his arm around my waist. Kyle steered us from interview to interview, engineering everything with subtle nods and gentle shoves. I declined to answer any questions, made Jeremy jump in and make stuff up whenever they asked about the ring. It was his lie. Let him chat to the reporters about it. I stared into space while I showed the ring off.

Going into the ballroom for the awards broadcast was a huge relief after the scary press of fans and photographers outside. The event was supposed to be a dinner, but everyone just socialized and drank. The Hollywood diet. I was long since desensitized to rubbing shoulders with the stars, so I didn't gawk very much, but I listened in to the conversations around our table and to the awards presentations, once they began. I felt Mason and Jessamine looking at me.

No. Not tonight.

I wasn't up for it. I hoped it wasn't something Jeremy would want. After Jeremy and Jessamine did their presenting duties and Mason picked up yet another Best Actor award, I leaned over to Jeremy and told him I was tired.

"It's not even nine o'clock," he said. "And there are more parties after this."

"Do I have to go?"

He frowned and looked away from me. "Yes, you do. If you like, you can go back to the hotel awhile and rest. But it's going to be a long night," he said, glancing over at Jessamine and Mason.

I got the hint.

He put me in a car outside the theater. "I'll tell Kyle to meet you there. But you'll only have an hour or two."

"Okay." I slid across to hunch against the other side. I wanted to curl up into a ball, but my dress was already wrinkled enough. I watched the bustle of Beverly Hills as we crawled through downtown, through brightly lit streets with all the beautiful people walking around. The hotel was nearby, and I was relieved to get upstairs to the room and collapse on the couch. A few moments later, there was a knock on the door and I stood up to let Kyle in.

But it wasn't Kyle.

The scowling woman in the doorway shoved a gun against my forehead and pushed me backward into the room.

"Lock the fucking door," she said, pressing the gun to my temple now. I hadn't ever in my life had a gun pressed to my head. I had never felt anything that felt so close to cold, hard death.

"It…it locks automatically," I stammered.

"The chain, you little bitch. No one's coming in until I tell you the things I need to say."

I turned to her. She was in her forties, heavyset, with nondescript eyes and drab, graying blonde hair. She wore a floor-length gown that looked like a bridesmaid's dress. She took in my dress with a malevolent chuckle.

"I don't know what my husband sees in a skinny, ugly bitch like you. That hair, ugh. You can tell it's fake, that awful red."

I shied away as she reached for a handful of my hair and pulled it. I clenched my teeth and swallowed a yelp of pain. I stared at the gun clutched in her other hand and felt nausea twist in my stomach. *A gun.* This was really happening. My mind raced through scenarios and outcomes, and none of them were good. Her finger was on the trigger, and it was shaking. *Talk to her.*

"I didn't—I had no idea Jeremy was married, I swear," I said. "I'll…I'll just go. I'll get my things. I'll leave him alone. I don't want to break up anybody's home."

"Go?" She laughed in a terrible voice. "You wish!" She shoved me away, wrenching my hair. I stumbled, and for a sickening moment the edge of my vision turned black. *Jeremy, I need you now. Help me.* I righted myself and turned to her. The gun was still trained on me, with both hands now. She gestured with a jerk of the weapon. "Sit down. Over on the couch. There's only one way you're going to go, and it's going to be in a way that's going to make it so you can't come sneaking back. Jeremy's always had a thing for the young ones. I love him, but he's not been the most faithful husband around."

"Men," I said, walking slowly to the sofa. "They always think with their dicks."

"You should know, running around to movie sets across the world with him. Did you think I wouldn't find out? Did you really think that? Did he fuck you? Did he fuck you every day and every night? Did you like it, you nasty little home wrecker? You know he was only using you, right? Jeremy loves me. I'm his *wife!*"

You're his stalker, I wanted to scream at her. *And he hates you!*

"They'll know," I said slowly. "If you harm me. They'll know you did it. Because you're his wife."

She laughed. "Maybe they will, but as you know, Jeremy is a very rich man. He'll use his money to get me off, and we'll be together again while you're rotting in your grave."

I stared at her. I had no idea what to do, no idea what to say. I just knew I didn't want to die, not this way. My heart leaped as a knock sounded at the door, but I realized just as quickly that Kyle couldn't be endangered too.

"I don't know who that is," I said. "Maybe housekeeping?"

He knocked again. "Nell, it's me, let me in."

The woman looked around frantically. I thought of jumping up and kicking the gun from her hand while she was distracted, as I'd seen Jeremy do in his action movies. With my luck I'd kick it right into my own face as it fired. I sat still on the couch.

"He'll go away," I reassured her. "This issue is between you and me. And I swear, I *swear*, I am going to leave your husband. I was actually planning to go back to school. On the East Coast. Far away from where he lives."

"Where *we* live," she said through clenched teeth. She nudged me into the bedroom with the gun at my temple. Once inside, she clamped a meaty hand over my mouth. Hot, clammy flesh, cold metal. "Not one sound, you fucking bitch."

* * * * *

I pushed my way through the drunk, chattering groups in the ballroom, searching for a quiet place to take Kyle's call. I crossed the lobby and ducked behind a coatroom.

"Tell me again. Slowly. Where is Nell?"

"I was calling to ask you that. So you put her in the car?"

I stared at the swirls in the carpet, eyes unfocusing and refocusing. My heart pounded in my chest. *Move.* I headed for the door.

"Jeremy, are you still there?"

"Yeah, I'm here. Yes. I put her in the car." My fingers felt numb, and my palm was suddenly slick with sweat. I grasped the phone more tightly and hailed the driver with the other hand. "She should be there. Maybe she's somewhere else in the hotel."

"I've looked everywhere in the hotel."

"Well, call the fucking police!" I said, climbing into the car. I barked the name of the hotel at the driver.

"I called them."

"Look around again. Where the fuck were you when she got there?"

"I was in the car, trying to get to the hotel! Why didn't you wait for me to get there before you sent her? Or call me to pick her up?"

"She was tired," I said. *She was tired of playing the game, and I was tired of watching her.* "Did you check the gym? The bar? The restaurant? The elevators?"

"Jeremy, I checked everywhere. Security is looking. She's not anywhere here. Maybe—"

"Maybe what?"

"Maybe she left."

I bit my lip. It was a possibility. One I didn't want to think about, but better than the other possibility…

"Check the room again."

"I checked. I knocked three times, but there was no answer."

"Just go in. Maybe she's sleeping."

"I left the key in my tuxedo jacket."

I cursed, noticing the black garment beside me on the seat.

"Knock again. Knock until she answers, or get security up there." I swallowed, my mouth suddenly dry.

I heard Kyle knock, and to my relief, I heard the door open and the clink of the chain catching.

"Put her on the phone, Kyle."

"Take the chain off," I heard Kyle say, and I heard Nell's soft refusal.

"Put her on the phone. Give her the phone! I want to talk to her."

Then I heard the sound of wood crashing and shots from a gun.

"Kyle! Kyle!" I yelled, but there was only terrible silence after that.

* * * * *

I cradled Nell in a private room at the hospital while she made her statement to the police. I tucked the blanket around her more tightly from time to time to distract myself from the terrible story she was telling them. No matter how close I held her, she still shivered in my arms. Underneath the hospital blanket, blood stained her ivory dress. Not her blood. Kyle's.

After everything we'd done, all the people I'd hired, all the police and private investigators, Leslie Gray had waltzed into the hotel room by knocking on the door. Nell let her in, thinking it was Kyle. It was too simple to believe.

"She had a gun. I wanted to run, but I was afraid she would shoot me. I was too scared to try to get away."

"No one expected you to get away," I said quietly. "That only works in the movies, not in real life."

"I tried to keep her talking, but she only got angrier. She said she was your wife and that I was a home wrecker…and a lot of other things."

I knew. I'd seen it all on her web sites, on the many letters she sent the last several weeks.

"She had her finger on the trigger." Her voice quavered, and she snuggled closer to me. She nudged her head under my chin. I stroked her hair and thought about how close I'd come to losing her. "She was going to kill me. She just had some things to say first."

"Thank goodness," I said. "It bought us some time. She always was very verbose in her ravings."

"When Kyle knocked, she freaked out. She didn't know what to do. She started acting really erratic...and when Kyle knocked the second time..."

That part I knew already. Kyle had broken in, and Leslie Gray had shot Kyle as he'd wrestled the gun from her, and then he had shot her. Fatally. Kyle was originally from Texas. He was good with a gun.

"It's okay. It's okay," I said as she cried. "Kyle's going to be okay."

Kyle's wound wasn't life-threatening, but he'd still taken a bullet to the chest. He'd come through surgery and was resting in recovery. Nell knew all this, but she still shook in my arms.

"I thought she killed him. I really thought she killed him."

"She didn't, but she might have killed you." I drew in a deep breath of her hair. Nell, fresh and flowery. Alive. It was redemption. A second chance to do things the right way. "I'm so sorry, Nell. This is all my fault. This is exactly what I was afraid of happening, what's kept me up at night. If she had killed you—" I stopped speaking. I didn't have words for what I might have done if Leslie Gray had killed my Nell.

"It was my fault too," she said. "If I'd stayed with you... I should have stayed with you. I was being selfish. I was tired."

"Hush." Why was she apologizing to me? Selfish? I was the selfish one.

I had been the selfish one all along. For my own purposes, I'd exposed her to this danger, but instead of blaming me, she was apologizing. She should have been throwing hateful accusations in my face.

"Rhiannon," I said.

"What?"

I looked down at her. "She should have hated her husband for what he did to her, what he put her through. But she forgave him. She still loved him."

She still loved him. Did she still love me? Had she ever loved me? I thought she had once, but how could she love me anymore?

She shouldn't love me anymore. I steeled myself to say the words I didn't want to say.

"You're like Rhiannon." I said. "But you shouldn't forgive me."

I watched her work that out in her mind. Small lines of tension appeared around her mouth, the mouth I wanted to kiss and soothe but wouldn't. She knew. My throat tightened to see the stubborn denial in her eyes. She kept her voice light and controlled. "Forgive you? It wasn't your fault."

"It was my fault. The only reason she wanted to harm you was because of me. I can't...I can't live like this anymore. I've never been able to live like this. That's why I don't let myself love anyone. That way it's easier not to get upset when the fans and press go after her. And it's easier to let her go...when I have to...for her own good."

She always tried not to cry but could never accomplish it. She blinked rapidly, and so did I. *Don't look. Don't let the tears sway you. Don't let the pain of this moment keep you from doing what's right.*

"You can't control who you love," she said. Her hands twisted in my shirt, and she looked up at me in supplication.

"I have a lot of control when I need to. You should know that by now."

"Jeremy—"

Steady voice. I had to be her dominant. I had to put the rest of it away and do this now. "Nell, I'm sorry. I can't anymore. I can't chance this happening again. I can't live with this. Someone like me—my girlfriends will always be a target. And making you my wife? Jesus. I might as well paint a target on your head."

"Jeremy—"

"No. I want you to start applying to colleges. Let me know how I can help. You can start in the fall, wherever you decide to go. I want you to go wherever you want. I want you to be happy. I want you to be safe."

I took her hand. She made a little fist that made my heart ache, but I pried it open anyway and slipped the ring off. I pushed her tear-streaked face under my chin so she wouldn't say anything further.

"I'll tell my publicist in the morning," I said, blinking back my own grief. "She'll make it all make sense."

* * * * *

She'll make it all make sense.

Nothing ever made sense in my life except for the truths I manufactured. Only they were unchangeable, exact, easy to provide and manipulate as needed.

And of course, the public and the press made their own sense of things no matter what you did. The confrontation in the hotel room turned into some quiet insinuations that Nell and Kyle had been having an affair under my nose that led to our highly publicized "breakup." Funny how far off and yet how close to the truth the papers got at the same time. But Kyle healed quickly and got back to working for me. Nell stopped working for me for good.

I still paid her, though. I took care of everything. I bought her a beautiful little bungalow in Hollywood Hills and a fuel-efficient Mini Cooper for her to zip around town wherever she needed to go. A nice, practical car for my nice, practical, quiet little student, and a mountain of mythology books that I couldn't resist sending every week. I found myself inexplicably buying them for myself as well, as though reading them might give me the answers I continued to seek. The answer to why Nell was still so heavy on my mind. The answer to why I couldn't let her go. What was it about her that had caught me? Why her, the simple, quiet, unassuming girl that she was?

You can't control who you love.

I heard her words in my mind a hundred times a day. And I think she was partly right, and partly wrong. I *could* control who I loved. I had the control to keep myself away from her at least. But I loved her still. So in that way, yes, she was right.

But I had control. I had the control not to call her, not to e-mail, not to invite her out to lunch, not to drive over to her little bungalow at three in the morning when I thought I would die if I couldn't sink between her thighs.

And I had the control not to beg on my hands and knees for her to stay in L.A. when I learned, through Kyle, that she'd be returning to Harvard to complete a program I'd never even known she'd begun.

Chapter Nineteen: Bravery

I sat on my back porch and watched the sun go down. It was so beautiful, but it would have been even more beautiful if I weren't alone. It was late April, warm spring, but I still felt cold. I thought I would always feel cold from now on.

The doorbell rang. My heart used to leap every time the bell rang, because so often it had been a package of mythology books, an anonymous gift I knew was from Jeremy. But the books had stopped a few weeks ago. I supposed Jeremy had moved on. I tried not to look at the papers, for fear I'd see him with someone new. Of course, what did it matter? More than anyone, I knew it wasn't real.

I walked to the front door and looked through the peephole. A nervous habit now, one I wish I'd had before, so I could have saved Kyle a hell of a lot of pain.

Speak of the devil.

I opened the door and threw myself in his arms.

"Oh my God! What are you doing here?"

"I wanted to come see you before you took off for the East Coast, you little slut."

I hadn't seen Kyle in ages, since the night at the hotel, although we'd e-mailed and spoken a few times on the phone.

"Come in!" I couldn't believe he was here. Part of me, deep inside, hoped Jeremy had sent him here, but I knew he hadn't. Even in our phone conversations, Kyle carefully avoided talking about him, I assumed at Jeremy's command.

"You look great. Wow. Like you never even got shot."

"Ha-ha," he said as I got him a beer from the refrigerator. He looked at it suspiciously. "Since when do you drink beer, Nell?"

"I don't. I keep it in the fridge because it...it reminds me of him. How he used to come home from work every day and go right to the fridge for a beer. I know, I know," I said at his derisive look. "I know I'm pathetic. God, sit down. Stay awhile. For real, you look great. And I've been meaning to thank you in person all this time. You know, for what you did at the hotel. I can't believe you took a bullet for me."

Kyle gave me that same old smirky smile, and it almost made me cry from the memories. "You know, Jeremy would have killed me anyway if I'd let you die. And it had nothing to do with that stupid crush stuff. Jeremy totally made that up."

"Oh, okay." I laughed. *If that makes you feel better.* "He made a lot of stuff up actually, didn't he?"

Kyle's smile faded a little. "The thing about Jeremy is that he does what he thinks he needs to do. Even if it hurts him. Even if it hurts people he really loves."

"Mmm," I said. "I guess."

"So you leave next Wednesday?" he asked, sitting back on the couch.

"Yeah, I'm starting summer session to squeeze a few credits in before the fall."

"You realize there's no hurry. He'd pay for your college even if you took ten years to get your degree."

"I know. I know there's no hurry. I just need... I need the distraction, you know? I haven't been working, and I can't go back to the clubs, thanks to you."

He looked down at his hands and then back at me.

"You know, Nell, he hasn't asked me yet to start looking again. For another one."

My heart leaped to hear that, but I pretended to laugh it off. "You mean he doesn't have a new girl yet? What has he been doing? That man needs it every day. Every hour."

"He hasn't been with anyone else," Kyle said, still serious. "At least no one I've seen. And as you know, I usually see them all."

I sobered. "Yeah, I know. I remember."

"Anyway, I'm pretty sure there's only one girl on this earth who would make him happy, and that's you."

I looked down at my hands. They were shaking. "I don't know—I don't think—I really don't think he wants me back."

"I promise you he does, desperately, but he won't admit it. He wouldn't know love if it came up and spit in his face, as someone once said." He paused and thought for a long moment. "He'd never in a million years ask you to come back. So you're going to have to ask him."

"Ask him what? How?" I was alarmed by the sudden, new hope rising in my chest. "I can't. I'm supposed to be leaving for school next week."

"So what? You think Jeremy can't set up a house in Cambridge if he wants? Fly back and forth? You'll be in school for what, two or three years at most?"

"And then what?"

"I don't know. You tell me. Do you love him or not?"

I was seized by desire and fear. I clutched my hands together. "God, I love him so much. But how...? But what...what do I say to make him see...?"

"I don't know. But you better figure it out, 'cause I don't feel like going back to scoping out BDSM clubs." He gave me a crooked smile. "You know it's never been my scene."

* * * * *

Kyle was my personal assistant, but we didn't do social things often, at least not the vanilla kind. I'd had a long day. I was frustrated and tired. The last thing I felt like doing was going out to a bar and fending off fans, but Kyle had insisted. At least he was pretty good by now at scoping out the empty, out-of-the-way bars so I could get down a couple of drinks and chat with a few women before the cell phones started popping out and the paparazzi amassed outside.

This bar was a dive. There was no nice way to put it, but it was so dark and small and smoky that it was actually easy to hide. I felt myself begin to unwind, begin to feel human again. It was a great feeling, to just relax and go unnoticed, a feeling I so rarely had. I leaned back in the booth and let the pounding music wash over me.

"Great, huh?" said Kyle. "I knew you'd like this place."

"I've needed this," I said, yelling over the music. "I've really needed a night like this."

I might even get laid. I saw a lot of freaky women walking around. Piercings, thongs rising out of barely covered ass cheeks. Tramp stamps as far as the eye could see. This wasn't exactly a kink bar, but it wasn't mainstream. The waitress tottered by in high heels and an obscenely short skirt. It gave me a small thrill, but she wasn't *her*. Not even close.

The waitress had long, frizzy black hair extensions, fake boobs, a nice, round ass, tarty lipstick. She might be nice to have for one night. I looked away a moment later. My heart wasn't in it. Aside from the driving desire to get laid, there was nothing about other women that attracted me anymore.

I probably just needed a little more time.

It had been almost three months since Nell left me. Well. Since I'd sent her away. I hadn't given her a choice. I couldn't have. If I'd given her a choice, I knew she would have stayed. My faithful one.

I took another drink of my beer, watched a few blitzed couples making out on the dance floor. Kyle kept looking around, as if he was waiting for someone.

I realized too late that I'd been set up.

She was there across the bar, and she was alone. She clutched her bag and bit her lip, searching the room.

"Jesus, Jeremy! Look, Nell's here!"

Great performance. He wouldn't have convinced a child. But there she was, and he stood and waved his arms to get her attention. She, too, pretended to be shocked to discover us here, as if she would have shown up at this tiny, hole-in-the-wall bar on the edge of town the exact same night we happened to show up. I would have scowled at Kyle, but I couldn't tear my gaze away from her.

She walked over with a lovely, wry, shy smile on her face, the smile I'd seen a thousand times, the smile that haunted my dreams. I drank in every movement, every muscle, every breath she drew in and out. I felt petrified with lust and fear.

Why would Kyle do this? I think he was starting to learn the art of sadism. I'd worked for months now to purge her from my mind. Unsuccessfully, but still. This wasn't helping. In fact, the ache was already unbearable. *No no no, you can't be mine.*

Perhaps Nell was the one who'd asked Kyle to do this. It didn't matter a moment later. All that mattered was that she was there, right there, close enough to touch. I could smell her faint flower fragrance, pick it out from the smoke and sweaty bar odor around us. I knew it elementally, like I knew everything about her. I stood up, feeling wooden, and embraced her. It hurt to let her go.

She had on a little black dress and textured knit stockings that ended just above her knees. She looked thinner and sadder than she had before.

"How have you been?" I finally managed to say, and it sounded mournful even though I was shouting to be heard over the music.

"I've been okay," I think she said.

"What? I can't hear you."

She leaned closer to me, resting her lips against my ear. "I've been okay. But God, I've missed you so much."

"You and Kyle engineered this," I said back to her in her ear, holding her head still with her lovely red hair.

She backed away and searched my eyes for displeasure, a skill all subs refined with their doms. I gave her a dry smile to let her know I wasn't really angry. Pained, yes. But I couldn't be angry with her. She dropped her chin and leaned close again. "I'm sorry. But I had to talk to you."

"About what?"

We sat down and put our heads together. I wanted to throw a grenade into the DJ booth. The music that had relaxed and hidden me before hindered me now, and I wanted it to stop. I wanted utter silence and stillness so I could hear nothing but the beautiful timbre of her voice.

"Let's go outside. Do you want to go outside?" I found myself asking. *Bad idea, bad idea.* Too late. She nodded, and we stood together. I went in front of her, reaching back for her hand. The feel of grasping her familiar little hand in mine almost destroyed me. Fucking Kyle. He was so dead.

"So," I said briskly, dropping her hand when we got outside. "It was loud in there, yeah? I can hear you now. You look great, by the way." I talked about inane things to keep myself from saying what I really wanted to say. *I need you. I love you. Come back to me!* "Is everything okay? Kyle told me you were leaving soon for school."

"I am." She looked up at me from under her lashes, another familiar mannerism that gave me pain.

"Harvard. That's really excellent. Wow. Impressive."

She laughed softly. "Expensive for you."

"Oh God, no. That doesn't matter. I wanted you to go where you wanted to go. Anyway, Kyle said you'd already been there. I had no idea."

"Your Ivy League submissive."

"I know. No wonder you were so good at it," I joked, but what I really ached to do was take her in my arms and kiss her and pull up that little skirt…

"They have a great folklore and mythology department," she said, oblivious to the indignities I was visiting on her body in my mind. "One of the best."

"Well, I'm glad. They'll be lucky to have you. I'm sure you'll do my money proud."

She frowned slightly, and I expected her to say something about how the money never mattered to her, which I'd come to believe looking back at our time together with a clear mind.

But instead she said, "I never told you the story of Svava, did I?"

"I don't think so."

"She was an obscure Norse figure, a valkyrie. Her father was a king. Do you know what a valkyrie is?"

I shook my head.

"Valkyries chose which warriors were most worthy to die in battle, and brought them to Valhalla after they died, to serve them mead and provide them...other pleasures."

I smiled. More sexy mythology.

"Svava took her job seriously. She looked out after the bravest men, both dead and alive. Then one day she came upon a man who was silent, so silent that no name had been given to him, nor did he have a family or any kind of life at all. But she could tell he was brave and steadfast, so Svava gave him a name, Helgi, and along with his new name, she offered to give him a gift, but Helgi said the only gift he wanted was her. They married, and with her support he became a great warrior, and she was always there protecting him in battle. She refused to let him die, although eventually he did take a fatal wound."

She looked off across the street in the dark night.

"Helgi called Svava to his side to give him one last kiss. But she couldn't give him up. Their love was so strong that, instead, they were reincarnated again and again to be together for all time."

She looked back at me, her eyes wide, intent. I shook my head. "Nell—"

"I don't want to give you up, Jeremy! I'm not afraid. Not like you. Life is scary sometimes, but being without you scares me so much more—"

"But don't you see?" I cut her off with a frustrated sigh. "Faithfulness, forgiveness, bravery...all the things you bring... What do you get in return? What can I give? Pain? Confusion? Danger? Fear?"

"Protectiveness. Kindness. Steadfastness. Handsome good looks."

She really meant it. I took her in my arms and held her close, breathing her in one last time.

"Nell. You gave me a name, your name. You gave me a gift. It's true I had no life before you, before you showed me what love can be. But if I lose you ..."

She shook her head. "Love can overcome all adversity, all fear, if you're only strong. If you can be brave, or let me be brave for you, like Svava—"

"Life isn't mythology," I said, drawing away from her. "Especially mine. But it was so wonderful to see you again." I forced the words out to send her away. "God, it really was. Now let me get you a cab."

* * * * *

The luggage he'd bought for me was all packed, sitting in the corner, the luggage he'd filled with delicious corsets and bras and stockings an eternity ago. But it wasn't an eternity ago. It had been barely half a year since I'd met him at Guillermo's restaurant.

Silly, ridiculous girl. He doesn't want you. Get over it already. Let him go.

I looked down at the book clutched in my hands, the copy of *The Odyssey* he'd given me in Portugal. Could I ever let him go? I didn't have a choice. I'd seen it in his eyes, that he wanted me more than anything on earth, and still he sent me away.

Let it go.

I sighed and put the book on top of my suitcase. When I got to school, things would be better. I could lose myself again in the stories I already loved, and learn new stories that illuminated the world and the strange things people did in it.

I couldn't wait to go.

I set the alarm clock and had just turned out my light when I heard strident knocking at the door. My heart stopped, even though it had been months now. I looked at the clock. It was after midnight. *It's not her.*

"Nell, it's me, Jeremy!" I heard in the darkness. "Let me in. I need to talk to you."

I opened the door to the humid night air. He stood on my stoop, his eyes intent.

"Nell."

He reached for me, and I threw myself into his arms. He kissed me hard and deep, and then he pulled away.

"I'm yours," he said, his voice hoarse. "I'm yours."

Tears spilled onto my cheeks. I couldn't believe he was there in front of me. He wiped them away and shook his head.

"No, don't cry. I don't want you to be sad anymore. I don't want to be sad anymore either. Not another minute."

He had something in his hand, a sparkling gold circle I remembered. He took my hand and slipped on the ring. "I don't want to pretend anymore that I'm not in love with you. If you can be brave, I can too. I promise you...I promise you..."

He searched for the words to say, but I knew already what he meant. I put my fingers on his lips and said, "It's okay, I know."

He put his hands on me again, first on my neck, then on my breasts, on my hips, between my legs. "The bedroom. Where's the bedroom?"

I led him to the stairs. He'd bought me this beautiful little house but had never even been inside. I would thank him later and give him the tour, but not now. His hand on my ass propelled me up the stairs. When we got to the bedroom, he drew off my cami and flung it in the corner. He slipped his hands under the waistband of my pajama pants and drew them down. When I was nude, he began to explore me. His hands swept over every inch of my skin.

His warm, rough palms were as familiar to me as my own face. I stood and let him stroke me, inspect me. Shoulders, breasts. A tweak of both nipples, and an approving grunt when each snapped to rigid attention. Down the side of my torso to my waist. His arms circled me there, then brushed down over the flare of my hips. His hands hovered at the juncture of my legs and caressed the ticklish flesh at the top of my thighs.

I trembled with the effort to stay still. I disciplined myself to the sedate presentation he liked, although I wanted to scream with joy, jump up and down. I wanted to leap up and wrap my legs around his hips. He looked down at me and the corners of his mouth curved.

He knew exactly how I felt.

His hand closed on my pussy. I closed my eyes and leaned against his solid body, then buried my head in the softness of his shirt. *Jeremy.* I could feel the tension in his muscles. One finger slipped into my slit. My grip tightened on his arms. I wanted him to take me, to subdue me, to put me back in my place. *Oh.* I gasped as his finger probed deeper. Another finger, and another. I was pulled off balance as he grasped my pussy hard, harder. "Oh please!" With a rough exhalation, he released me and stepped back. I felt like I was falling without him. In the split second he released me, my heart raced in panic. I made a frightened sound.

He pulled me close again and fumbled in the pocket of his jacket with the other hand. He drew out another circle I remembered, but this one was black leather instead of gold. Instead of a diamond, this circle was affixed with a large silver ring. He held the collar in his palm, ran his thumb over the rough leather. I stared. *For you, Nell.* I wanted to touch it, kiss it. I wanted to fall to my knees. I wanted to grab it and wrap it around my neck, but I couldn't. I waited and bowed my head.

"Down," he said.

I sank to the floor. His thumb pressed under my chin, and he forced my gaze to his. His face was set in rigid lines, but his eyes and mouth were soft. He placed the black collar around my neck and drew my hair aside to fasten it. The gentle feel of his fingers on my neck contrasted with the pull of the tightening leather. I was truly going to be his. With or without the collar, with or without the work contract. He owned me through and through.

He stepped back and looked down at me. One light fingertip traced around the unfinished edge of the collar, then insinuated itself into the ring at the front. I felt the tug as he grasped it, and then the pull. I came to my feet and tripped behind him, dragged to the bed. I moaned as he bent me over. He delivered stinging slaps to my thighs until I parted them to his satisfaction.

Behind me, I heard the familiar sounds of him undressing, the clink of his belt buckle, the quiet whoosh of his shirt sliding down his arms. The swish-snap of his pants being dropped and kicked to the side. I stood, spread and collared, bent over. I waited to be taken, my heart in my throat. I could smell my arousal like an intoxicant. I sneaked a peek behind me at Jeremy. My gaze slid over his bunched abs, his waist and groin. His arms hung at his sides, powerful arms that hurt me and held me in turn. His hands were open, relaxed. Was he thinking about the same things I was? *I own her. She's mine.*

He moved forward and splayed one hand on the small of my back. Slight pressure. *I've got you.* His other hand probed my pussy again, greater pressure this time. Two fingers, three...pushing, exploring. His hand prodded me. I leaned forward, then lifted one knee to the bed. He made a sound of denial and pulled me back by my hips.

"Stay."

He stood closer behind me, so his cock nudged at my entrance. His warm, virile strength and vitality felt so familiar to me, so comforting, I nearly sobbed. How I'd missed him, how I'd craved his hands. And his cock. Oh God. I made the slightest movement, a hair of a shift backward, searching.

"No. Bad girl."

I lowered my head and clutched at my floral bedspread. He teased, he tempted. He dipped the head close to my slit, then withdrew. A soft whine communicated my indignation. He laughed and slid his fingers into the back of my collar. He pulled me up and held me clasped back against him.

"Question, girl. Have you been with anyone else?"

I shook my head, aghast at the idea of it. "No, Jeremy. No."

His fingers burned a trail up to my breasts. He squeezed one tit. "Neither have I." He squeezed the other, then his fingers brushed over my sternum to once again grasp the collar's O-ring. "Are you still on the pill?"

"Yes." A good owner protects his property. He was letting me know that he was still safe, checking that I was too, before he came inside unsheathed. The idea of it touched some deep part of me. The care he gave me, it was remarkable. If it were me, I would have already speared myself on him, disease or pregnancy be damned. But not Jeremy. "Please." My voice was shaky with emotion. *Please, I love you. Please, come inside.* I pressed my ass back against him and got a little shake at the collar.

"Wait."

"Yes, Jeremy." Melting with desire. Tortured. He turned me around by the ring.

"Lie down." He half pushed, half helped me lie back on the bed. My hands skittered around, unfettered. I almost put them in my crotch, desperate to assuage the ache. I finally grasped the covers at my side. He buried his fingers in my hair and leaned forward. I felt his warm breath tickle my clavicle, then felt his rough cheeks brush the soft skin under my chin. I smelled his aftershave and hummed with pleasure at every sensation, every familiar scent. I hungered for his cock.

"Give me your hands," he ordered.

I held them out and he gathered them up and pushed them over my head. He arched above me. I stared up at his golden torso, the sculpted abs. I lost control and pulled forward to put my mouth on him, to taste, to lick.

"No." His reprimand was delivered with a trace of a smile. He stroked a finger down my quivering middle. "Have you become so poorly trained? In such a short time?"

"Yes!" I was wild. I bucked my hips against him. "I need…I need…"

"You need me to teach you a lesson?"

"I need you to fuck me!"

Jeremy laughed and kissed me. I thrust my tongue in his mouth and tasted him. I wanted him so much. He pulled back and took my lower lip between his teeth.

"As uncontrollable as ever."

"Worse," I said. "It's been so long. Please!"

"Little grabby sluts who beg are sometimes not given what they want." I shook my head. No, I couldn't bear it. He continued, leaning down to nuzzle against my cheek. "But sometimes, they are."

He slid inside me, all the way to the hilt. My whole body reacted to the astonishing pleasure, the feeling of being stretched by him. I remembered it, the delicious pleasure, and yet it was totally new. My hands flew wild. My arms came up off the bed. He caught them and held me down with his hard, immovable body. He arched forward again, then back. His pace quickened. I felt possessed by him, unable to move, giving up my will to the invasion of his flesh. My walls felt ready to explode, the pleasure was so intense. His pace quickened. I pressed against him and arched my back.

"Yes, yes!" He drove me on as my incoherent noises rose in intensity. His pelvic bone ground against my clit. His fingers pinched my nipples, and the hot pressure sparked right to my center. His hips drove into me, dragged me across the bed. He gathered me up, and I pressed against him, dying for release.

"Not yet." He was gasping. "Not yet. Look at me." It took a moment for his words to register. "Look at me, girl." The tenor of his voice drew me back to attention. My gaze met his. He grabbed the collar and thrust his thumb into the ring. "You're mine. Now come for me, girl. Let me see."

My pelvis convulsed. He yanked on the collar and I struggled against him. His gaze held mine, and he fucked me hard, banging against my pussy. I thrust my hips against him again and again as he held the collar tight. "Oh, oh!" My pleasure was growing, spreading wide. I felt a new closeness pulling us together, and not just where we were joined. My body and mind opened to him, and he gazed back at me. His other hand cradled me, squeezed my shoulder. I stared into those clear blue eyes and let everything go.

I cried out as the orgasm shook me. The intensity was terrifying, white-hot. As the pulsing waves took over my body, I felt the part of us that was connected grow into something more, something bigger. A concordance of hearts. I felt hot tears on my cheeks, but I didn't remember starting to cry. I was afraid. I was replete. I was aware, more than anything, that he held me tethered by the thick silver ring. The black circle. The gold ring on my finger. He had me. The circle was me and him.

His hand tightened around the collar and he rocked against me, growling. His pelvis jerked in fits and starts as he rode out his own intense climax. His thick member pulsed inside my rippling walls until we both came to rest. My pussy contracted in soft, rhythmic aftershocks. With each wave, his cock seemed to swell anew inside me. My nipples still tingled with lingering sensation.

After a moment his fingers unwound from the collar and moved up my neck to twine in my hair. I felt the soft pull, the caress of fingertips. His hot breath teased my ear. We both realized at the same time that my arms were still stretched over my head. We looked at each other and laughed. His chest hair tickled me, and I laughed harder. He thrust his tongue in my mouth and kissed me, then drew back. He smiled down at me.

"You're mine," he said, as if I didn't know it.

When we woke in the morning, his finger was still crooked through the ring at my neck.

* * * * *

Jeremy groused about having to move to Cambridge, but we both agreed a long distance relationship wasn't going to work.

"I want you by me, for me, under me, every fucking day," he'd insisted as we lay together the night he came to take me back. "I don't ever want to be away from you. Can you live with that?"

"Yes, Jeremy." I snuggled as close to him as I possibly could.

I'd slept that night wrapped in his steel embrace, neither one of us willing to let an inch of space between us. We spent the next day alternately making plans and fucking. We'd be in the middle of packing or making notes or phone calls when he would pull me down and take me. If the woman at the electric company wondered at the short, urgent gasps peppering our conversation, she was too polite to inquire what was going on.

And I didn't mind it at all. It felt absolutely perfect to be available to him again, to be filled with him when he wanted it. I'd felt empty in so many ways without him.

The truck came for my things on Tuesday, and on Wednesday we flew out. We arrived in Boston and drove straight to the charming little house he'd bought me adjacent to campus. I didn't even want to know what he'd paid for it, but I figured money could buy just about anything.

Anything but love.

And it must have been love between us, for Jeremy to leave his luxurious L.A. mansion to move into my tiny, modest house. In fact, it suited us perfectly, and we both felt strange whenever we returned to the L.A. house, like two kids wandering around in some museum. The only thing he missed about his L.A. house was the state-of-the-art dungeon there. Before the summer session was over, he had Kyle arrange to move the equipment here.

Kyle visited us regularly. He still arranged Jeremy's trips and photo shoots, although his job now was to streamline these duties into the shortest possible time. He was good at doing it too, just as he was good at doing everything else. He seemed inordinately pleased that everything had worked out for us. Without him, I suppose, it wouldn't have. As I told him once, he had saved both of our lives.

For now, Jeremy was taking a break from filming. He planned to look at scripts that could be set in Boston or possibly New York. I told him I could always take a semester off if he needed me to. We both agreed that spending more than a week apart was absolutely impossible.

Most mornings when he was there, Jeremy walked to class with me. We held hands, ignoring the paparazzi who crouched behind the bushes to take their shots. It didn't bother us so much, now that we had nothing to hide. Although the silly, cloying TOGETHER AGAIN! headlines were a little ridiculous for a while.

"Beautiful day," he always said as we walked, and I always agreed with him, because now, even the rainy, muggy summer days seemed beautiful and wonderful. He would walk me to the courtyard outside my classroom and kiss me lingeringly.

"Be a good girl today, Miss Ashton," he'd say.

"Or what?" I'd ask, whispering in his ear.

"Or you know what," he would reply, nuzzling me softly. "You know what," he'd tell me with that smile that always made me shake.

Epilogue

I hurried down the sidewalk toward our little house. I looked ridiculous in my short, pleated schoolgirl skirt and skintight Harvard sweater, but I didn't care. I'd been studying for exams like crazy the last week while Jeremy stood over me supervising, and now I was about to get my reward.

As soon as I'd turned in my essays, I headed to the bathroom and locked myself in a stall to change into the little outfit Jeremy had tucked in my bag. The toy was there too, with a little trial-size packet of lubricant, like he'd fixed me some kind of twisted kinkster lunch. I inserted the plug gingerly, feeling like his naughty slut even though he was nowhere near, which I'm sure was what he intended. Next I pulled on the silky crimson thong.

Ha, Harvard colors. He must have been planning this for weeks. I pulled the stockings on last, the ones made like knee socks that ended just above my knee. They drove him crazy. I don't know why, but I was happy to wear them for the reaction they got.

I was so close now. Only three more nicely manicured yards to pass before I reached our den of depravity. I felt like running, but that wasn't something I really liked to do when I had a toy in my ass, even with a thong over top of it. I slowed down instead, in case he was looking out the window. I tried to look like a well-behaved but slightly-in-need-of-correction coed on her way home from acing an exam. By the time I neared the house, Jeremy waited in the doorway.

"Come in, Miss Ashton. You're a little early."

"Well, I...I didn't want to be late, Professor Gray."

"Have a seat over there by my desk." He pointed to a wooden chair against the far wall, then shut and locked the door.

I sat down on the hard seat and squeezed my knees together. I was so wet already. I had been since the moment I'd turned in my exam. He crossed to sit behind "his" desk, which was actually mine, then leafed through some papers with a frown. I sat and waited, buzzing with lust. Finally he sat back and fixed me with a hard stare. I squirmed as his gaze traveled lower. He cleared his throat.

"Penelope, if you sit on that lovely skirt like that, it's going to get wrinkled in the back. Perhaps it would be better if you pulled it up and sat with your bottom directly on the chair."

"Oh, okay," I said, rearranging myself.

"Much better. Now let's talk about your test results. I looked over your essays..."

With a flourish, he took out a pair of fake, intellectual-looking glasses and perched them on edge of his nose. I tried to stifle my laughter, but one wild giggle escaped.

He looked up at me from over the lenses. "Too much?"

"They're awesome, Jeremy," I said, trying to compose myself. "Please leave them on."

"Stop laughing, then, you little goofball."

"Okay." I schooled my face back to a serious gaze.

"So these essays..." He went on, scowling at me through the glasses. "I realize you're a highly intelligent girl, and a Harvard student," he added, nodding at my tight-fitting sweater, "but the ideas in these essays are just, well, far too scandalous and temerarious for a young girl like you to express."

I totally cracked up again at *temerarious*, but being the actor, he was somehow able to keep a straight face and not fall out of character every thirty seconds like I did.

"Young lady, I don't find this situation at all funny."

I made a great show of trying to collect myself. "I'm so very sorry, Professor Gray."

"Have you been drinking, Penelope?"

Oh my God, he was going to kill me. I burst into helpless laughter again.

"Very well," he said. "I see now your essays are not the only thing completely uncontrolled and lacking in discipline. In my opinion you are a very ill-mannered and saucy girl." He took off the glasses and fixed me with a dire look. I tried to look partly apologetic and partly scared.

"I'm afraid this kind of behavior needs to be dealt with strictly. I wouldn't be a good teacher if I allowed this sort of thing to go on. Stand up, Penelope, and bend over the desk for me. And turn up your skirt to expose your bottom." The stern tonality of his professor voice resonated straight to my clit.

"Oh, Professor Gray, I can't! That would be so humiliating!"

"Nevertheless," he said, putting his glasses aside, "I think a very strict paddling is the only thing that will bring you in line. So I'm going to have to ask you again to stand up, bend over my desk, and turn your skirt up."

I sighed and draped myself over the desk, sulking and pouting. I stole the opportunity to press my clit right against the edge. While I'm sure he noticed, he pretended not to.

"That's right. Bend right over," he said as he opened the drawer and pulled out a thick, broad wooden paddle that I knew very well. I shivered with the familiar thrill of anticipation, excitement tied up in knots of dread. "Your skirt now, please."

"Oh, Professor, please paddle me over my skirt. Please, I'm so ashamed."

"You'll be more ashamed before this is all over. Your face will be as red as your behind when I'm done with you. Quickly now. The longer you make me wait, the more licks you're going to get."

Licks. God, I hoped I got some real licks later. After scenes like this, I often did.

"Yes, sir." I lifted my skirt to expose my crimson thong and the toy planted between my ass cheeks.

"Good Lord Almighty," Jeremy said. I muffled my laughter in the desktop as he paced back and forth behind me, tapping the paddle against his hand. "What on earth have we here?"

"It's…it's an anal plug, Professor Gray," I whispered, pretending to be ashamed.

"And you are wearing it because…?"

"I don't know, Professor. I can't explain."

"Perhaps because you're a horny little cum slut."

"Yes," I said softly. "That could be why."

"And you love to have your little asshole violated, because you're such a little fuck-happy whore. You love to have a cock shoved up inside there, drilling you and using your ass until it's full of cum. Is that it?"

"Yes," I confessed in a whisper. My clit throbbed and my tight hole clenched around the toy. "I love to have my ass taken and used."

"I bet you do. And to tell the truth, sometimes there's no other way to put a headstrong little coed like you in her place."

"Yes, Professor." I pressed my clit against the edge of the hard desk again.

"Stop fidgeting," he snapped, running his fingers up the inside of my thigh and then back down to trace the top of my schoolgirl stockings. "Spread your legs and brace yourself for a nice, hard paddling. Afterward I'll take that naughty little toy out and give you exactly what you deserve."

"Oh no, please, Professor. You won't...you won't take me...*there*? Will you?"

"I most certainly will. And I should warn you, my cock is much larger and much less forgiving than that little toy you play around with."

"Oh, no!" I pretended to be distraught. "What if...what if your big cock hurts me?"

"I sincerely hope it does, since you are in such severe need of correction." He brought the paddle down hard on my ass. "I have no intention of going easy on you."

Ouch. Tell me about it.

Whack. He brought it down again. "Owww!" I yelped, not totally faking. "Ow! Please!" The more I squirmed under the paddle, the more my clit rubbed against the desk. I spread my legs farther and arched my back as the sting of the paddle spread across my cheeks. I loved every second of it, but yes, it really hurt. It was easy to play the squirming, chastised student getting paddled hard by the stern professor because, well, that's exactly what I was.

"Please, oh please, Professor! I'll never write anything so...so...inflammatory again!"

Inflammatory got a soft chuckle from Jeremy, a real victory since he hardly ever broke character in our role-playing scenes. "Just hush," he said, landing a sharp one. "Don't make me put the glasses on again."

I half yelped, half laughed as he paddled me harder. I could barely feel the stinging pain now, I was so aroused.

"Please, please, please," I begged in earnest. "Please, I've been punished enough now. Surely you don't even need to take my ass! I know my place now, and I won't be disrespectful again, not ever. I promise. I swear!"

I wiggled my red-hot ass in hopes of distracting him from further discipline, but well, he was a sadist after all. My horny asshole had to wait until he landed a few more stingers. *Crack.* The fire in my cheeks combined with the fire in my ass until I was one shuddering mass of aching girl goo.

"Okay, Penelope," he said finally, laying the paddle down. "That will make it hard for you to sit down for a while."

I put my hand behind my ass to rub the smart away. He took it and shoved it back down on the desk. "None of that. I want you to feel every bit of that pain. When you sit down, and you feel that lingering sting and ache, you will remember the proper way to behave for an intelligent Harvard girl like you." I brought my hand to my lips and started sucking my fingers. I was so horny. I craved the taste of his cock.

"Absolutely, Professor Gray." I nodded. "I've learned my lesson now."

"You've almost learned your lesson, Miss Ashton. Now please lower your undergarment to your knees so that I can teach you a little more about proper behavior for an unabashed anal whore like you."

"Please, no!" I shifted on my feet so my ass swung back and forth. I was rewarded with Jeremy's soft intake of breath. "Please, I'm afraid your huge cock will hurt me!"

"As well you should be," he said, coming around to stand before me. He undid his belt and then his pants. He whipped off his shirt and pushed his pants down, shoving his hugely erect cock in my face. "I think this will be enough to teach you a very effective lesson."

"Oh no, Professor Gray. Please...please let me suck you off instead!"

"Suck me off? A girl like you probably couldn't even get a cock this thick past your lips."

"I'll try! Let me try—" My words cut off as he shoved his cock down my throat. I sighed and took it deep inside, swirling my tongue around the swollen head and then bobbing up and down on its length. I was so hungry for him, the salty taste of him, the musky, masculine fragrance. The satiny texture. I pressed my clit against the desk harder, twisting my hips back and forth.

"Take your panties down."

I reached back, not losing a beat, and worked the thong down over my hips, letting it fall to the floor. His cock bobbed in my mouth as he reached back and took the toy out. He left me and positioned himself behind my ass.

"Please!" I pleaded one last time. "I promise to be good. I'll do extra credit! Whatever you desire!"

"Here's your extra credit, you naughty little whore," he said as he held my hips and eased the head of his cock into my ass.

I moaned. In twenty seconds or less I would come.

"Oh please…" I begged as he slid slowly all the way in. "Please teach me a lesson, Professor! I don't know why I'm so naughty."

"I think it might be the red hair." His voice sounded jerky and strained as he spoke the words in rhythm to his thrusts. His fingers dragged across my scalp. "I find red hair in young ladies very subversive. Especially your particular shade."

My laughter cut off in a gasp as he wrapped his hand in my curls and pulled my head back to plant a kiss on my temple. "But I'll try to look past the things you can't help."

"Thank you, Professor. But oh God, oh…please—"

"Please what?"

"Please may I come, Professor?" I gasped.

"Young lady, must I remind you that you're being punished?"

"Oh please, please!" I'd been masturbating against the edge of the desk since he'd first bent me over it. If I didn't get release soon… My clit was so hot, my nipples were aching from rubbing back and forth against the wooden surface, sliding across papers and books. "Ohhh." I moaned as he ground his pelvis against my ass.

He leaned forward on the desk to brace himself. I grunted and bucked against his swollen cock. The desk started sliding across the floor.

His hands grasped at my neck and then slid down to squeeze my breasts. He pinched my nipples hard. I cried out and scrabbled for purchase, tensing as he drove faster and faster into my ass. Papers flew, pencils scattered. A pencil sharpener was batted to the floor.

"Holy fuck!" I screamed. Jeremy clamped a hand over my mouth. Pleasure shot out to every part of me like a thunderbolt. I pounded on the desk, riding the waves of orgasm as my ass clenched around his cock. He gave one last pummeling thrust and shouted through his own orgasm. The desk nearly toppled over. I swiped for the lamp as it fell and managed to save it. He collapsed over me, his hand still over my mouth. I lay still, his body around me. His cock remained planted firmly in my ass. His chest hair tickled my back. His thighs trapped mine. My dominant, powerful and strong. Warm and loving. Hilarious. I loved him. A few seconds later he planted a soft kiss at the back of my neck.

"I guess I'm going to have to accept that fact that you're incorrigible," he said against my ear.

"Yes, Professor Gray," I agreed with a sigh.

* * * * *

I peeled off her sweater and sucked her tits before I dragged her to the shower. I wasn't done with her yet, but I was finally getting to the point where I could show some restraint. I was finally coming to realize she wasn't going to leave me.

She was mine forever. My faithful one.

Oh, I was still going to marry her. Not that she needed that piece of paper any more than I did. We would do it sometime. Maybe after she was done at Harvard, maybe before, if we felt like it. I'd already set Martin to drafting the prenuptial agreement, more to amuse Nell than for any practical reason. It was much less explicit than the first document, since not much needed to be spelled out between us anymore. I didn't need those black and white words on paper the way I used to. I could see all the promises I needed in Nell's clear, beautiful eyes.

Penelope Ashton (hereafter wife*) agrees to live as partner and lover to Jeremy Gray (hereafter* husband*).*

The wife agrees to provide loving faithfulness, as well as sexual submission upon request.

The husband agrees to provide dominance, protection, kindness, and handsomeness.

The wife will offer bravery and forgiveness as needed…hopefully not too much…

Later, in bed, I spread her out in front of me and tied her down. I knelt between her legs and started to lick her all over. She sighed and arched her back and made those small, urgent noises I loved.

"So how did you do on your exam?" My tongue fluttered against her clit.

"I did…I did really well—I think—" She was having trouble finding her breath.

"You think?" I asked, raising my head. She moaned and nodded quickly.

"I…I know I did…I did really well—"

I smiled and resumed licking and teasing her swollen clit. I loved to play with my little toy. My comfort object. My submissive. My soon-to-be wife. I loved to feel her writhe against me and give up control to me. Oh, I craved for her to lose self-control. I could do this for hours just to feel her jerk under my tongue, just to drive her lust higher. I tasted her musky juices and breathed in her scent. She twisted under me, then whined softly. I didn't reprimand her for being fidgety. Sometimes I did, but not today. I devoured her swollen slit until her hips bucked against my chin and I could tell she was close to the edge. Then I stopped and smiled at her guttural protest.

"You studied hard, didn't you?"

"Yes..." she said. "Oh, Jeremy... Oh God... Please!" Her wrists and ankles pulled helplessly at the restraints.

"I'm so proud of you," I whispered. I fell on her once more and lapped around her clit, then took it in my teeth and gave it a tug. I worried it delicately between my lips and then soothed it with a broad, lingering stroke of my tongue. I felt the tension release, heard her quick exhalation. I stroked her all over as the orgasm racked her body, stroked her until the tremors subsided, then untied her and drew her into my arms. "Nell. I love you so much. Good girl."

The wife will act as comfort object at all times to her husband, Jeremy.

The husband will be brave enough to love his wife, Penelope, and worship her like the goddess she is.

A Final Note

I hope you enjoyed Nell and Jeremy's story. If you're wondering about their happily ever after, please check out the other three books set in the world of *Comfort Object*—*Caressa's Knees*, *Odalisque*, and *Command Performance*.

Caressa's Knees picks up a year or so after this story ends, and tells the story of Kyle and his quest for love after the heartbreak of pining for Nell. In the course of Kyle's romance with a talented yet tormented concert cellist, Jeremy and Nell make several appearances, and you learn more about their life a few years down the line.

Odalisque tells the story of Kai Chandler, Mason and Jessamine's friend, who acquires an odalisque named Constance to fulfill his sexual needs. But the two lovers soon find that sexual slavery leads to a much deeper emotional connection—whether they want it or not. Mason, Jessamine, Jeremy and Nell all appear in this book.

Finally, *Command Performance* relates some serious life changes for Mason, including a new, trumped up, PR-driven relationship that turns poignantly real.

You can buy all these books separately or take advantage of my promotionally-priced Comfort Series box set, available from the two largest online book retailers.

Please turn the page to read an excerpt from *Caressa's Knees*.

An excerpt from *Caressa's Knees*, a sequel to *Comfort Object*

She froze at the knock on the door. It wasn't her aunt's knock. "Go away," she yelled.

"Open the door," he said in a calm voice.

"I said go away!" God, his stupid voice. She hated how it sounded like caramel, all smooth and melty around the edges. Where had he said he was raised? Louisiana? Texas? Again he knocked, two sharp raps in succession.

"I'm trying to sleep!"

It was a lie. She was huddled beside the bed where she'd dropped and pulled her knees up to her chest, trying to forget about the mistakes, the patronizing applause... She heard the knob rattle and knew he was picking the lock. The door swung open and she turned her back on him.

"Caressa—"

"Get out!" She screamed it, the same way she'd screamed at him that morning. "Get out, get out!" It felt good to scream at him, or rather at the wall, because she couldn't look at him and scream the way she was screaming. "Get ou—" The final 't' was muffled by a large hand and his hiss against her ear.

"Stop it, you diva."

She hit out at him, turning and attacking with everything she was worth. He parried, pushing her back and pinning her down with embarrassing quickness.

"You're an angry little girl, aren't you?" he asked, his hands flexing on her wrists.

"I'm not a little girl, you jerk. I'm not a diva."

"No? You act like one."

She fought with renewed energy. He slid his hands from her wrists to cover her palms, still pinning her with his body.

"Let go of my hands!" No one touched her hands. Ever. But he ignored her shrieked command, his fingers closing around hers. His chest was pressed to hers, a cage. An anchor. He waited for her to look at him, but she wouldn't do it.

"Go away!"

"No."

She finally chanced a sideways glance at him, and what she saw devastated her. He admired her. Still. "You don't understand, Kyle. It was terrible."

"I liked it," he said without pause.

"Because you don't understand."

"No, I don't," he agreed a moment later, with an ironic lilt to his voice. "How can you say it was terrible? The applause went on and on. They were shouting 'Bravo!'"

"Yeah, they're idiots. They do that every time. Dress up and go listen to the pretty music from the fancy orchestra in their flashy tuxedos. They're like you, they don't know. The reviews will tell the story tomorrow. You fucking idiot."

His face changed then, and his fingers tightened around hers until she squirmed to pull them away. "Apologize."

"Let go of my hands."

"Apologize. *I'm sorry I called you a fucking idiot, Kyle.*"

She shook her head.

"Say it. *I'm sorry I called you a fucking idiot. I'm sorry for trivializing your experience and ranting at you like a shrill bitch.* Say it."

"Fuck you!"

"Say it. I can hold you here all night. Do you need me to repeat it?"

"I want to go to bed."

"As soon as you apologize."

She pouted. Damn, she had an itch on her arm. He wouldn't let go of her hands no matter how hard she pulled, and she had to scratch it. She squirmed against him and…oh my God.

He smiled down at her. Smug asshole. "Say it, Caressa."

He was hard, and he was pressing against her in a way that had her body rebelling against what her mind was telling her to do.

"No. Go away," she insisted, a little less forcefully this time.

"*I'm sorry...*"

"Jesus. Fine. I'm sorry I called you an idiot!"

"*And ranted at you like a shrill bitch.*"

Caressa heard a snort and a laugh and realized it had come from her. And then more laughter bubbling up before she could stop it. She wanted to be angry. She hated him. She *despised* him. No. She adored him.

"Say it." He was laughing against her lips, kissing her. "Say it, you crazy little wingnut."

"I'm sorry...I'm sorry I ranted at you like...like...a shrill...hahaha...bitch..." She could barely get the words out, she was laughing so hard. Tears were streaming from her eyes and then she wasn't really sure where her laughter ended and her tears began. Kyle kissed her again and again, licking the moisture from her cheeks and nibbling at her lips. Their bodies bumped together in laughter and a deeper, more intent purpose. He was groping at her pants, pulling at the waistband.

"Don't rip them," she said.

"Take them off."

She scrambled up, still not sure if she wanted to hate him or worship him. The conflict of her feelings lodged somewhere in her middle, near her heart, but between her legs there was warmth and wetness. She undressed and he undressed too with a complete lack of self-consciousness. She stared because she still couldn't quite get over the sight of him—the sculpted perfection of his torso, his muscular legs and his hard, upstanding cock.

She made a sound and backed away as he advanced on her, condom already in his hand and quickly rolled onto his thick length. His eyes never left her. In fact, his eyes were so intent they frightened her. She started to fight him as he backed her to the wall, for no other reason than the shit storm he stirred in her. He ignored her half-hearted slaps and shoves and pressed against her, slipping his hands beneath her knees to draw her thighs up and around his hips. She braced herself and bumped her head back against the wall, holding on for dear life.

"Say you want me, Caressa."

She gazed at him with bared teeth. "You're always telling me what to say."

"Then say what you feel. Say *yes*, or *no*—"

"Oh..." She moaned. "I don't want to talk." She couldn't summon words. She heard music, banging clashing chords, and felt his cock parting her, easing up into her. Why did he need her to talk? Couldn't he hear it? She gave a sing-songy whine and shifted her hips to take him deeper. His knees, or her elbows perhaps, thumped against the wall in the silence of the hotel suite as he began to move in her, each thrust lifting her higher. She banged her head again but she didn't care. His teeth closed on her neck and she wanted him to bite instead of nibble. "Kyle…"

She arched her hips into his thrusts, wanting to urge him on, but not knowing how. She ground against him and his fingers tightened on her hip where he held her. His cock pinned her and possessed her, and then found a spot that had her falling faster, rising higher. Her moans intensified as she sought satisfaction.

"Shhh…"

She heard his shushing as if from a distance. She grasped his shoulders and dug her nails into his golden skin. "Help me. I can't— Closer, please!"

With a groan, he slid an arm under her and turned, carrying her to the bed and collapsing over her. The force and rhythm of his thrusts increased as he plundered her, his hips pounding against hers. His pubic bone contacted her clit, rubbing over it in an unbearable tease. She pulled her knees up to draw him closer, to urge him on, and then he delivered a stinging slap to the outside of her thigh. Another, and another again. The sound was loud and she jerked, at the same time the chaos inside her transformed into a single strain of completion.

"God, Kyle!" The orgasm came on her like a gunshot, an explosion. Every nerve seized and her thighs clenched around him as he stiffened above her. He gripped her thighs where they still stung from his blows and pressed her down, down, down. She wanted him to hold her down forever, to fill her and not let her go. Her pussy clamped down on his hard thickness, a jolting release made even sweeter by the way he shook and shuddered above her.

When he fell against her she lay still, not wanting to stir and cause him to move. A moment later she heard a chuckle and a soft gasp of breath against her cheek.

"I suppose we could have been quieter."

Caressa didn't answer. Quiet was the last thing on her mind. God, the way he fucked her, like an animal rutting, like a wild man. He had slapped her thigh, hard. She still felt the warmth of his handprint.

And she had liked it. Very much.

He finally drew back to lie beside her, turning questioning eyes on her. "So…you got your spanking. Did you enjoy it as much as you hoped?"

She looked past him, over his shoulder. "What do you think?"

He tweaked her chin and tsked at her. "Don't be a smart ass. Tell me if you liked it or not."

She forced her gaze back to his, stared into those blue eyes that pinned her as effectively as his cock. "I still feel it." She didn't know what she meant by that...if she meant the burn on her thigh or his cock still firm and stirring in her. "You've got quite a libido working there."

"I do all right," he sighed, pulling away from her. He kissed her, not gently, and rolled off the bed. He stood over her and she felt suddenly naked, vulnerable. She pulled the sheets over herself and looked past him again.

"Can I sleep in here with you?" he asked.

"No."

He studied her a moment longer, then shrugged. "It's late, and if I sleep in here I'll probably keep you up later than I should."

"You've already done that."

He stretched his gorgeous limbs, refusing to rise to the bait. She watched and pretended he didn't make her heart beat faster and her mouth go dry. He started to dress and she turned on her side, remembering everything that his ruthless seduction had driven away for precious moments. The concert, the horrible flubs. The undeserved applause. The piece had slipped ahead just out of her fingers. She'd thought she had it once or twice, but overall the performance was average at best—

Ohhh... He was leaning over her, licking up the side of her neck. She shivered and almost reached for him, reached to pull him back down beside her, with his spicy, manly smell and his voice like caramel.

"You still taste like tears," he whispered. His tongue slipped behind her ear, teasing and tempting. Then he kissed her gently on the forehead and was gone.

The Comfort Series

#1 Comfort Object
#2 Caressa's Knees
#3 Odalisque
#4 Command Performance

About the Author

Annabel Joseph writes emotionally intense stories about the romance of dominance and submission. She has published erotic fiction with Ellora's Cave, Loose Id, and her own indie imprint, Scarlet Rose Press. You can learn more about her books, read reviews, and find contact information at **www.annabeljoseph.com**

Made in the USA
Middletown, DE
06 January 2016